# I HAVE LIVED TODAY

## Steven Moore

For Leslie

When we met I claimed I loved to write,
yet hadn't written anything.

So you said write a book, and I said okay.
Here it is. For you.

Thanks for your inspiration and understanding.

Thanks for your kindness and encouragement.

But most of all…

Thanks for being you.

## The Names

The family in my story is a Cornish family hailing from Penzance. I've decided to use a traditional Celtic Cornish name for each of them that in some way reflects their innate personality and character, or at least demonstrates aspects of their life.

**NANCARROW** is a medieval family name that means 'valley of the deer.'

**TRISTAN**, a hero of Arthurian legend, was a noble and gallant young man.

**BLYTH** is the Cornish word for 'wolf.'

**KERRA** in Cornish means 'dearest one.'

**AILLA** means 'beautiful one' in traditional Cornish

Other names

**BELLA** is a short form of the Cornish name Belerwen, the regional word for Venus, Roman goddess of love.

**MARK** is Margh in old Cornish, and is the local word for 'horse,' and the name of the King of Cornwall in the tale of Tristan and Isolde.

# CONTENTS

# Part I

# Cause and Effect

*Chapter One*

To a boy's ears, the growls during the beating sounded more wild animal than human; raw anger and menace, like a prowling lion. Tristan always thought his father savage as he raged down upon him, crashing through his slender, futile arms like fragile grass on an African plain, as the snarling beast attacked its prey with dreadful, unhinged ferocity. "Get up and fight you little shit…get up," he drooled as the punches rained down. "Fucking fight me, boy." His dark hair was dirty, the olive eyes, rabid. With chest heaving he edged back, heavy boots echoing off the cold stone floor.

Tristan curled on his side, the foetal position automatic. His arms wore angry bruises. One eye swollen shut. His head pounded and he wanted to run, but experience had taught him to play dead…it would be over quicker that way, as his father's feral rage subsided.

But not yet.

The boy stared at the scuffed black work boots now inches from his pale face. Expectant. Certain.

Blyth Nancarrow grabbed his son's neck and yanked him to his feet. But now he was weak and worn and drunk, and their bodies spilled heavily to the floor as the stench of stale whisky filled Tristan's bloody nostrils. He rolled slowly away and closed his good eye.

And waited.

Unhurriedly, his old man rose to his feet and stood nonchalant, his long frame towering over the broken boy below. "You will fight me, boy," he taunted, voice coarse and low, ominous. "One day you will fight me, or that day might be your last."

Tristan tried in vain to turn away, but with a last ounce of rage Blyth crashed a fist into his son's temple. Tristan crumpled motionless to the unforgiving floor and held his breath. He could feel his body against the ground, stone and grit piercing eggshell skin; a knee cap, the knobbly bit of an ankle, a grazed elbow, a smashed cheek...all screamed in protest. Yet he couldn't remove himself, almost as if his frail body had been dumped from a mold and spilled into the cracks like a liquid child, now a fallen actor at one with the cruel and pitiless stage. Through piquant tears he saw his father retreat calmly from the room.

It was an old cottage, and in moments like those the immovable, thick stone walls seemed to close in around him. Through sickening quietude he listened, the air as thin as the time seemed long. An owl hooted somewhere beyond the window. There, finally, the welcome slam of the bedroom door. Only then could he breathe, short painful breaths as a cracked rib let itself be known. The dark walls receded too, now, as if letting out their own sigh of relief. He shuffled into the deep corner shadows of his room, tender cheek pressed against cool stone. Eyes shut tight, one forced and the other chosen, bruised arms wrapped tight around himself.

Battered and helpless, a young boy yearned for the night to take him.

Tristan didn't understand why his father beat him with such vitriol, conditioned to assume it was natural, accept it as deserved. But innately he knew it was wrong, for children are not immune from sharing their parents' shame, and there, forsaken in the darkness, the sobs came. At first slow and sporadic, they soon became the strong and pitiful cries of an abused child. The tear fell unseen, his pain unheard...wasted. He knew no one would comfort him that night.

A drop of blood dripped silently from his nose and splashed black on his forearm. More followed, and they soon mixed with the flow of teardrops to create a trickling cocktail of sorrow. Alone and neglected on his bedroom floor, Tristan imagined that just once his mother would come to him. His was a lonely life, and with no one to cry to, he faced the slow path of time alone.

He was thirteen years old.

His sleep was rarely peaceful, and during the night Tristan awoke with a start. Instinctively his muscles tautened, and his heart raced as a discerned fear of his father kept his nerves shredded. His eyes stretched wide but were rendered useless by the swallowing darkness, and suddenly he gasped, unaware he hadn't drawn a breath in thirty seconds. Once sure he was alone, Tristan laid back and screwed his eyes shut to the world.

It was a dream that had woken him. He dreamt about a house resounding with the sounds of unhappiness.

Shouting and crying. Furniture breaking. Glass smashing. The noise of violence. These sounds haunted his dreams, and all shared a simple commonality; they terrified him, and more so in dreams than in reality, for when awake he could choose not to listen.

His dreams often involved a girl, though he didn't know her name, just a face from his imagination and a face that was never clear. In the dreams the girl would disappear, and that was always when the violence started. When he thought of the girl beyond the nights he imagined her as a close friend, but Tristan had no real friends and those rare happy moments were priceless, for the next beating was always on its way.

Tristan longed for his mother. She was so afraid of her husband that she rarely went to her son's room. She never stayed or said anything, but it was enough for him to know she had checked on him in the night. In the pre-dawn blackness he imagined her sad, pretty face, her lonely dark eyes smiling inwardly because they'd both made it through another night.

Kerra Nancarrow endured hell at the indifferent hands of her truculent husband. She was a beautiful young girl when they'd met, but time and Blyth were not kind, and years of battery and psychological abuse had reduced her to a stress whittled and heartbroken woman. She existed within a mean and smothering fear, and knew that the most trivial thing could provoke a corporal or emotional onslaught, and often both.

It was nineteen sixties England, a liberal and forward thinking nation, yet she lived like a slave, a Victorian housemaid who spoke only when spoken to and obeyed her master's every whim. Kerra suffered in silence, too afraid to complain, and learned that her subservience might just make her son's passage through childhood less barbarous. If she protested Blyth often vented on the boy. She could suffer the beatings…she'd suffered them for fifteen years…but it broke her heart to see a father abuse a son.

Yet she was powerless to stop it, and couldn't bear to imagine the consequences for Tristan if she tried to escape. She had made that mistake only once, and her memory of the backlash had tortured her since. Eight years on, and she hadn't dared try again. They were prisoners of those accursed, stone-clad cells, and their guard was malicious.

Hours later a horizontal rain drummed harshly against the window. Tristan awoke as the murky dawn emerged under a heavy storm, and though October was mild, November had banished the sun. He lay still for an age, and listened for familiar sounds throughout the soulless cottage. Nothing. He waited.

Running an aching hand over his long, lean body, he winced at the tapestry of nefarious bruises. The puffed eye saw nothing and a grotesquely split lip stung like acid. He breathed short, shallow breaths, his cracked rib firing lightning bolts through his chest. Still, he waited.

Finally the sound he hoped for arrived; the heavy slam of the cottage's big wooden door. That grimly impressive barrier, constructed from the reclaimed timbers of a once stricken fishing boat, served as an impenetrable portal for Tristan. It kept him locked down like a forgotten prisoner, and when it closed it closed with terminal finality. He was always on the inside.

Ten more minutes, just to be sure. Then, and with considerable effort, Tristan dragged himself out of bed and edged gently towards the window in painful, shuffling installments. Despite the hour it was still almost dark, and he strained his one seeing eye into the gloom. The truck's low growl and demon red back lights slowly faded from sight and sound, leaving only silence in the oily black. Its departure tranquilized the young boy's soul.

He stood at the small window a long time, oblivious to its warped rotting frame and cracked glass. He stared out into the dimness, though there was nothing to see. Tristan had lived his entire life in that bleak and isolated beach commune of three, and had rarely left. He often wondered what he might find if one day he could leave the island of St. Mary's, which seemed prehistorically remote, though Cornwall's busy port of Penzance had evolved just forty miles across the sea. He yearned to go there...to go anywhere...but he was just a kid, too weak, too naive and too afraid to escape that tyrannical kingdom.

But Tristan could dream, and no violence would ever inhibit that. He imagined a faraway world, somewhere he needn't fear, perhaps a world where he and his mother could be safe. He might even have a friend, like the faceless girl from his dreams.

And he dreamed of a world where his father didn't growl like a wild animal as he beat his thirteen-year-old son like a dog.

*Chapter Two*

The girl suffered no religion, having long since dismissed the reality of religious fairytales, but she knew as she wrote that her message had a New Testament feel to it. She didn't care. It might help.

The letter was written with a specific person in mind,

and though she knew they'd never read it, the symbolic act of the writing comforted her. The guilt she'd kept hidden for more than a decade, a remorse that sometimes crept like a sickness to corrode her happiness, was a constant yet unwanted companion, but her actions today would take her a few small steps toward emancipation.

The train out to Long Island from Penn Station was quiet on a Sunday morning, as was Long Beach when she arrived, and she smiled, satisfied, because it's where she went to be alone. She often spent hours there, just walking the beach or sketching in her notebook, and one day she hoped to be an artist…it was in her genetics, she believed…and daydreamed about the future as she kicked her feet through golden sand a million years in the making. But she had a more present issue, and when she neared a familiar and isolated spot, her hand subconsciously felt the smooth envelope deep within her shoulder bag.

Sitting down she took out that envelope and removed the single piece of folded paper from inside, then slowly read the message for the last time. Images from a distant past brought on a swell of sadness, but she knew that writing and sending this note was positive, and though some guilt would remain, *shit, it always remains*, she thought, *clinging to me like a loyal stain*, she imagined that at least a little would ebb away, carried out on a strong Atlantic tide.

The girl accepted she was probably being hard on herself over the guilt, because, after all, she too had been a victim. But the remorse she felt for the person she had written to was real and potent. The letter was for them, but symbolically, equally, its poignant message was for her. With a subtle nod to herself and the world, she returned the note to its envelope.

White clouds scudded low across the horizon's elegant arc, and the only sound came from harmless waves ending their long one-way journey by drenching her shoes. She didn't care. Gazing out across five thousand miles of ocean, and speaking loudly as if to carry her voice the entire distance, she said aloud the first line of her message:

"Don't be alone any longer, for I am here with you."

There was nobody to hear and nobody to see her glistening teardrops catch the sunlight, as they slid from big inherited blue eyes. The intended recipient would never see his message, and those tears fell for the boy she would never meet.

She rode the train back to Manhattan, and arrived as Penn Station swarmed with smiling people on a luminous Sunday afternoon. She stopped next to a mailbox outside and smiled also, as she placed one envelope inside another, the second on which she'd written from memory an address that had witnessed years of her happy childhood. Then she raised the envelope to her lips and with her eyes closed, kissed it delicately, and in an instant the letter was gone, slipped into the mailbox with the rest left to fate.

How did she feel? Happy with a tinge of sadness? Or sad with a hint of happiness? It didn't matter. It was done, a small, simple gift to herself.

Today was her sixteenth birthday.


*Chapter Three*

The screeching high above of constantly dissatisfied gulls roused Tristan from his aloof reverie. He angled his gaze to the wide sky and envied the birds their freedom.

*Freedom.*
In his fifteen years he had never once considered his own liberties and license, and as he pondered the alien concepts he kneeled back down on the damp, blackish soil and resumed tending to his plants. In a tidy kempt corner of an otherwise neglected garden, Tristan cared for the aster flowers he'd nurtured from seeds his mother gifted him many years past, and the pink, purple and blue star bursts were his pride and joy. But those flowers were a source of immense pain too, for when they became an easy outlet for his father's despotic anger, it hurt Tristan as much as a fist upon his own flesh. He vowed to never let them die, and each autumn they returned was a small and cherished victory.

Blyth Nancarrow dwelled in a state of immortal depression, and no matter how hard he had tried to destroy it in its formative months and years, it could not be killed. He knew his failures as a man were down to bad luck and the hand he'd been dealt, and this knowledge mixed with whisky intoxicated him into trancelike acts in a coliseum of violence, with his wife and son cast as unwitting commissioned comrades and helpless victims upon whom he bestowed his relentless abjections.
When Kerra wasn't convenient to play the role, the boy would suffer, and when Tristan was out of sight, his beloved asters were cruelly and coldly trampled into the earth like retired theatre props. Each time this happened Tristan wished it was him, and the seed of his own anger grew unchecked, though he was still no physical match for his father. He'd learned in the very hardest way that to resist his father meant his mother bore the brunt of the bloodletting hostility, and it was a writhing, vicious cycle.
They both knew it, he and his mother, and together they

suffered in a diseased silence. It was spoken of only once. "Ours is and must be a silent love, my son, and that bond is stronger than life itself and which no fist can ever break. It needs no voice yet it's here, like a pendulum constantly swinging, from my heart and mind into yours and back again. No one else deserves its power, and that power is in our silence."

Since that day they'd barely spoken, their relationship forced mute and he mutilated by it. But their veiled bond endured, and Tristan hoped that one day soon he'd unearth enough courage to confront his father and claim back his mother's freedom. With irrational shame he knew that day was distant.

Tristan was drifting absently amidst his swirling thoughts when his mother came and stood by him. After a few uninhabited, hollow moments, she leaned close and whispered five words that ignited a spark in his undeveloped pride. "Your flowers are so beautiful."

Over his neglected hands she placed her own, and with no further words necessary or dared, they looked out into a passive twilight and imagined.

When Tristan was seven, mother and son sat at the old oak table, piecing together their favourite jigsaw puzzle, a Constable landscape with galloping wild horses that injected a sense of adventure and colour...and escape...to the insipid, lifeless evenings. For Kerra those moments were at least peaceful, and they smiled and laughed quietly together. Sometimes in those days, if they stood at the window when Blyth was out they'd see the occasional large deer, even the odd stag, over by the woods beyond the property, but those rare and wondrous sightings were becoming more and more sporadic, as if the sounds of violence from within were warning the skittish animals away from the dangerous humans inside. It had been months since they'd seen one of the magnificent creatures, and it was yet another sign to Kerra of the deterioration of their once peaceful lives.

But that evening their calm was shattered when the front door flew open then slammed shut with its foreboding thud. Immediately Kerra stiffened, and Tristan though young sensed the impending threat. Blyth in those days still visited the pub a couple of miles into the village. He would set off after lunch, wordlessly leaving the cottage behind and often getting home only after the landlord had kicked him out, always sullen, his ignoble mood as dark and heavy as the cottage door.

He'd returned home earlier than expected, as a late summer sun threw ethereal spears of light slicing through the cottage as if through the bars of a prison cell. Tristan heard his father's footfalls, slow and ominously erratic, and glanced at his mother. Under a spell of fear, the hazy half-light made a gargoyle of her face, and though she forced a smile to comfort the boy, it was weak and easily betrayed by eyes as wide as a rabbit's when an eagle swooped.

Never was a wife more afraid of a husband, and as the kitchen door creaked open on its ancient hinges, the author and architect of her horror story life staggered into the room.

"Ah, fucking at it again are we?" he growled, and the stench of his whisky breath spilled into the air. "Planning to take the boy and leave, were you? Fucking bitch! I know your game, always scheming when I'm gone."

He stumbled a little and cursed as a lamp wobbled then fell to the floor. Blyth wobbled too as he edged nearer the table. "Admit it, woman," he spat, and swung a powerful open hand at Kerra's face, but all she felt was a rush of air as the cruel slap narrowly missed, and Blyth almost fell, such was his whisky fueled momentum.

Tristan jumped up and stood brave in front of his mother, wise to but naive of the very real danger he faced. At this demeaning show of defiance to his power by a mere child, the magma of his father's volatile rage surged, and in an eruption of fists and grunts and flying spittle, he shoved his young son viciously to the floor, smashing the fallen lamp to pieces.

Next Blyth grabbed a fistful of his wife's coppery auburn hair and dragged her screaming from the kitchen, sending chairs and the table tumbling, the door crashing shut in his wake. Tristan was locked behind it, with pieces of fractured jigsaw strewn all about him like fallen volcanic ash.

With his skinny hands balled into useless fists and crying out for his mother, Tristan pounded on the door as if it was his father's rugged body.

"Leave her alone. Please leave her alone!" As hot and helpless tears fell and his feeble child muscles waned, he was aware of only one sound; the sickening muffled thud of fist striking flesh.

Then he heard the scream, and his heart broke.

Beyond that door and the next, Blyth beat upon Kerra with chilling vengeance, and when he ripped the belt from the loops around his waist, her scream could be heard for miles except, there was no one but her son within miles to hear, and now even he clamped his bloodied bruised hands over his ears to block what he thought were the sounds of her death.

Kerra slumped unconscious to the ground, the twisted, inert form settling beneath the legs of her destroyer. The injury index was long: fractured cheekbone; cracked ribs;

two black eyes; belt gashes seeped blood like split fruit; her pale skin a winter sky painted with purple clouds.

Blyth sat heavily on the bed, breathing hard. All around him was still and silent, and a sweet metallic scent of blood laced the air. In a daze he stared at and beyond the wall, and though he couldn't see them, autumn leaves fell like rotten stars from an indifferent sky.

After a moment his tired eyes dropped down to his victim. She wasn't moving, other than the slow rise and fall of her chest. He saw blood drying black on his wife's skin, and a blank, distant look passed over his face, as if realising for the first time what he'd just done. But that lapse of compunctious emotion was fleeting, and by the time he wiped the sweat from his brow, it was gone.

He kicked off his thuggish black boots and threw down his mucky trousers and whisky stained shirt, and finally, with a piggish, sardonic grunt, Blyth Nancarrow turned his back on his sins and rolled over on the bed. He was asleep in seconds.

Neither parent heard their son's anguished cries from the kitchen, and as minutes stretched to hours and the earth's slow revolutions stripped the last light from the sky, the voice melted first to a whimper and then ceased completely, as a devastated young boy curled against the door and found himself, as he would so often be in years to come, cold and alone in the darkness.

That memory, that unspoken moment from their shared past, virtually forbade them from speaking together when Blyth was home. Neither dared trigger his demons, and though the understanding was mutual, it tortured them both. Kerra didn't want and no longer expected much from her own life, nothing more than to love her son as a mother should, to hug him, and tell him she was proud.

But the violence this might incur meant her love was unemployable, and she couldn't...she wouldn't...display the affection that she longed to give and he craved to receive.

So for now, and when seldom the chance arose, they simply stood together and relished the calm, because too well they knew that, just like a palm on a beach or a sailboat on the Pacific, their lives were subject to the whims of a brooding tempest looming vengefully just beyond the horizon.

Blyth's heavy drinking furnished him with anger and paranoia. When he drank he always believed Kerra would leave him, and he knew that she should. He understood what a failed husband he was, but he couldn't control his drinking and the violence that shadowed him. His sober self knew sorrow, but the whisky bullied him, its grip unyielding, and plunged him deep in a downward spiral of drinking and violence and depression and remorse. It was an endless dark tunnel with no light at its end.

Today was one such day. Blyth slept late and woke only when the midday sun penetrated the tattered incompetent curtains. Hearing nothing, he stalked the dark corridor that dissected the dead cottage like a redundant artery, and stepped out into a clear late summer's day. There they stood with their backs to him, wife and son together, hand upon hand and thin shoulders barely touching, and for a brief moment he was awash with happy reflections. A thin misplaced smile even stole onto his worn face.

He'd been handsome once, tall and lean and with strong and confident features, and was popular with the girls in school who loved his olive green, intelligent eyes. It was a couple of years later that he met and fell in love with Kerra, a beautiful young artist working at a gallery in their seaside hometown of Penzance. They adored each other, and she quickly fell for the good looking and assured young man, much to the dismay of her legion of suitors. One in particular, devastated by the news, reluctantly kept his distance.

They married young and perhaps too soon, but they didn't care and were oblivious to the world. They were carefree and happy times. But life had not been gentle to Blyth's features, and where on broad shoulders once sat a pleasant and righteous face, that face now was worn and thin and held behind it a worn thin collection of misery and morals.

Blyth's trance was broken by the ocean breeze ruffling his dark and untamed hair, now flecked with grey at his temples. He looked up into a sky the colour of dead coral, and saw shadowy clouds forming miles out to sea. As if the dark malevolence in those clouds was some unconscious trigger, his happy moment evaporated, and what flooded in instead was anger and resentment. Much as he fought to quell them, his demons were far too strong an adversary for his weak mind, and rose at will with not a damn thing he could do to stop them.

As time and whisky were unkind to Blyth's appearance, so they took a heavy toll on his character and stability, and when his demons rose as they did then, there was only ever one result; a blinding, choking red mist laced with danger. The mere sight of them standing there and scheming together in whispers was too much to bear, and he strode forward, vile intensity stripping the peace from his face.

With apparent sixth sense his prey turned their bodies to face the storm. Time slowed. Tristan saw with clarity his father's tightly balled fists, skin strained white over clenched knuckles, glazed eyes focused on retribution for an imagined violation.

Tristan once more looked to the sky, the shrieking gulls now mocking him from above, and as the tornado struck, his last thought was of freedom, and what that really meant.

## Chapter Four

Tristan couldn't open his left eye. Through his squinted right he saw that the sun was high, but he heard nothing other than the blood pounding through his temples. He was in pain...a lot of pain...which he ignored; his only concern was his mother. His father had come at him first, and only a blur had followed, but without doubt his mother had born the brunt, for the look in his father's rancorous eyes screamed vengeance.

He stepped from his bed and placed his ear against the door, and was met with a quiet so deep it seemed as if the whole world had died. A sense of foreboding crawled over his milk white skin as he advanced queasily to the kitchen. The relief he felt to see his mother sitting there was demonstrated by a slow expulsion of long held breath, the first sound he'd heard that day. But she sat so torpid and silent, arms folded nervously in her lap, that goosebumps rose in earnest.

Not wanting to startle her, he called out softly. "Mum. Good morning." Despite just yards between them she didn't hear. He called again, a little louder. "Mum? Are you alright?" Her slight, sallow hands twitched a little in the faded folds of her dress, then gripped the worn fabric tight. Her knuckles blanched white under the pressure, and her slim chest heaved as if sucking in the island's last air. Tristan moved to place a comforting hand on her shoulder, and she turned to face him.

What he saw made his blood run cold.

Her slitted left eye shone purple black. Above it, running from her ear to the centre of her lined forehead, a deep red slash glistened. Her pale skin, more ghostly than usual. Her weak frame, more fragile than ever. Teardrops of despair spilled onto swollen, quivering lips. She stood shakily, faced her son, and looked deep into his eyes. Tortured. Mauled. Impaled at once by love and hate. Unable to speak the words she longed to say, she turned and hobbled to her room, the door bolted hard behind her, like the last nail in the coffin of her hope.

Far from the cottage, Blyth Nancarrow stood alone at the top of a high cliff. He squinted out at the nothingness before him yet saw everything. Hung-over, the world flickered harsh and bright, and the troubled man shed rare tears. He stepped forward, dangerously close to the cliff's edge, turmoil ripping his heart, first one way and then another, and in a barely intelligible voice that was lost forever on the breeze, said to nobody, *who am I?* and *what have I become?*

Tristan followed after his mother, but it was a futile act knowing she would muzzle her anguish the way she always did. Blyth was so dominant after so many years of pernicious torment, that she'd become as tractable as a hungry dog, and the power of his paranoia was such that the two of them, mother and son, were critically circumspect. He called to her again anyway, and when only the familiar heart wrenching sobs of desperation resounded from beyond the door, the same familiar helplessness clenched at his guts. Those solemn sounds haunted Tristan at night, for in a house of near silence, his mother's pain echoed through the darkness like a sonorous sermon of tribulation.

He trudged from the house with his spirit in shreds, and worry hung from his slumped shoulders like a veil of iron. Though he knew what he would find, he walked slowly to the scene of yesterday's savagery. But even he was surprised at the extent of the destruction; all his flowers were destroyed, with not a single one of the pretty asters left undead.

A creeping rage infiltrated a heart shorn of affection, and took root for the first time where once it had only visited. He tried to deny it, vainly refusing to become hateful like the man who deserved his hate, but it grew, sorrow growing where sorrow had been denied, feeding on its own absence until it entered his veins like a slinking trickle of ice. Refused entry before, now it was welcomed.

Planting his hands firmly on the low wall, as if trying to ground his anger and store it among the ancient rocks, he thought of his mother. Hushed and alone in her room, he worried about her as he always had. Recently though, he'd noticed an aphoristic shift in her surface demeanor. Despite her emotional disablement Kerra had always greeted her son with a smile, and her eyes shone bright when they were together. But that shine had vanished, and the abandoned look in its place scared him more than anything.

She was frightened…how could she not be? But the adopted stoic facade had deserted to leave her exposed to Tristan's incipient observations, and with no dialogue between them he felt paralyzed. He needed to engage his mother, to find a way in which they could speak alone and with freedom and without the scepter of *Him* shrouding them in fear. He had to help, had to be strong to fulfill the unlikely role of soldier leading his fallen mother to safety, and he imagined himself as nature and tried hard to picture stone or rock or even oak, but instead saw only fallen leaves or dust or trampled grass, and he knew he was no soldier and never would be.

Tristan didn't know where his father was or how long he'd be gone, but in his desperation, he didn't care and felt reckless. The sky promised him nothing good as he crossed the almost sacred cottage boundary to the beach, and he was in no doubt of the fate to befall him if caught. But today he had to go to the forbidden sanctuary, and allow the coastal rawness of the air to scrape the debris from his mind.

To Blyth it mattered little that they lived miles from any other house in a deserted corner of a near empty island. It was irrelevant. They must never leave, because if they left then they might never return. He knew he was mean to them, aware of his failures as husband and father, but he couldn't change. Alcoholism swamped him with depression and stirred his emotions into a dark fermenting maelstrom.

But despite what he knew of failure, Blyth was a tortured man who felt all the world conspired against him. Life and circumstances had polluted his good nature to spawn an angry, untethered soul, yet in the ugly face of it all he loved his family, and the despair at what he'd become charged violently to the surface. He too was a victim, and he knew it well because despair can break a man unlike any physical force ever could. Rocks can smash bones, and bullets maim. Poison steals life in silence. But those enemies use violence and pain, a man fully cognizant when it happens. Despair is a cruel and vicious foe, lurking and spiteful, doing its worst in the dark where it cannot be seen or felt. It's a patient and cold enemy that rarely loses.

Yes, Blyth was as much a victim as his wife and son. They just didn't know it.

Once he'd even considered ending it all. Because he knew that they all suffered, he would kill them in their sleep, then slit his own wrists and wait patiently, gratefully, for death. But Blyth was a coward and they suffered still. Morality for Blyth was a virtue he could reach but could not hold onto, so a dictatorial inner fury gripped his heart like a vice, twisting any thoughts of remorse into uncontrollable rage. They, his family, were the guilty, manipulating his weaknesses, against him, the innocent.

Tristan had ventured just a few hundred yards from the cottage, but already the cloak of anxiety had slipped away, and aside from his mother, there was no other living soul within miles. *So little life*, he thought, but as he walked along the beach's barren dunes he realized that the title of life in itself was a misconception, for to be justifiably known as life, one could safely assume some semblance of living. And for many years, even the most generous witness could not label their existence as living.

Surviving. Tristan knew they were merely surviving.

With only the endless ocean stretching out beyond his imagination, there on the beach was as close to freedom as Tristan had ever been. That he was so naïve to the basic essence of freedom meant he couldn't fully appreciate the truly awful state of his and his mother's desperate lives. And he was never at liberty to witness their contraries, because invisible yet ruthless harnesses kept them intrinsically bound, as if in a sane asylum where only the guard was crazy.

He knew very little of the faraway world only forty miles across the sea, and once, when he questioned his father about life beyond those desolate shores, he was told in no uncertain terms that *he didn't know how lucky he was*. And there was no good reason to disbelieve that, other than an inherent consciousness that life consisted of more than he knew. And all Tristan knew were the beatings and the loneliness and the polarized accompaniment of silence and screams.

On the rare occasions he had broached the subject with his mother, a dusky shadow settled over her face as she considered her response. With reluctant sadness, it seemed to him, she always replied in the same way; *your father is right*. She could never hold his gaze when she said this, and although he noticed, he couldn't yet interpret the connotation. These evasive answers and his father's dismissals only nurtured further the sprouting thought that there was another world beyond the restrictive water of the bay.

Sitting on the beach then, and looking out over that unusually flat water, Tristan mused as to how far he would get if he swam straight out, unsure even if he could swim or not, having never been allowed to try. If he did make it to the mainland, what would happen to him? Who would he meet? Would they hurt him too?

Today, questions that usually scared him didn't, and Tristan felt strange, dully aware of a new and subtle disturbance within, something alien, like a tingling in his guts of some emotion never before felt. Was it bravery? Was that how it felt to have some form of control over your actions?

A sense of purpose stilled the air around him, and for a moment he actually considered wading into the sea, until he recalled the extent of his injuries and the idea was painfully snuffed out. Even here his father controlled him, as if some remote conjuring master of puppets, and his anger inflated just a little more.

Besides, he knew the consequences for his mother if he left the island. Blyth would hold Kerra responsible and beat her until she confessed, and his frightening and unwelcome knowledge of what his father would do to him if he was caught, and to his mother if he wasn't, set his blood surging with an adrenalin laced throb of fear and anger.

Tristan reluctantly dismissed the sudden and brief fantasy of leaving St. Mary's. Over long static minutes his pulse had slowed, but now the lack of dispatched adrenalin allowed a swathe of claustrophobic, vestigial despair to settle once more upon his back.

He didn't know how long he'd been standing there, but noticed with alarm how the sun had set fire to the horizon. He panicked. His father would get home before him. But he stared as the fire dropped swiftly in a western sky that seemed lifetimes away. *Just follow the sun over the horizon, and escape the cottage and its living nightmares.*

One day, he thought, but he wasn't convinced.

Tristan hurried home with aching, uneven strides. He made it in time.


*Chapter Five*

That night, as he often did, he dreamt of the girl with the obscured face. In the dream they spent hours playing at the beach, launching stones into the waves and hiding among the grassy, billowing dunes. They were happy dreams when the girl showed up, and they brought him rare unconscious smiles. But when the girl left and the dreams faded, Tristan was accompanied by the only companion he could ever rely upon not to desert him.

Loneliness.

The next day Tristan awoke late and slowly, and there was no rush because there was nothing to rush for. He attempted to recall the hazy dreams of the faceless girl, to relive that happiness, but try as he might he couldn't penetrate the opacity of his lethargic mind. But then, and with frightening clarity, yesterday's events came crashing through the opaque morning like a barreling Atlantic wave to leave him feeling washed up and struggling for air. In time the wave receded, and he staggered dazed from his bed to gulp thirstily from the glass of water beside him.

It was mid-morning and the sun fought the dense clouds valiantly. Tristan sought out his mother, and found her sewing, perched delicately on the edge of the bed. As he hovered in the doorway she glanced up, and her forehead's angry gash blazed red. His parent's bedroom was out of bounds for him. His father had once thrashed him for stepping inside. So he paused in the threshold and noticed the chipped doorframe, and knew it was caused by repetitive, violent slamming. From the door his eyes scanned the room, and he noticed for the first time how drab it seemed. Faded wallpaper peeled sadly in corners, and small achromatic rectangles revealed where pictures had once hung. Threadbare curtains dangled limply on too few hooks, and dust settled everywhere like ant sized deserts of dead skin. The very room breathed a sadness that reflected the now permanent atmosphere in the humble, dilapidated cottage.

But his mother's smile allayed his uneasiness and assured him he was safe to enter, that *He* wasn't home. Tristan glanced nervously down the narrow hallway, but her gentle patting of the bed beside her convinced him, and he at last stepped inside.

Though he had few women to compare her to, Tristan

had always thought of his mother as pretty, and recalled something his father used to say often back in more peaceful times. "You should have seen her, boy," he'd say, "she was really something. The prettiest young girl in all Cornwall. And she fell for me." Blyth would chuckle, his eyes emitting a genuine sparkle of wonder when he spoke of the past, his soft voice emotional as he withdrew into the recesses of his fractured memory. Then the clouds would roll in from the capricious ocean of his mind to censor that shadowy recollection, the moments once more lost to time.

Tristan faced his mother and searched her eyes, saddened to see how thoroughly worn down she looked. She still bore fine features, and when she smiled, a little of the old glint returned to her eyes. But she was fading, and had become the embodied form of her intangible surroundings. Her forehead, once smooth, was now scarred by deep wrinkles, as if a plough of despair had been dragged across it, and her slim shoulders sagged, while her gaunt wrists looked so deathly against the brown bed clothes that Tristan had to blink away the image of bones in earth.

Grave of heart, he took a seat on the bed. She took her son's right hand in her withered left, and they sat in their usual reticent state. The only sound was of their slow breaths, for no clocks chimed within those walls. Motes of dust shifted lazily in the sluggish light, as if waiting for something. Waiting to escape. Tristan turned to his mother. A single tear caught in her long lashes. She looked back at him as she fought the swell of emotion.

This was his moment.

"Mum, we have to leave." He gripped her hand tighter. "We could go right now, hide out somewhere and go to the mainland tomorrow. He'll never catch us…he'll never hurt you again."

From Kerra's eyes then weeped unabridged tears, and her lips trembled while her breaths became strangled, as if choking on words that refused to be spoken. He looked on alarmed.

"Mum, what is it, what's wrong? We have to leave now, before he comes home."

Composure eluded her for a long, uncertain moment, until at last she forced shut her eyes with fierce determination. Kerra had always known this day would come. But now, she somehow managed to swallow down the words she knew she should say but also knew she never would, and was ready with her response. She only hoped that it would not return to haunt her.

With all joy purged from her heart, Kerra Nancarrow straightened her back and looked intently at her son.

"No. You're wrong, Tristan. We cannot leave. I know you're scared, and I'm scared too. But if we leave, he will find us, because there is no escaping from him. It's too late for that. And, my brave boy, he's my husband, so it doesn't matter what he's done to me, because I have my duty as a wife. I took an oath when we married, 'until death us do part,' and I will not betray it."

Tristan wanted to protest, but the stony look that bore out from his mother's eyes, damming what was just moments ago a flood of sorrow, froze his jaw and shocked his voice into silence.

When she next spoke, it was with objective authority. "We cannot leave, no matter what he does. No matter what!"

Tristan was staggered, in utter disbelief at what he was hearing, and if it weren't for the bed beneath him he may have collapsed in frustration. With numbing clarity he knew that by staying, his mother had not only guaranteed, but in a way assented to their continued abuse, almost as if the sheer consistency of her suffering had embedded her acquiescence.

He longed to, had to, protest about this irrational foolishness. But she was his mother, and Tristan so badly wanted to believe that she knew the best path for them. There was something in her tone, too, a fortifying of stoicism absent too long, and it gave him something to cling on to. Tristan knew only two emotions, fear and love, and regarding his parents he feared one and loved the other, and he trusted her judgement implicitly, despite his contrary heart. They looked at each other for a long moment. Eventually he forced a smile, unaware that although her face had softened, the smile she returned was equally forced.

With a subtle hesitance she didn't miss, Tristan reluctantly nodded his own submission.

He stood to leave, but paused in the damaged doorway to look back at his mother, unable and perhaps unwilling to recognise the look on her face that appeared somewhere between austere and agonized. With his head down, he stepped from that dank and decayed room, and felt his mother's eyes on him long after he had left.

Though she could no longer see her son, those glassy eyes followed him for an age after he'd gone. Kerra in that moment was nothing more than a defeated, broken woman with a face stained by pure agony. Such pain had been incubating within for years, but under the strain of the harsh and onerous decision she'd just made, that pain now hatched and came forth fully fledged. Sitting in that infested air, the vile decision made, Kerra didn't know when she would see her son again.

Stalked by his mother's haunted eyes, Tristan heaved

open the weighty wooden cell door and padded out of the prison cottage once more. Autumn clouds continued their perennial battle with the sun, and a taut breeze angled long arthritic shadows down that estranged shore of raw, handsome coastline. A sad wind whistled as if to lament its human void.

Edging away from the choppy shoreline, Tristan glanced back over his arced shoulders to see one solitary set of footprints following him sadly up the beach, and he felt as lonely as he ever had. Onwards he trudged, sandy footprints creeping up behind, and in the lee of a low sandy cliff he found the usual shelter which, during his infrequent visits, had become the one place in his young life he felt safe. In that secret sanctuary he was alone, as he was everywhere, but at least there he could breathe a little easier, if just for a while. The fresh air and welcome taste of security allowed him a rare opportunity to think clearly, yet good thoughts usually eluded him. Sometimes his sadness and emotions got the better of him, and he'd start to think of how he and his mother suffered, and once that seed of indignation took root it was difficult to shake off.

Tristan's parents were the only two people he knew. There had been occasional visitors to the cottage over the years, usually his father's friends from the village coming by to borrow tools, or to walk with him to the pub. But those visits dried up a long time ago, as one by one his father's friends stayed away until they ceased coming altogether. The odd tradesman or salesperson passed through, to chance their arm at some work or other, but they were always swiftly dismissed, Blyth ever wary of their motives and intention. There were even sporadic visits by religious types, preaching the so-called *good book*. Tristan remembered a time when Blyth welcomed them in, made them tea and listened carefully before contributing to their bulging pockets or collection pots. But like everything else, his father no longer believed, and began to growl invectives at them from the door before slamming it in their well fed faces. They no longer came.

*How can two parents be so different?* Tristan thought, and then thought of his mother. Though adrift from her now, when he was younger she'd been so serene and placid, kindly and wise. Then his father, who was perpetually morose and intolerant, often brutal and angry. Blyth barely acknowledged his son's existence, and beat him whenever the urge seized him. And his mother could not and did not love him like he yearned to be loved, remaining aloof and incognizant of her alienated child.

And that is how Tristan felt; like an abandoned orphan who shared a roof with his own parents. *Who am I?*

Eventually enough wind had stolen into the shelter that his melancholy had blown away along with his footprints, and by the time he stood to leave, the sun had melted below the horizon. His stomach grumbled in protest.

Something caught his eye. He peered into the near dark, and saw a cast off sheet of newspaper tumbling on the breeze towards him. Stretching out a long arm he grabbed it and, ignoring his hunger, backed again into the shelter. It was the cover page of a local paper, and reading the headline, his pupils dilated in surprise. In bold, black letters:

**MISSING BOY: PENZANCE- October 29th, 1962**

*Just last week*, Tristan realized. He read on.

**Unnamed boy, 15, reported missing.**
**Last seen Wednesday at the beach near his home in**

**the village of Mousehole, Penzance.**

**A weak swimmer, and authorities fear the worst after last week's wild storm.**

**Locals encouraged to stay alert.**

**Report any sightings to Penzance Police Department at first instance.**

The story was a shock to Tristan, and he wondered what had happened. *Did he really drown? Snatched by bad people? Maybe he just ran away from home?*

Run away. It seemed so simple. Something roused as he considered the prospect. He was sad. Beatings were common. He was always lonely, and had nothing to look forward to, ever. *Why don't I just run away?* he thought. *Why can't I simply disappear?*

But as thoughts of escape squirmed and inflamed the very air around him, Tristan knew he didn't mean it. He once made a personal and solemn pact never to leave his mother, despite his own bleak consequences. He was sure his mother had made a similar vow long ago, and she had confirmed it just hours before. They'd suffered alongside one another for many years, and they would stick together. *No matter what!* That is what she said. *No matter what!*

From afar Tristan saw the familiar dark bulk of the low roofed cottage. The day's dying light flickered for a second on the roof's apex, and then it was gone, swallowed by the night and sucked at last across new longitudes.

Beneath that thickening darkness he walked, hoping his father was still out, though he doubted it, and unease slowed him as he approached the boundary wall. At that wall, he paused. His shoulders tensed while a knot tormented his stomach. Instincts told him something was amiss. *It feels different*, he thought, as the knot tightened.

The kitchen light glowed bright. His father's truck dormant in its usual spot. A bat swooped on an invisible feast. He listened; *too quiet*. Then the metallic clash of pots and pans from the kitchen broke the silence, perhaps a little louder than normal, but not unusual. *What is it?*

At that moment he noticed; no smoke billowed from the ancient chimney. Aside from two months in the summer, smoke wisped permanently from the crumbling stack, and a silent alarm sounded as his guts clenched. He was used to that; living with a violent alcoholic shredded his nerves. But an inauspicious impulse disclosed some dire happening, and he broke into a jog.

When a chair smashed through the kitchen window in an explosion of glass and splintered wood, that jog became a sprint.


*Chapter Six*


Injuries forgotten, Tristan flashed through the gate as an image of his mother's battered body flashed before his eyes. Heart pounding his ribs, he skidded to a halt just shy of the gaping kitchen door. Warily he looked inside. Horror entered his soul.

Even from afar he saw anarchy in his father's incandescent eyes, and they stared unseeing as he hurled furniture in a blind agenda of destruction. Blyth didn't see his son at the door, and as Tristan scanned the room he saw his mother wasn't there. A small mercy, he hoped, amidst that febrile, inflammatory atmosphere.

Blyth stood stock still in the centre of that crippled room, teeth grinding as his chest rose with the intake of electric air and fell with the expelling of putrid whisky breath. And then, with a chillingly subtle tilt of the head, he locked eyes with his son.

The primitive look that warped that graceless face was more frightening than anything Tristan had ever seen. Strong wiry arms hung limp by his father's side, dangling fists clenched tight. He blinked rapidly. The man was unhinged, and Tristan flinched as his father stepped forwards.

Abruptly though, he stopped, and with a loosening of muscles, the deranged mask slipped from his face. Tristan couldn't discern the expression that replaced it, rare as it was. But slowly, frame by frame, and for the first time in his life, he bore witness to an extrinsic sadness that ironed flat those wretched and asperous features. Tristan saw sadness, and as shocking as it was, he saw shame.

Blyth stepped a little closer, and the dire perfume of stagnant whisky drifted over. Usually that smell was a reliable portent of pending violence, and to Tristan its association with pain was habitual. Yet to his great surprise he didn't feel afraid. Blyth remained mute and unmoved, green, narrow eyes fixed on the wide blue of his son's. His once proud shoulders sagged, as if all muscle within had quit. He wept.

And then, in a raspy inaudible whisper, he spoke. "She's gone. Your mother has gone."

Blyth Nancarrow was destroyed.

Tristan could not apprehend the words. He heard them clearly enough, but their meaning escaped him. His father said *She's gone. Your mother is gone.* But his voice was so weak and shaky and the words so unexpected that he thought he'd misheard. Looking at his father, though, and at the destruction before him and beyond, he instinctively knew it was true. Tristan's heart plummeted into his stomach.

"What do you mean she's gone?" he pleaded, "gone where?" But even as the words came out, the hands of bleak reality clamped round his throat.

"She's gone." The reply came in a vacant monotone, stripped of passion and barren of emotion, as if it too was ignorant of the implication. "Gone!"

Tristan recalled the stoic authority with which his mother had spoken earlier that day. She told him they could not leave. *No matter what*, she said, and with granite veracity. He trusted and accepted those words without condition, albeit with elemental reservations of their wisdom. Now though, Tristan understood what she'd done. His mother had deceived him. She said she could never leave. Yet now she had left. And he was there alone with his father.

The mother he worshipped had betrayed him, and the deceit tightened the boreal grip on his neck and wobbled the boy on his feet. Queasy, he reached an arm against the door frame to steady himself. His mind spun, bile rising in his ever constricting throat. Crestfallen, an abandoned son plunged to his knees, the world turned upside down, and his fragile heart shattered into a thousand pieces.

With his back against the wall, Tristan clutched his knees to his chest. Oblivious to the chill infiltrating the open door, his body shook from both cold and shock, numb both inside and out. He couldn't comprehend the contradictions, and did not want to face up to the betrayal. But to witness his father's face, contorted first with rage and morphing into regret and sadness, proved his fears beyond any doubt.

His mother had left him. That was his truth.

Tristan roused from his melancholic inertia as cold as if

the whistling icy wind had seeped into the very marrow of his bones. Like emerging from minutes stuck beneath killing ice, he drew an expansive life-giving breath, and shook so violently as if to shake away the grisly remnants of a horrific dream. A disordered hour had passed in which his addled mind swirled hypnotically, first one way to the light and then another into darkness, and had settled somewhere in the twilight grey middle of incomprehension, and that is the state he found himself then, the lone, washed up survivor on the deserted wasteland of the cottage floor.

He struggled to his feet to close the door, and for the first time appreciated the depth of the destruction. Chairs destroyed, the kitchen table broken in two. A window obliterated. Pots and smashed crockery littered the floor like an abstract minefield. To stand amid that chaos, and despite his injuries, he being the least broken thing in view, Tristan knew one thing with clarity; he was impossibly lucky to have been out when his father's storm ripped through the room.

*Chapter Seven*

Amongst the aftermath, the dim realisation of his predicament slowly began to settle, as did his nerves. His mother had left him there, alone with his violent father. That much he knew. But there was much more he didn't know. Where had she gone? Was she hiding somewhere close? Was she safe now? His riven heart was crushed by questions that would not get answered.

*Maybe she's left me a message? Somewhere secret, hidden from him?* It was a glimmer of hope that might ease the pain of his betrayal. If there was such a note it would surely be in his room, far from those wolfish eyes. He had to check, and on weak and weary legs he walked from the gutted kitchen. Stopping outside his father's room to listen, Tristan recognised the familiar lion's purr of drunken snoring, and knew he could search in safety, at least for now.

Once his whisky rages had subsided, Blyth would often sleep unbroken for ten hours or more. He drank so much, no one could wake him and nor would anyone try, as those bland moments were priceless in their tumultuous home. But Tristan knew, as his mother had known, that calm almost always heralded a storm.

In his sparse room Tristan worked fast. Beneath a lone flickering bulb that cast eerie shadows, he wrenched covers from the bed and tossed over pillows. Nothing! He pulled open drawers and rifled through clothes. Again, nothing but dust and disappointment! He hauled boxes of junk from the cupboard, spilling crumbled books and faded papers across the floor, and once again came up empty handed. With a growing aversion to the equally growing reality, Tristan was loath to believe as truth that not only had his mother abandoned him, but she'd left no trace of a message. Hot teardrops blurred his vision, and lying back on his creaking bed, Tristan was consumed by his conscious nightmare.

A glass exploded against a wall. Tristan's arms shot unbidden to his face, taut muscles expecting violence. All was black. He was freezing, and when he reached for blankets none were found. *A dream,* he thought, *yet so real.* In that dreadful dream his father had smashed up the kitchen in a ruinous rage and his mother was gone. He blinked away the traumatic scenes. But image by awful image, the events of the previous day germinated, and sprung clearly into his mind. He grabbed his covers from the floor and wrapped them tight around his trembling bones.

With daybreak still hours away, at four in the morning darkness and silence reigned over the cottage. It was so cold now, and Tristan remembered the absence of smoke from the chimney yesterday that had set internal alarm bells ringing. Keeping the hearth stocked and the fire alight was strictly his mother's chore, but now that lack of smoke meant no fire, no warmth, and worst of all, it meant no mother. He recalled the words from their last conversation, and his conflicting emotions raged from desperate sadness to acute anger. By lying, she'd broken a solemn bond never to deceive him, and her escape must have been planned. But he also hoped she must have his best interests at heart, and was protecting him with her secrecy. That was what he wished. And in the gelid destitution of the coming dawn, that one warm thread was all he could cling to.

Tristan was scared and confused. His father had demonstrated what appeared genuine remorse, and the surreal anomaly had perplexed the boy who had seen it maybe twice in his life. But at some point later that coming day he would have to face him, and he knew too well what to expect. To approach his father when he first awoke, in light of what had happened, would be to swim among hungry sharks. It was little more than suicide, and he considered making a run for it there and then, take his chance in the darkness and thrust himself and his fate headlong into the wind.

But despite his naivety, Tristan understood the simple realism. With no money and no transport, he could not escape the island. Within hours he'd be found, probably injured, probably frozen half to death. It wouldn't matter;

the outcome of a failed escape made him shudder. No. He would wait until the guaranteed hangover had had some time to disperse, and with time himself to evolve into his new reality, he would face his father then.

After a restless few hours buried deep in the blankets, Tristan roused to the raucous barrage of yet another resentful storm. Windows rattled and a constant weighty thud echoed down the hallway. He guessed correctly that the battered kitchen door still swung wildly about on stressed hinges. It also suggested Blyth was still asleep.

In the harsh light of day, the chaos Tristan found in the kitchen shocked him again. As if deposited by some fierce tornado, which in many ways they were, twisted furniture and crockery and shards of lethal glass lay strewn about everywhere. A sharp wind screamed at him through the smashed window, and as it clung gamely to its screeching hinges, the heavy old door slammed time and again into the unforgiving stone wall. Rain water puddled the floor, and autumn's fallen leaves flashed gold and red among the dismal grey. Distant thunder added to the mournful soundtrack, and sporadic lightning cast an ethereal glow onto the otherwise depressing stage.

The harrowing sight of the carnage and the grievous nature of the storm tilted Tristan's thoughts to his mother. Where had she slept last night? She had no friends on the island, her husband never permitted that, and unless she had made it to the mainland yesterday, his fearful assumption was that she must have spent the atrocious night without shelter. His mother was smart, Tristan knew that much, and as he considered all that had occurred it became apparent that she couldn't have managed the escape alone, and must've received some help. And although Tristan was reluctant to admit it, it was clear that her escape was premeditated and planned…and did not include him.

Eying the wreckage keenly, as if it posed its own organic threat, he considered his scant options. To attempt to clear up the mess and straighten out the scattered furniture might somewhat placate his father, whenever he finally emerged from his cavelike room. That way, it was just possible that the inevitable confrontation might be less brutal. Or, in a heated moment of asinine hope, he thought about just stealing some of Blyth's money, hiking all the way to Hugh Town and boarding the ferry to Penzance. He could do it. It was possible, at least…wasn't it? Then he wouldn't have to face his nemesis, face *Him*, at all.

But the immediate weight of his oppressive dilemma was too much, and an exigent tingle of fear and frustration crawled with small but salient talons down his spine. Dimensionally he was growing, almost a physical match for his father. Yet compared to Blyth's frothing ocean temper, Tristan was as passive as a duck pond by nature, certainly a trait from his mother, whether inherited or by osmosis he didn't know.

Years of abuse had nullified his spirit, and like a rock down at his cliff sanctuary, Tristan was worn smooth by his father's constant erosion. Blyth had strived for and succeeded in contriving a weak and docile child through his iniquitous behaviour, and the result; Tristan was simply too afraid to run away. It seemed his mother was braver than him, and he longed for some of her courage. *But if she was so brave, why wait until now to leave?* Tristan's confusion brought forth more unanswered questions.

He lit a fire in the hearth, and once a blaze took the chill from the air he started tidying the mess, immersed in his own shame and the shame of his father. He brushed out broken twigs and rotting leaves, then mopped out cloudy pools of rainwater. The deluge had at last abated, but the wind still blew with relentless ego, whistling and whining, and whipping the broken door about with powerful disdain. Hefting a couple of rocks from the garden, Tristan wedged that door as far shut as it would go, and relished the relative calm it created.

He made tea, and moved a chair, its pine back broken off, in front of the hearth. Sitting slouched and forlorn and bereft of joy, Tristan's uninhabited gaze saw nothing of the dancing flames, as images of his absent mother danced into and out of his mind.

Blyth stirred, slothful at first, as if to procrastinate the pending hangover. But he too sat suddenly upright, just as his son had hours before. Like a sledge hammer to his churning stomach, the realisation that his wife had left him hit hard. His clanging head resonated from the whisky. His mouth ached for water.

At forty-three years old, time had not been kind. On mornings after whisky Blyth felt like a train wreck, more sixty-three than forty-three and, dropping his leaden feet to the floor he stood, wobbled, then steadied himself against the wall. *How bad was it yesterday?* The domestic and familiar smell of fire smoke drifted down the hall toward him, and a wrinkle of confusion formed a crooked, elongated *M* of his dark brows. *Was it her? The boy?* But he knew it could only be the latter, and with the beginnings of an old man's gait he made his way to the kitchen.

The snap of splintered wood and crackle of the lively blaze masked the sound of his approach from Tristan, oblivious to his father and rapt by some unseen image beyond the flames. Blyth knew his son feared him. He had victimized both his son and wife to such an extent, that they visibly cowered when he entered a room; paranoia and depression had banished love and kindness from his hands. But beneath his volatile exterior he himself was spineless, and like the worst kind of coward he capitalized on the weaknesses he'd cultivated.

Today was different. Blyth's heart throbbed with remorse, and when he saw his young son sitting dejected and alone, a solemn look of lament softened his obdurate stony face.

Tristan remained unaware of his father's presence, as he dwelled on what now seemed a dangerous and fragile predicament. The kitchen was squared up a little, and he was warm and fed. But he was also more vulnerable than ever, and a zoetic and unpredictable peril lurked nearby. Nerves on edge, he stood from the hearth and turned. Jarring surprise shocked his eyes wide open, as the master of his unbalanced fate stood just yards away.

The principal instinct was to bolt from the inevitable savagery. But as he looked upon his father's face, smoothed were the harsh lines that corrugated his nettled forehead, and tender were the predatory eyes that so often bore coldly into his own. Instead, only a weak man stood there, older than before, whose moist eyes pleaded, and whose posture betrayed a freshly broken spirit.

For just a brief moment, Tristan believed he was witnessing his future self. He knew that *he* himself was no good, that *he* would never amount to anything. He knew this because his father had barked it at him often. And if what he knew of heredity rang true, enough of his father's blood coursed through his veins that he believed it wholly. All his life he had kowtowed to his father through fear and compliance and ignorance, and that bitter realisation both chilled him with sadness and burned him with anger.

But something was altered today. A subtle shift in the dynamic, in the very atmosphere that engulfed them. Tristan himself felt older, bigger even. And though wary, because experience was a ruthless educator to his father's cruel moods, that fear, both cerebral and of the flesh, had vanished along with his mother. He glared back at his father, and waited. For the first time in his life, he would let the drama unfold.

Through bloodshot eyes, Blyth tiredly scanned the room. He saw and appraised the damage, diminished as it now was. Then he looked at his hands. With a shudder at the havoc they had wreaked, he closed his eyes. He stood still, the moment stretching, the distress evident and evolving, mixing with his hangover into a concoction of convulsive pain. It took him many more long moments and some long, deep breaths. But at last Blyth stationed his gaze back upon his son.

"Tristan…my boy."

Tristan didn't respond, and held his nerve as he held his gaze.

"Son, will you talk with me? I've a lot to say to you."

The boy breathed hard. He knew to stay on his guard, be ready for anything. But he was prepared to listen. Blyth motioned to a chair, and grabbing the least damaged two, placed them facing each other. Looking from his dad to the chairs, then back again, Tristan nodded his accord.

Blyth fixed them a hasty breakfast of bread with jam and tea, and with the upended table in two uneven halves, they sat down to eat from plates on their laps. The storm had quietened, and as they faced each other, heads down, a thick silence stifled the room.

Tristan sensed a nervousness about his father, a radiating tension that pinched his gnarled features. That was positive. It was too long since he'd been nice to the boy. Tristan studied the man before him. He looked awful. The grey sweater was grubby and slept in, his thin hair unkempt, ruddy face twitching and fidgeting like a guilty man in court.

Tristan might have enjoyed this moment, watching his father...his tormentor...squirm, but it wasn't his nature. He was aware of new feelings, emotions never before felt, at least toward his father. What he felt was pity. Finally, Tristan saw the man for what he truly was; a drunk, weak and lonely bully. He pitied him, only because he empathized with that acute loneliness. But he did not feel sorry for him; he could not and would not forget who the real victims were.

After what seemed like forever, his father finally spoke. In a cracking, frail voice that rose barely above a whisper, Blyth Nancarrow bared his soul. "My son..." He paused, laboring within. Eventually, he continued. "My son...I've done some terrible things."

Tristan held firm his gaze. He said nothing.

"Tristan, I love you. I love your mother. And I love..." He wavered a moment, then continued. "I always have." He was really struggling, and the boy knew it. Tristan remained silent.

"Son, I'm sorry for everything I've done to you...for every time I've...I've hurt you." His shoulders hunched low, stooping his head in ugly shame.

Tristan couldn't see it, but pain etched his father's corroded face, and for once the mighty king was defenseless. Moving his hands from his lap, knuckles scarred from the administering of violence, he wedged them beneath his legs to control the shaking. His moist eyes, usually so hard and fierce, were now wide as a child's, as if he had lost everything. He had. Almost.

The squirming would not relent, but through trembling

lips he went on. "I don't expect you to forgive me. Not yet. But I've some big issues…it's the whisky, see, I can't control it." The words came expedited now, as if in hasty confession or defence. It could easily have been both. "But I'm not blaming the drinking. I get so depressed, son, so sad about the past, that sometimes drinking is the only way to forget."

Blyth at last raised his head, hopeful of some acknowledgement, of a little condolence. It never came.

"Sometimes?" It was Tristan's first word of the discourse, and it surprised them both with its spat out hostility. "Did you say sometimes? You always drink, every day."

Blyth's head slumped again under the forceful reproach. He had no answer to that truth. An aeonian minute passed before he lifted his head once more. Shame, undeniable shame, sat guilty and uncomfortable on that disgraced, dishonored face. It had been twenty years in the making.

"You aren't to blame for any of this, and nor is your mother. I've treated you both so badly, and I'd do anything to wind back the clock and undo all the pain, all the suffering." At this last word, Blyth's final ounce of dignity died, the last light of honour extinguished. His dark, asperous chin fell heavily to his chest, as his once proud shoulders heaved in discordant spasms of robust grief.

Tristan looked on, unflinching. He'd barely said a word during this extraordinary show of emotion. But he felt that at least…perhaps at last…his father had spoken the truth. His own heart roiled in turmoil. He loathed his father at times, wished he would leave them. And in his darkest moments, he had wished him dead. But he was still young, his passions unseasoned, and he'd not yet learned to hate.

Tristan calmly observed his father, whose face wore an expression of acute sorrow. Blyth, unable to bear his son's detached, judicial gaze, entombed his own face in the arm of his soiled sweater. But regardless of his external facade, Tristan's heart strained at the contradictions. He would not forgive his father for what he had done, what he'd put them through. How could he? He had caused his mother to flee, possibly…no, probably…for her life. And those cruel hands had left painful signatures on his own skin since he was a toddler. However, he was prepared to listen. He would transcend his own feelings of acrimony and disgust, and give the man a chance to rationalize his dissolute behaviour and gain some comprehension of their tragic lives. With luck, he might just get some indications as to where his mother could have gone.

Tentatively, Blyth stood, and took an uncertain step towards his son. Tristan stood too. To stand willingly in front of the man that had beaten him so mercilessly was unnerving. But he was calm, steady. Blyth held out his hands, palms open in a gesture that willed his son closer. Tristan stayed still, used to seeing those jittery open hands as fists. His father took another step forward.

"I know how you must feel, son. I understand. I'll stop drinking, and then I'm going to find your mother. I've always loved you both, and I'll prove it. I need her. We need her. Give me a chance. Please."

Tristan stood still, as if nailed to that very spot. He was determined to stay strong, but despite it all his stoic resolve was fragile. His father moved even closer, until he was near enough to reach out his arms and draw his son to him.

"Just give me a chance. Let your father hug you." There was an abyss of sadness in the shallow tone of his voice, and Tristan's stoicism, whether convinced or not by the sincerity, dissolved. Blyth embraced his son.

Tristan wavered. It was the first time his father had hugged him in twelve years. It felt like a thousand. It felt good. His mind was in turmoil, a flurry of bewildered thoughts and conflicts.

Ultimately, he accepted that hug the way he accepted the violence; unflinching and without emotion.

Blyth Nancarrow held onto his son tight, reluctant to let go, as if to do so would be to let go forever. The sobs that emanated from deep within his chest vibrated through the boy's, and although he was more or less unresponsive, Tristan couldn't deny the warm joy of human contact that didn't involve fists.

After what seemed like enough time but was less than a minute, Tristan slowly eased out of the embrace, and took a gentle step back to study his father's face. Hidden among the creases and stubble and the dark, introverted eyes, he saw what he believed to be real emotion.

It was a critical moment, and his experiences with the unhinged man before him advised caution. His father looked up at him, those grey green eyes beseeching for some sign of clemency. Despite everything Blyth had done, all those vicious acts of violence he'd committed against both Tristan and his mother, it was difficult for the boy to ignore the pain in those despondent, heartsick eyes. With his resolve stretched to its farthest limits, he made a choice; his father would have a chance at redemption.

Tristan still thought of himself as weak and was acutely aware of his naïvety. But over the last twelve or so hours there had been a shift in his mentality, some evolving transition that gave him a new sense of self. He knew his father could still beat him, had the ability to hurt him, but the cold, sickly fear was gone. He had witnessed the dictator reduced to a shuddering wreck, and the frightening, almost mythical beast was dead. In its place was simply an old man.

The fall of power had in turn empowered him, and despite himself, Tristan found his voice.

"I can't forgive what you've done to my mum...to us both. You treated us like animals. She's your wife, and I'm just a child...your only child."

Blyth flinched at the words, as if an ice pick were jammed into his ribs, and Tristan paused, letting the weight of the condemnation hang in the air.

"But I want to believe you regret it...that you're sorry. I believe at least some of mum's goodness has rubbed off on you."

Though his nerves were taut, so too were his muscles, tendons poised ready for action. He held his gaze steady. But Blyth averted his eyes, desperate to escape his son's judicial glare.

"Dad, look at me!" The depth of his shame meant a father obeyed as meekly as a son once had. Tristan truly was empowered. As if his willowy body had been taken over by some unknown force, he stepped closer, affronting the man that had for so long dominated him through violence and fear. Tall as an oak, he stood, backbone a steel girder, and for the first time ever his eyes aligned with his father's. Everything rigid, and at the end of long arms flexed both hands, open and shut, open and shut. He was ready, and the voice that spoke did not sound like his own.

"If she ever comes back, and if you ever touch her again, I'll kill you."

His pulse raged like a flash flood through his temples. The air felt inflammatory, as if his words were coated in diesel and could ignite at any moment. The tension was manifest, a heat haze between them. At least that is what Tristan felt. For Blyth it was a barrier of glacial ice.

Though just three feet apart, there remained a gulf between them, an epic desert of wasted kinship. Tristan looked through almost sixteen years of history into his father's eyes, and in that barren wasteland saw something glimmering there that he'd never before seen. Across that limitless expanse, he thought he saw respect.

An abused, alienated son had stood up to an abusive, alienating father for the first time, and in that second, in that exact, frozen moment of time, Tristan resolved never to be beaten again. Not by his father. Not by anyone.

Blyth though seemed to have shrunk, wilted in a drought of shame. He nodded, a vague dip of the head, and had neither the grit nor the energy to look at his son. Turning slowly, quietly, he walked out of the kitchen, guilt trailing him like the muddy tails of an undertaker's coat.

Tristan's eyes didn't leave his father until he was inside his room and the door was closed. As feeble as Blyth seemed those last minutes, Tristan knew not to show his back to a wounded animal. But, and keeping a healthy prescription of vigilance at hand, he couldn't help but know the undeniable truth; it was no longer a tyrant that stepped so tame and solemn into the former king's chamber.

No. Now it welcomed a broken and pitiful man.

Whereas Blyth's spirit had faded beneath the enormity of his sorrow, Tristan was awash with raw and new emotions. But what was it he felt, what could he sense? Relief? Pride? Possibilities? He stepped outside for some welcome air and slumped down to rest, long legs pulled in close, head resting on shaky knees. Exhausted, mentally drained, nervous tension had fleeced him of energy. The last hours had overwhelmed Tristan, and he willed himself to calm down.

Mid afternoon, and the low sun offered little heat as it contended with rushing, restless clouds. Restless. Tristan could relate to that. Those clouds may not have a predetermined destination, but they moved, because if they stopped moving, they would fall to their death as rain. Movement equals life, he realized. Of course. His mother had known it too.

Yes, he was restless. Tristan had to move to live.

So as he sat there, unaware of the sharp, gnarly stones digging into his lean legs and back, one swirling thought began to solidify in his aching mind, until its edges became as hard as flint. Eyes narrowed in gritty determination, mind as clear as he'd ever known, Tristan knew in that moment of clarity one indisputable fact; that whether or not his mother had betrayed him when she escaped, he would leave that accursed island to find her, or he would die trying.

*Chapter Eight*

Summer was now a distant memory on St. Mary's, and the isolated cottage was at the mercy of the merciless, apathetic autumn. Tristan dreaded the year's dark half, and asked himself the same question as always when the darker seasons came around; why do we even live here? It seemed that only the foolish would choose to, or only the banished, and he sensed his father was probably both.

Once the winds started, it felt like they would never stop. They whistled under doors and rattled through eaves. The low roof often shed its slates, which gaped unfixed for months. The wind often brought rain, but not the vertical rain that fell in spring; it was a hard-edged horizontal rain that evicted birds from the skies and stung faces as it chilled bones.

He had known no other home. His first faint memories were of those cold stone walls and the blaze of the kitchen hearth. They were not good or bad memories, just snapshots from a time lost beneath a grainy sadness. He was still only fifteen, but it felt a lifetime since it had been a happy place. His mother rarely smiled, though she had once had a bold and carefree smile bright enough to illuminate any room. But that too was a long faded memory, snuffed out like a candle as a new day dawned.

A week had passed. Blyth was largely silent and ascetic in the days since his wife had run away. Thankfully for Tristan he remained almost always in his room, leaving only occasionally, slow and laggard, like a bear in mid hibernation, to use the bathroom or chop firewood, the latter exertion of energy laying him down for many hours after. He barely ate anything, looked sick, and smiled only weakly when they passed in the hall. Tristan believed that it was a genuine attempt at recovery, but he knew that a volcanic rage boiled just below the surface, and an eruption back to normality was possible any moment.

When he eventually emerged more permanently from his room, looking slightly healthier but still wearing a dismal countenance, Blyth set out to scour the island. In the old truck he drove for hours, knocking at doors in tiny scattered villages, and quizzing former acquaintances in Hugh Town and Penzance. But there was no sight or sound of his wife, and not a single hint of her whereabouts. At the end of each excursion he would report back to his son, not that there was anything to report.

To Tristan, this devastating news could mean one of only two things; either his mother had successfully carried out an existing plan of escape with the help of an unknown ally. Or, and this possibility chilled him to his core; maybe she'd ended the suffering by taking her own life? His imagination ran wild, with images of her jumping from a nearby cliff cutting him like a guillotine. But no matter what his mother endured, he could not believe she would kill herself. Not with a young and loving son to take care of.

As lost and abandoned as he felt, Tristan took some comfort in his belief that she was okay, finally safe and free from her cruel husband. Even if she did betray him, he understood her need to run, and was totally justified in doing so. The beating a couple of weeks back was the last straw, and she probably, understandably, feared for her life. To live, he now knew, she had to move. And so he forgave her. Her courage amazed him, and in a perverse way he respected her now more than ever. The amount he missed her grew daily, as the pressure and uncertainty of his own situation grew. But for now it was just him and his father, and he, Tristan Nancarrow, would have to fend for himself.

Over the following days and weeks, though, Tristan's dilemma clutched at him and bound him in knots. He sunk into a morose stupor in his mother's absence, and moped about the dim cottage as if in a subterranean labyrinth with no way out. He dragged his feet about, scuffing dust from unclean floors. Dishes piled high, and flies buzzed at the dirty plates. He gazed unseeing out of windows. With no ears to hear him, he had no voice. His shoulders, so broad when he stood up to his father, were once more slender and hunched. He was desperately alone.

His birthday was coming soon. His sixteenth. Although

celebrations of any kind were always scowled at in Blyth's house, his mother had promised him that this birthday would be special, with cakes and gifts, and even a day out in the car, no matter what *He* said. That happy memory, like so many before it, had now evaporated in the decaying atmosphere of the cottage, and he wondered if his mother even remembered her promise. Worse still, that she'd forgotten about him entirely.

He would spend not only his special birthday alone, but perhaps his entire life.

But what did his birthday matter, anyway? It was just another number on the forgotten page of an unturned calendar, and the transition from fifteen to sixteen was as insignificant to him as having a black left eye or a black right. Like birthdays, he'd had plenty of each, and Tristan put it out of his mind.

His mother was not there. That was all that mattered.


*Chapter Nine*


Life now seemed shrouded in a perpetual grayness. The bleak sky matched the mood below, and autumn knocked heavily at the cottage door, which Blyth had finally repaired weeks after almost smashing it from its hinges. But after his enquiries had yielded nothing but disappointments in the search for his wife, he remained astray, adrift from the world and skulking like a ghost behind closed doors, curtains permanently drawn, and hiding his ongoing internal battle from his son.

This self-imposed lockdown began to have an effect on Tristan. With the haunted shadow of his father now abeyant, Tristan grabbed at the welcome advent of relative freedom. More and more, he spent longer and longer outside, ignoring the cold and grateful to be away from the void in which his mother's absence still echoed.

Out in the liberating air he at last began to feel some form of safety, and observed the gulls as they drifted by, graceful and in control, despite the strong winds. They called to each other, and in his searching, yearning mind he heard them cry *destiny*, time and again. His imagination was to blame, but he accepted that and embraced the word, and pondered its meaning as the gulls screeched on. *Destiny!*

The word offered him nothing in that isolated and listless place. And yet here he was, unsure of what was to come but certain it was coming. Over the days and weeks something was growing, invisible but present, intangible but pressing in. He felt it; his life was changing.

And sometime soon, his destiny, whatever that was, would come calling.

On the breeze his questions swirled among the gulls. Could his father really change? Could a real father son bond repair fifteen years of estrangement? Was it possible for a broken man to undo what he himself had broken?

Tristan had no answers. And right then, there alone on the beach, he didn't care. His sadness and anger were what had really grown, twisting together as conflicting allies, knotting him tight, strong and yet still weak, waiting but afraid to wait, urging him forward but holding him back.

The beleaguered, cloistered young boy hoped for just one thing in those confusing times; that his mother missed him as much as he missed her. Despite the brutality of his youth, he was still a child, and he missed his mother as any child would.

Time passed with no word from or about his mother, each day gloomier, longer than the last. He was desperate, and over those few weeks, daylight became his new enemy, illuminating the missing, as darkness became his only friend, concealing his loneliness.

That his father could become the man he promised was unlikely, and Tristan just could not see how it could happen, so far down the road to ruin as it seemed Blyth was. Thus, he was on his own, and finally, after weeks of plummeting into a well of self pity, he started to consider the very real prospect of a life without his mother.

When he stripped it bare, free from the shredded remnants of his hope for her return, and facing up to the evident reality that she wouldn't, his prospects were grim. So, it came down to a simple choice; if he ever wanted to see his mother again, he would have to follow in her unknown footsteps, escape the island and find her himself. And, perhaps most importantly, he would have to do it soon, if only for his own sanity.

Tristan had never once set foot off St. Mary's Island. He knew nothing of life beyond its rugged, incarcerating coast. And he knew nothing of caring for himself, other than how to subsist on a diet of tea and toast and boiled vegetables from the fast dwindling larder. His mother until now had been his cook, cleaner and nurse, and at the moment his father, who rarely left his cave, was devolving into his not so distant neanderthal ancestors.

He would have to grow up, evolve, and it had to start now. But he faced many problems. How would he physically leave the island? And how could he leave in secret? Where could he get money? If he did manage to escape, what about transport? He had no friends to call upon, and no idea as to who had helped his mother. Anxiety swamped him and drained his confidence.

What would he do? It seemed as if it was him against the world in a battle he could never win.

*Chapter Ten*

The day of his birthday, or, at least, the anniversary of his birth, came around suddenly. The slow days when accumulated passed in a confused blur of pain and plans, and he awoke early, the sky tar black beyond his window. In his punctuated sleep he dreamt of his mother. Stepping through some unknown door, the faceless girl appeared, indistinguishable but familiar. He had no idea who she was or why she visited him when he slept. But the night was better when she did.

In the foggy waking-up moments after a restless night, something felt different. He recalled the sound of a faint knocking, and assumed it involved the door in his dream. Those sounds had faded and then stopped, but the hazy echo of them lingered on. At this point Tristan would usually burrow deeper into the bed and try for more sleep, ignoring the fact that it was his so-called birthday. But, as if urged by some obscure, unseen presence, he extended his long arms out in a mechanical stretch and eased from the bed, bare feet numbed by the gelid floor. On a hunch, he made four quick steps to his window. Disquietude tensed his meagre muscles as he pulled aside the flimsy, useless curtain. He leaned close to the rain lashed glass, and his breath caught in his throat.

There, on the rotting sill beneath his window, bound tight and sealed in plastic, was a small brown package.

He knew it was from his mother. In his heart of hearts, Tristan knew. He threw open the window and peered into the darkness, wide blue eyes straining, searching, though he knew it was futile. His breath held just a little longer.

Just in case. But once he accepted what he knew…that nobody was there…Tristan snatched up the parcel. Cold rain stung his face, and before he closed the window against the elements, nature's tears streamed inharmoniously with his own.

It wasn't yet six o'clock. Whoever left the package during the night had to have known which was his window; it could only be his mother. But she'd be crazy to return here alone, he thought, and risk being caught. It had to be the anonymous ally. Tristan scuffed away disappointed tears on his sleeve, and by torchlight tore carefully through the outer package. A sturdy envelope sat inside. He opened that too, and his fingers trembled as they revealed a thin pile of cash and a postcard. The picture was of a strange circle of giant upright stones, and before he read the words, Tristan remembered: Stonehenge. He turned over the card, and saw through misty eyes his mother's tiny unmistakable handwriting:

*Dearest Tristan,*

*I miss you, my son. I'm so very sorry for leaving that way, and I can only imagine how betrayed you feel, but in time you'll understand why I had no choice. I'm free and safe, now, and if you're reading this, then you'll soon be free and safe too. At 4:00 a.m. on Friday, go to the old lighthouse on South Cliff. Dress warm and <u>do not be late</u>. You'll meet a man, and you must trust him. He helped me, and he will help you. DO NOT say a word to your father. I can't tell you where I am, but I promise you'll know soon.*

*I love & miss you. Stay strong. Happy 16<sup>th</sup> birthday,*

*Your loving mother*

He could barely breathe, as tears of relief spilled down cheeks puffed with joy. She was safe. She had sent for him. And she remembered his birthday. *Of course she did*! Tristan was ashamed he doubted her.

He looked again at the money, and slowly counted out the notes. £21. Tristan was staggered. He'd never seen so much money. And the picture? Was she near Stonehenge? Was it a clue?

Now he had to untangle his braided thoughts. His mother had arranged for him to leave in secret. The thought terrified him, but pleasant stabs of electricity fizzed in his fingertips. How was it possible? But even as he thought it, he realized that it's exactly what she herself had done. And now she was helping him.

"Movement." Without realising it, Tristan had whispered the word aloud. *That's it,* he thought, intoxicated now by the certainty of it all. "Movement equals life."

His pulse raced with this new possibility. Could he actually succeed? After his mother left, he swore that he would leave St. Mary's and find her, or he would die trying. But in the days since, both his nerves and the reality of the situation had got the better of him, and he'd more or less given up on the idea. But now...now things had changed. Only physically had he been abandoned, but emotionally and in matters of the heart, his mother was right there beside him. He would not be doing it alone.

Adrenalin surged, and as the day's first light seeped through the translucent curtain to his room, the very world seemed to open up before his eyes. But most importantly, Tristan's hopes at seeing his mother were renewed, brought back to life by his birthday message like the proverbial flaming phoenix. It was the best gift he could ever have imagined.

Even though Blyth was slowly winning his battle with sobriety, or so it seemed, Tristan was more than wary of his father's unpredictability. Any hint that his son planned to leave could unravel everything, and Tristan knew too well what would transpire if he was found out. His choice was simple; destroy the evidence.

He turned the postcard over with nimble fingers that still buzzed with nervous energy, and once more looked at the megaliths of Stonehenge, standing so high and honorable in the verdurous open landscape. Tristan was in awe of their sheer size...he of course had never seen anything like it with his own eyes...and his mind wandered, retreating to happier times when he and his mother travelled the planet vicariously via the spectacular and mysterious images of an encyclopedia. Happy memories, and yet so distant.

Though he recognised the place, Tristan had no memory of where Stonehenge actually was. But he knew, was somehow certain, that those stones were a clue, a signpost leading to his mother. Soon he would destroy the card and the package in the fireplace, and the money he would hide deep inside his cupboard, so Tristan took a last look at the enigmatic image and smiled. It was the wry, lopsided smile of a young man who knew his life was changing, but didn't yet know how.

So, he would finally leave the shores of St. Mary's island. The thought sent equal measures of wonder and trepidation shivering through his bones. The feeling of relief that his mother was safe and had made contact was overwhelming, but Tristan was also anxious about the coming days. How could he keep the secret from his father? And how could he make it to the old lighthouse without getting caught? Tristan was daunted by these dilemmas. But he knew one thing for sure. He simply had to try.

Morning had barely dawned, but any attempt to sleep was futile as his thoughts about the days ahead frothed like churned milk. He stepped from his room and listened; the stillness and quiet in the cottage was deafening, and brought into acute focus a glaring fact; leaving the house undetected at night was impossible. As he walked down the hall, every creaking floorboard echoed like thunder, betraying his progress to all humanity, and worse than that, to his father.

Tristan paused to listen by his father's door, and heard the steady breathing of a deep sleep, untroubled even by the dual foes of paranoia and shame. Blyth's demeanor had altered, and although it was a slow, ongoing process, the change was dramatic. Tristan was still genuinely surprised at the polarities between now and just weeks before, and it was almost as if his father was reborn. Fleetingly, he even wondered at the prudence of actually discussing his desire to leave. But this he soon dismissed as foolish. Blyth had recently lost his wife, though the fault was entirely his own. Because of that, he had left alone the whisky, and his roiling ocean temperament was passive for perhaps the first time in a dozen years. It was too risky, and Tristan dare not cast any stone whose ripples might disturb that calm. After all that had happened, he knew, Blyth would not willingly relinquish his son.

Tristan shoved some stale bread on a plate and settled down to the meagre breakfast. Blyth's door whined on worn out hinges, and when he tottered unsteadily into the kitchen, his face was jaded and gaunt. But then he smiled, and it was wide and real.

"Good morning, son." The pleasant tone was alien to his son. And then; "Happy birthday."

Tristan was in shock. It was at least a decade since his father had said that. *He's really trying*, he thought, and despite himself felt a brief pang of guilt about his secret plan. Small talk ensued.

"Listen son, I didn't get you a present. I know you're not surprised. I'm sorry." This time the smile was weak, and his rutted brow betrayed explicit shame. But he battled on. "Why don't we take out the truck, drive to the cliffs and go for a walk. I could even teach you to drive?"

Tristan thought quickly, ignoring the bewildering exchange. It was an opportunity to ride the coast and visit the lighthouse, to gage how long he would need to get there.

"Okay...thanks. That sounds nice." He willed himself to smile. It was only half faked. With determined volition, he went one step further. "Thanks, dad."

"Look son, I've a lot of making up to do. I know that more than anything I've ever known, and I promise I'll make everything right between us, starting today."

"I know you're trying, dad, I can see it. I'm glad." And though he was glad, he doubted the ravine like rift could ever be fully bridged. Besides, if all went to plan he would be long gone in three days.

For many seconds Blyth gazed at his son with soft, dewy eyes. "Did I ever tell you how handsome you are? You certainly take after your mother." Blyth chuckled a little at his own joke. It was unintentionally callous, but he missed the sadness flash in his son's eyes.

"My mum is gone." It was barely a whisper, and Blyth missed that too. Tristan's melancholy wavered, reforming readily...a little too readily...as molten anger. It simmered, briefly threatening to bubble over. But somehow he held it down. He would not follow the path of his father's violent footsteps. For now he would keep the peace. For now, he would be a happy and supportive son.

For now.

After finishing their modest breakfast they climbed into Blyth's old truck. Like everything, it too was neglected, and the decayed and rust covered body reflected the decay and broken down structure of his family. Blyth made a mental note to repair that truck, a good start to repairing the torn fabric of his severed family.

He drove careful and unhurried through the dense morning mist, sometimes whistling a pleasant tune, and at others stealing brief, somewhat shy glances across at his son. The last time Tristan was in a car with his father was four years ago, and to be so proximate with a man who had so often kicked and punched him was unnerving. Though he tried, he couldn't relax. Instead he concentrated on the road, clicking off the minutes in his head. He could afford few mistakes when he made this journey alone, and he had to be in no doubt of the route.

Blyth was a man of few words, always had been, and they drove largely in silence. That suited Tristan just fine. Blyth was a simple man who believed in two things; one, that his opinion was not worth sharing, and two, that when he had an opinion, few people were worthy enough to share it with. Once upon a time he believed with all his heart that a home, an honest job and a family were all any man needed. He had a steady job, and when he met Kerra, the love of his life, all he needed then was a child, and he, Blyth Nancarrow, would be content forever.

Then it all changed. He changed.

They drove along narrow country lanes that snaked half

a mile inland from the gnarly coast, and Tristan tried hard to pick out obvious landmarks as they passed by his window; an oak tree here, a farm gate there. They pulled over for the occasional farmer, and Blyth raised a hand in greeting, rarely returned, causing Tristan to wonder if they were the anonymous ally. He was actually relieved he didn't know their identity; that way he couldn't let it slip. St. Mary's was a small island, little more than six square miles, and just over a thousand people called it home. So few, he thought, yet among them must be his mother's mysterious philanthropist. *Had they ever met before? Did his father know them?* Sometimes ignorance was best.

Like falling leaves his thoughts swirled, as the battered old truck climbed toward the abandoned lighthouse, derelict for years since the building of a newer one in Hugh Town. As they drew near, the faded paintwork stuck out amid the gloom, and the red stripes on whitewashed walls echoed the image of his mother's horrific gash across her pale skin. Tristan struggled once again to suppress his rising fury, and clenched his fists tight in his pockets. There was no doubt that Blyth was trying, but moments like that made his opportunity to leave more resolute and right.

Blyth stopped short of the crumbling tower, which seemed held together only by the mass of blackish ivy that crawled menacingly up its side, and they walked the last, rocky stretch. It was bitterly cold up at the cliff top, and the wild Atlantic wind bit deep. Tristan would wear all his clothes when he came back at night, though he knew they wouldn't be enough.

Creaking like a wrecked ship, the lighthouse door was ajar, and a freezing father and son stepped into a circular room littered with damp debris and rampant with congeries of twisted ivy, the half-light of winter failing miserably to penetrate the darkness. Progress was slow on the slippery stone corkscrew of stairs, the thud of their footsteps bouncing back at them off ancient, mossy walls.

Tristan was making the ascent a few seconds behind his father, when, in the obscure light, he spotted something extrinsic on the floor. His heart omitted several beats, and he paused, his breath held. Partially buried beneath moldering rubbish and fresh cobwebs was a glove. And then he saw its match. Despite the gloom, he could see they were blue, and not only blue, but the blue of vast, wide oceans full of promise. His mother's favourite colour. Those gloves were hers!

So that was where she'd met with her collaborator during the escape, and had somehow lost her gloves in the dark. Tristan wanted so desperate to grab them up and take them to her. But it was reckless, he knew, for if Blyth saw them it would only cause problems, and Tristan had to avoid that at any cost. He lingered just long enough to cover the gloves with a discarded plank, and with bittersweet emotions he hastily scaled the stairs after his father.

They entered the tapered round room that once housed the giant lifesaving lamp. From high up in its cold lonely home, for decades it had protected sailors upon wild winter seas. Tristan marveled at the simplicity, but this time he did catch the irony; that, despite his years of close proximity to that beacon of safety, it had done nothing to protect him and his mother from the storms that raged right beneath their own roof.

Staring out at the panoramic view, he saw a sky growing dark when it should have been getting light. But it wasn't only gloom he saw on that distant horizon. Somewhere out there, he believed, somewhere beyond his repressed and shadowy life, a light was shining for him.

He just had to go out and find it.

Two hundred miles away on the mainland, another young boy sheltered from the same storm. He had slept in that cold, filthy barn for three nights, and was weak, demoralized and hungry. He didn't really know where he was, and nor where he was going. He only knew that he was fifteen-years-old and his name was Richard White, and that a search party was possibly out looking for him across southern England.

He had been on the run nearly three weeks.

Further east at that same moment, a beautiful young girl fed a sick baby boy. She didn't know the child's name, and was simply helping out as she often did. Her art gallery business was thriving, and she enjoyed a good, safe and healthy life. Once in a while, though, when the guilt that she kept deep within her heart rose unbidden to the surface, she went down to the orphanage and helped take care of the many unfortunate kids that needed it. Her unselfish yet selfish act…it was for her as much as for the poor children…went at least a little way toward alleviating those deep stores of irrational yet steadfast limpets of guilt.

*Chapter Eleven*

The night of Tristan's planned escape loomed. Each day, as the early winter sun sat lower and lower in the western sky, his nervous excitement rose more and more. He was desperate to leave the island and begin the search for his mother, and since the message he'd got on his birthday his confidence had also grown. She was out there, somewhere in the expanses of the endless planet, and he would find her.

If this scenario had arisen in different circumstances, maybe one where his mother hadn't had to flee for her life, he might be looking forward to the coming adventure. But it wasn't a game, far from it, and he had to tread carefully through the next few days and beyond. His father's volatile nature could not be trusted, and leaving him was simply the first and probably most difficult of many more difficult steps.

His life was changing, shifting somehow, morphing into something he could begin to control. But to call it *life*, he needed to start living. In reality, Tristan had merely been enduring time, instincts and his innate resilience his only guardians, sole protectors from the daily threats of violence. He was probably tougher than he realized, and the fact that he was ready to stand up and leave testified to that. And now he was moving forward, despite the odds.

He smiled as he thought of *Darwinism*, a lesson learned from his mother in a distant memory, and *survival of the fittest. Life will always find a way*. Where had he read that phrase? Back then he had no comprehension of their meanings. But now he was on the cusp of something, striving, and more than that, evolving.

Soon he would take his maiden, fledgling steps toward liberation. Tristan was evolution in progress, with unknown and unlimited potential. That thought, coupled with the burgeoning determination to see his mother again, empowered him greatly.

He felt an unnerving sense of impending movement, and the days passed so fast that, without actually going anywhere, he had to run in his mind to keep up. For too long he'd been kept prisoner on that island, locked up by an imaginary key forged from naivety and fear, and despite his growing sense of self, that constitutional ingrained fear remained, hanging in the air like some malignant, intangible menace. Unless he kept his sense of reality in check, his entire world, or at least that of which he knew, could fatally unravel.

Blyth had made substantial strides in his battle against the odious whisky, and those cursed bottles of pain remained hidden and locked away in the outdoor shed. And for now, at least, so did their incumbent agonies.

He and the boy communicated little, but a calm atmosphere settled about the cottage like dust. Dust. Tiny particles of dead things. Appropriate, mused Blyth. As they each came to terms with recent events in their own ways, Tristan's mind simmered with angst and notions of escape, while Blyth's focused only on sobriety and finding peace with the world. Neither wanted confrontation, especially Blyth, and it was a welcome standoff for them both.

It was a long and arduous challenge, but to Tristan his father seemed valiantly committed. He didn't fully understand the crippling disease of addiction and its itinerant demons, but a small layer of respect had grown for his father, or at least for his father's newly acquired discipline. How it would effect him long term, if at all, he didn't have the time to consider.

Deep within his bruised heart, Tristan knew that the evident progress and positive strides were too little and too late for his father to win back his mother…much too little, and much too late. Tristan only wished he himself had found some courage and stoicism sooner. Perhaps he could have even helped his father, encouraged him to stop drinking? Maybe even intervened during his mother's beatings, and somehow protect her?

He was being harsh on himself, and he knew it. He was just a child, really, and shouldn't have had to witness and endure all that he had. But he was learning. Tristan knew life was the teacher, and that life's lessons were never scheduled. He was aware now only to obey his instincts, even, and perhaps especially, if he doubted them, and be prepared for anything that life threw at him, both the fair things and the foul.

Tristan was ready to grow up.

Aside from everything else that flooded his thoughts, Tristan now faced the very real dilemma of how to leave the cottage unnoticed, and his home of sixteen years was most definitely not an ally.

If he tried to walk out quietly at night, the screeching floorboards and whining hinges would betray him in a second, as if they too lived under Blyth's imperial control. If he was caught at night with his backpack...well, he didn't want to think about that. Blyth would never allow him to leave.

He considered simply asking permission to explore the island. He was sixteen now, he'd insist, and he just wanted to have some fun, perhaps a solo camping trip at the beach or in the nearby hills. Blyth had softened appreciably, and he might have just agreed. Then, if he made it off the island, he guessed it could be days before his father's suspicions were roused. But it was far from perfect. Blyth, in his efforts to get closer to his son, might suggest a bonding, father-son excursion, and that was risky. At the very least, he might miss the 4:00 a.m. rendezvous with...well, with whoever it was.

He even, if only momentarily, considered somehow locking his father in his room. He could snatch the key, lock the door, and in one way or another fashion some kind of barricade. But as quickly as the thought formed in his mind it was summarily dismissed. He was simply not brave enough to attempt such an endeavour, and besides, if he resorted to that kind of behaviour, regardless of the circumstances, wouldn't that relegate him to the same moral standard as his father, the very person he was trying morally and ethically to transcend?

No. After many, many hours of stressful consideration, Tristan had made his choice; he would take his chances and gamble on the night. Of course it was risky, dangerous even, but under the cover of surprise and darkness, he figured, it was his best and only chance of success.

By the following lunchtime…Tristan was alarmed to realise it was Wednesday already…his plan had solidified. He knew what he needed to do, and he would need a trial run. With Blyth still laying low in his room, Tristan slipped out of the cottage.

He set off casually at first, so as not to arouse any suspicion if his father was spying from the window, but once out of sight he was eager to put as much distance between himself and that place as possible. The sun was high and the day was bright and mild, a very welcome break from the almost permanent chill. Tristan's spirits rose with every stride away from the prison cottage, and he started to revel in his mini adventure.

But the two days and nights until Friday's escape were still fraught with danger. So many things could go wrong, and as quickly as it had lightened under those clear skies, his mood darkened with acerbic thoughts of his father. Nothing could undo the enduring pain of the past, and, that one man had caused so much suffering made him doubt that such a man could ever fully change. Tristan felt sure that with even minimal provocation, the whisky could come screaming back into their lives like a scorned phoenix, setting fire to the fragile threads of peace that for now held everything together.

It was simple really. He had to leave before that could happen.

Somewhere along the beach, Tristan was suddenly stopped in his tracks. It was something in the awful sound of his feet crunching against shingle that had caused him to pause. He stared out across the vast expanse of water before him, and tried to imagine where his mother was, and how she was doing. But all his mind's eye saw was the man who'd so violently forced her to leave.

So passionate was his desire to escape his father's tyranny, and so feverish the desperation to see his mother, that one more reality would became clear and final before that day's end: If his father somehow learned of his plans, and he had to actively disable him before he could leave, then he, Tristan Nancarrow, was prepared to kill.

The beach narrowed at its eastern end, and Tristan edged away from the water and up into the grassy dunes. He'd settled himself again, letting the red mist drift away on the slightest of breezes. But he was glad to have those sporadic moments of fire in his belly, because they would help keep him alert, and focused on his objectives.

The countryside surrounding his home was beautiful, and he began to truly appreciate it for the first time as he made good ground east. It was so peaceful out there, a far cry from all the turbulence he'd known, and the only sounds were of tiny waves performing their forward rolls onto the shore, and the lazy gulls gliding overhead, calling out to each other, calling out to him. That word again; *destiny*.

He wasn't sorry to be leaving. Innately he knew that

beyond the shores of the island, a pretty but forgotten patch of land that to a young boy was little more than an abandoned penal colony, and he the last remaining inmate, was a better world, a better life.

Tristan pushed on for another hour, and soon the old lighthouse emerged up the hill ahead. He took a reflexive, expeditious glance behind him, as if his diligence might have suddenly betrayed him. But satisfied that he was still alone, he jogged the last half-mile with purpose.

He breathed hard as he stepped through that rusty old door, and took a final look over his shoulder before dashing up the stairs. In a second he had pushed aside the wooden plank, and salvaged his mother's gloves from the debris. For long moments he held them tight against his chest.

But he couldn't linger. Tristan stowed his few items in a dark corner and hid them with the same plank, and wasted no time in leaving. If he was to be seen by his father, it could not be there. It had taken almost two hours to reach the lighthouse, though he could have made it in ninety minutes had he rushed. Tristan guessed he would need a further hour to make the journey after dark. So a midnight departure, he calculated. His expression in that moment was unreadable, perhaps fear, maybe determination? But most of all he felt anticipation. He was ready.

Tristan ran most of the way back, not because he wanted to be back, but to reduce the chance of suspicion. Once safely inside the cottage, and confident that his plan was still unknown, the relief he felt was immense. The first part of his mission was completed.

*Chapter Twelve*

On Thursday morning, and remembering how cold it could be in the dead of night, Tristan laid out all his clothes on the bed, what few there were, and sat down to consider his plan. Quite naturally he was nervous; after all, he was on the brink of a dangerous prison break. But he also felt an aberrant calmness settle over him, like that feeling you get when you've done everything in your power to prepare for something, and the result is no longer in your hands.

His thoughts flitted to his mother. How must she feel right now? This was her plan, her idea, so of course she must be nervous too. She'd taken some huge risks so far; first, by leaving, and then arranging the birthday message. He still had no idea how that had transpired. But, he assumed, she no longer had any control over the situation either. They were on the same emotional ride.

Grainy yet familiar, the image of the dream girl also drifted into his thoughts. He'd never seen her face clearly, but felt certain that she smiled her encouragement to him. *Maybe one day I'll find out who she is*, he thought, as weariness sucked him back down into a midmorning doze.

"Tristan? Son, are you in there?" His father's jaunty voice snapped him from his weary reverie, and his heart pounded. Despite a growing confidence, the boy was still edgy. Blyth was in the garden, he realized, right outside his window. He called again, followed by two gentle taps on the glass.

"Tristan, why don't you come outside? I've a surprise for you."

Though his curtains were drawn, Tristan panicked, quickly stuffing his clothes under the blankets. He could not arouse a single shred of suspicion, however innocuous it seemed.

"Yes dad," he called back, "I'm coming out now," and he breathed deep as his father's shadowy figure moved away from the window.

After hiding his paltry collection of worn out clothes, Tristan made his way to the garden. He approached his father slowly, as years of violence had trained him to tread cautiously. Blyth turned to face him. He'd been tending to Tristan's asters, so callously destroyed by his own insensate actions too many times. Now, his features were mild, his smile temperate, and moist green eyes spoke heavily of regret. Blyth was unrecognizable, a transformed entity far removed from the wild creature that wreaked such carnage just weeks before. He seemed rewired, morals renewed. But was he reformed? Tristan couldn't know.

There was conflict hidden in the lines of Blyth's face and buried in the folds of his eyes. They were eyes swamped with guilt, but that sparkled just a tiny bit with an equally tiny sense of pride. And those lines were lines of sorrow, but that arched just a little with a subtle sense of dignity. Those two facets, both that glimmer of pride and that shred of reconstituted dignity, had long ago been drowned and rendered extinct beneath the killing flood of whisky.

"My son, I'm so sorry about your flowers. I've been caring for them this week, trying my best…see, look," he said, sweeping his arm over them, "they're coming back nicely. Hardy little buggers, eh, just like you." There was a definite flicker of anticipation in those eyes, a despairing wish for some form of pardon.

Tristan studied his father, and just like his beloved asters, he thought, his old man looked healthier. He hadn't had a drink for three weeks, an eternity for him, and colour livened his pallid cheeks. His eyes were less hollow and empty. His gaze was steady. It was obvious to Tristan he was trying hard, and making some progress in his recovery. His efforts were undeniable, and it caused Tristan a moment of anxiety. Should he still proceed with his plan? Would it undo his father's valiant efforts? Blyth had neither shouted at nor hit him since his mother had left, and there'd even been some limited dialogue, strained as it was.

Tristan glanced down at his precious flowers, delicate splashes of pinks and blues against soil and stone. He planted them himself as a young boy, and now marveled at the way they had grown up alongside him, facing up to nature's rages and surviving, as he had survived, the unnatural rages of his father.

They were indeed hardy, as Blyth had said. But... Tristan was just a child, and a child should never have to prove he was tough whenever a father got drunk and beat him.

Vile memories from a recent past swamped his thoughts, and before he could control them, they overran his mind; the thud of crashing furniture; glasses smashed against walls; sickening purple bruises; the crunch of breaking bones; blackened, crying eyes; agonized screams as his mother was beaten; pitiful weeping echoes that followed in the night. Those noises and worse formed the sound track of his childhood, and it frightened him now as it had frightened him then.

"Tristan," said Blyth, "you alright?" The boy's eyes had anchored upon something he couldn't see. "Son?"

Tristan's body went rigid, spine erect and muscles taut, and that momentary compendia of doubt was superseded with a cast iron determination. He locked eyes with his father, while in his mind's eye he saw his mother's terrified face, its awful red slash stoking the fires in his furnace of anger. Adrenalin exploded though his arteries, and a volition previously unknown saw a boy stand tall.

He stepped forward. This was his moment. In a voice he barely recognised as his own, a boy spoke his first adult words.

"I'm leaving the island."

It was as if Blyth hadn't even heard the words, let alone registered what they meant. He simply stared unaffected back at his son. Tristan's muscles clenched further, prepared for sudden violence, but Blyth just looked at him. Unmoved. Unblinking. Time stalled to create a tableau of raw tension. Tristan heard his own heart thumping. *Didn't he hear me?*

Then the most subtle of movements as Blyth's jaw set like stone. A slight twitch of the shoulder. A single blink, and then his eyes, solemn just moments before, narrowed into a sincere, familiar scowl. That glare, those slitted wolfish eyes, bore deep back at Tristan, and the skin of his knuckles strained white as they clamped shut into fists.

The boy braced against the coming storm.

For Tristan it was a titanic battle of wits to hold his father's flinty, unyielding gaze. His heart thumped louder still. His throat arid. Guts churned. And then, with a chilling tilt of the head and a smirk to match, Blyth spoke one word in a voice so cold that it froze his son's heart.

"No!"

Seconds slipped by. Five. Fifteen. If Tristan wanted to run, he couldn't, movement and coherent thought eluding him. His father had grown taller before his eyes, his shoulders grown stronger. The contrite gaze dismissed, glowering menace in its place. A smirk of pure ice.

Blyth edged forward, leaning in close to his son's face. "Why? Why do you want to leave, eh?"

Numbness possessed Tristan's body. Words evaded him and teardrops welled, as that flirtation with stoic resolve deserted him. Eventually though, and with great industry of will, he somehow forced a reply, hoping beyond hope that the spurious calm in his voice might hide his far from spurious fear.

"I'm sixteen, dad. It's time I left. There's nothing here for me now, and I want to leave." He daren't mention his mother.

Beyond his father's head he saw a pair of sable-tinted crows fly by, joyless and malevolent, as if winged harbingers of chaos. If it was possible, Blyth's eyes seemed to darken, matching their melanoid colour.

"You can't leave now, boy. We're doing well together. I've cooked, I've washed your clothes, and I haven't drunk in weeks." The words came out caustic and indignant. "It's all for you, son. Your mother has left, and we have to stay together...we *will* stay together. You need me. You will not leave!"

Tristan too was indignant, and fire blazed back into his belly. The two ominous black crows took flight. He took a deep breath, and like the wildest flow of lava, relished the blood that flooded his temples.

"No! I'm not leaving in spite of you, dad, I'm leaving because of you! You've destroyed this family. You've ruined my mothers' life. You are weak, and you're a bully. I was afraid of you. But I'm not afraid anymore. Drinking has torn the goodness from you. Mum didn't need you, and neither do I. I'm leaving this island, and I'm not..."

He paused, and for just a moment shifted his gaze back at the cottage, the small stone house that cast a permanent shadow over his young life. His wide blue eyes opened wider still, as if to elicit as much courage from the world as possible. He needed it for what he was about to say.

"I hate you, dad, and I'm never, ever coming back!" Dizziness threatened to send him sprawling, his shaky knees weakened almost to buckling. He blinked away the sick feeling and sucked in gulps of cool air. He didn't buckle. Tristan had planned to sneak away and escape in the night, and not say anything about his plans. But now Blyth was in no doubt as to his son's feelings, and Tristan had said what he though he'd never dare say. It could not be undone, and he knew a sequence of events had started which could only end one way; the beating to end all beatings. He was ready.

But for a brief instant Blyth's gaze lost its grim intensity. He staggered momentarily, and a solitary tear escaped from an almost closed set of eyes. His mouth, shrouded by weeks of dark stubble, opened and closed like a landed fish, but no words came forth. A watching psychiatrist might have labeled it as some kind of mental breakdown, but Tristan had never before seen the likes of it from his father, and was at a total loss. Was it real grief?

Tristan couldn't know it, but he was witnessing his father entrenched in battle against his old foes; demons of rage that never left him, no matter how hard he fought. They desired only that Blyth lash out at the kid, batter him with his gnarly clenched fists. They would show the boy who really controlled his destiny, and it was not him.

Blyth was in turmoil, toe to toe with his habitual nemeses, masters versus slave in an invisible clash of unequal warriors. He fell to his knees. Looking up at his son through beseeching eyes, and by utter conation of will, he managed to splutter out: "No, son, don't leave, everything'll be okay, please…I beg you.'

Tristan remained unmoved, frosty certitude lacing his

veins. *Do not buckle*, he told himself. *Not now. Not ever!*

"I'm begging you son, please stay. I'll make everything right, just give me a chance, please!!" That last word echoed with desperation, then hung in the following silence a long time, eventually lost to the wind and to the world. His urgent, frantic petition had fallen on unsympathetic ears, and Blyth knew it, knew he'd lost his battle. His head slumped on limp shoulders, and for the longest moment he remained silent. Blyth Nancarrow knew it was over.

The air had fallen still as death. Black clouds roiled silently, and no gulls called out. Tristan's throat was dry as bone, his breaths rapid. He ought to run, he knew it, he ought to run now. But run where? He glanced about for inspiration, perhaps intervention. None was found.

And then, as if unfolding himself from a crouch of shame and defeat, Blyth stood up tall. Once more the crows flashed by, and he watched them until they were two tiny black dots in the distance. Then that old malignant look settled across a face, that to Tristan seemed to change its very shape, contorting under the twisting pressures of rage. It was a face plagued with enmity. Blyth, or the demons that controlled him, glared, eyes refocused and intense. Malicious.

The demons had won and Tristan knew it, and at that very moment, as if all the foundations of life were about to crumble to dust around him, he took flight. But with the appalling speed and ferocity of a Nile crocodile, Blyth and the demons struck in a sickening collision of flesh and bone. In that sudden flare of violence he was knocked to the ground, the air sucked from his lungs and his face in the dirt.

From his chronic position splayed on unkind ground, Tristan's inborn survival mode kicked in, and through raised arms he saw more than felt the brutal attack. Snarls and grunts resounded, and the punches arced down in a relentless barrage. Some landed, others deflected, but down they came, until at last they slowed, and finally, they ceased. Blyth withdrew, breathing hard and sweating, despite the season.

Tristan lay still, and took a second to appraise the situation, to appraise himself. He wasn't hurt. Not at all. A few scuffs and scratches, but no real damage. It was a defining, momentous realisation. Everything had changed.

He had one searing thought, then; get up and fight. He had good reason...many good reasons. Undeniable truth. How much pain had he suffered by his father's cruel fists? Too much. Way too much.

But over recent weeks Tristan had come to understand something. His father hadn't drank anything in that time, at least that he knew of, and the rages had stopped. That those rages were caused by drinking was obvious, now more than ever. And Blyth had said more than once in that time that his drinking was caused by depression.

Looking bleakly now at his father, standing unsteady only yards away, Tristan wondered just how accountable Blyth was. Did he have some unknown mental issues, an inner torment that warranted sympathy, pity rather than apathy? He didn't know. But now was not the time for sentiment. He himself was in danger, and had to make the right decision for both their sakes.

Stand and fight? No. That was what his father wanted, what his father would do. It was wrong. Or play dead? Feign submissiveness, morals intact, and survive to carry out his plan?

And he chose to survive, just as his father descended with a second wave of fists and boots. Tristan made himself compact, and absorbed the punishment as if his very life depended on it. And for all he knew, it did.

Blyth's energy ebbed, and sporadic blows arrived with little force. Eventually, his demons' bloodlust waned, and they deserted him, just as all others were deserting him. He sat down heavy as a felled tree. Finished.

Tristan was okay, nothing more than a few minor bruises. He sat up, linked his arms around his knees, and looked sadly at the man before him. He would be more than justified to seize the advantage, reap a revenge on the man who had controlled his life with the dual weapons of fear and pain. But that was the easy option, the choice of a coward. That would be his father's choice. Tristan didn't stand up. He waited and, as the minutes passed, he watched.

Blyth stood now, and it took great effort. He backed away several yards, but despite the distance between them Tristan could see his face clearly. His father was crying. The demons were gone, and he wept from despair and relief.

Tristan rose too. He sensed a shift in atmosphere, a singular tranquility, and edged closer. The crows, dark and dire, were gone. Nearby though, a tiny robin sat calmly on a rock, red breast aglow against the encompassing grey drabness, eyes fixed on Tristan, almost as if checking up on him. Its small head bobbed left, then right, and apparently satisfied, flitted off beyond a hedgerow. Tristan hoped that the omen was good.

There was no fight left in Blyth, physically and, perhaps, even morally, and they both knew it. Tristan stood directly in front of his father.

"Dad, it's over," he said, in a composed, almost sympathetic voice. "I'm leaving, and there's nothing that you can do or say to stop me. I've taken all of this for too long, and I've survived. You no longer control me. I'm sixteen, and I'm not a child anymore. Goodbye, dad."

Blyth Nancarrow looked into his son's anguished, innocent eyes, and knew he would never hurt him again. His weathered forehead scrunched up into tight furrows, and from distraught eyes sprang tears from an untapped well of emotion. He'd never meant to hurt his family, yet he knew that it was all he'd ever done. Guilt and remorse gushed freely down cheeks that burned with shame.

He wiped his eyes on a filthy sleeve, and looked imploringly at Tristan. For the first time, a young man looked back, and he saw a face no longer afraid. His gaze dwelled on those wide blue eyes for a long moment...and they were not his own.

He was a bully for the simple reason that he could be, a bully of the worst kind, the kind that preys on the weak. For so long, his wife and son could not defend themselves, with no choice but to suffer his wrath. But that had changed. First, she had left him. And now, only weeks later, his son would leave him too. He was a terrible man, he knew it, and that he'd made too many terrible mistakes was a sharp maxim that cut deep.

Beneath it all, though, he was just plain old Blyth Nancarrow, whose life had tied itself in cruel knots that he'd never managed to undo. *How did this happen to me?* he thought and didn't say, because no one was listening and no one cared.

Blyth was wretched with grief, and as the narrowing ash grey sky above descended into a smothering black, a ruined man heard the whisky calling from the darkness.

Tristan knew what he must do, and the fact was clear and simple; he just had to walk away, and by turning his back on his father now he'd be turning his back on tyranny forever. But Blyth looked so pitiful, stood off balance, like a scarecrow in a forgotten field, ragged clothes hanging from wilted muscles, and a conscience crushed by the weight of his own treachery.

It didn't matter. Tristan had to go. But he'd taken just a few steps before he turned to face the man who had placed sanctions on his happiness for the last time. A random gust of wind swirled tiny yet turbulent eddies of dust at Blyth's feet, as if to show him that his own private storm of chaos would follow him forever.

That mattered little to Tristan now, and with a steady gaze, he said three words that condemned a broken man's heart to perdition.

"I forgive you."

Torment contorted Blyth's face. His movements were sluggish and unsteady, and as if powered by unseen forces, he angled towards his shed.

Beyond that flimsy door he knew what he would find; nothing but oblivion.

With the deepest of breaths, Tristan at last turned his back, and as he did he heard an all too familiar sound; the long slow sobs of a tortured adult. Though this time it wasn't his mother, the wretched noise still discharged shivers up his spine.

But all had changed and, composed and unperturbed, Tristan went into the house.

The boy had come of age.

Dark had fallen fully now, and as the night engulfed Blyth, so did his shame. The long overdue comeuppance for the perpetual abuse of his family had arrived. But one more ghost haunted him, and was about to scream back into his conscience. The single tool he had to fight that demon, the one that had held him captive almost twenty years, was to surrender himself to the whisky. That one event that he now recalled so vividly was the catalyst for his depression these last years, and such was his all-encompassing remorse that he was virtually insane with regret.

That Tristan remained oblivious was his only comfort.

Head bowed, Blyth stepped inside that dilapidated wooden sanctuary and bolted the door. Whether it was to lock the world outside or himself in he wasn't sure, and it didn't matter. He flicked on the one feeble light, and from a cracked mirror that hung on rotting string his face glared back at him, features twisted into a grimace of pain, the splinters evidence of too much violence, its fractures echoing the fractures in his mind. In the silvery orange glow, the face he saw oozed blame and contempt from every pore, and developed over long years, it challenged his bravery about what needed to be done. Blyth slumped into his battered old deckchair and unscrewed the cap from the first bottle.

The decision was made. Over the coming hours and days, he would finally drink himself to death.


*Chapter Thirteen*

He knew his father would drink, he'd seen it clearly in those unclear eyes, and he'd probably be passed out and impervious within a few hours. But Tristan could not let his guard slip. These were dangerous hours, and it was a wounded lion that lurked in the shadows of that unlocked cage of a shed.

Ten o'clock came around, and the night was cool and still. Tristan sat at the hearth for a final time, making the most of the heat before his mission in the cold of the small hours. As he looked about the room, his mind buzzed with edgy excitement, and he thought of his father, slumped yet always threatening, and considered actually barricading the shed door. His father was callous and coldhearted, especially when drunk, but too many times Tristan himself had been locked behind doors for reasons he never understood, and he had vowed never to act that way, no matter the circumstance. He would not treat his father like an animal, despite his own maltreatment. He left the shed alone.

Tristan knew now that his father had a sickness, the disease of alcoholism, and it wasn't just a feeble excuse to act tough. He understood this, but knew also that little effort at atonement had been made during more sober times. *He's still a bad man*, he whispered, as if to consolidate his thoughts as well as convincing himself of his decision to leave. In just a couple of hours, he'd be free of that cottage, that prison of sixteen years. He would leave, and he would never, never, return.

In the damp and dark decay of the shed, Blyth was distraught. Black bugs scuttled about, and one, either brave or foolish, crawled up his sleeve. He flicked it off, and watched idly as it floundered on its back in the mud. Helpless. About to die. He crushed it, unaffected. Blyth tipped back his head and poured the whisky for long seconds, stopping only to draw breath. He sank lower in the chair. Mould infected the walls and vast cobwebs laced every corner. Much of the wood was rotten, and at least one rat ran over his muddy feet. He was oblivious to it all, and drank on.

As the whisky flowed, his emotions swung like a wild pendulum, rage and remorse, anger and guilt. But despite getting what he knew to be his just recompense, Blyth clutched desperately to the last thread of dignity he felt was his. Not everything was his fault. He too was a victim, perhaps more so even than his family. Why should he be the one to suffer? He fought hard to stay in control, but teetered dangerously close to losing his mind completely. Skittish now, he looked around him, rigid with paranoia, as if his wicked, shameful past lurked nearby in the murky shadows of the present.

Suddenly, he lurched forward to grab a knife, fully intent on slicing deep into his veins, thus ending his own anguish and finally setting his wife and son free. But those hidden demons, his own nemeses that slithered and slipped around the weakest parts of his mind, mercilessly focused his rage onto the boy. *Why not turn the knife on him instead,* they breathed, *he who dared defy you? You, Blyth Nancarrow, master of their fate and ruler of their lives!*

The whirlpool like maelstrom of conflicted thoughts plunged him further and further into an abyss of hostile depression, causing the tortured man to pitch back his head and let out a long, deep bellow that might have been heard as a desperate cry for help to his son, had it not been swallowed by the shed and the night beyond, and dispersed into the world unheard.

Forsaken, he wept as the blade dropped to the ground, submerging into that second bottle of whisky like a rock in a pond, plummeting swiftly to the muddy bottom where he stuck for so long that time and the world would no longer miss him.

Pacing the cottage, Tristan noticed just how unkempt it really was. Dust gathered in great drifts on skirting boards, and cobwebs hung thick in every corner. Curtains were torn and limp, and the walls hadn't seen a coat of paint in his lifetime. There wasn't a trace of pride to be seen.

Pride. He knew his mother's pride had quite literally been beaten from her, and it inspired him to find his own. He'd need it for the daunting task ahead.

At last, and after a tense few hours, the time had come to leave. There'd been no drama with his father since he'd holed up in the shed, and apart from the occasional muffled, incoherent shouting, all was quiet. He was ready.

He put on all of his clothes, what few he had, and hoisted his small backpack onto shoulders loaded with burden. Along with a little food and the slim envelope of cash was the one possession he treasured above any other; a solitary photograph of him with his mother.

Taken on the beach when he was about six, their smiles paid testimony to happier times, and she indeed looked pretty and relaxed. Mostly, he noticed, she didn't look afraid, and his heart ached at her physical demise. It was just a decade, but because of the misery she'd endured, Kerra had aged nearer twenty years in that time. When she dared to smile she was still pretty, but for the most part she looked worn out and tired of life. Tristan wondered if she smiled more now, wherever she was. He was more determined than ever to find out.

Tristan glanced once more around the kitchen. He edged towards that kitchen door, a barrier that had always been symbolic to Tristan. That door, with its heavy permanence that kept the harsh outside world beyond, and the harsher, loveless world within, and beyond it a life he could scarcely imagine.

When he was younger, his mother had spoken of the places she longed to show him, but as the years passed she'd evidently accepted both of their miserable fates, and no longer taught him anything. He assumed it to be a defence mechanism, a tactic to protect him from his own imagination. So the only life he knew was on the inside of that door, its dark strong wood symbolic of his crippling lack of freedom. And he'd heard it slammed so often, its echoes causing both him and the walls to shudder, that the very sound of it was enough to keep him locked and bound within.

But on the night his mother had left, he saw that door, with all its innate power, clinging to that power by a single twisted hinge. His father's rage had smashed it to within an inch of its indomitable life, and only now did he appreciate the symbolism of that moment. If that door, that icon of oppression, was fallible, and could be changed, then so could anything.

And there, right at that moment, he was the proof. He'd changed, and was changing still, and he truly believed his metamorphosis was just beginning. It was a comprehension that breathed life into his lungs and blood into his veins.

Tristan heaved the door open on its strong new hinges with newfound strength of his own. He breathed deeply of the crisp autumn air, and stepped out into the night. The world beyond that door was pitch-black, and he sensed more than saw the eerie mist as it crept along the ground. Heavy, unforgiving clouds concealed the moon, and a storm threatened. That's how it always felt, he realized; in his life, a storm always threatened.

But right then, Tristan felt as alive as he had ever known. He flicked on his torch, and with purpose, boldly strode off into his future.

*Chapter Fourteen*

It wasn't long before the first few drops of rain fell,

stinging his face like hail, while his flimsy clothes, gear that hung loosely over his angular and underfed frame, failed to keep him dry. He was freezing, but the time to worry about that was later. First he had to get clear of the cottage.

To compound his woes the wind picked up, dragging ghostly, wraith like swathes of fog from the sea. Though his torch was bright, it barely penetrated the thick, swallowing fog, and progress was slow, but he knew the route well enough, and was still confident he'd make good time. Nevertheless, he proceeded with caution, because if he twisted an ankle now, all his plans, his growing purpose…everything…would be ruined.

An hour passed, and because of the obscure haze he hadn't covered enough ground. As the fog thickened and swelled, so Tristan's anxiety swelled with it, and despite the numbing cold, he felt a trickle of sweat slide down his lower back. *I must not be late*, he thought, and stopped to compose himself. Standing still he felt his pulse race, and saw his breath hanging in the air before his eyes, just about all he could see. The rain had solidified now, falling as cruel hail, so he set off again, and timed his strides to match his pulse; One, two. One, two. He moved on, pace urgent yet steady.

Another hour though, and he started to panic. Tristan knew he was close. But where was the lighthouse? A cruel sky pelted him with icy bullets that crunched underfoot as he walked, and the cold penetrated his clothes, forcing itself deep into his bones. He paused, his breath ragged from both the frigid fog and creeping anxiety, while trees as barren as death swayed ominously in the wind. This was not the place for a youngster.

But then, straining his eyes to infiltrate the thick dark, he saw it, like some mercurial giant, the smooth curved walls of the old beacon emerging like a ship as it cut through the mist. Relief waltzed over him in a warming sweep of emotion, and he sprinted the last fifty meters to the retired edifice.

Despite his success, Tristan hesitated before entering, as too many dire experiences had damaged his trusting instincts. But after a moment, and feeling the icy wraiths once more at his neck, he stepped out of the maelstrom and into silence, the door closing with a creak behind him.

The darkness surprised Tristan. He'd expected whoever was to meet him there to have a light on, so quickly shone his own beam about the black room. Nobody! *Was it a trap?* Adrenalin buzzed like the bare end of a live wire, and a familiar knot throbbed in his guts. A sudden noise, and he turned, just in time to see the lighthouse door swing back open to reveal a shadowy figure that filled the doorway.

In that instant, Tristan's native fear, his abstracted sense of imminent peril, made him feel as if his stomach had given way. He knew it was his father.

The giant figure stared at him for a long moment, as trails of that cloying mist drifted in around him. But once Tristan's eyes had adjusted to the artificial half-light, he saw with temporary relief that it wasn't his father there, but a total stranger. He looked back at the man, and noticed his eyebrows arch and eyes flash wide open, as if getting the surprise of his life. But a smile then cracked across the man's face, and in that smile Tristan felt his anxiety firmly erode away. Everything was going to be alright.

A flux of questions spewed forth at the unknown goliath before him. "Where's my mother? How is she? Is she safe? When can we...?"

"Tristan, it's okay, I'll tell..."

"Can I see her? Where is she?"

The stranger listened patiently. There was tenderness in his face, at odds with his strong body, and he'd clearly expected this barrage, smiling gently as he raised his palms to say *calm down*. He pointed to a step. Tristan sat, and the man crouched down and faced him, their eyes level. He exuded a composure that pacified the frantic kid, and with his kind blue eyes set on Tristan's, he introduced himself.

"I know you're wondering who I am. My name's Mark, and I've known your family for a long, long time. I've some answers for you, but first I've a message from your mother."

"What is it, what did she say?"

"She said she's so sorry to leave you the way she did. She misses you dearly, and she longs to see you. And I can tell you this; your mother is very proud of you. You're here now, which means you've been brave. And Tristan, the hardest part is over. You're safe, and your father can never hurt you again."

At the mention of Tristan's father, a subtle frown darkened the man's face. But the next second it was gone, and the bright eyes returned.

"We can talk more on the way, but now we have to leave. You've got a ferry to catch."

Tristan did feel safe, and he appreciated the man's help, and knew now who had helped his mother. For that he was grateful, but he wanted answers. Now he'd had a clear look at the man, there was something very familiar about his face and his chestnut colored hair and stubble, and he ventured one more question.

"I understand," he said, "and thanks for your help. But please tell me honestly…who are you?"

"Me?" The big man looked at Tristan seriously for a

moment, deep in thought, as if caught off guard and unsure of a truthful answer. But after a moment he chuckled, and replied, "I'm just the driver."

*Chapter Fifteen*

Tristan remained silent as they crept through the fog toward Hugh Town. He couldn't understand why the stranger seemed so familiar. He hadn't met him before, he was certain. So who was he?

It wasn't a long drive into town, but in the wretched conditions it seemed to take forever. The darkness had yielded to a maelstrom of granite grey and pink tinged white, and beyond the fog, an autumn gale coiled clouds into a kaleidoscopic swirl of peace and power.

At six-thirty they finally arrived at the island's only port. Tristan was there once before, albeit many years ago, but he didn't remember it that way; everything had grown.

Mark noticed his surprise. "Big town, huh?"

Tristan didn't answer. He looked about him in awe, admiring in silence the large houses lining the quay. He saw shops and a post office dotted between fancy looking hotels, and a pub and a petrol station sat side by side a florist. But it was like he'd never seen them before, and he knew why; he was viewing them now through contemporary eyes, the eyes of a boy who for the first time could sense the safety of freedom. That was the big difference, he knew, and his smile was tangible evidence.

Just then something caught his eye, and he craned his neck to see better before it slid out of view.

"Please stop the car, Mark" he yelled. They'd just passed a bus shelter on which had been stuck a poster showing a boy's face, a face Tristan instantly recognised.

Through the gloom, the grainy black and white image was a portrait of the missing boy from the newspaper he'd found on the beach. Mark reversed up a little.

"That boy, the boy on that poster, who is he?" Mark knew whom Tristan was talking about.

"That's Richard White, poor kid. He went missing from the beach near Penzance, and he's not been seen in weeks. Everyone fears the worst."

Mark pulled slowly away, but Tristan was unable to take his eyes off that face. There seemed to be a depth of sadness about the boy that captivated him. Perhaps he thought it echoed his own innate sadness. *Richard White,* he muttered to himself, *where are you?* Just as he'd sensed on the beach, Tristan felt the eerie notion that the boy's story was somehow intertwined with his own. It was impossible, of course, but the thought wouldn't leave him.

As the truck approached the entrance to the dock, a patchwork of images rushed around Tristan's head, like trash in the wind. He saw his father, and his mother with eyes closed. He saw Richard White, and the unknown girl from his dreams. His trampled asters. Black crows. The cottage.

His own eyes closed as he tried to focus, the big night finally taking its toll, but soon Tristan was nudged from his momentary rest, the collage of colour and shade fading as Mark's big hand tapped him on the shoulder. "Time to go, kiddo."

He pointed to a large boat someway along the dock. The sun had just climbed into view over the horizon, shunting the clouds apart with apparent difficulty. It was almost seven now, and Tristan was hungry and worn out. He grabbed the food from his bag and offered some to Mark, who declined.

"Inside this envelope is your ferry ticket," said Mark. "I

won't be coming with you. You'll go on from here yourself."

Tristan's anxiety roared back upon hearing that he'd once more be alone, but Mark pushed on, unperturbed.

"There's also a second envelope, but you can't open that one until the ferry has departed. It's your mother's wish, and she said that if you didn't agree, I'm not to give it to you at all."

Tristan didn't understand, and his gut's knot of fear once more tightened. But his mother had trusted this man, so he had no choice but to trust him too. "Alright."

"Do you promise?"

Tristan paused, and the man smiled with patience. After a moment, Tristan smiled back.

"I promise," he said, and he meant it.

Mark handed Tristan the envelope, and patted him warmly on the knee.

"Your mother told me you were brave," he said. "She was right. You're going to be just fine out there in the world, believe me. I can see it in your eyes. Your father is a coward, always has been, but I can see you're different from him, stronger, and better. You're going to be a good man, Tristan. A good man." He jumped from the truck, and rushed around to open Tristan's door. He stood squarely in front of him now, and held out his big hand.

"I have to go now. You won't need it, but I'll say it anyway...good luck."

Tristan took the hand in his own, enjoying the warmth and strength of it and wanting it to never stop. Blyth had never shown him any tenderness, and this stranger had shown him more kindness in a few hours than his own father had in a lifetime.

"Thanks for everything, Mark." He looked up into the big man's face again, the rising reddish sun two bright

91

dots in big blue eyes. Those eyes. *I know you,* he thought, *but who are you?* He had to ask. "Now we're here and you're about to leave, can you tell me who you really are?"

The huge shoulders seemed to slump a little, and those eyes blinked a few times in quick succession. He looked as if he might cry.

"I guess I can tell you now," he said in a voice laced with emotion. "I'm the man who wished he was your dad."

He grabbed Tristan in a tight bear hug, and a second later had jumped into his truck, and was gone.

Tristan stood immobile, impotent in thought and movement, cold, alone and bewildered. After long moments the fierce chill forced him to move. He glanced at his ferry ticket...fifteen minutes until departure. He had no time to think about what had just happened, and on willing legs walked swiftly towards the boat, a vessel that would emancipate him from that island bastille for the very first time.

Walking now he cast an uneasy glance back at the road, half expecting to see his father's truck racing towards the dock. Of course it wasn't there. Deep down he believed that at that moment his father would be unconscious after a severe whisky binge, but his nerves were still chafed, and until he was miles out to sea, Tristan knew that everything could still unravel to a ruinous end.

The ferry's formidable engines roared to life, and its funnel belched dense black smoke. Bellowing three times, the horn signalled its imminent departure, causing Tristan to jump. *This is it...I'm finally leaving,* he thought, and scanned the sea wall for Mark. But he was long gone, vanished from his life just as quickly as he'd arrived, and

Tristan felt an incomprehensible sadness for the absent stranger. But there was no hint of his father, and for that he was relieved.

With a pair of violent shudders, the big boat crawled away from the harbour wall, turned a slow, wide circle, and faced towards the open sea. The dark water beyond the harbour mouth churned under tide and tempest, but the ferry, with Tristan safely on board, surged stubbornly forward into the channel.

There were two key reasons why Tristan was leaving the island behind. Primarily, it was to find and be reunited with his mother. But in doing so, he would finally be escaping the long suffered abuses of his father. Aside from this, and in spite of his keenly felt apprehension at being on this journey alone, Tristan was also aware of a vibrant, tangible sense of pending excitement, and his pulse sped with the promise of adventure.

He stood at the bow, ignoring the rushing cold as the boat cut through the petulant waves at surprising speed, and with the dim glow of a gallant sun trying to illuminate his passage, he banished all thoughts of St. Mary's from his mind and peered across the murky sea to a brighter horizon.

*Chapter Sixteen*

All across the south of England, an ireful storm lambasted the coast. Bitter sideways rain lashed everything without judgement, while relentless winds tore down trees and ripped the tiles from roofs. Huddled against the elements beneath a sturdy stone bridge, a young boy buried his face in his sleeve.

He shook uncontrollably from the cold, and his vacant

belly ached with hunger. His mind ached too, because his next decision was his biggest yet. The boy was struggling. He could make himself known to the police, who he wrongly supposed were still out looking for him. That way he'd be warm and fed, and could sleep in a real bed for the first time in weeks.

Or, he could battle onwards, unsure of his destination. As cold and hungry and tempted as he was to go to the police, the thought of returning home to his parents sent a powerful, more sinister chill shuddering up his spine.

"No!" he said aloud, piquing the curiosity of a nearby tramp. Then, more quietly, "I'll never go back!"

The boy knew just what awaited him if he returned home. The darkness and cold and the bleak loneliness of his current situation were still better than the life he'd known, and he resolved there and then that the flimsy uncertainty of the future was better than the rigid certainty of the past.

He heard footsteps and looked up, and when the smiling old tramp with the impressive beard offered him a steaming cup of tea, he took it.

A grandiose discharge of forked lightening lit the London skyline, silhouetting the city's shining towers of ambition and the unambitious drabbery of its flats. Several people on the bus gasped. A little boy cried.

Every few weeks, the daydreaming young woman rode the bus into the sprawling capital to procure supplies for projects at her art gallery in Brighton. The ninety-minute drive north gave her time to plan upcoming events, or in this case, a well earned nap. She missed nature's electric show, enveloped deep within a drowsy lull, but the following eruption of thunder unceremoniously shook her from her melancholy.

In the moments before the sky's rude outburst, she'd been lost in memories of her childhood, painful images that always came to her during a storm. She'd escaped her troubled early life at a young age, and knew she'd been lucky, but the hurt came when she thought of the one less fortunate. That hurt, that shaded phantom from an undulating past, often clawed at her heart, and though the nasty presence was invisible, she felt it throughout her entire being.

The last time she saw the boy, the sky hemorrhaged rage as it did now. The baby was too young to understand, but she'd never forget the look of fear on its tiny face as the lightning cracked through the darkness. She was the charmed one, and she wondered often about the baby that was left behind. Shivering, she fought hard to suppress the guilt that stewed just below a surface rendered delicate by experience.

She had survived. She only hoped that the poor innocent boy had survived too.

*Chapter Seventeen*

Blyth lay prostrate in the dirt of his shed floor as storm water seeped beneath the rotting timber and pooled around his head and body. At some unknown point during the night he'd drained the second bottle of whisky, and having staggered for a third, slipped cheaply to the ignoble and unhallowed ground. He remained conscious then, but had neither the strength nor desire to stand up, muttering incoherently and almost choking in the filth. He heard the storm growing, and sensed the danger, but sputtered something that sounded like *justice*.

Blyth was distraught about all he'd lost, and his depression weighed so heavily that he attributed no further value to his life, not that he ever had. He would simply lie there and await his fate. For hours he lay amongst the muck and glass and unused tools, as forgotten and alone as a person could be, an exile in his own home, while his destiny, in the guise of an icy inglorious death, came seeping ever closer.

Dawn broke, and sent crawling tendrils of gold and orange through ever stubborn clouds, yet the sky clung to darkness as the ferry trenched through jagged seas. The storm was upon him now, and as thunder clouds thumped nearby Tristan's stomach turned somersaults, not only from the rolling uncertain ship, but from the fissure of uncertainty ahead. In a couple of hours he would arrive at the mainland, but for Tristan it could be the moon, so little he knew of it.

Until now Tristan had kept his promise to Mark, but the envelope burned a new hole in his already holy pocket, and he couldn't wait any longer. Taking care not to rip it, he tore it open. The note inside was short, and as he read, his trepidation surfaced again.

*Dearest Tristan,*

*Be patient my love. You've come so far already, and you must come further still. I'm so sorry for the secrecy, but in time you'll understand why. The wonderful lady you'll find at this address will help you:* 34 Broad Willow Lane, Odstock, Salisbury. *You have to trust her.*

*Please stay safe.*

*I love you, my son x*

Each word stung like a needle, and he nearly choked on the growing tumor of dismay in his throat. He would not see his mother today...maybe not even soon. *But*, he thought, *I must be strong,* and he blinked away the pooling teardrops. This was more than just a journey to his mother. It was a journey of self-discovery upon which he'd learn of the real life so long denied him. *He* was doing this, and it was *he* who was now living. Tristan vowed that the message would not drag him down, and he breathed deep of the cool, salty air.

Despite the setback, he knew his mother must have valid reasons for this latest disappointment, and accepted it with a determined nod. Staring out through the indifferent and unwelcoming gloom, Tristan fortified himself for the burgeoning storm and whatever trials lay ahead. But there was one thing he knew beyond any doubt; that no storm's fury could ever match that of his father's, and in possession of that knowledge, that he'd somehow withstood those abuses for so long, meant he could withstand anything that now presented itself. At least he hoped so.

Three turbulent hours across unstable seas, and Tristan finally saw land. Penzance! His heart galloped as the port's lights, blurry through the relentless downpour and howling wind, slowly approached like a wintery oasis, and the astonished boy's eyes grew wide. The only town he'd ever seen before was Hugh Town, and from his position a few hundred yards out at sea, Penzance dwarfed it in every way, sweeping east and west in a panoramic grey mass of boats and buildings and church towers that merged coarsely with the crushed slate sea in front and dismal flattened hills beyond.

Tempest winds assaulted the port as they'd done for millennia, rendering hardy its native souls. Despite the slashing deluge, Tristan saw scores of traders enduring; fishermen hurried to unload catches; dockers shifted containers left and right; drivers flitted vans here and there, their horns, it seemed, honking at everything and nothing. It was a mad flurry of organized chaos the likes of which he could've scarcely imagined. Tristan was in awe.

And yet, in the broader picture of the world he knew Penzance wasn't that big. Other names he'd heard of came to him; Plymouth and Torquay, Birmingham and Oxford, big important towns and cities that were relatively nearby. But one place he had always dreamed of stuck out beyond all others; London. In the note his mother had instructed him to make his way to Salisbury, and he would obey. But deep down he was destined to go to London, he somehow knew it, and the thought filled him with a palpable sense of wonder.

London, so big and so busy, so many opportunities, and people, and museums…and life. So much life!

Perhaps that was his destiny, to live in London. To find life in London.

The ferry's horns boomed with a triumphant flourish to snap Tristan's attention back to the present. On adrenalin fueled energy he roused, and had almost cleared the gangplanks before the ferry was docked, such was his desperation to set foot on what for him was the hallowed safety of the mainland. Drenched but oblivious to it, he ran by the waiting passengers, whose expressions spoke of mild curiosity. But Tristan neither noticed nor cared, and with the form of a newly emancipated prisoner, he reveled at his first sniff of freedom.

It was a cold and hard earned freedom, but it was his.

Only he and his mother knew what he'd endured to reach this juncture. And Blyth of course, but he was the sole cause and didn't count. Barely sixteen years old, and he'd suffered so much, but Tristan had evolved so significantly in those last weeks that now he felt almost anything was possible. The world around him had become, for the very first time, that longed for oyster, and once the dust had settled from both a recent and long-lived turbulence, he would grasp it with young and eager hands.

But he had to find his mother above all else, and in doing, so the troubled opening chapter of his decade long story of pain and misery would slam decisively shut.

At the exit to the grey port he stood beneath equally grey skies that fell to earth in an endless onslaught. To a bystander, to pause in such an exposed spot seemed ridiculous. But to Tristan, who breathed in the fresh air as if it had been denied him forever, was savouring every second. He looked around and saw unhappy people scurrying for shelter, and worn out buildings whose heyday was long forgotten. He saw no smiles and little joy in the old port town that had seen prosperity once but now harbored broken dreams and little else. And it was the most beautiful place Tristan had ever seen.

"I am Tristan Nancarrow," he shouted into the soulless void, "And this is my life!"

The empowered boy hoisted his backpack tighter across shoulders that felt stronger even than yesterday, and headed out into the town as the newly commissioned scribe of his own unwritten destiny.

# Part II

## Seek and Destroyed

*Chapter Eighteen*

Deep in a dismal underground cellar beneath the storm beleaguered streets of east London, Kerra Annis sat aching and uncomfortable at her workstation. Her weary eyes looked all about the cold and lifeless room, and saw dozens of other woman she assumed must feel cold and lifeless too. The icebox cave they occupied wore a woman down, not that most of the browbeaten women there weren't worn down already. They were a pitiful bunch, yet under the duress of their individual plights and their collective work conditions, they maintained a rowdy spirit and a sense of humour that defied their harsh realities.

Kerra had secured her job in that squalid backstreet garment workshop soon after she'd arrived in the city, and though it was monotonous and demanding work that paid little and did nothing for pride, she earned enough to share the rent of a small flat with her feisty co-worker Mollie.

It was a start, at least, and Kerra was coping well enough, but it was far from what she imagined now she'd made it so far from the hell of St. Mary's. Reverting to her maiden name, she'd vitiated the anathema Nancarrow to her past, and now Kerra Annis thought of only one thing; her precious son Tristan. If the daring plan that she'd made for him in collaboration with her friend Mark Trescothick all worked out, then Tristan should now be safely away from the island and on his way to Salisbury. And more important than anything, she hoped, he was on his way to freedom.

He was brave enough, Kerra truly believed that, and she trusted Mark wholly. But now she felt vacant and powerless, as distant as she was in London, and as a mother she had to trust in her son's guts and tenacity to pull him through. That helplessness was painfully familiar.

It was because of her weaknesses and helplessness throughout the previous years that they were in that situation in the first place. Why couldn't she have just been stronger? Why did she wait so long to leave? Why didn't she take Tristan away sooner? These agonizing doubts cut into her like a rough blade of judgement, and she was writhen with guilt about the difficult choices she'd had to make.

Sliding swiftly down into what was her lowest moment since reaching London, Kerra almost didn't notice the wicked and wiry supervisor stalking toward her along the scarcely lit aisle, until from behind she heard an urgently whispered, "Oi! Heads up." Lacking an empathetic bone in his lean and angled body, there was no time for self-pity while he prowled nearby, and quickly she lowered her head and wiped her eyes with a subtle raise of the sleeve as the sullen factory overseer moved on, thankfully unaware.

Kerra breathed a stifled sigh of relief, and a swift look back granted her a friendly wink from Mollie. For the rest of the long and arduous shift the repetitive toil acted as a tonic, as she busied herself pinning down collars on a never ending stack of cheap and ugly shirts.

At least she was safe now, and she'd made a friend in Mollie, her first in too many years. Plus she had steady work and a roof over her head.

But above all else her heart ached for Tristan, and as the days passed by in a dilatory haze, her son was all she could think of.

*Chapter Nineteen*

Through sleeting rain, rain that came at him like arrows in some ancient battle, Tristan rushed towards the busy streets of Penzance. At a zebra crossing, he paused, tentative, having never seen anything move so fast, amazed as sleek cars sped by, despite the treacherous conditions; surely destined for carnage, he thought. With his growling belly and ever more powerful shivers of cold, Tristan hustled across the street into the nearest tavern. At sixteen, he'd never been in a pub, and having experienced first-hand the multitude of suffering caused by his father's drinking, he'd long ago vowed never to touch alcohol. But he was intrigued as he pushed through the ornate doors and sought refuge from the ongoing battle outside.

Through a sickish haze that hung languid throughout the place, he saw it was already packed. Though it wasn't yet midday, serious middle-aged men in sharp suits drank ale and read newspapers, while older men sat at the bar alone and, hunched over tankards, looked as if the world might end that very day. Beside their pints, chaser glasses sat newly drained. Huddled at other tables were brightly dressed clusters of people, laughing and chatting loudly, their accents alien. Brown and black and white skinned men, some with curious hats and others long beards, spoke together in languages Tristan couldn't understand.

But amongst all these strangers, some clearly from foreign lands, it was Tristan who felt strange, an alien in his own country, and it dawned on him in that moment just how isolated he'd been and how naïve his deprived childhood had rendered him. A gnawing sadness began to swell, and for an instant he thought he might cry. But a flush of taut anger rose up from his chest to quash the sadness and clench his jaw shut, and it was an anger born of all the despicable things wrought upon him by his father.

And yet he grew angrier still for all the things his father hadn't done, for the things he hadn't shown him, and for all the things that he as a child had clearly missed out on.

Tristan fought against weeping and looked about him. He stood there unnoticed, the rowdy patrons oblivious to him and his woes. And suddenly, as if the blurry fragments of his life merged to form a lucid and welcome picture, he understood with clarity that he was finally free. Liberated from those restrictive yet destructive shackles, he had a whole wide world to learn from. And what better place to start learning, he thought, than in a room full of strangers.

Over in a dim corner he spied the last empty table, and jostled his way to it through the legions of drinkers. The moment he sat down and picked up the greasy menu a young woman approached, and in a perky voice, said,

"What can I get for you, young man?"

Tristan's cheeks blazed the red of apples as he managed only a mumble in response.

"...erm..er, maybe...uh..." Aside from his mother, he had never spoken to another woman, and his stumbled reply was met with a pleasant chuckle.

"You're not from round here, are you lad. Cottage pie, how does that sound?"

Tristan nodded, his shyness painfully obvious.

"Where did you roll in from?" Her smile was warm, but instincts told him to keep the details of his journey to himself.

"I'm from...I came in from out of town, miss."

"Okay love, suit yourself." Still she smiled. "One cottage pie, coming right up."

Her bubbly countenance matched the bubbly shape of her body as she strode away, and when she looked back over her shoulder and winked, Tristan's cheeks flustered from apples to plums. *I'll have to get used to this*, he thought, and gradually relaxed back in his seat, for now content just to sit and observe, and breathe in his surroundings on this, the first day of his new life.

Tristan ate slowly, relishing the simple pleasure of a meal without his father's intense presence rushing him. Content now and with a full stomach, and the chill at last defrosted from his bones, he began to notice things for the first time.

With his newly tuned senses, beyond the pub walls he heard the constant thrum of engines, and through steamed up windows he saw impatient riders making their powerful machines growl as huge trucks thundered through town, causing the walls to vibrate and trailing their thick exhausts in the air. Inside he heard the droning rise and fall of animated conversation, each group of customers intent on drowning out the next. Foods he'd never heard of filled the menu; Korma and masala, pizza and risotto, and words he could barely pronounce, like enchilada and biryani. He vowed to try them all, as their myriad smells enticed him from nearby plates and cast his imagination to other worlds, while the constant choking smoke of a thousand cigarettes stung his eyes, their toxins swirling upwards to paint the ceiling a rotten yellow.

The multi-colored winter clothes the people wore, and the pub's vibrant yet aging décor, all seemed other-worldly in comparison to the cold grey stones of his recently escaped prison cottage. All was effervescent, living, when before, all was decayed, dying.

And at the bar, old timers waited for judgement in silence, oblivious to it all.

Beautiful paintings hung about the pub, their dramatic scenes of wild coasts and ships on stormy seas reminding Tristan of his own recent voyage. But then his eyes fell on one particularly enigmatic image, and his heart missed a beat. He navigated the thronged pub, and was soon standing in front of the picture, eyes wide in awe.

"Stonehenge! Amazing, isn't it?" He turned to see the bubbly waitress. "My name's Barbara," and, with a grin added, "but friends call me Bobby."

"Hello...Bobby?" he ventured.

"Bobby it is." They shared a warm smile.

"Do you know what the stones mean?" asked Tristan.

"Nobody really knows, but some believe it's an ancient clock, or a signpost of some kind. Thousands of years old, they say."

"It's beautiful," he replied, and there was real enchantment in his tone. He turned to face her, and spoke with certainty. "I'm going there soon."

Bobby looked at him with compassion, her lovely face awash with understanding. An unexpected teardrop glistened in the corner of her eye.

"Yes, Tristan," she said without joy. "I know you are."

Bobby's shift was over at four and, now changed out of her stained apron, was sitting next to Tristan, each embracing a mug of tea.

"How did you know my name?" he asked, "I didn't tell you."

With a nod she smiled. It was a smile that could warm the coldest of hearts.

"I've been expecting you. Mark asked me to look out for a good looking young lad that looked a little lost. He described you pretty well, I'd say. I was to keep an eye on you, though it seems to me you don't need much looking after. It's nice to meet you, Tristan."

They shook hands.

"Mark's my husband. Big handsome lump, isn't he? We've a flat just up the road."

"But how'd you know I'd come into this pub? I could easily have gone in another."

She chuckled, and it was a joyous sound. "With that disgusting weather, there was a fair chance you'd come in here first to escape the storm. Mark is very well known around these parts, and if you went somewhere else first, word would've gotten back to me and I'd have come and found you. And you can trust me, Tristan, the same way you trusted Mark. He's known your mother a long time, and we really want to help you. Which reminds me...we'd be honored if you'd stay with us tonight. Our place isn't much, but it's warm, and you can sleep on the couch. It's very comfy, and you can stay tomorrow too, if you need a bed, though I expect you'd like to be getting along."

There was a subtle pause, and a shade of sadness colored her cheeks. "I know you're looking for your mum."

"Have you met her? Is she in Salisbury?"

"No, I haven't met her, and I'm sorry, but I don't know where she is. All I know is that I'm to help you however I can. You're a nice boy, Tristan, as I was told you were." Bobby seemed to struggle to find the right words. "I'm...well, I'm really sorry for what's happened to you and your mother. Truly I am. I just want you to know that...well, that not all people are like your father. There are some really nice people in the world...good people, like Mark."

"Like you too, Bobby. You and Mark have been so kind, and I'm very grateful. I know my mum is, too."

"It's our pleasure, and we just hope you get to see her soon. I wish I could help more. Look, why don't we go back to the flat now? You can get some rest before tomorrow. What do you say?"

"Thanks. Actually, I'd like to walk around for a while...explore...explore the town a little." His head bowed, covering his face as if ashamed of his obvious naivety.

"Of course, love, you take your time." Bobby knew that the poor kid had hardly seen anything beyond the cottage where he'd grown up, and she pitied him his sheltered and fractured childhood. "Just come back whenever you like," she said, and explained how he could find the flat, just half a mile up the hill from town. Winking, she added, "By the way, be careful out there. There are plenty of ruffians in these old port towns. Hold on tight to your bag."

Bobby had the kindest, most sincere face Tristan had ever seen, and he did trust her. He left the pub, and wandered through town with his backpack strapped extra tight to his shoulders. He passed shop after shop, their lights inviting in the descending darkness. The shops sold everything; fancy cakes, expensive clothes, luxury furniture. And myriad restaurants with strange names; *Lim's Chinese Diner; Mario's Pizza and Pasta; Namaskar Curry House*.

The gaudy lights of a car salesroom caused him to pause, and inside, the magnificent Jaguars sparkled like mirrors behind windows that stretched from floor to ceiling. A stiff man whose suit was as shiny as the cars, circled them with nonchalance. *Too shiny* thought Tristan, disliking the man and his cars instantly.

Walking on he found a book store, which to Tristan was like finding a horde of treasure. As the miserable rain would not yield, he stepped inside.

"Good afternoon, young man," said a rotund and well seasoned old lady as he entered, "Is there anything I can help you with?" It looked to Tristan as if she'd worked there a hundred years.

"Hello, miss. I just came in to look around." He began to move further into the shop, but then turned. "Actually, do you have an atlas?"

The timeworn assistant chuckled. "Well, that's our specialty. Where are you heading to?"

"I'm going to Salisbury first, and then to London."

Muriel, or so her name-badge declared, looked at him for a moment, a curious expression on her powdered, puffy face. Then she shuffled out from behind the counter and led him to the travel section. Tristan followed behind, and saw reams exotically titled books; *Explore Provence; Go Down Under; Island Hopping the Bahamas.* Muriel selected a book and, peering over tiny spectacles at the title, nodded to herself with a satisfied blink. She handed it to him. *Atlas of The World.*

"I think this is what you're looking for," she said, and ushered him to a seat. Over her shoulder as she walked away, she said, "We'll be closing in fifteen minutes, love."

Tristan turned the pages delicately, as if he was looking at a priceless and ancient manuscript. To him it was an object of beauty, a treasure from a museum, and indeed the musty old store had a museum feel about it, or at least that's how Tristan imagined a museum would seem, having never been to one.

Traversing the pages, long and brightly colored roads zigzagged cross county, thick blue ones linking cities like Birmingham and Newcastle and Edinburgh, and thinner ones in red and yellow, like an intricate spider's web, linked smaller towns from east to west, from Carlisle to Lowestoft...and Penzance. Tristan marveled at seeing it all there on the page, and tried to imagine zooming in from above to the very spot where he was now sitting. He was even more amazed to see his tiny island just off the coast, one small green dot among many more. *St. Mary's Island*, he whispered to himself, *so near, and yet so very, very far*.

And then, with a lump in his throat, he saw Salisbury. He traced a slender finger along the road from Penzance to where he was heading. *Not far*, he thought, *and there I'll find my mum.*

Back at the counter the antiquated old woman looked cheerily at him.

"Son, do your folks know where you are?"

He considered for an extended moment before committing to his first ever lie. It was justified.

"Yes, miss, they certainly do."

Muriel clearly doubted him, but he was polite and, more importantly perhaps, he had the money to pay. She bit her tongue as she searched for a bag beneath her counter. When she rose back up, she noticed he was listening intently to the soft music coming from the radio. It was a well known song that everyone and his dog had been singing lately.

"Miss, who's singing this? It's amazing!"

A look of genuine disbelief arched her considerable brow.

"Where've you been these last couple of years, son? You're listening to the most popular group of boys this side of the Atlantic. They're handsome too, in a shaggy, modern kind of way." She chuckled, and her lumpy shoulders jiggled under her blouse.

"Who are they?"

"They, my dear, are The Beatles."

"They sound great. And in answer to where I've been... well...I've been living in the past. Thanks for the book. Goodbye." With that, Tristan hurried out of the store and went in search of Bobby's flat, leaving Muriel more than a little bemused.

"Kids these days," she said to the empty store, but couldn't keep the grin from her face.

He found the place easily, and soon he and Bobby were chatting over a cuppa as he warmed himself by the fireplace. Tristan was surprised at how at ease he felt, not only in Bobby's company, but in general. The last few weeks and days had been upsetting and traumatic, and today was a milestone in his young life.

Yet he'd taken it all in his stride, and had learned more about the world and, in turn, about himself, in just one day than he had in sixteen years on St. Mary's. Once more, that sudden gush of anger towards his father. How could he have denied his own son so much? And though he understood how difficult it was for his mother, married to a drunk who quelled her spirit and stole the light from her eyes, he also felt a twinge of anger at her. He knew she could have...should have, taught him more about life through the books that they both loved.

But despite that, Tristan longed to see her now, far from the dominant, dangerous shadow of her husband. He might at last get to see the real Kerra Nancarrow.

Seeing his faraway yet intense gaze, Tristan's momentary lapse eased when Bobby placed a gentle hand on his knee. She didn't probe his thoughts, guessing at his reluctance to talk about whatever had irked him. Instead, she took up the reins and swerved the conversation onto her and Mark and their life in Penzance.

"Did you know Mark was an old school friend of your mother's? They grew up together in a small village just outside this scrappy old town. They were never really boyfriend or girlfriend, but they were very close...like sister and brother, Mark used to say. He once told me about when Kerra first met your father. Mark was jealous of him, but not in a bad way. He just wanted Blyth to take care of his good friend, which he did at first, until they moved over to St. Mary's...until everything changed. But that was long before you were born. He also told me about..." Bobby cut off abruptly, and her face took on a strange look, as if she'd almost said something she shouldn't have. Tristan didn't miss it.

"What is it Bobby? He also told you what?"

"Oh nothing, just my silly mistake. I was confused... forget it."

He sensed there was more, and he pushed her, emotion straining his voice. "Bobby, please tell me. What were you going to say?"

"I'm sorry. Mark told me never to mention it, ever, not

under any circumstances. I promised I wouldn't. I'm really sorry but I can't." She yawned, and Tristan thought it was faked. "I'm tired love, reckon I should get off to bed."

"Please," he begged, certain now that Bobby was holding something back. "You have to tell me Bobby, please."

The transparency of his emotions was painful for Bobby to observe, and she knew it rendered him susceptible to deviants that preyed on the weak and fed their corpses to the vultures. And there would be plenty of vultures going Tristan's way.

"Goodnight Tristan!" she said sternly, although it didn't suit her at all. "Help yourself to anything in the cupboards tonight, and I'll cook you a big fry-up in the morning, bacon and eggs, the works. Sleep well." And she was gone.

Deflated, Tristan knew he'd missed out on some important information. Bobby was kind, but he knew she'd made a mistake. Exhausted from the day, he had no choice but to let it go.

As he bedded down on the sofa he realized that it was the first time he'd ever slept somewhere other than his own bed. Also, since he'd left the cottage everyone had been kind; Mark, Bobby, the chubby old lady in the book store. With so many nice people in the world, and despite Bobby's warning words, Tristan felt confident about quickly finding his mum and, feeling safe, he nestled into the cushions and closed his eyes.

Weary, Tristan's addled mind drifted to his mother, and he hoped that wherever she was at that moment, she was safe and warm like he was. He wondered about his father, and whether he was drunk? Probably slumped in his deckchair, he guessed. Richard White, the boy from the very town he was now in, whose face he saw on posters… *what is his story? Had he really drowned?* That's what he'd overheard from the gossips in town that afternoon, and the thought made him cringe. He'd never met the kid, but Tristan hoped with surprising and unexpected fervency that it wasn't true. He didn't really understand why he cared so much about a total stranger, but the thought of that kid alone in the world echoed his own tribulations, and that he might be the only person who did care about him instilled in him some kind of a responsibility to do so.

A million questions blinked at him from the darkness, sketches eddying before his eyes, but just before exhaustion claimed him for the night, one final image shone bright. The background was blurry, but in clear focus for the first time, Tristan saw her face. His eyes shot wide open in the dark. The golden red hair…the wide blue eyes above rosy cheeks…the tall, slender figure…and on her face the familiar look of sadness he'd seen so often in the mirror.

He actually heard his heart beat and felt it hammer against the inner wall of his chest, because if he hadn't known better, a sister that didn't exist was the unknown girl haunting his dreams.

*Chapter Twenty*

Unfamiliar smells of toast and bacon roused Tristan from his slumber. His muscles tensed, and he kept his eyes closed tight. He waited, hands over a chest that rose and fell with rapid, nervous breaths. But the expected shouting and clumping about of furniture never came. Eyes still closed, he reached for the glass of water he always kept beside his bed, and almost fell off the coach.

Peeling open his eyes, he soon understood. He wasn't in his bed. He wasn't even at the cottage. And he wasn't even on the island. He leapt from the couch and rushed to the door, remembering just in time to pull on his trousers and sweater. Now clothed, he burst into the kitchen, and startled Bobby so much she almost dropped the tray of food.

"Good morning, Bobby."

"Whoa there, love. Careful will ya," she laughed as she struggled with the tray. "Sleep well?"

"What time is it? It feels like I slept for days."

"Well young man, it's almost eleven. You looked so peaceful so I left you to sleep in, and I reckon you deserve it with all that you've been through."

"Thanks. I guess I did need it." Tristan eyed up the enormous breakfast. His stomach growled in loud anticipation, causing a glow of embarrassment to warm his cheeks. Bobby wobbled beneath her infectious chuckle as she joined him at the small table.

"So you're going to Salisbury, eh." It wasn't a question.

"Yes, that's where my mum is. I'll leave today, and hopefully see her tonight."

A shadow crossed her rounded face. "Look, Tristan, I hope she's there, I really do."

"Of course she is, she sent me the address."

"I know love, and I'm sure you're right. But you should be prepared, just in case."

Tristan was confused, unsure of her meaning. "Prepared for what, Bobby? I got a message from her with an address of where to go, so she must be there. Why wouldn't she be, if that's what she told me?" A trace of desperation crept into his voice.

*You poor thing,* she thought, and her heart ached for the kid who had suffered so much. She knew he wouldn't find his mother there. She knew it, but she couldn't tell him. Mark made her promise, and besides, she couldn't bear to tell him the truth.

"I know she *was* there. I'm just saying it's possible she's moved on. Mark said she was looking for a job, and there aren't many jobs in the South West these days. I hope I'm wrong, but you still have to go to this house. I'm sure you won't regret it."

Bobby stopped, knowing she'd already said far too much. Though she didn't completely understand the need for secrecy, according to Mark, Kerra had valid reasons, and who was she to question them? She wished Mark was there with her now, but he was still on St. Mary's taking care of business. She hoped it was going smoothly.

Bobby looked at Tristan. He seemed such a frail kid, but she sensed a degree of durability and toughness about him, and despite his youth his eyes were sharp. Now she thought about it, he reminded her of a much younger version of Mark. And she felt that the kid was a survivor... he just needed some long overdue good fortune in the coming weeks.

But Tristan was adamant. "I believe she's there, Bobby. But even if she did have to leave I'll be following right behind her. I *will* see my mum soon."

Bobby admired the kid's conviction. But fate hadn't been kind to that boy, and she feared...no, she knew, there'd be more disappointments ahead before he found his mother. Tristan was brave, but she sensed that alongside his resilience there lived an inherent naivety within him.

"You know, Tristan, I'm not a prophet and I won't

preach, and I definitely don't mean to scare you, but here's a gentle caution. There're some amazing people out there in the world, and on your journey you'll meet all sorts, both good and bad. I know you've suffered, and it must be difficult for you to trust people. But that can be a good thing, believe you me. You can never be too careful, especially these days, because everyone wants something from somebody, and usually for free. Saying that, most people deserve a chance to be trusted. They're not all bullies like your father, and most people are kind. All I'm saying is that you should be careful. Real life is tough, though I know you've had it tougher than most. You've an amazing future Tristan, and I wish you and your mother all the best."

She was right, and Tristan knew he had to be careful. He had little knowledge of the real world, and resolved to make every new day a lesson in life. Experience would be his teacher.

"You're right Bobby, of course you are, but I'm ready for the challenge. Not just about finding my mother, but whatever comes my way. But..." He paused, and looked a little abashed.

"It's okay, love, you can tell me." Bobby smiled her encouragement.

"It's just that I'm...well...is it normal to be scared?"

"Oh Tristan, of course it is. Everyone's scared of something, even if they can't or won't admit it. If someone says they're scared of nothing, well that's an admission that they're scared of something, maybe scared of being scared. There's no shame in fear, only in denying it. To be brave is to admit our fears and face them, and that's the hardest part. Now you've done that you'll be just fine."

Out on the street, Bobby hugged Tristan tight. He

thanked her for her kindness and walked with purpose up the hill. After about fifty yards he turned, and Bobby was still standing there, watching him leave. Surprised, he waved at his new friend, and though he couldn't see it, she wept.

Bobby was happy for him. She knew all about what he'd been through as a child, and was relieved that he'd at last broken free from the abuse. But she couldn't shake the notion of further disappointments ahead for him. She waved once more, and quickly went inside.

As he walked he realized with arrant sadness that Bobby was his only friend, and that all his life he'd been blind to the tragedy of his loneliness, ignorance his compassionate saviour. His mother Kerra had mastered her loneliness, passing the monotony of time creating fantastical works of art in her mind, though it ripped her heart in two that the art was only imagined. His father also understood his loneliness, though he dealt with it by drowning in whisky, his long time confidant. Blyth spoke more words alone and to himself when accompanied by the bottle than he'd spoken to his wife in ten years. But Tristan had never appreciated the isolation of his previous life until now, and every minute spent since then demonstrated with stark clarity just how sequestered and alone he truly was and had always been.

Penzance seemed dreary now, the novelty of its effervescence overcome by Tristan's downcast eyes and attitude. With a heavy heart he trudged on, with nothing but hope and a shadow, to the bus station on the outskirts of town. The wind had swept away the storm, and with it his positive mood, but at least it was dry as Richard's familiar face stared out at him from the posters, his melancholic face echoing Tristan's own. *What's your story?* he thought again, and loped on in long and languorous strides.

Just five minutes later, or perhaps it was thirty five, Tristan didn't know or care, he was nearing the edge of town when a sound drifted on the breeze unlike anything he'd ever heard. He wasn't sure why, but a wash of emotion resounded deep within, and without thinking he changed direction in search of that sirenic sound.

Tristan had never been to school. His mother would tell him that his best education was at home with her, and he remembered fondly those younger years. They would sit together at the kitchen table, and she'd teach him about history and geography through the stories of kings and queens and oceans and mountains. They'd sketch or paint together, something they both loved, and she'd create such wonderful scenes of landscapes and rivers and forests, all from distant memories or a bursting imagination.

As those years passed, Blyth's drinking began to dominate their lives, and the lessons dried up as his mother's spirit was cruelly and effectively beaten from her. When he did venture an enquiry about attending school, she simply told him it was a bad idea. In truth, his father didn't allow it. He feared that Tristan would one day talk to someone about his life at home, and rightly raise the alarm. Blyth would never let that happen.

The melodious noise grew louder, and he soon understood its origin; it was the elementary yet heart breaking sound of carefree children playing. Tristan slowly approached the school's rusting iron fence, and he saw so many happy faces chatting and laughing that his last shred of positivity was conquered by a desperate sadness. All these years, and he'd never experienced that basic fundamental joy of sharing fun with his peers. Small clusters of boys kicked about well worn footballs. Girls skipped rope. Others swung conkers on strings, cheering wildly when one got smashed into pieces. More still strolled about and spoke in smiles with friends, oblivious to the knife they twisted in his heart.

There and then, Tristan vowed that if ever he had children of his own, he'd be the best father a child could ever have.

Undignified rain began to fall as he cowered beneath a tree by a rusted fence. From the warped steel dripped brown rain into pools of oily sorrow, and it seemed as if today, even the ground shared his misery.

Unable to extricate himself from the torturous spectacle of innocent fun, what had felt almost like grief soon morphed into an anger directed at just one person; his father. He didn't like the word revenge. It sounded too much like his father speaking. *No*, he thought, *not revenge. Comeuppance! I'll show him the pain he's caused. I'll show him what he's lost.* He didn't like the way he felt, that bitterness that hinted at retribution, but nonetheless he felt it and didn't to try to quell it. He would use it as motivation.

At the bus station Tristan checked the schedule. A service to Salisbury was leaving in forty minutes, so he bought a ticket, found a bench and huddled deep into his inadequate jacket. As he waited, shivering, he spotted a man perhaps fifty yards from the entrance, oddly standing by the edge of the main road. *Strange* he thought, *bit dangerous to cross there.* The man then held out a sign, and written in bold letters, its message was simple: 'EAST.' Intrigued, Tristan waited and watched. Cars zoomed past, dozens of them, ignoring the man as if he wasn't there. But after maybe ten minutes, one car, a large, rusting heap of a ford, slowed down and pulled over twenty yards up the road. The man grabbed his bag from the ground and ran to the car, climbed in, and in the space of ten seconds, he was gone.

Amazed, Tristan wasn't sure what he'd just witnessed. But whatever it was it seemed easy, and an idea quickly materialized. If he tried to emulate the man, he could save money, and at the same time get the chance to meet new people. He walked over to where the man had stood, arriving at the same moment as another, older man, who swiftly picked up the traveler's discarded sign.

"Damn hitchhikers," he said, "no respect, throwing their rubbish around."

"Excuse me sir, but I'll take that sign." The man eyed Tristan suspiciously.

"What do you want this for? Aren't you a bit young?"

Tristan took the sign and smiled at the man.

"Sir, I'm a hitchhiker."

The bewildered man shook his head and walked off, as Tristan appraised the big letters; EAST. *That's good for me! With* a deep breath, he stepped to the kerb and hoisted the sign toward the oncoming traffic.

After only two minutes and to his further amazement, a tiny green sports car pulled over. The gentleman inside wound down the window and spoke over the din of the traffic in a loud, jolly voice. "Where are you heading to, sonny?"

In the back of his mind was Bobby's caution, but Tristan felt no danger with this old man. He went with his instincts.

"Well sir, I'm heading to Salisbury?"

"Hop in out of the drizzle, my boy, and I can take you as far as Truro, if that might help?"

Tristan folded his long frame into the car's tiny passenger seat, knees almost to his chest and his bag and sign stashed beneath his legs.

"Thanks a lot. My name is Tristan, Tristan Nancarrow."

The man's smile was barely visible beneath a bushy white mustache that curled daintily at either end.

"And my name is Ernest Fredrick Harvey, sixty five years young, and I'm delighted to make your acquaintance. But Tristan, you must call me Ernie, since we're now friends."

Ernie's eyes were intense, his accent as refined as his immaculately trimmed mustache. Within a few miles he'd explained how he'd spent thirty years in the Royal Navy, but had long ago retired to a sedate and more peaceful life in Truro. He recounted tales of himself as a young lad, both in and out of the navy, and Tristan listened with intent as if they were the first stories he'd ever heard.

"Cars were a real novelty back then, lad, and hitchhiking was difficult though not impossible. But we used to ride the train if ever we went to the 'Big Smoke."

"The what? The Big Smoke?" Confusion showed on the Tristan's face, as Ernie's eyes sparkled with excitement.

"My boy, I'm talking about London, the greatest city on Earth. Oh, the times we had in London. Of course, that *is* where I met my wife." Those eyes fairly glistened at the happy memories, and if Tristan had any doubts whether he himself would someday visit, Ernie had dismissed them in an instant.

"So, young man, what is your plan, if you don't mind me asking?"

Tristan's answer was muted and vague, and Ernie just caught a line about searching for something. He gathered from the boy's reticence that it was a subject best left alone, and accepted it without question.

"Well my boy, I wish you all the very best, and I hope you find everything you seek on your travels."

He was a real gentleman, and Tristan was glad he'd trusted his instincts, especially when Ernie invited him to have dinner with his wife and spend the night at their house. Despite the early hour, the winter sun was already fading below the season stripped trees, and the day's light was soon to be extinguished. Tristan accepted gratefully.

They arrived after dark at the modest semi-detached house in quiet suburbia, and when Ernie introduced his wife Vera she smiled warmly beneath a shock of white curly hair. At dinner Tristan divulged a little of his tale, as his kind hosts listened intently and with genuine compassion.

Vera's response was tender. "You poor, poor dear. If there is anything else we could do to help, please, just ask."

Tristan had never met his grandparents, all having died before he was born, but if he had known them, he hoped they were as lovely as these folks. He felt secure with them, and without realising it he'd opened up, revealing what had happened to him to another person for the first time ever.

He was glad. It was part of the process of putting it all behind him. At least that's what he hoped. He thanked them for their kindness, and added sincerely that Vera was an excellent cook. It was in fact the nicest meal he'd ever eaten. He knew it's because it was eaten in peace.

Not long after nine the two old timers said goodnight and went to bed, leaving Tristan at the dining table with his atlas. He found the section on England, and then located Truro and assessed his route to Salisbury. A bus would be the quickest, maybe the safest choice, but he'd enjoyed his first hitchhiking experience and decided to try again tomorrow. He should still make it to Salisbury that evening. *Tomorrow night mum*, he thought, *I'll see you tomorrow night*. He'd waited so long already. He could wait just a little longer.

Closing his eyes, Tristan opened the atlas at a random page. Opening them again he saw the eastern coast of North America. He followed the coastline, and starting at the northern edge of Canada, he read the names moving south, all of them unknown; Labrador to Halifax. Bangor to Portland. Boston to Providence. And then, in bold black letters, he read; *New York*. It was the first name he recognised, and he lingered over it.

New York! He wasn't sure why, but Tristan had a vaguely peculiar feeling that the city was important to him, an elusive sense of allure that, like London, his destiny linked him intrinsically to it. Yet rather than make him nervous…after all, New York was an entire ocean away, the idea provoked him, spurred in him a sense of adventure that was as alien to him as hitchhiking had been only yesterday. His new life, a life that had started free from shackles, was beginning to take shape, and for the second consecutive night he tumbled into a deep untroubled sleep, safe and at peace in the presence of strangers.

A round of warm hugs and goodbyes followed an early breakfast, and with a promise to send Ernie a postcard from 'The Big Smoke,' the spring Tristan sensed in his stride as he left the house the next morning was just one more unknown phenomenon.

*Chapter Twenty One*

The highway roared with mechanical life, and without hesitation Tristan wielded his sign before the snarling traffic. Today's sky was unusual in that it spread all ways in an agreeable blue, appropriate to his rehabilitated mood and, he mused, good for his unwitting friend Richard. But anxious to press on, hundreds perhaps thousands of cars passed in a blur to threaten his good spirits. For an hour he felt invisible, as no driver gave him a second glance, until eventually one car did slow a little, and the young woman driving stared at him as she passed. She didn't stop.

He wondered if yesterday's ride had just been good luck, and that he should have taken a bus. But then that car again, the one that had slowed, driving back the other way and distinctive by its intense red colour and the girl who again looked directly at him but again drove on. Tristan was more than surprised when a few minutes later he saw it again and it stopped right where he was standing. The girl looked beyond miserable.

"Do you want a lift?" she asked curtly.

Tristan hesitated for just a second, and then climbed in. The girl was pale and she didn't look well, but seemed somehow familiar, and the sadness in her face was unmistakable.

"Hello miss. Thanks for stopping. Where are you heading?"

She stayed silent for a while, eyes fixed straight ahead and lost in thought. When she finally replied it was tired and subdued.

"I'm not really heading anywhere. I'm…I'm looking for someone." She couldn't disguise the pain in her voice. In his mind's eye Richard White's face loomed large on a weather worn poster, and something clicked. With a subtle shift in his seat in order to get a better look at the girl, the recognition became clear.

"Are you looking for your brother?" he enquired gently. Her head jerked left, eyes wide.

"What? Richard? How did you know? Have you seen him?"

"I saw his face on posters all over Penzance. They're everywhere. You look just like him."

"When I first spotted you by the road, my heart fluttered because I thought you were him, but I realized you look nothing like Richie when I came back round to double check. It's just that when you want something so badly, your mind sees what it wants to see. It's happened a lot." She was on the verge of crying. "He's been gone so long now…almost two months, but I know he's out there somewhere. I even quit my job to look for him, and every day I drive around just hoping I'll find him. I know he's okay…I just know it."

Teardrops fell, and Tristan understand her anguish, echoing how he felt when his mother had left.

"He's such a nice boy, and so passive. It's my stupid father's fault because he always picks on him, and sometimes…sometimes he hits us." Her narrow shoulders rose and fell with her sobs, and she dabbed at a tear that tickled her top lip. "I know my brother didn't drown in the sea like the police believe, like my father believes. Richie's just too sensible to go swimming in that weather. My mother's heart is broken. Now she's helpless, and I'm ashamed because it's almost like she's given up and lost all hope. But I know he's alive, I know it, and I won't stop looking until I find him."

He'd seen those tortured expressions on only one other person before, his mother, and to once again witness such despair had Tristan's heart aching for that devastated young lady.

"I'm really sorry for what you're going through, but I think everything will be okay. Just keep on looking and you'll find Richard soon. I know about the pain and confusion of being beaten by a father, and I ran away too. I'm here, alone and far from home, searching for my mum, and I have to believe that I'll see her soon. She's all I have in the world, all I've ever had, and I won't stop until I see her again. We'll both find what we are searching for, I know it. We've just got to believe it enough."

Through blurred eyes the girl looked into his blue eyes and saw they were clear and honest. She believed in her heart he was right.

"Thank you," she said, and with a deep breath smiled for the first time in too long. Driving east she told him about Richard. "He's a quiet boy and really smart, but doesn't have many friends. Other kids tease him in school because he's a bit different."

"Different? How do you mean?"

"Richie's kind of a…well, I suppose he's kind of a mummy's boy, but it's not his fault he doesn't like sport and instead prefers to read. Dad hates that, says it makes him weak, and is why he's so unpopular." A scowl pinched her forehead and wrinkled her nose. Tristan felt for the boy, and believed that if they ever met they could become friends.

"I don't have any friends either," he said, "because my father wouldn't allow it, but I think your brother and I would get along very well. I hope I get to meet him some day."

She smiled, and Tristan saw renewed hope in her eyes. He wanted to make her feel better, but had meant what he'd said.

"I'll keep a look out for Richard on my travels, and if I see him I promise to tell him that you've never given up."

Richard was hungry, he always was these days, but the

drier weather had lifted his spirits at least, and he'd decided to try and make it to London. In such a big city, he guessed, he'd have a better chance of forging a new life. He hated his father, and he didn't care if he never saw him again, and though he thought his mother didn't do enough to protect him at home, he loved her and felt guilty for not making contacting. I will soon, he kept telling himself, but he never did.

The person he really missed was his sister, and as his only ally, they were very close. Unlike him she had a lot of friends and was popular in school, but she was always there to look out for him whenever he needed it. For all of those reasons and more, Richard loved her implicitly. But though it was justified, when he ran away he left without saying goodbye. If she was aware of his plan to leave, she probably would have understood. But as his sister, he knew she'd have tried desperately to talk him out of it.

Richard had no choice but to leave in secret, yet he was conscience stricken, because he knew how devastated she'd be and that she'd blame herself, thinking she hadn't done enough to protect him from their father. Richard also knew that she wouldn't believe that he'd drowned. Until the police recovered his bloated, dripping body from the water, she would never accept it.

But the thought that she might be out searching for him choked him with both love and concern. If she found him, she would surely be duty bound to tell their parents, and then the police would come and take him home. He was not ready for that, and would not let it happen. *No, I mustn't contact her yet.* Though he agonized about the pain she must be in, it was an onerous but justified decision.

Down on the promenade Richard walked into a public bathroom. Just behind him, a small red car took the corner and pulled up opposite the toilets. The young woman driver and the boy beside her seemed to be admiring the seaside view, and saw families enjoying the rare sun and people walking dogs. Some boys were flying kites high on the ocean breeze, and one old lady was even braving the chilly English Channel to take a swim.

They saw many people, but they didn't see Richard White.

Pulling up on Torquay's sun doused promenade, Tristan and the girl gazed out across the calm scene. It was a few minutes before either one spoke, as if both were trying to extract energy from the sun and the happiness they were witnessing in every direction. It gave them both renewed hope that they would find what they wanted.

It was Tristan who broke the spell. "This looks like the perfect spot to thank you for the ride, but, forgive me, I didn't even ask your name."

"Anne-Marie."

"Well, Anne-Marie, Richard is lucky to have a sister who loves him so much, and I must say I'm a little envious." It was said with a smile and no trace of jealousy or bitterness. "I hope you find him soon, and I'm sure you will. Thanks again for the ride." He unfurled himself from the cramped car, then leaned down to look inside again. "And don't forget, Anne-Marie…stay strong."

They exchanged smiles of real warmth and a mutual understanding of loss.

"Thanks. I will. Well I guess this is goodbye then… um…?"

"Tristan. Tristan Nancarrow."

He watched until the car disappear out of sight, and then sat on the promenade wall, his long legs dangling above the beach. Although he honestly believed that

Richard was safe somewhere and that Anne-Marie would eventually find her brother, Tristan felt a great sadness for both of them. They'd been through, and were still going through, a difficult time, and he sincerely wished them well. But he had his own issues to contend with, and centered his jumbled thoughts onto finding his mother. Looking down at the beach he marveled at how long it would have taken to break down rocks and shells to create the fine sand below him. Millions of years, he knew, and with a wry smile, Tristan hoped he'd see his mother considerably sooner than that.

Richard emerged from the public bathrooms refreshed, and under a clear sky he was ready to push on to the highway. But suddenly his ears pricked up when he heard the diminishing yet familiar sound of a distant engine that sounded surprisingly like that of his sister's beat up old mini. He often teased her about that car; to him it looked more like an overgrown toy, though he loved to ride around in it with her. He listened, but then the sound was faded and gone. Yes, it did sound like her car, but he knew it couldn't be her, not this far from home, and shook his head with a slightly ashamed sigh of relief.

Richard crossed the street to take a last look at the ocean, and spotted a boy of similar age sitting alone on the wall. It was moments like these that he sometimes wished he was braver, wished he was less shy. What would be the harm saying hello to the other boy? Nothing, he knew it, nothing at all. But he was shy, painfully so, and swiftly stepped back over the street, and was soon making easterly strides in the general direction of London.

Oblivious to their close encounter, Richard, Anne-Marie and Tristan had missed each other by seconds.

*Chapter Twenty Two*

The worn out cottage on St. Mary's was still tormented by heinous skies, with voluptuous, mushrooming clouds spitting hail that drummed hammer like against the shed's timber roof. Blyth awoke on the floor, shivering from cold and half choked in the mid and filth. But he didn't die as he thought he might.

During the previous two nights he'd been blasé about his fate, indifferent to his life or death. But he lived on. In the night, and being in a small gully, the water rose knee high in the shed, and at its drowning mercy he almost succumbed. But it didn't take him. Blyth had lost everything. Yet all that remained was the one thing he didn't care about losing; his life.

Blyth had always considered himself an unfortunate man, and for two decades he'd believed that all the iniquitous world conspired against him. It was a selfish fantasy. True, he'd lost his promising career as an engineer. He had also lost all his inheritance and most of his land. His sister had turned her back on him. His wife had now left him. And lastly, now too his son.

The reality was that Blyth's only bad luck was first discovering and subsequently getting marooned by his dependence on whisky. It served as the unsympathetic catalyst for his dramatic change in character, and soon became the vindication for most of his actions. For so long he'd been under its damaging influence, that he no longer knew what was right and wrong.

Until now!

Both during the storm and as he surfaced in its aftermath, Blyth was experiencing a revelation, and it was a simple notion; that the sole blame for his abandonment lay with him. When at last the silent declaration solidified, the immediate guilt he felt struck him like a sledgehammer blow to his wheezing chest. Struggling up on weak legs, he stood there for a moment in wide eyed appraisal, and as the draining storm water flowed in deathly dark rivulets around his ankles, he was shocked to be alive.

Blyth didn't believe in God, and early in his marriage had rendered all mention of it in the marital home taboo. Kerra, although never devout, for years held onto the hope that there was something more than death, especially as her marriage, indeed her very life, started to unravel. It always seemed so final to her, so sad, and she wanted something to believe in, some spark to cling onto in her darkest hours. But Blyth was stubborn and uncompromising, and in the vain hope of retaining some semblance of peace, she accepted his rules, while keeping her version of faith quietly in her heart.

But as he looked about, the very fact that he hadn't drowned right there on the grungy swamped floor of his shed, seemed to Blyth some kind of miracle. When he shoved open the door, pushing hard against the build up of sediment, the first thing he saw was the obliterated stump of an old apple tree, destroyed by what could only have been a very recent lightning strike. Duly amazed, Blyth took it as a further sign of his deliverance.

Feeble and dangerously cold, he trudged with difficulty across the flooded garden and went inside. Nausea racked his twisted guts as he struggled to light a fire, and his head throbbed relentlessly from the whisky.

With dry clothes on and the fire now lit, Blyth felt better. But it didn't last. As he set about trying to make sense of his ruined life, he was soon as depressed as he'd ever known. A burgeoning hangover descended, and withdrawals from the whisky ruthlessly highlighted his savage emptiness, both of the body and of the mind.

For the first time ever neither his wife nor son where there. The void was cavernous, and where once before two more souls occupied the joyless rooms of that perpetually negative space, now only the memory of their broken spirits remained. Thunder echoed nearby like some belated malefic caution, and Blyth stole a skittish glance through the window. *So dark,* he thought, *the shade of my heart. How did I become so wretched, so unworthy? When did I lose control?*

He knew the answer, had always known, but not once had he ever admitted it, especially to himself. Emotionally, Blyth was a drowning ship a million miles from shore, while both selfishness and vanity, the twin weights that would drag his ship to the very depths of despair, convinced him that nobody else had ever felt so alone.

"What have I done?" he murmured into the void, his heart a fractured lump of ice.

"What've I done?" Louder now, as his debilitated body convulsed with despair and his violent fists shook with shame. Teardrops stained his dirty face. He was a man on the brink.

And then a final time…

*"WHAT HAVE I DONE?"* This time his plea exploded throughout the cottage, its raw force barely human. In the nearby woods a fox darted for cover, and roosting crows flashed out of naked winter trees. He stared with distorted eyes into the now raging fire, but only demons looked back from blackened, twisted faces, daring him to leap from the last fragile rung on his ladder into insanity.

"What am I?" he screamed. "WHO AM I?"

Like a crazed scarecrow shifting errantly in a gale, his

shadow danced demonically on the wall, swaying as if to some unheard pagan music seconds before a sacrifice, and somewhere in his mind, a wolf howled as it chased him through dark and hostile woods, so he ran, and a young girl screamed, her face begging *no* right before his eyes, and he scratched wildly, vainly trying to scrape that heartbreaking image from his vision as he ran until he collapsed in a heap on the unyielding and crypt like floor.

Blyth Nancarrow was a broken man.

Mark Trescothwick drove to the isolated beach community in a hurry. It was the first time in fifteen years. Rarely, he visited an old aunt in Hugh Town, but this was business. Unfinished business that didn't involve money. He'd come to settle an old score, as enmity raged through his veins.

Blyth cowered against the wall in turmoil, mind inhabited by unconstrained thoughts that weren't his own. Unhinged. The very edge of sanity. Oblivious to the new storm headed his way.

Before the day was over, he would know its wrath.

*Chapter Twenty Three*

Up in the tiny flat she shared with Mollie, Kerra clutched the bedcovers tighter to fend off the chill, and though the heating was on high, she just couldn't stay warm. And she'd just had a bad day. The factory she worked in had just completed an order, and without warning she found herself out of work. She still had a little money, but most of what she had was sent back to Tristan. Despondency once more shrouded her days while loneliness troubled her nights, and above all, the guilt she harbored for leaving him alone on the island acted as a lethal foe to her spirit. Like a dagger between her ribs; that's how she felt, knowing he'd arrive in Salisbury to find her gone.

But she was just too vulnerable back in Salisbury, and knew for sure that only in a big city like London could she find safety through anonymity. In the south west Blyth's reach was long, and she feared...no, she knew...that somehow her psychotic husband would find her. Of course Tristan would be devastated, and he might never trust her again. But she did what she had to do, for both of their sakes. The secrecy of her leaving in the first place was imperative, and moving on from Salisbury was best for them both. That knowledge was all that kept her afloat in the rapidly filling lake of despair.

Things began well in London. She got on well enough with the factory girls, most of whom were in the city for the same reasons as her; escaping from something or someone. Until yesterday the work had been steady, and Mollie was a good fiend. But now Kerra was worried. There were a few other jobs about, but she'd been warned by the disgusting supervisor, and in no uncertain terms, *that if you work for us, we expect loyalty.* The slimy bastard said everything with a sly wink, and her skin crawled thinking about him. Other women had crossed that line, only to be kicked out of their flat and occasionally beaten, just to set an example. With few options, Kerra decided to sit tight and wait for the work to resume.

Mollie was a wise cracking, feisty character indicative of the tough East End. She spoke loudly and from the heart, and the two of them were an odd match, or as Mollie was fond of saying with what amounted to a cackle, *you're the cheese to my chalk*. Kerra was still an edgy, nervous wreck after years of subservience to Blyth. Mollie however was a handful for any man, and though younger she'd seen it all. On the rare occasion when Kerra opened up about her past, Mollie nodded knowingly.

"Poor, poor thing," she said as she sat beside Kerra on the bed. "Don't you worry my love, cos' Mollie's here to take care of you now, and we'll get work soon enough, you mark my words, cos' that slimy boss Billy has a soft spot for me and can hardly take his perverted eyes off my peachy arse, and we'll be back lighting up those factory lines in no time, you'll see."

Finally she paused for breath, and Kerra couldn't help but crack a smile. Mollie was a good sort, and her spirit and energy were infectious. She'd been born and raised, or as she told it, dragged up, in the roughest part of the East End which she'd never left, and her coarse accent, intrinsic to people from that area, was true cockney.

"Everything's gonna be alright love, just you wait'n see. I'll fix us a nice cuppa tea, shall I," and it wasn't a question as she danced the few steps into the kitchen.

But in her absence Kerra's smile soon faded as she switched her thoughts to Tristan. He was out in the world for the first time, and she was sick with worry about him. But he'd escaped the violence and the oppression, which was the most important thing…that is, if he made it away safely, and her heart clenched under the strain of not knowing. In her gut she knew, but without confirmation there'd been many sleepless nights. She didn't want to cry in front of her friend, but as Mollie returned she found Kerra curled in a ball and weeping from puffy eyes.

"Come on love, there there, things'll work out in the end, they always do, 'specially with a shot of me finest 'joy-juice' in yer tea." With a wink she added a generous splash of scotch to the brew. "Reckon you could do with it too, and someone to sit and shoot the shit with. Come on love, you can talk to Ol'Mollie, she's all ears."

Kerra sighed, forcing out a weary smile, and between sniffles told her friend about when she'd first met her husband.

"Blyth was a good man, he really was, so nice and kind, and very handsome, but things started going wrong and his whole personality changed, turned him into a different man…a horrible man. And he drank." Clearly shaken, her dainty shoulders shuddered at the memories.

"I know I've made mistakes, far too many, but my first was…well, I should never have spurned Mark when he asked me to marry him. We were barely seventeen…just kids really, but he was…he is…such an amazing man with a pure heart." Overcome by what might have been sadness or regret or both, the tears streamed, but she managed to add, "but you have to know, I would't change anything, because my Tristan is an angel."

She hid her face from Mollie, but couldn't hide the shame from her voice. She struggled on. "Everything we've been through, all the suffering we've endured, and despite it all he's an amazing kid, untainted by it all, almost as if Mark was his real father." Kerra now fell silent for a moment, contemplative through the jarring sobs. Then, "I really don't know how he turned out so well." Her face contorted as she wept.

"I miss him Mollie, I miss him so much," and for the briefest of moments Mollie wondered if she meant Tristan or Mark.

## Chapter Twenty Four

An artery clogging feast of sausages, eggs and bacon, mopped up with a side of fried bread drowned in dripping, disappeared from the plate as Tristan chewed over his next move. Bright sun gave the beach at Torquay an illusion of summer, and a few souls braved the sands to walk their dogs in the early afternoon glow.

Up until now his luck had held. Hitchhiking had brought him this far, and looking out over the placid channel waters Tristan noted how happy and energized he felt, and if this was the happiest he'd been since he left St. Mary's, then by default, it was the happiest he'd been in his whole life.

The calm sea, reaching out before him like shining blue glass, reflected the calmness he himself felt, perhaps for the very first time and, on a whim, he decided to stay in Torquay for the night. The day was already drifting by, and even if his luck continued he might not reach Salisbury before midnight. It was best to stay.

The sun, making its subtle daily descent into the west, was closely followed by the languorous evening shroud as Tristan searched the sea front for a hotel. One place caught his eye, its fancy facade set fifty yards back from the promenade inviting him in. And having never before stayed in a hotel, he was excited as he pushed through the brightly colored doors that opened with a stubborn and creaky protest. The threadbare carpet and deep layer of dust on the reception counter went unnoticed. He waited a full minute.

"Yes boy, what do you want?" grumbled a crumbly old man as he hobbled from a door by the counter. Tristan thought the door might have led to the last century.

"I'd like a room please, sir. How much is it?"

The man leaned almost comically to his left, as if one leg was longer than the other.

"Are your parents here?" the inclined relic enquired.

"No sir, I'm here alone. I have money though."

The man's dewy eyes now focused beneath a bushy monobrow that raised in a wide arc of expectancy. This too went unnoticed by Tristan.

"Very well. Room 101, first floor. Last door on the right. It's one pound and eight shillings per night. How many nights?"

"Just tonight, thank you." Tristan took the key from the staring, eldritch old man, who didn't let go for uncomfortable seconds. His face resembled a weathered stone statue.

Tristan climbed the dark stairs, footsteps echoing from artless walls. The entire hotel seemed deserted, and despite it being almost winter, he still expected more guests. The key seemed to turn with great reluctance, but yielded after a significant and forceful twist. With great anticipation Tristan stepped inside and flicked on the light. That the hotel's pleasant facade betrayed its shabby interior was a major understatement, and a zoological mustiness caused an immediate sneeze. The dingy room had no window, and the provenance of its furniture might have been the local dump.

But it was okay, he thought with an ironic smile, and appreciated quickly that if a worn out room was his biggest worry, life had drastically improved.

Upending his backpack, Tristan poured its meagre contents onto the bed. They were modest; a few patched up clothes, his new atlas, the photograph of him with his mother, and the money. *What else do I need*? Scooping up a little cash and his atlas, he smiled as he locked up, and left the room in a buoyant mood.

A cold malaise accompanied him through the drafty reception as the aged clerk gave him a long, appraising look. Though he said nothing, Tristan felt a strange uneasiness he didn't understand. Hotels were safe, he assumed, and that curious old-timer surely couldn't wish him harm?

Shaking his cynicism aside, he strode out to the promenade just as the sun vacated the day to illuminate western skies. Tristan jumped down to the beach, and stood where the ocean tickled the shore. This is Torquay, he thought, but across that thin silvery stretch of sea is France, and beyond that, the rest of the world. The grody grump back at the hotel didn't get a second thought.

Tristan's gift of insulation was his naivety, impenetrable barriers of ignorance and zero expectations that had served him well until his escape, but now perished with the very recent advent of warmth and kindness as yet unappreciated and scarcely imagined.

It should have been a good thing for Tristan.

It wasn't.

*Chapter Twenty Five*

Blyth stared at the fire. Did it stare back at him? He no longer knew nor cared, and though physically a little better, the whisky finally purged from his system, mentally he was beyond exhausted.

Guilt and remorse bore down relentlessly on shoulders that had carried his split personality too many years, and wrapped up within his ragged state of withdrawal Blyth teetered unbalanced on the cliff edge of sanity. He stood as a toddler stands, tentative and unsure, nervously scanning the room with bloodshot eyes that darted left and right. He was alone…and yet…he felt a presence nearby, an oppressive force that held him in distinctly malevolent distaste. He said a swift and silent prayer for protection to a recently remembered god, but no one was listening. He fought to ignore it, suppress the nascent feeling of being watched. He failed.

Vexed by the chimney's breeze, flames leapt wildly from the fire, and from those flames emerged his shadows. Blyth's shadows didn't just follow him but stalked him as if prey. They paused when he paused. They crept when he crept. He kept moving, shuffling from corner to corner, knowing that if he stopped even for a moment the demonic black-souled beings that haunted his stride as they haunted his mind would make of him a grisly sacrifice.

A crushing headache woke him. He raised a stiff arm to his forehead and found a prodigious lump caked in dried blood. He'd no clue as to how long he'd been unconscious, but the fire now was nothing but dying embers, and the shadow demons were gone. Blyth sat up. From his floored position near the hearth he hunched for long minutes in a somnolent daze, numb to the bruising press of the cold stones beneath.

The intrusive beams of approaching headlamps shone fierce yet unnoticed through the cottage windows. By day visitors were an absolute rarity, but by night…well, nobody came at night. Yet Blyth didn't register the unmistakable thump of a slamming car door, and not until a heavy hand pounded the cottage door for a second and third time was his oblivion replaced by consciousness in his umbrous mind.

With his head cocked at a strange angle Blyth had the

look of a man who'd heard something that may or may not be threatening, like a deer, hearing either the snap of a twig or the death click of a hunter's rifle. Delirious, he was slow to react, as if rousing from the depths of a heavy anesthetic. But when the next round of pounding shook the door in its frame, an unlikely glimmer of hope soon focused his attention.

He fantasized that beyond that door waited his wife and son, ready to forgive him his callous mastery, exonerate his cruel torments both physical and mental, and absolve his miserable failures as a husband and father. It was a fantasy born deep within his corroded remnants of reality, and he toppled towards that imagined reprieve on enervated legs, grabbed the handle, and upon heaving that weighty timber barricade inwards, his myopic self-deception was immediately and unceremoniously smashed to death.

He froze as if gazed upon by medusa herself, for standing there on the cottage threshold was a spectral nemesis from his past.

Mark Trescothwick!

"Nancarrow! It's been a long time."

Shock seemed for a moment to set Blyth's bones like granite. Mark too was in shock, as the man standing before him was nothing more than an emaciated collection of rag and bone, whose lifeless eyes stared vacant and unseeing from deep recessed sockets. For a long minute neither man moved, one unable, the other unsure; *has Blyth finally lost it?* wondered Mark.

But suddenly Blyth took a gasping breath, as if emerging from below the surface of a long and terrifying dream, just as all the world around him rushed back into focus and all the years of waiting for that exact moment had at last arrived that very second. Survival instincts took, over and with a surge of desperate energy he tried to slam the door, but Mark was quick and shoved a strong leg forward, over-powering the weaker man as if he were a child.

Blyth backed away slowly. Tractable. Like Tristan.

"What do you want? Why are you here?" Blyth's voice was as defeated as his body, and he knew for certain this was no friendly visit.

"Come on Blyth. I've not seen you for fifteen years, but you're as stupid as ever. Sit down!"

To resist was futile. Physically he was no match for Trescothwick, never was, and he knew him to be an honest man. Anything he'd say now would be the truth.

Although Blyth had somehow spirited Kerra away from Mark when they were much younger men, Mark had, at Kerra's request, long ago forgiven him. A truce ensued, and had endured for a decade and a half. Mark had honored it. Actually, he had merely honored Kerra. But he had never forgotten.

Deep down Blyth knew that Mark had helped Kerra escape. But now he was there before him the questions arose; how long had they been in contact? Months? Years? Had she always loved him? And of course he'd helped Tristan too, but that was okay because the boy deserved his freedom.

Right now though none of that mattered. His wife had left him and it was with great justification. So only one question remained: why was Mark Trescothwick there? But he already knew the answer to that obvious question, and it didn't bode well; with Kerra now out of the equation, Mark wanted revenge.

"What are you going to do?"

"You think I'm going to hurt you?"

Blyth simply looked up at the colossal man, but he

didn't speak.

"No Nancarrow. Violence is for bullies and cowards, and the lord knows you're both. I'm not here to harm you, though you deserve to be harmed. At least not yet. I'm here with a warning." Mark's face betrayed no emotion. He wasn't glad to be there, and to intimidate someone was out of character. But that miserable human Nancarrow had gotten away with his uncivilized barbarism for too long, and he was there to stop it once and for all. It bought him little joy, but he'd waited for the opportunity a long time.

"The rules are mine, and they are simple. If you ever break them, you'll die. If you're even caught trying to break them, you'll die." Mark took a step nearer. "Are you ready to listen?"

Blyth looked into the stony eyes bearing down on him. He'd never seen eyes as intense or honest as those, and Mark meant what he said, he knew it. His head dipped, and his eyes saw only the coldness of the floor. After long, silent moments, in which images of his lost family occupied his mind, their sad faces an epitaph to his sins, an imperceptible nod gave Mark his answer.

"For many years you've made their lives intolerable, picking on them because they were weaker than you and afraid. You've beaten them and hurt them both physically and mentally, and you've ruined their lives. But you've hurt them for the last time."

Blyth knew it was the truth. Most of it. There was one factor, one secret that only he knew, and for so long he'd fought to keep its destruction entombed deep down in his heart and in his suspect conscience. It perpetually tore at his soul to escape its violent restraints, and as difficult as it was, he'd valiantly kept it hidden. At least for now.

"Nancarrow, if you ever try to leave St. Mary's, I'll know about it. And I will find you. Your face is well known around Hugh Town and Penzance, so it's impossible for you to leave unnoticed. I'll have people check in on you from time to time, see what you're up to, and if I hear it's no good I'll visit you again. And you know the consequences." Mark stepped closer still. "Look at me, Blyth."

Blyth raised his head, face pale and shamed. Mark pressed on, his voice strong and sincere.

"Know this! No one will miss you. No one! You'll stay the rest of your pitiable days on St. Mary's, and you'll grow old and then you'll die, a sad and lonely bastard. You've kept Kerra and Tristan as prisoners here, but now you become the prisoner. I've made a promise, and only over my dead body will it be broken. You will never leave this island, never, that's my oath, and do not try me, because I will do anything to protect it. Do you understand?"

Blyth swallowed hard, his adam's apple prominent against the taut skin of a parched throat. His breathing was labored. When he saw Trescothwick at his door he'd expected a severe beating, but what had transpired instead was so much worse. Blyth knew he was sick. Alcoholism was frowned upon and few accepted it as a bonafide disease, but he'd been at its mercy for many years, and he'd battled it alone. In his heart of hearts he wanted to recover. And then, when he regained control of his anger and was secure in his emotions, what he desired more than anything was to go and find his family. He'd find them, and convince them he was a good man, a changed man, who was at last worthy of their love and worthy of a second chance. They were all he had in the world.

But Mark's was no idle threat. Blyth always feared he would come back into his life someday, and now it had happened. Despite his secret, one that if revealed would change everything, he still he didn't warrant that longed for second chance, and he understood that. Regardless of the reasons and his disease, nothing could justify the terrible way he'd treated his family, and after surviving his almost deadly night in the shed, that miracle, his revelation of a reemerging God had made everything so clear.

This was what he deserved, his comeuppance, and he had neither the will not the courage to protest. He would accept Mark's rules, and not because he was afraid of the consequences. It was, quite simply, everything he deserved.

Blyth was determined to do the right thing by his long suffering and now estranged family. To accept Trescothwick's decree would be the first and only positive thing he'd done for them in too many years, and though few would believe it, it was done out of a long buried and dormant love. He looked squarely at his accuser, inhaled deeply, and spoke in measured and humble words.

"I understand, and I concede to your commands. I know what I've done, what I am, and I receive my fate, my punishment, without protest." Blyth, who felt as if he'd aged twenty years overnight, let his stubbled chin fall to his chest.

Mark watched on passively, taking no pleasure in seeing a grown man so thoroughly dejected. Patiently he waited for him to say more, but he had to be sure that his threat was truly absorbed, and he pushed a little further.

"You know, Nancarrow, a small part of me wishes I was a bully like you. Lord knows you deserve to be beaten… fuck, what kind of man abuses his wife and son? Disgusting men, like you. But your loneliness will be a just punishment. I do hope you recover from your so-called disease, because only then will you know the true nature of your despicable behaviour. And I say this to you, Blyth, don't for a moment think that I won't keep this promise…I will! You've my word on that."

There was no doubting the truth in any of that statement. Blyth knew Mark would keep his promise. He had done despicable things. He deserved his punishment.

His loneliness was nothing new. Alcoholics often faced their demons alone, as he had done for more than fifteen years. But now he would die like some forgotten hermit, crushed by loneliness, and forsaken by the world with only the hope of God to keep him sane. The though terrified him.

Mark looked down upon the pitiful man before him, and felt nothing other than an abject sadness for those whose lives he'd ruined. He had said what he came to say and, duty done, he was confident his message was clear. He took a final glance at Blyth, and with an expression somewhere between contempt for him and contentment that he'd never again hurt anyone, Mark turned his back and walked out of the cottage.

As if to signify that Blyth's final show was over, the sky pulled down its vast black curtain, leaving a final crack of daylight beneath its all consuming veil to show Mark his way to the car. From the corner of his eye he noticed the door of a shed swinging open, the broken glass of its window catching that last spear of light. On a hunch he turned toward it, and when he yanked the suspended switch to light the dank space, he wasn't surprised at what he saw; a horde of more than two dozen bottles of whisky filling two shelves, below which stood crates of wine and home brewed ale. It took only one second to decide his next action.

Within two frantic minutes, not a single drop of alcohol remained in those numberless bottles, and the stench was potent as smashed glass crunched beneath his big boots. He backed out of the shed and looked toward the cottage. In the doorway stood Blyth, a slim silhouette against the hearth's orange glow.

Unmoved Blyth looked on, and knew exactly what was about to transpire.

Mark cupped his hands and scratched a match down its box, watched as it caught and continued watching as it burned slowly toward his fingers. *Nancarrow will never drink again,* he thought, *not if I can help it,* and threw down the match in anger with something akin to morbid glee radiating from his blue eyes.

Vertically flames erupted as fifty liters of effervescent alcohol combusted in a wild holocaust. The small wooden structure soon ignited in a violent, swirling wall of fire, and both men looked on, each aware of the significance and finality of the event. Once satisfied by the destruction, Mark didn't look back as he drove away into the night.

Blyth watched and didn't flinch as he focused hard on the flames. They rose high, and still he gazed, deep into the inferno, more than watching…looking, searching for his demons. The shed walls eventually crumbled, quickly followed by the collapsed ceiling, and when only a smoldering heap of charred wood and splintered glass remained, he blinked several times, as if to clear his eyes and his mind of any doubt, and nodded with a solemn air of contentment; *the shed is destroyed, and beneath that blackened pile of misery and destruction, so too are my demons.*

In that very moment, the weight of fifteen years of suppressed agony slipped from his sagged shoulders, and with a massive sense of relief Blyth turned his back on the carnage and went inside. All around him was silent. Even the fire in the hearth had died. Just the faint glow of the single exposed bulb above cast any light on his life, and he relished the darkness and closed his eyes.

He felt his heart racing, could feel the blood in his temples, and knew that he'd at least been given a chance of personal redemption if not that of his family.

*Tomorrow,* he whispered into the void, *tomorrow I'll start to rebuild that shed. And when that's done, I'll start to rebuild my life.*

Then, and for the first time in thirty years, Blyth Nancarrow dropped to his knees and prayed.


*Chapter Twenty Six*

Huddled in a deserted seafront café, Tristan was happily exploring the world through his atlas. The waitress who'd served him earlier approached. "What's your name?" she asked in a voice tinged with acute boredom.

"Tristan. What's yours?"

" Stephanie. Friends call me Steph."

"That's nice." He didn't look up, which did little to lighten her sour mood.

"Suit yourself," she huffed, and skulked off to stare out of the window.

He flicked through the pages, mentally exploring continents he knew little about. He saw Australia, and couldn't imagine the distance between him and it. He spotted Korea and Japan, and tried to guess at what kind of clothes their people wore. Argentina and Chile, so long and thin compared to England. The island of Borneo, massive, and he compared it in size to tiny St. Mary's. He was in awe. So many places full of mystery, and he wanted to visit them all. What did they eat in Spain? How were the schools in Nepal? Were the girls pretty in Mexico?

All those questions and more clogged his mind, and he wished his mother was there to answer them. She'd know some of the answers, and if not she'd invent some funny story which they'd laugh at together. At least, that's how it was before his father started drinking, and his heart sank at the distance of the memory of much happier days. *But*, he thought, *maybe she's even happier now?* and a wave of hope cracked a big smile across his face.

"What're you so happy about," asked an even grumpier Steph as he paid his bill.

"I'm sorry I was rude and didn't say much before." He smiled, and she smiled back. "I'm going to see my mum tomorrow…I can't wait," and he didn't wait for a reply either, and left Steph bewildered as he sprinted grinning all the way back to the hotel.

*Does he ever leave*? Tristan mused as the flaky old fellow dozed behind the counter. Unerringly, as he passed his eyes shot open and followed him across the lobby. That uneasiness again. *What's that look on his face? Guilt?* The man gave him the creeps, and he rushed to his room. With a nervy glance behind, he closed the door and relaxed. *Just your imagination* he told himself with a wry smile, and clearing the few scattered things from the bed, he climbed in and switched off the lamp.

"See you tomorrow, mum," he whispered, and was asleep in less than a minute.

Well rested, Tristan stretched out easily, ready for the day ahead. But then, bothered by a strange sense of disquiet, he looked about the musty, decaying room. Something just didn't feel right, and his steady pulse quickened. What was different? His bag was where he left it, and so was his picture. He breathed a little easier. So what was it? And then it hit him, as the icy weight of realisation clutched at his throat.

"My money!"

Frantic, he scanned the room with wild eyes, but he knew it was gone as butterflies swarmed in his guts. Tristan felt sick. *Nobody knows I have any money.* But in his mind's eye he saw himself paying the creepy old man for the room. *He must have noticed. But he wouldn't have taken it? Would he?* He checked the room again, but the money was nowhere to be seen. Tristan had rarely felt his own anger before, but as he felt the blood boil he savored the adrenalin that surged through him. He took the stairs to reception three at a time.

He found the the old man sitting there, as he knew he would. The clerk didn't move, hardly looked to be breathing, but Tristan thought he detected a faint smile in his eyes, and was about to approach him with his accusation when he summarily stopped in his tracks. Colossal in both height and width, another man sat quietly and unmoved on a bench to the right of the counter. With a shaved head that glinted menacingly under the lights, and a crisp suit that strained on oversized muscles, the giant looked devastatingly tough. Tristan again felt the blood hammer through his temples and, though the man looked treacherous, he was angry and he wanted answers. Empowered by adrenalin, he faced the old man.

"Where's my money? You've stolen it! I know it was you, and I want it back."

The diminutive old timer stood up. Tristan dwarfed him, yet his smile was haughty and arrogant.

"Young man, it's dangerous to accuse innocent people of stealing." His voice was sly and pompous. "I'd take it back, if you know what's good for you."

"But I know it was you," he cried, anger now mixing with growing desperation. "There are no other guests here, so it must've been you. You saw my envelope."

"You're right, boy, there is no one else here, except my good friend over there." He nodded toward the Samson-esque figure in the corner. "So if I were you, I'd be more careful who you accuse."

On cue the thug stood, all six feet six of him, and as he approached, Tristan thought he looked capable of anything. Including murder. Tristan had to think and act quickly, and knowing that his anger would get him nowhere, he addressed the old man in a more passive tone.

"But sir, that's my money," he said in a quiet tone. "It's all I have in the world."

"And now it's mine. Boy, let this be a simple lesson for you, to never flash your money around and not to leave it lying about in your room. And besides, it could be a lot worse…young strays have been known to disappear round here."

It was a barely veiled threat, and Tristan's flesh crawled as the giant stepped a little closer. But he had one last hope of getting his money, and he tried appealing to the man's conscience, if he even had one.

"The thing is, sir, my mother has disappeared, and I'm using that money to try and find her. We're all each other has left in the world. Please sir, give me back my money."

The old man laughed out loud at the boy's determination, and for a moment Tristan thought he had a chance. But when the laughing ceased, those pale eyes bore into him like daggers of ice.

"I don't know who you are, boy, but my patience is thin. Yes, I took your money, and I thank you for your kind ignorance. But don't think of it as theft. Consider it more, shall we say, of putting someone's belongings to better use. Indeed, what does a young boy like you need so much money for, anyway? What are you going to do, buy sweets?" He grinned, but it soon twisted into a sardonic sneer.

"Time for games is over. Get your things from the room and disappear, quick sharp. Otherwise Terry here will really help you disappear, right Terry?" Terry nodded. "Do we understand each other?"

Tristan knew then it was hopeless, and anger threatened to shame him with tears. But unsure why, rather than leave he stood still and stared evenly at the ignominious clerk. He wasn't quite through yet.

Tristan knew not where it came from, but his audacity shocked even him, as he took a step forward and scowled at the thug, who in turn glared back, though it seemed a glare was the only expression his huge face was capable of. He was more than surprised when the boy held his gaze, especially when a hint of a smile curled the corner of Tristan's mouth. Tristan then turned to face the old man, and when he spoke his voice was calm and measured.

"You can keep my money. I don't need it. What you've taught me is more valuable anyway. But rest assured, one day I will return…and maybe you'll be here alone." He flicked his head at Terry. "Then I'll take what's mine, and I *will* have my revenge." Tristan's smile was serene. "Do we understand each other?"

Both the ancient clerk and the overgrown lump were stunned. They did not expect that, and remained speechless as Tristan showed them his back and calmly disappeared up the stairs.

Tristan leaned against the inside of his door. With legs

like jelly and a heaving chest, he waited for his breathing to slow from its galloping rate. After a few calmer minutes he looked back on what had just occurred, and felt an unusual emotion; something akin to pride. He'd changed, divergent from that other boy, evolved somehow; had he become a man?

An acute sense of injustice still niggled at him, but he ignored it. Tristan couldn't know, but if his parents saw him then, they'd have seen a different son before them, a young man whose posture was straight and whose head was, for the very first time, held high.

He stopped once more in reception. The crooked unscrupulous pair stood close, waiting to see what the boy might do next as he fixed his eyes on them. Their expression's had changed from surprise to bemusement, but Tristan didn't care. He had taken a lot from this bitter lesson, and as he left and stepped through the doors into the bright but chilly morning, he barely registered the sound of riotous laughter from behind him.

*Chapter Twenty Seven*

Dawn greeted Brighton kindly, and the sun crept over the town like a cosy blanket. Ailla knew that mornings like this would be rare as winter approached, and she relished her early walk along the beach while the town still slept. A busy day loomed ahead, and she cherished those moments of solace before the workday began. Her gallery of fine art was getting a lot of attention, far more than she expected, after a couple of successful exhibitions by local artists had generated a lot of interest since her spring opening.

But now she was nervous. Ailla herself knew she was a

talented painter, but had yet to fall in love with painting. Jack, her boyfriend, had finally convinced her to exhibit some paintings of her own. Until now painting was little more than a fun hobby, a distraction from the business side of her work, but Jack insisted she was as good if not better than the work she'd been showcasing and, somewhat reluctantly, she agreed.

When they first met, Jack was fascinated by her childhood growing up in New York.

"My foster parents were very hip," she told him, "and we spent many long and lazy afternoons exploring galleries and shopping at art fairs, so I guess my passion for art stems from them, and although they had no real ability themselves, they loved to try. I'm not sure where my little talent comes from? 'It's god given,' my step mother would say, always with a wink, as she knew I didn't believe in fairytales."

"But why did you leave? It seems strange you'd come back to sleepy England after New York…though of course I'm happy you did." Mutual smiles.

"I love them dearly and miss them a lot, and New York is a wonderful city, but I just felt compelled to return. It was a difficult decision which I thought about long and hard, and if it wasn't for their support and encouragement to follow my heart, I might still be there now. But we celebrated my eighteenth birthday together and I left the following week. And here I am."

Ailla soon felt at home in Brighton. The town's thriving art and music scenes satisfied her sensibilities, and she loved living right by the beach. London was close, and she and Jack spent many weekends in the city to scour Spitalfields market and go to concerts.

She was happy, yet she fought an ongoing battle with her often disabling guilt. It got so bad at times that she

Steven Moore

would slip into a morose and unhealthy doldrum for days
on end. Jack knew only some of the secrets she kept from
the world, but the two were close, and slowly they were
falling for each other. He loved her personality and the
way she looked, but most of all he adored her spirit. She'd
had a tough childhood prior to New York, and he
respected her desire to keep her secrets. But the way Ailla
dealt with everything, and the manner in which she stayed
positive about life and her desire to help others despite her
own painful issues…he was simply in awe.

And helping others was how they met, volunteering at
the orphanage outside town. Jack was blown away by the
red-haired girl that walked in one Monday morning, and
although she seemed shy, he sensed a tough inner
strength. He enjoyed art too, and recalled Caravaggio's
Pre-Raphaelite women when he saw her. The first time he
told her that she blushed, also believing those paintings
were beautiful. A close friendship blossomed, and within a
month they were inseparable.

That their childhoods were so different meant little to
them. Jack hailed from a stable and loving family, while
Ailla had been fostered more than once. His was a settled,
peaceful upbringing, while Ailla was moved between
homes and families, even continents. It simply made them
respect each other all the more.

And, of course, Jack was her biggest fan. Her paintings
were an eclectic mix of dramatic coastal scenes with
turbulent skies that hung alongside brightly colored
flowers and children playing. To a stranger's eye there
was no apparent theme to her work, only random images
of random subjects. Ailla alone knew they represented her
life story, and that was one secret she kept purely to
herself.

As the show approached she painted with verve and a

156

definite glint in her eye, and at last unleashed the passion she'd had as a child. Upon her canvasses emerged scene after scene of children playing, and within those scenes one face reappeared often; the melancholic portrait of a ten year old boy. Ailla didn't have a brother, but Jack thought that if she did it must be him in these paintings, such was the resemblance. He wondered who the inspiration was for the lean angular boy with reddish golden hair and big blue eyes.

He didn't know. But he was sure Ailla did.


*Chapter Twenty Eight*

Adversity was something Tristan had known all his young life, and the disappointment of his stolen money was soon forgotten. A few pounds remained, and was enough to see him through until he reached his mother. She once told him that whatever didn't kill him would only make him stronger, and Tristan felt strong. He smiled sheepishly at Steph as he returned to the café, and ate with gusto as his eyes drifted over the horizon into a world he now felt a part of.

*SALISBURY.* Just seeing it written on his board filled Tristan with keen anticipation. Cars, trucks and an almost constant stream of white vans sped past, and it wasn't long before one of the white transits stopped for him, he'd jumped onboard and, hardly missing a beat, the van accelerated into the fast lane and was again hurtling east.

The driver must have sensed Tristan's surprise, because he had a curious smile on his face.

"What, you never seen a black man before?"

"Actually, I did a few days ago, but I've never spoken to a black person."

With that the man roared with laughter. "Well kid," he managed, "turns out it's a day of firsts, cos' I ain't never picked up no hitchhiker before, neither." Tristan joined in the laughter.

Winston was from London, the first and only son of second generation Jamaican immigrants, and he'd driven vans along the south coast for a decade and loved his job.

"I really don't know why I picked you up, kid," he said, "been ignoring thumbs for years. Policy, the governors say, but you look harmless, and I reckon there's a nasty storm coming in 'cross the channel. And today is your extra lucky day, 'cos good old Winston 'ere just so happens to be driving right through Salisbury and all the way to sunny London. What d'ya make of that then, my friend?"

"It really is my lucky day. Thanks a lot. By the way, I'm Tristan. Glad to meet you."

"The name's Winston, but most folks call me Winnie. Choice is yours, and it's a pleasure to meet you too, kid."

From that second on Winston didn't stop talking, as if all the conversations he'd missed by refusing hitchhikers now spilled forth in a stream of ultra verbose consciousness. And Tristan couldn't have been happier. He heard tales of Winnie's adventures as a pickpocket on the mean streets of the East End. He learned how he should really have been a famous cricketer, and that barring his mother's clumsiness, when she dropped him from the bed as a baby and he broke his shoulder, he'd now be the West Indies' greatest ever bowler. He grinned with shiny eyes as he told Tristan of his dream to play in a test match at Lords, and bowl bouncers at the heads of famous English batsmen, like Boycott and Knott. Tristan had no idea what he was talking about, but thoroughly enjoyed himself as Winnie spewed tale after tale upon him. And he barely even noticed as the rolling green fields of England flashed majestically past his window.

A couple of hours and a hundred miles later, Tristan knew more about Winston than any other human. It was also by far the longest time he'd ever spent on the road, and his eyes were getting tired. But just then, during a wide and satisfying yawn, he spotted something out the window that made his heart leap for joy.

"There, look, do you see it?"

"See what? What are you talking about?" He was oblivious, but Tristan strained against the windscreen for a better view, and Winston was startled by the passive kid's sudden flurry of activity.

"What is it kid, what's wrong?"

"There, there, can't you see?"

Winston strained his eyes too, but saw nothing of any interest.

"Okay, you got me. What's given you ants in your pants, eh?"

"Stonehenge. It's Stonehenge. I've made it."

Minutes later Winston pulled into the car park, and as he always did, shook his head in bewilderment at the sign:

*Parking for Stonehenge Tourists.*

"What else could it possibly be parking for," he began to ask, "all the way out…"

But the kid was gone, immediately sprinting over to the giant monoliths.

"Woah, look at Jesse Owens go." Winston was amused but not surprised. If the kid had never seen a black man before, it's perfectly understandable that he'd never seen that old pile of rocks either. The novelty of Stonehenge had more than worn off for him…he'd probably driven by it a thousand times…but he was enchanted by the kid's enthusiasm and followed him over.

"Aren't they amazing, Winnie? Just look at the size of them." The stones did indeed tower above the tiny humans. "Isn't it some kind of ancient clock?" he asked as he reached his arms out as if to embrace one of the stones. Winston had heard several theories about the mysterious arrangement of the rocks, but he had one of his own and was quick to educate his new friend.

"You see kid, it's like this. Ten thousand years ago, aliens came to Earth from Mars and saw some Jamaican kids playing cricket in a field. The aliens loved the game so much that they wanted to play. However, they were big, actual giants, you know, so when they played they accidentally stood on the boys and killed them. Those big stones right there are their graves. The brainy leader of the aliens, who had seven eyes by the way, noticed that the graves resembled cricket stumps, and for many years stupid tourists believed Stonehenge was some kind of ancient clock, when all along it was a giant, alien cricket pitch."

Speech finished, Winnie's face was as deadpan as Tristan's eyes were wide in mock wonder.

"What kid, you don't believe me? Hmm!"

The new friends cracked up in fits of laughter, and slumped down on a nearby bench. For a few more minutes they sat quietly and enjoyed the view, both lost in their own thoughts. Eventually though, Winston faced Tristan, and for the first time since they'd met he spoke in a serious tone.

"Look kid, yours is a sad, sad story, and I really hope you find your mother. But you know what? I truly believe this will all have a happy ending."

"How do you know…how can you be so sure?"

"You know how I know, kid? You know how I'm so sure it will turn out right for you?" A huge grin spread across Winnie's face, and his eyes shone like pearls.

"I know, because if aliens can fly to Earth and make a cricket pitch out of stones in the middle of nowhere, then anything is possible."

Tristan doubled up laughing, his chest heaving over aching ribs, and while teardrops streamed down his reddened cheeks, cramps knotted his stomach. These were familiar symptoms; tears, aches, cramps. But they usually signified a recent beating by his father. Not this time. His life had changed, and Tristan had never laughed so freely before, and though he didn't realise it, not only did he weep with unbridled laughter, but with relief at his new and unbridled freedom.

Tristan was truly happy. And in just two more hours, he'd see his mother in Salisbury.

*Chapter Twenty Nine*

Winnie's van disappeared down the busy high street and was soon lost among the swarming traffic. Tristan's new friend was gone, and he felt a momentary void of sadness because of the great time he'd had chatting with and learning from him over the course of the day.

But it also taught Tristan another crucial lesson; that he was capable of making friends. When he first left the island he feared he might be awkward socially, having never before interacted with other youngsters, and although Winston was older, they were of the same generation and got on famously. Yet another fear allayed, and one more step in his continuing development.

Tristan was getting so close now, and he could feel the

adrenalin begin to surge. Winston had dropped him in town so he could buy his mother flowers, and as he selected some pretty asters, both of their favorites, a shiver of emotion elicited an outbreak of goosebumps across his fair skin. He figured the walk out to the address he had would take thirty minutes, a good amount of time to compose himself and conquer his nerves.

That he was nervous was sad to Tristan, and he guessed it was due to the mixture of emotions he felt; the joy at being reunited with his mother after so long, and his anger towards her for leaving him in the first place. It was confusing, but the most important thing, he knew, was that they'd be together soon. With his mother around, everything would be better.

A thriving breeze shook dead and dying leaves from trees, which disintegrated under his feet with a dire crunch. A descending chill kept him at a good pace, and before long he turned onto the wide and peaceful Broad Willow Lane. On seeing the faded and overgrown street sign, Tristan's already long stride lengthened as he walked faster still. She was close.

Appraising other houses along the tree lined road, he could see it was going to be a big house. Wide open spaces separated the properties, but their numbers told him he was getting near. Twenty-eight. Five minutes later, 'Duck Pond Cottage: Thirty.' Five more minutes, Thirty-two.

And finally, partly hidden by a stand of giant swaying willows, number 'Thirty-four.' His heart thumped, and in the ebbing light he moved slowly towards the house.

An air of dour neglect hung like a stain about the place, and the wild garden hadn't been tended in months, if not years. The house was overgrown with slinking ivy, and despite the early hour all its curtains were closed. Tristan's good mood cranked back a notch, and he read and reread the address on his postcard, just to be sure. But it was right, of course, and a dismal feeling constricted his throat like the twist of a maleficent scarf.

He shuffled forward into the dark and shady porch, and shivered at the sight of cobwebs that held captive so many dead or near dead creatures. It was as if the door hadn't been used for a very long time…too long. Dismayed, he breathed deep and rattled the rusted knocker.

A slow minute passed. Then another. He banged again and an upstairs curtain twitched. Tristan backed up in a vain effort to see, but the curtain had fallen still. Within the house all was quiet, the dull silence heavy, and he raised his arm to knock again when he heard the soft tinkle of keys and the grinding slide of a weighty dead bolt. His heart almost stopped.

"Mum?" he cried, "is that you?" The door slowly whined open as if itself in pain, and the weathered and stooped old woman that stood inside wore a look of sheer sorrow.

"Where's my mother? Is she here? I'm Tristan, and I want to see my mum."

With great effort the aged lady straightened up, and a face that had forgotten happiness laid its pitying eyes upon him.

"I know who you are, my dear. You'd better come in."

She cast an apprehensive glance past Tristan and, after re-bolting the door she ushered him into the darkness of the living room. A stale and musty smell hit him immediately, and much like the shabby Brighton hotel, deep layers of dust coated everything beneath an entrenched and decayed shroud. Throughout the room a palpable sadness seemed to ooze from the very walls.

"Open the drapes, please dear, and let me look at you."

Tristan obliged, and looked out onto a wild garden made infinitely more ominous by the swiftly dying day. He turned back to the withered woman.

"Where is she? Where's my mother?" He already feared the worst.

"Please dear, take a seat. I know you've had a long journey. I'll make us a cup of tea, and then I promise to answer all your questions."

He sat and looked forlornly at the flowers he still held, their pretty colors dull and wasted amidst such cheerless surroundings, and certain now that his mother wasn't there.

The rumpled, rickety old lady shuffled from the room, as claustrophobia pressed in on Tristan in the dank and airless lounge. He opened a window, hoping for a breath of fresh air, but it yielded nothing more than the ripened stench of rotting vegetation. After an age she returned, unsteady on legs stripped of all muscle and tray shaking in fidgety hands, and as tea cups clinked together in a dissonant, chaotic chorus, the sickness she tried but failed to hide became clear.

"Milk and sugar, dear?"

He nodded, and for a full minute she stirred the tea as if cranking up some much needed energy. She sat opposite him, and when she spoke it was with surprising familiarity. The resolute voice betrayed her frailty.

"I'm so happy you're here, Tristan, and that you are here means you're no longer on St. Mary's and have left that desolate place behind. I'm sure you must be wondering who I am, so let me introduce myself. My name's Bella, Bella Patrick. I'm your aunt."

Tristan was stunned. "My aunt? I don't have any aunts."

"There are many things you don't know about your

family, Tristan, shameful secrets kept from you for too many years. But it's true that I'm your aunt, and I'm ashamed to say, your father is…" She stalled, struggling to finish her sentence.

Tristan pushed a little. "What about my father? What is it?"

"I'm sorry. Blyth is…Blyth's my brother."

Tristan was utterly confused. He had no knowledge of any family beyond his parents, so it was a real shock. However, for now it was of little importance compared to his real concern. He put down the flowers, and pushed on to what really mattered.

"Where's my mother?"

"Your mother isn't here, and believe me when I say it breaks my heart to tell you."

"Why isn't she here? Tell me where she is."

"Tristan, please, let me explain. Kerra was here, as you thought. She was here to wait for you, but for a very good reason she had to move on. Your father of course knows where I live, and Kerra, being a savvy, sagacious woman, was too afraid he'd come here to look for her. She left in a hurry, fearful of that wretch Blyth, and the poor girl had very little money, and had to move on to find work. I wish I could have helped her more in that regard. I'm so sorry she's not here, truly I am. She left you a message which I'll fetch shortly."

Tristan was deflated, as if all the positive air had been sucked from his lungs. When he first saw the place from the outside he feared the worst, but it was still a bombshell. Bella continued.

"You have to know that Kerra's priority was always you. Everything she has done was for you, and though it may not seem that way now, you'll soon understand." She smiled in an attempt to reassure her nephew, who had visibly receded deep into the puffy couch as if to back away from reality. But the effect was minimal.

She tried again. "You know, you look just like Kerra, with your golden red hair and those big eyes. It's the first time I've seen you in fifteen years, and you've grown into such a handsome young chap. I understand why she's so proud of you." Bella looked weary behind her labored smile, and it was almost as if she'd been waiting many expectant years for that moment. She wanted to elicit something, some response from the clearly distraught boy. Nothing.

"Your mother didn't know exactly where she would end up, only that she was heading to London. She left two weeks ago. London is a big place, Tristan, and she'll find the anonymity she needs there, what with all those millions of people and all that hustle and bustle."

*Anonymous to the world,* he thought, *anonymous to me.*

He slumped, depressed even further into the couch and causing a small puff of dust to infiltrate the air, as if there wasn't already enough. What Bobby had said to him back in Penzance was ringing true. She warned him there may be further disappointments, and she was right. He closed his eyes and saw his mother's smiling face, encouraging him to trust her and for him to be brave. The former was proving difficult.

But he'd learned many things since his new life had begun, and that the real world was also difficult was one such fact. He'd come so far, and he knew that he could continue. He had to. His mother had made another difficult and brave decision herself, so he would make one too. *I will not let this beat me,* he thought, *I will find her.*

Becalmed slightly he chatted about his journey to Bella, who listened intently and with growing admiration. She was happy he'd met some nice folks so far, but was sad and not shocked to learn of the robbery. Tristan's bravery and stoicism to leave the island, and his tales of hitchhiking and the way he dealt with the theft of his money, infused her with long lost pride, and a waxing moon of warmth from her broken heart added equally long lost colour to her pallid cheeks.

Tristan's remarkable tale had arrived in the present, so Bella thought it a good time to prepare dinner, adding a firm decline to his offer of help.

"You look exhausted. Why don't you take a nice nap? Dinner will be an hour, but first I'll get your letter."

Tristan thought he'd never seen anyone more exhausted than Bella, but he himself was shattered, and accepted the chance to read his note and then close his eyes.

With a conflicted heart he read his mother's flowing and familiar handwriting, and though the gracefully written words were few, the message clear; she loved him, and was so sorry she wasn't there with him now. He wasn't to despair though, because they'd see each other in London soon. She believed in him, and she missed him.

It was a simple message, at least until the last sentence, which he didn't understand. It implored him not to blame her for some of the things he'd learn from Bella. *Blame her for what?* It didn't say. *I have to show understanding and forgiveness?*

Tristan was unnerved and at a total loss. What did it all mean? Now he expected some terrible news, or some heinous secret about his mother. Once more a barrage of wild butterflies billowed in his guts. *Don't blame me*, it said. *Understanding? Forgiveness*? A maelstrom of confusion and dark potential clouded his mind, and the oppressive room shrank, suffocating him of air and of clear thoughts. He stepped outside and stared into the blackness.

Two hours later and dinner was over. With a combination of the cool air and a hot meal he had forced himself to relax a little, but now he couldn't wait any longer. Across the table, he fixed his aunt Bella with an implacable look that would not be denied.

"I think it's time you told me the family secrets."

## Chapter Thirty

Kerra was scared. Work had dried up along with almost all the money. Unpaid bills meant the gas was cut, and no gas meant she shivered constantly from the cold. The truth was simple; Kerra was impoverished and the straits were dire. Added to that, Mollie hadn't been home in two nights. A couple of evenings earlier her friend had got drunk on cheap wine as they discussed their options and, feisty as ever, she spoke from the heart as she derided their boss.

"Well, we don't need shitty old Billy Boy anyway, because he's nothing but a worthless, slimy scumbag, and there're plenty of other ways to make money round here, 'specially for a couple of lookers like us." She winked with a flourish that would have been at home in the Moulin Rougé, and her loud, hearty laugh was impossible to ignore.

Kerra smiled, but beneath it she was troubled by Mollie's comments. *What did she mean? Other ways to make money? Lookers like us? Is she saying...no, she wouldn't.* With a long drink of the cheap and nasty wine, she dismissed the idea as her increasingly sensitive imagination running wild.

But, two days later Mollie hadn't been seen or heard from since. The more she thought about those comments, the more it seemed Mollie had referred to prostitution, and she just couldn't outright dismiss it. It was, after all, the East End, notorious for gangs and criminals and, as she'd heard often, London's seedy side where criminals often acted as pimps for the hookers. Kerra winced at the thought. *No matter how bad it gets, I'll never do that. Never!*

She curled her ever slenderizing body deep beneath inadequate blankets, and tried to derail that sordid train of thought as she drifted into a fitful sleep. That night Kerra dreamt of her son. She dreamt of her husband. And, in the darkest pre-dawn hours before the sun spread its useless winter rays across London, she dreamt of Mollie and her beaten and bloodied body found in the alley just yards from where she slept.

Mollie was dead.

*Chapter Thirty One*

Tristan assured himself that whatever Bella had to tell him, it couldn't hurt him more than he'd already been hurt. He was ready for his aunt's secrets.

"What I'm going to tell you will be painful and, moreover, difficult to understand. You'll be confused and angry, and you'll want someone to blame. But please consider everything before venting your feelings. I'll be right here for you. Are you ready?"

*Surely she's being over dramatic*, he thought. *What could possibly need such a solemn build up? Let's get this over with.*

"Tell me whatever it is you need to tell me," said Tristan, trying in vain to keep impatience from his voice.

Bella appraised him now, unsure whether to proceed or

not. She knew she must, knew that he had a right to know, and she had promised Kerra. No doubt, what she had to say would come as a bombshell, but she also knew that if she waited the chance may be lost forever. It was now or never, she believed, and took a deep breath. Bella began her story.

"Do you know where you were born Tristan?"

"Of course, at the cottage...on St. Mary's." Eyebrows arched, he wondered what Bella was talking about.

"Then this is my first secret. You weren't born on that island, you were born at your family's home just outside Penzance. Your parents moved to the island a few months later."

"I don't understand. Why would that be a secret? Why keep that from me?"

"That's not it. That's...it's not the most important thing." She swallowed hard. Her brow furrowed in concentration, and deep shadows crimped her forehead. In the dim light Bella suddenly looked a decade older. But impatience took over, and he pressed her without sympathy.

"Bella, please, what is it? Come on, what could be so difficult to say?"

Bella struggled. She raised a hand to her chest and screwed her eyes tight shut. Tristan fought his frustration, but out of deference to his old relation he waited. After endless seconds, his Aunt Bella finally looked at him, and with a hint of a tear in her eye, she spoke four words that would change his life forever.

"You have a sister."

As if in a dream, the light above swirled and he stared distrait as a cold sweat accompanied the rising nausea. He foundered in the chair, and Bella moved as quick as her debilitated frame would allow to put a frail arm around his suddenly frail shoulders. Unmoved, they sat that way for countless minutes. Finally, and satisfied he'd recovered a little from the shock, Bella retook her seat.

Tristan looked into the haunted eyes of his aunt, and the tortured expression that looked back told him she'd spoken an absolute truth.

"It's not possible," Tristan at last uttered, his voice a verbalized agony. "It…it can't be possible."

But the sympathy etched on Bella's face left no doubt.

"Where is she?" It was less than a whisper.

A lugubrious look hung loosely over her impossibly jaded face. In that moment they saw, felt and shared each other's pain. But Tristan knew there was more to Bella's story. He leaned across the table, and reached out his hand to hers.

"Bella, please tell me more."

She saw he was ready, but how ready only time would tell.

"From the beginning, then. You have suffered terribly by your father's hand, and of course your mother has too. But my brother wasn't always so disturbed, far from it. When we were kids he was a kind and loving boy, and it didn't matter that I was a few years older than him because he always looked out for me. He was bright, and believe it or not he was a sensitive young man. Popular, too, especially with the girls. But when our mother died young after an old illness, something changed in him, some internal imbalance driving him down into a guarded, circumspect depression. Morose became Blyth's standard attitude, and he spent a lot of time withdrawn and alone, and for a long time I worried about him, but he just shrugged it off. Then one day the beautiful Kerra entered our lives, and the old Blyth returned, rebalanced, and his smile reinvigorated. They married young, and for a few years they were happy. Blyth had his workshop and Kerra her art, and you know, she was so talented and dreamt of opening her own gallery someday. My word, Kerra was a stunning young woman. So many admirers, but one lad in particular stood out...Mark, I think? Anyway, Blyth was always a little jealous of that, and to hide it he..."

At that moment Bella inhaled in the short sharp bursts of a powerful sob, the pain of the aroused memory clear. But a dab of the eye, and she continued.

"Sorry dear...he, your father started drinking. Too much. Then out of the blue he lost his job at the workshop...cutbacks, they said and he slumped, reminiscent of when our mother died. Your mother tried hard to make him happy, and she was a good wife. Kerra surprised us all one day when she announced she was pregnant. She hoped, we all did, that having a baby would snap Blyth out of his misery, but he just deteriorated. And that's when the abuse started." An involuntary shiver shook the old lady's thinning white hair.

"It wasn't a lot to begin with, you know, just a lot of whisky fueled shouting and threats that didn't really amount to anything. But as the drinking clasped hold of Blyth's ever weakening emotions it escalated into physical abuse. Blyth's glare cut you where you stood, if only his eyes could focus long enough, because whisky unbalanced him from day one and he never saw clearly again until it was too late. When the baby was born, your sister, the rages took on a more sinister edge. Sometimes when the poor thing cried, Blyth would hit Kerra, and even threatened to hurt the baby if your mother couldn't stop it crying. She was terrified and, at her wit's end, she came to me for advice. I loved my brother, but when I saw what he put her through..."

The strain showed itself over Bella's entire being. She

grew paler by the second, and her body was in a gentle but constant shake.

Tristan considered telling her to stop. But he wanted… he needed, to know it all if it might help him understand who he himself was. With a subtle nod to let him know she was okay, she continued.

"It was difficult for me to betray Blyth like that, but I had little choice, and said we should report him to the authorities. But by then the poor thing was so afraid of your father and what he might do to both her and the baby, that she bravely suffered his abuse in silence for the sake of your sister."

His eyes were closed, but Tristan listened with rapt attention. For his mother his heart ached. But for his unknown sister, the swell of sorrow blossomed darkly like a cancer. Bella waited until he opened his eyes, and when he did she saw a potent mix of sadness and rage. On she pressed.

"On one occasion Kerra had to go shopping. Blyth was too lazy to ever help her out. Of course she was loath to leave the baby with your father, especially as he was drinking, but she was out of baby food and it was freezing outside, so she reluctantly decided it would be okay if she was quick. Inevitably, as soon as the door was closed the baby wouldn't stop crying, and Blyth just as inevitably lost his temper. In a drunken mania he held a pillow over her tiny head to make her quiet. Because of the slow icy roads Kerra knew she'd been gone too long and rushed panicked back to the house, only to walk in to her worst nightmare. She launched herself into Blyth and somehow managed to snatch the baby up just in time. Your mother saved that baby's life. Later she said it was as if Blyth was in a trance. When she pushed him off the baby he looked through her as if she wasn't even there. Luckily the baby was more or less unharmed, but your poor mother was beside herself with fear and guilt, so, out of total desperation, she came to see me again. I had no choice other than to confront him, but a few days later when I arrived at their house he was steaming drunk. Kerra had a nasty black eye, but when I saw the baby, my heart broke. She had bruises on her arms and legs, and blood trickled from a cut on her face, so I screamed, *'what have you done?'* but he just shouted back at me to mind my own business and stay away, even threatening me, his loving sister and last ally, with violence, so I knew then that Blyth was a devolved and afflicted man."

Breathless and upset, Bella paused once again and wiped at a flow of teardrops with her sleeve. That they were painful memories was obvious, and Tristan empathized with his aunt.

"I just didn't know what to do. I thought that if I reported him to the welfare authorities they would take the baby away, and I'd heard terrible stories of children in care being abused. So my husband and I discussed it. Will was a quiet and peaceful man whose morality was born of the old school, and at first he refused to get involved in another man's business. We always wanted our own children, but for whatever reason we were never blessed. For a long time we agonized over what to do, and after emotionally evaluating our own morality and ethics we finally came up with the idea to adopt the baby as ours. We wouldn't report Blyth to the authorities or the police, we told them, but we did have one important condition, and that was that they had to move away. We suggested The Scilly Isles, knowing Blyth could find work and Kerra could open a gallery. The idea met with angry protestations from both of them. Kerra cried, saying she'd rather die than give up her baby, and despite what he'd done, Blyth said that only over his dead body would he give the baby up to anyone. But after a few days spent searching her tortured soul, a devastated Kerra had to admit that it was better to give her daughter over to us than risk Blyth hurting her again. She was wretched with sadness and guilt, and I don't think she's ever stopped hurting. Your father agreed too, but I remember thinking then that his decision came a little bit too easily. He was acting strange, not drunk though, as he had managed to lay off the whisky for a few days. Rather, it seemed to me as if he welcomed Kerra's decision. I think that in her state she didn't notice Blyth's apparent lack of contention, because deep down she believed in her husband, and with the isolation of the island, she must have hoped Blyth would recover, and that she'd soon be reunited with her baby. What that poor woman has been through, both then and ever since, well, it's a wonder she has kept her sanity."

If a bomb had fallen from the sky and destroyed everything around him, Tristan couldn't have been more shell-shocked. One revelation after another had been told, and just when he though it was over, still there was more.

He just could not believe that he had a sister. Everything was changed, and his worn out mind could barley contain it all. But he realized something else, then…Bella hadn't even old him his sister's name. He had to know.

"What's her name?"

"Pardon dear?"

"Her name? What's my sister's name?"

"Oh, I'm sorry. Ailla. Her name is Ailla."

*Chapter Thirty Two*

The short and turbulent history of his family was much worse than he'd known, and it was all just so surreal to Tristan that he wasn't even sure how he felt. There was the obvious joy of having a sister. Not long ago, happiness was waking up and not seeing his father's bloodshot eyes glaring at him. And at least now he was safe.

But he also felt a profound and abject sadness. For so many years...his entire childhood...he'd been alone. No one to play with. No one to talk to. To now learn he'd had a sister all along put into context just how lonely he'd really been. *How could they do it? How could they give up a baby?*

And his father. He knew he was a drunken and tormented bully. But the fact that he could harm a tiny child took that knowledge to a much darker level. The blood surged through Tristan's veins like broiling lava, and at that moment he wanted to kill his father, the earthquake of hate he felt shaking him with rage.

Under the trying circumstances, Bella thought it was best to give Tristan some time alone, and had stolen off into the kitchen for a while. But now she returned to the lounge, and as she regarded the boy she sensed a definite shift in his demeanor. The kid that arrived a few hours ago was a young, naive boy of sixteen, but now an intense look hardened his eye, and that *boy* Tristan was gone. In his place sat a toughened and serious young man. With alarm she recognised that inexorable and adamantine look in his eyes, and an involuntary shiver crept through her bones, as it was the same look she'd seen too often in the eyes of her brother. Cold and calculated. Sinister. It troubled her greatly. She had more to say.

"What I've told you must be so difficult to take. But

nevertheless, you have to believe me when I say that, in regards to your sister Kerra had no choice. It took amazing courage for her to give up her daughter, even though she believed it was a temporary solution. Things were bad enough with Blyth. But imagine if Ailla had fallen into the hands of someone worse than your father, only the Lord knows what could have happened. There are too many bad people out there, but at least with us Kerra knew the baby would be safe. And that brings us onto the next part of the story."

Sitting with his back straight and arms on the table, Tristan clenched and unclenched his fists and watched distractedly as the blood drained to leave his knuckles white. He fantasized of piling those fists into the skinny, bristled jaw of his father, and listen to the bones in his face crack while watching the blood spill. He'd never entertained such thoughts of revenge before, because in truth he'd never really appreciated the magnitude of abuse he'd endured. In such isolation and with nothing to gage against, he'd be forgiven for thinking it acceptable for a father to punish a family.

But there and then his mind was swamped with thoughts of retribution. It was wrong; two wrongs didn't make a right. He knew that. But there it was, a tumor of revenge swelling in his mind, and for now he was content to let it fester. Bella couldn't be sure how much more Tristan was capable of hearing, but she had little choice but to persevere.

"Ailla was such a sweet and beautiful little baby, and what your father did to her was criminal, but luckily there were no lasting physical effects. After your parents moved to the island, and soon after she came to live with us, Ailla quickly became a happy child. Will and I loved her so much. We watched her blossom and, via her friend Mark I occasionally sent secret letters to Kerra, just to let her know how her daughter was doing, but she couldn't reply of course, because Blyth would surely have found out. During one of her Blyth sanctioned annual visits to see Ailla back in Penzance, she assured me that things had improved somewhat. She was still desperately sad, she said, but told me not to worry. A few years had passed and they had settled into a sedate, quiet life on St. Mary's. Blyth had enough work to keep food on their plates, and Kerra occupied herself with housework and sometimes even a little painting. She stayed just a few days with her daughter, Will and I, and then she returned to the island. She surprised us all some months later when we learned she was once again pregnant, this time with you. Blyth went absolutely crazy, and he started drinking again, more heavily than ever. Obviously Kerra feared for the safety of her baby, but over time Blyth's anger abated a little until eventually he became entrenched into a severe depression. None of us knew what had caused those violent outbursts when Kerra got pregnant, and maybe it was just coincidence. I was sorry for Kerra, but I couldn't help but feel for my brother too, because by then it was clear he suffered from some unknown emotional torment."

Just for a moment Bella's eyes drifted off to some other place known only to her, and her skin had never been more pale. Under the low lamplight she looked half dead. Tristan was listening, but in an effort to keep from boiling over he kept his eyes closed. He was unaware of his aunt's distinct deterioration.

Still she continued. "Ailla knew we weren't her real parents, and of course she knew Kerra was her real mother, but at just four years old she couldn't really have understood the situation. She was such a bright kid, but after you were born she became more and more withdrawn. Strangely, she started to have nightmares about her baby brother, about you, and would run crying into our room, screaming that you were being hurt. It really was bizarre as she was so young, and she couldn't possibly have known what was going on across at St. Mary's. Anyway, you were born, and from what we understood you were as cute as a button, with wide blue eyes and a shock of red hair. You never cried, not ever, Kerra told us, and you were the quietest most content baby she'd ever seen."

At those words the hard edge of Tristan's features seemed to fade a little, and in its place was a mask of acute sadness. Beneath the mask though, Bella knew that rage still awaited a chance to escape. But for now he was calm.

"At that time Blyth slipped into a dark and dangerous depression, and because of his now serious drinking problem, his anger had evolved into something far more sinister. That's when the regular beatings started. But Kerra learned that if she didn't retaliate and just absorbed the punishments, then at least Blyth left you alone, and that's the awful pattern all your lives took for many years. Blyth drank because of his depression, and when he was drunk he got more depressed. It was a terribly vicious wave of downs and more downs, and my brother just could not break free of the drowning swell of whisky. It was hell for Kerra, but for a while you were safe. Mark tried to intervene, but your mother forbade him for fear of the repercussions and he stayed away, reluctantly I'm sure. But it wasn't long before Blyth turned his fists on you."

It was late, and except for the one dim lamp that barely cast a shadow the room was in full darkness. Beneath the surface Tristan was seething, but he was determined to keep control and welcomed the soothing gloom of the lounge. And for now he'd heard enough about his mother and father's misery.

"Tell me about my sister, please."

Bella nodded. She seemed to have been talking for hours and was clearly exhausted, but she had to push on. The old lady knew time was short.

"Ailla flowered into a pretty young girl, and her fiery orange hair shimmered in the sun. And what a talent! My goodness that girl could draw, and she would sit for hours just sketching and painting anything that came into her mind. Such a natural talent, just like her mother. Oh Tristan, Will and I loved her so much. He was such a kind and gentle man, but he was always a little sickly and had been ill for some years before we took care of Ailla. He simply adored that girl, but the sadness he felt for Kerra and the silence we kept in terms of all the abuse, well, it just gnawed at him constantly. Will of course worried about you over on the island, too, and he got so stressed about it all that his health deteriorated more than ever…in the end it was just too much for him to bear." She fought against crying, and like Tristan she was glad of the diminished light.

"It's okay, Bella, take your time." He gently took her hand.

"Thanks love. I'm okay, just a silly old woman sometimes. He was just fifty-two when the stress combined with an already weak heart sadly caught up with him, and he suffered a massive heart attack. Will died that day, and a major part of me died too, because I was devastated. I'd lost my husband and my best friend of thirty years, but he had been sick for a long time, and deep down we both knew that he might not live into old age. No, it was Ailla who was hardest hit. Despite her youth she felt responsible, believing that the extra burden of taking care of her had caused his heart attack, even though I explained that it wasn't at all her fault. I told her she'd given us years of pleasure and so much joy. But she never really got over it."

Tristan listened with a mix of admiration and sorrow for Bella. "My uncle Will sounds like an incredible man, and I wish I could have met him."

"Yes, he was, and he would have loved to have met you too. Ailla became more subdued over the next couple of years, more withdrawn, like a moon that had lost its sparkle. She stopped painting, and retreated into the solitude of her room. Of course she was as grateful and courteous as always, but there was a definitive shifting of vitality deep inside. Our lambent little girl was gone. As for myself, well it was a big struggle for years after losing Will's income, and times were tough. My health also suffered."

Bella laughed a quiet and accepting laugh that surprised Tristan, who shot her a concerned look.

"To be honest, I'm surprised I've lasted this long. I have cancer, you see, and not just any old cancer, but terminal. At least, that's what they said, but so far I've outlived the doc's forecast by five years, though there'll not be too many more sunsets for me, now."

She smiled, and Tristan smiled back. That woman and her husband, an auntie and uncle he hadn't known existed, had given their lives to protect Ailla, and he was overwhelmed at their kindness and generosity and about how far some people went to do what was right. But he was also struck by the polarity of human nature. Blyth and Bella, two siblings that couldn't be more different, one troubled and shaped by uncontrollable fits of jealousy and rage, and the other strong and humble, guided by love and almost saintly in her actions. He himself was humbled as Bella continued, and hoped he'd inherited at least a tiny part of her golden and inspirational nature.

"Ailla had just turned twelve, and I'll never forget the day she came and sat beside me. I could see sympathy in her eyes, and my heart beat fast as I saw her young face wracked with regret. *I love you*, she said, and she told me how grateful and lucky she was to have Will and I in her life. Such a sweet girl, and so wise. She said she understood how difficult it was for me now that I was alone. She knew about the money issues and my health concerns, though it wasn't the cancer back then. I was just so tired all the time, and the doctors could do nothing other than tell me to take things slow. Ailla said she wanted to find a new family to take care of her, so that I could spend more time at rest, and of course I protested with all my heart. She needed me, or that's what I thought. But she was right and I knew it. Just cooking a simple dinner left me drained, and your sister was only thinking of my health. Though I hated to admit it, it was the best thing for her, too, because she was such a bright young thing and her potential could only thrive by living with younger, healthier guardians. I wondered at the time why she didn't suggest being reunited with her mother, though by then she understood the problems Kerra endured. But she never asked, and I like to think she was just wise beyond her years. After much anguish we contacted the local fostering agency, who found her a lovely family in Brighton. A couple of months later and she was gone. They truly were nice people, and perfect for Ailla. Although it breaks my heart…I have…" This time Bella took a long while to compose herself.

"I'm sorry…it's just that, well, I've never seen or heard from her since."

Tristan was yet again stunned by what he'd heard.

"You mean that once she left for her new family, that was the last you heard from her? After everything you did for her? And you've no idea where she is?"

"I'm so sorry to say it, but it's true. I lost all trace of her, and of course that meant your mother did too. We decided when you were a baby that you should never know about your sister. If you had known, you could never have visited her anyway, and that would have meant only more disappointment. I know you won't feel that way now, and I can see you're hurting, but please believe that we thought it best for you both, and I stand by it. Forgive me, Tristan, and please forgive your mother. As for your father, I can't and won't ask you to forgive him. The Lord knows I never have."

A tsunami of emotions confronted Tristan as he struggled to stay afloat amidst everything he'd learned. Anger allied with bitterness to combat the joy and love he felt for a sister he'd never met, and his pride at having a benevolent relative like Bella contradicted the shame he felt over the malevolence of his father. But amid that maelstrom of turmoil that threatened to overwhelm him, he also recognised the years of torment that Bella had suffered, and he leveled with his aunt.

"It's okay Bella, I understand why I was never told, I really do. It was the right decision…no, it was the only decision you could have made at the time, and I respect both you and my mother for making it. It must have been difficult."

Bella glowed with pride at her nephew's maturity and compassion.

"But now I know about my sister," Tristan continued, "I have to find her. You've really never heard anything about her since?"

"Thank you, my dear, and what a fine young man you are. But about your sister, well you probably shouldn't give it much heed, but there was one rumor, though it was such a long time ago, and despite my enquiries it was never verified. In my heart of hearts I doubt it's true."

"What was it, Aunt Bella, what was the rumor?" He had to know.

"Well dear, an old friend of mine heard that maybe, just maybe, Ailla had moved abroad. After a short but happy time she moved on from the family in Brighton, and was fostered by another family from London who apparently moved away on business."

"Where?" It was a simple question, but his tone left no doubt about his desire to know.

"Remember, I said it probably wasn't true?"

"Yes."

Bella sighed deeply, and then she met his eye.

"New York."

*Chapter Thirty Three*

The last dregs of Tristan's energy ebbed away into darkness. Just weeks ago life was so simple. It wasn't a good or happy life, but he understood his small place in it. There were no surprises, and no shocks, and the only variation was when no abuse came his way. But in just thirty minutes, all he'd ever known about his family was undone.

That was his new reality. And Tristan was in chaos.

He liked Bella a lot, and though he'd only just met her he trusted her every word. So fresh was the knowledge about his family that he could barely digest it, and yet he felt the need to discuss it further with his aunt. Maybe she could help him understand his feelings. He was sapped emotionally, and she looked terrible. He felt bad. But he needed to talk.

"Bella, how did things go so wrong?"

"There are so many factors that caused you and your family to suffer, but it all stems from my brother's mental weaknesses. As I said, he wasn't always like that. Blyth was made...forged, really...in a kiln of his own paranoia and insecurity, and he went into meltdown, constantly on the edge of erupting. I never really understood why, but I always suspected it had something to do with Kerra's short high school relationship with Mark Trescothwick, and your mother's continued fondness for him. Silly, really, as your mother stopped seeing Mark once she fell in love with Blyth."

"But that doesn't excuse him, does it? There must be a mean streak in him, to beat us like he does."

"No love, it doesn't excuse him, and there can be no excuses for the way he treated you all. But he really changed so much when Kerra became pregnant, and it seemed to be the catalyst for all the suffering he caused. The man he became was unrecognizable to me."

Fear entered Tristan's eyes, and when he spoke his tone was desperate.

"My father's blood courses through me. He's in me, and so his weaknesses and shame are in me, too. I'm afraid. I don't want to be like him."

Sympathy for the boy tugged at the strings of her conscience.

"Listen. You need to know something. Your mother is a good and kind person, and though I'm just a silly old lady now, I have a good heart too, just like Will did. And your sister has a lovely soul and a heart of gold. What I'm trying to say is, that no matter what your father has done, no matter his mistakes, it doesn't mean you'll turn out the same. Blyth is a weak man, and his weakness is what made him drink. Once the whisky ensnared him, the Blyth we loved was lost to us forever. But you aren't like him, I sense it. And your mother was right when she said you have an inner strength. After all you've been through, the bravery you showed to make it this far is incredible. Your mother will be so proud of you. I'm so proud of you. You have a long and happy life ahead of you, Tristan, and I know you will never hurt anyone."

"I wasn't scared of him, and I never feared the beatings. I just thought they were a normal part of life, something I deserved."

Bella's face contorted in anguish. "You must never think that, Tristan. Never! You were an innocent child, and no adult has a right to harm a kid. You have to remember that."

He nodded weakly. "But I was afraid of the emptiness afterwards, when I knew my mum wouldn't come. I knew she loved me, and I felt that love, despite the silence. But she was too scared of him. I understand that now."

"Your mother has had a very troubled marriage, but she's an intelligent woman, and everything she did was to protect you. She always felt she failed with Ailla, and she tried her very best to shield you. In the end she knew that the best way to make life better…the only way… was to leave. You'll see. Once you find her in London, all this stress and sadness will disappear, and you two will be together again. Nothing can stop that now."

Bella's words eased his angst, but sadness still reigned over his thoughts. He missed his mother.

"When she left, I just didn't understand. For the first few days I assumed she'd come back, that she was trying to scare my father into changing. But when it became clear that she wouldn't return I felt betrayed. For weeks I was lost and just moped around the house, waiting and wishing for her to come home. But I knew she never would, so I knew I had to find a way to change my situation, but I was afraid and didn't know what to do. Then my mum's birthday message came, and at least then I knew she was okay. It made me feel better, and I started to believe things might be okay."

"And here you are. And Tristan, the hardest part is over. You've left that island behind, and I can already see the smile on your mother's face when she sees you. Poor Kerra was so desperate and sad when she arrived here, and though she herself was safe at last, she never relaxed knowing she had left you behind. The moment she arrived I saw and felt her suffering. Pure pain, that's the look she wore as she told stories of a recently remembered past. The memories flashed in her eyes, and the pretty smile, once so permanent, was absent. But she is happier now, I know it, and she'll be delirious when she sees you. As for Blyth, I pity him. He has had some time now to consider what has happened to him, and to understand what he has lost. He deserves it, that's for sure." A pause. "How was he when you left?"

Tristan considered for a moment. It seemed so long ago. It was just days.

"When I told him I was leaving he acted strange, I mean at first he begged me to stay but then he got angry and…well, the usual. Overall I think he expected it and just couldn't accept it. I even felt torn for a while, especially when he stopped drinking, because he made a real effort and even told me how much he regretted everything. He promised to repair all the damage, and I believe he was sincere. I felt for him." His eyes hardened a little, his voice softer. "But it didn't change the facts of what he had done to me and my family."

Bella nodded in acquiescence. Until now she'd reserved a tiny bit of sympathy for her brother, understanding that not all he'd done was in his control. But when she replied to Tristan, her voice was firm.

"No amount of parental remorse or even demonstrations of their love can lessen the amount of pain a child can store in their mind, and sadly, those dark memories could last forever. But you must not forget, not yet. One day in the future, when all of this is over, then maybe you can forgive your father his mistakes. It might be possible to forgive him his sins. But for now rest assured that you've done absolutely the right thing by forsaking him on that miserable island."

*Chapter Thirty Four*

Bella Patrick suffered. She'd anticipated yesterday's events for many years, though in some ways...selfish ways, she thought...she hoped that the day would never come, that she would die before it could. But arrive it had, knocking at her door on a cold and wintry afternoon, and she had done what she knew she must do; break a poor boy's heart with wrenching family secrets.

And now she was tired. The cancer was diagnosed several years ago, and had been eating away at her ever since. The doctors gave her less than a year, but she had stubbornly defied their forecasts, and only she knew the reasons why she continued to suffer through unimaginable pain on a daily basis. When she saw the doctors on scheduled visits they would huddle together in amazement and discuss the scientific *miracle* of Bella in hushed tones, unable to accept the idea that she just wasn't ready to die.

*Too much pain*, they said, *why prolong it?*

Bella's truth was very different. She did want to die, and had for a long time. The only joys in her life departed when she lost both her husband and then Ailla. Her own health left her weak and broken from pain, and she lived in an endless cycle of misery. She endured for two reasons only; first was her simple promise to Kerra, that when the time came she would help the boy. And second, having kept that promise, she lived on to see the day when Kerra, Ailla and Tristan would be reunited.

But Bella had finally done all she could do for them. She simply could not do any more, and all she craved now was to be reunited with her husband. Together they'd raised Ailla, and after Will died she had coped for a long time on her own. She later supported and harbored Kerra, and helped her on her way to London. She'd done her duty by Tristan, who would now follow his mother to the city.

Bella had played her part, and the colossal millstone around her neck was lifted. Now it was time to rest.

She had taken too many powerful cancer drugs for too many years, and was sick of the side effects. The moment Tristan arrived at her door was the moment she decided *no more pills*. That night, while he slept, every last pill got flushed down the toilet. She looked in on him in the night, his eyes darting about beneath heavy lids, and she knew his dreams were dark. He would be okay, she knew that too, but she felt for him. So much torment at such a young age, and now one bombshell after another, just like the German bombings she'd witnessed herself as a child. He was a tough kid, and brave, and his heart was good, but she remembered his very real worry that he was just like his father. That bothered her, too, but hoped with all her heart that he was not. With a heavy soul, a soul that was more than ready to depart life as she knew it, she closed the door on Tristan for the last time, and for the first time in many long and Godless years, she said a prayer for her entire family. Not even Blyth was forgotten.

She climbed with difficulty into bed. Maybe she would wake up tomorrow. If she didn't, her agonies were over. If she did, one way or another she'd make sure it was for the last time.

No longer for this world, Bella Patrick was ready to die.

## Chapter Thirty Five

Left and right he rolled in the hour before dawn, troubled by shadows and the weight of newly learned knowledge. And when he at last broke free of sleep's stubborn grip, he awoke with the usual moments of fear and uncertainty. Today though those emotions were confounded by a cloudy confusion as to where he actually was, but when the echo of last night's bombshells resounded again he fell back onto the pillows, as if hit by a real physical force. Tristan lay still for an age, as he once more recovered from the impact of all he'd learned. Finally, and surprising even himself, he sat up and found that he was smiling.

"I have a sister," he whispered into the stuffy and silent void. *Ailla*. Anxious to learn more he dressed and rushed down the stairs; *what does she look like? What's her favourite food? What books does she like?* But downstairs there was no sign of his aunt, and although it was early, he felt an exceptional stillness about the large house. Tristan stood in the hallway and listened. Nothing.

"Aunt Bella." His voice was absorbed by the mouldy walls. "Bella, where are you?" The only noise was the creaking of the old house itself, as if the illness suffered by his aunt had contaminated the walls and ceilings around him. Uneasiness crept along the dark corridor until it lodged in his mind and told him something was wrong. The kitchen and the living room were empty, and looking in the laundry room and the adjoining garage left him perplexed and worried. Tristan climbed the stairs and called softly at his aunt's door. A stair creaked in response. Not wanting to startle her if she slept, he knocked gently, but as the seconds passed his anxiety grew into a cold chill across his skin. He opened the door and went into the room.

Bella had looked sick and weak when he arrived yesterday, but the little colour that was in her cheeks had now gone, and though her eyes were open, they saw nothing. Panicked, he rushed over and tried in vain to wake her, but she was unresponsive. He scanned the room for a phone to call an ambulance, but there was no phone and now he was afraid and he grabbed Bella and shook her shoulders, desperate for any sign of life, but she was lifeless and he wept onto her faded nightgown as the heavy realisation of what he knew to be true hit him with the weight of a falling tree. It was all futile.

Bella was dead.

Numbness cramped his legs and it was all he could do to stay on his feet. Last night she was alive, and now, just hours later, his aunt Bella was dead. Suddenly lightheaded, Tristan half sat and half fell onto a bedside chair, and he tried not to look at his stricken aunt but he couldn't take his eyes from hers, open and vacant and unaware he was even there.

Though the longer he looked at her, the calmer he felt, and he soon realised why; Bella looked at peace.

He barely knew the woman, yet he owed her

everything, for she was the one who'd given him the greatest news in his short yet tumultuous life. He had a sister. With a deep breath Tristan took hold of his aunt's cold hand, and absent the strength to resist a flurry of helpless tears, he sat that way for a long time, gripping tight to her hand as though to let go would be to also let his sister slip away from him. In that position he drifted off into an exhausted sleep.

When he woke up an hour later he slipped gently from the grip of Bella's seized hand and rested it respectfully by her side. But what should he do now? Of course he had to hurry and tell someone. Maybe a neighbour had a phone? He would call the police and explain what happened. Something niggled though, and the more he thought about it that niggle became an itch he couldn't scratch, and he hated himself for it.

It's why he hadn't fought against falling asleep before…he didn't want to face the unfaceable. The way he saw it, if the police came to the house he would have to answer their questions. They'd demand to know who he was and why he was there. He wouldn't be able to lie to them, and thus would tell them the truth. Ultimately, and against all his wishes, he knew they would scoop him up and deposit him back to St. Mary's, no matter what he told them about the hell he'd so recently escaped.

But Tristan had come so far, and he would not be sent back.

Not now! Not ever!

There was only one option, and it was abhorrent. Nothing He must do nothing. He would wait until dawn and leave the house unseen, and when he was safely out of town, and only then, he'd make an anonymous call to the police. It was wrong, and he felt wretched. Bella was a fine woman who deserved better than being left to rot in an already rotting house. But his decision was made.

Something in his aunt's right hand suddenly caught his eye. She clutched a small envelope and with it an old faded photo, its edges curled and both now bent in half from the rigour inflected hand. Prying it loose he saw an image of Bella herself with a young girl on her lap. They smiled as if all the world was safe, and Tristan's heart raced. He had never seen this girl before. Just a few hours earlier she didn't even exist. But now he knew; it was a picture of his sister.

His own name was on the envelope in fine and flourishing handwriting. He sat down to rest legs that could stand no longer, and though he wasn't cold his hands trembled as he unfolded the delicate and worn paper.

*Dear Tristan,*

*Don't be alone any longer, for I am here with you. I know you've suffered, and you suffer still, but don't be afraid, for I hold your hand in the dark. Share your pain with me, and share your suffering, for I have known them both, and I know them still. And together, you and I will walk on, side by side, hand in hand, and no more will we be alone, for in each other we'll find comfort and solace. Be strong my brother, for I watch over you now, as I know you watch over me.*

*Forever by your side,*

*Your sister,*
*Ailla.*

Thunderstruck. That was the effect of that short letter. Just hours ago he believed he was an only child, but now, not only did he have a sister, but a photograph and a personal letter from her. And what a letter! It was written as if she'd known everything about him all along; all the suffering, all the loneliness. And the comforting words she used; so thoughtful, so necessary. If only he had got that letter back when it was first written, how much stronger and less alone he would've felt, and another uprising of anger toward his parents and his current situation threatened a full scale mutiny against his usually passive nature. The pale cheeks that had so often been struck now blazed fire at his father, and he paced the room with his long and agitated strides while silently admonishing his mother.

Internally he seethed, and without knowing it his teeth ground together and his hands scrunched into fists bent on fury. But, and only after his breathing had slowed to a normal rate, he remembered where he was and who lay stricken next to him. That anger at his parents quickly subsided, replaced by shame at himself for the almost hysterical reaction. It was an unwelcome yet timely reminder that his father's poisonous blood gushed through his arteries, and desperate not to become his father's son, in that moment he resolved always to hold dominion over his emotions.

It was amazing to Tristan just how little he'd known about his family, and even more so how they'd managed to keep him so in the dark about his sister. And the letter which Bella had kept safely for him for so many years, well that changed everything. Now there was no longer just the issue of finding his mother, though that was still his primary and overriding ambition. But once they'd had what would surely be a relief filled and heartfelt reunion, then he would do everything he could to find his sister. To first meet Ailla, followed by the reunification of mother, daughter and son, would be the beautiful golden nail in the coffin of his tormented childhood.

Beyond the damp and miserable walls the long day had faded into an early winter dusk, and Tristan's thoughts circled back to his tragic aunt. The decision he'd made about not reporting her death plagued his nerves and conscience, and he was torn between what he should do for her and what he needed to do for himself. Bella should not be left alone and neglected like that. It was simply wrong. But he had considered long and hard and knew he had no choice. Tristan's heart ached for his poor brave aunt, and as much as she deserved better, he too deserved a chance to find his mum...was due his chance at freedom. If he notified the police now, that freedom might be short lived, yet he took little comfort from that and spent a cold and anxious night waiting for the dawn. He clung to his only consolation amongst the debris of what had happened; that wherever she was, he had a sister that loved him.

The milky dawn finally crept out from beneath a stubborn, endless darkness, and after a sleepless few hours Tristan paid his last respects to Bella. He offered a silent prayer, though he didn't believe in God, and had long ago disregarded the miracles of Jesus as Sunday School fairytales. Tristan knew about Sunday School, and his mother had even dared take him once, but when Blyth turned up drunk and caused an embarrassing scene, he was never allowed back. It'd had a bearing on his thoughts about Christianity ever since. But he needed to say something. Stood bedside her bed and with eyes closed, he spoke directly to an aunt he wished he'd known all his life.

"Dear aunt Bella, thank you so much for all the selfless things you and Will did for our family. You stood up to my father more than we ever did, and you were so kind to care for Ailla. The burden...the curse...you carried so lovingly for so long is now gone. On behalf of the three of us, my mum, Ailla and me, I give you our heartfelt gratitude and love. May you at last rest in peace."

Tristan laid down the flowers he brought for his mother and quietly went down stairs. The day was almost upon him. With a heavy heart he closed the door on the worn out old house for the last time, his aunt's inert eyes imprinted into his mind. Yet somehow he knew that behind those eyes was a soul that encouraged him to move on, and to leave his conscience and even memories of her behind. He was doing the right thing, she seemed to say from beyond the grave. *The right thing!*

So move on he did. Unseen and fleet of foot Tristan headed directly out to the highway. What had seemed lifetimes ago since Winston had dropped him off was only thirty six hours, but in that brief time his whole world had changed. So much altered, and so quickly, and as they had so often lately, difficult questions and inevitable doubts surfaced. *Has my mum ever tried to contact my sister, or visa versa?* It seemed impossible they hadn't. *Does Ailla want to be found? How would she feel about a mother who gave her up?*

With Bella gone Tristan was once more alone. But as the cold November rain stung his cheeks and the shivery drop in temperature snuck beneath his clothes, the photo and letter in his chest pocket and his searing determination to find what he sought did their best to warm his heart.

*Chapter Thirty Six*

Numbness afflicted Richard's bones. For several consecutive nights he'd endured the full wrath of the autumn elements, and he was getting desperate. So many times he'd contemplated contacting his family, yet he refused to give in, and although he didn't consider himself a strong or even a brave kid, the last couple of months had made him tough. He was always hungry, and the cold...he never got used to the cold. But he would not go home to Penzance. Not while his dad was around.

For three nights, or maybe it was four, he wasn't sure, Richard had slept beneath an underpass on the outskirts of Southampton. It was dirty and the concrete walls were caked in slimy moss, but at least it kept the incessant rain at bay. Sharing the shelter were a couple of older and seemingly permanent residents who'd been kind to him and shared what little food they had, and despite the cold and bleak environment, he felt welcome.

One man in particular intrigued him. During the evenings in that tiny community, Richard sat huddled in an old blanket and listened while the man told tales from what he labeled his 'gloriously inglorious' past. He'd spent many years living on the streets, he told them, yet despite that Richard had never met a happier, more content man in his life. The haggard grey beard and shabby clothes betrayed his handsome face, and his intense eyes shone with a sparkle that belied his surroundings. And when he spoke, people listened, rapt at his adventurous tales and eager for more.

Something about the man, with his erudite speech and graceful manner, seemed wildly out of place in that gloomy underpass, but Richard was grateful to him and his friends for their hospitality, and at least for a while he was happy to stick around. He knew he could learn from these people about life and living on the streets, and in particular, he thought, the manifestly wise old man.

But more important than any of that was that he felt safe. These few chaps that shared the bridge were as nice as anybody he'd known, and the occasional new face that came by was always welcomed by the residents as he himself had been. The days were peaceful and calm...fun, even, and despite the unlikeliest of scenarios, Richard was happy.


*Chapter Thirty Seven*

The exhibition space was now almost ready, after Ailla and Jack had spent a giggly day adding the finishing touches. Now exhausted, they sat against a wall an empty wine bottle nearby and another well underway. On the opposite wall hung a painting of the boy whose face appeared often in Ailla's recent works, and though the late afternoon light was dim there was an unmistakable sadness etched into the boy's face.

"I'm so proud of you," said Jack as he turned to face his love. "You've worked so hard these last few weeks, and I know it'll be a roaring success."

Ailla in turn faced him, and her smile was radiant. "I hope you're right. And thanks for all your help and support. It means so much, and I couldn't...no, I definitely wouldn't, have done it without you."

He returned the smile, but as she returned her gaze to the boy opposite Jack fell silent, and for a few moments they both just sat enjoying the quiet. Finally he looked once again at the pretty young lady beside him, and with a deep breath he took both of Ailla's hands in his own. His pulse raced.

"You mean so much to me, and I've been thinking... well, we've been together six months this weekend, and you're everything to me. Ailla Annis... I want you to be my..."

Suddenly she turned her face away, cutting him short a second before completing his momentous declaration. She was going to tell him about the boy in the painting, the secret she'd kept for so long, but out of the blue came his proposal and she couldn't bear to hear it. It's what she wanted, what she had wanted for a long time, but she was scared. There were so many reasons to say yes, and none at all to say no, but despite that, she knew that it was no she'd say, and that was an answer Jack didn't deserve. Ailla had her reasons, as weak as she believed they were, but for now she'd keep those reasons to herself.

For so long she stayed silent. Too long. And poor Jack's heart ached.

"Ailla...what is it? What's wrong?" He gently turned her face towards him, and in the soft light he saw silent silvery tears stream like liquid mercury down her cheeks.

*Chapter Thirty Eight*

Once more the foul weather followed him east, and the rain was so heavy that he could hardly see the natural beauty of the countryside from the car window. *Will it ever stop?* he wondered. After two hours of painfully slow progress due to the conditions, Tristan's latest ride terminated on the green outskirts of Southampton. He had only one plan now; get to London, and ducking into the first café he found, he looked at his map while practically hugging a mug of tea for warmth. Still a long way to go.

But, if he hitched the coast to Brighton…three or four hours, with a little luck…there would then be just a short hop north, straight into the capital.

His priority would always be to find his mother. But the revelation of his sister loomed larger by the moment, and he took out the photo and her letter. They looked alike, he couldn't deny it. But she was so pretty. *Does that mean I'm handsome?* he mused, and smiled bashfully at the ridiculous thought.

Then like a beautiful thunderbolt it struck him. For long years Tristan had dreamt of an unknown girl whose face was almost always obscured to keep her identity a mystery. A few days ago he'd had the weirdest sensation that it was a non-existent sister he dreamed of. He didn't have any siblings, so he figured it was exactly that…just a dream, a fantasy even. But now it was so obvious. The girl really was his sister, and she'd existed all along. But there was something else that troubled him, though it was of a more curious concern; how could the dream girl and his sister look so alike? Coincidence, or some kind of sixth sense? He had no idea, but the two girls were undeniably one and the same.

This profound knowledge gave Tristan a renewed purpose and confidence about the search ahead, and he no longer felt alone. He gulped down the last of his tea and paid his bill with a smile, and, stepping outside the café strode forward with intent, oblivious to the rain and ignorant of the wind howling at his ears. Tristan was on a mission.

Despite the energized pace at which he'd set out, Tristan hadn't gone far when suddenly he stopped. Something had registered in his sub-consciousness, some hazy notion of recognition, and he looked around him but saw no one or nothing of interest, and shook his head, bemused. But on a hunch he retraced his last few steps, and turned a corner just as a flash of red slipped from view, apparently in a hurry.

A vague image began to take shape. When it solidified, he couldn't believe it. The grainy black and white image so often seen on the missing boy poster slowly melted into colour...red! It was Richard White.

*Was it really him?* In reality, it was unlikely, and probably just his under-developed imagination trying to make up for lost time, but he set off after the red jacket anyway. He reached the next bend at a jog and turned but the street was deserted. But then, over in the far corner where a bridge rose up and over a wide highway, there it was, a glimpse of red, and he raced across the street towards that brilliant burst of colour so clearly projected against the sea of endless grey.

Tristan slowed as he approached, and from a distance he saw half a dozen people sat in a tight group sheltered beneath the bridge. The tempting heat of a fire blazed in an old oil drum, and flickered bright on the darkened concrete ceiling. Small piles of belongings sat nestled under the dry eaves, and he counted six people, five men and a woman. And standing beside them was the jacket. In a second Tristan knew that his intuition was correct, and instantly recognised the boy from the posters; Richard White.

He hesitated, unsure how to proceed. Because Richard was on the run, Tristan assumed he wouldn't want to be recognised, so he took his time, and as he stood there thinking of how he could approach the runaway, the sad and forlorn face of Anne-Marie drifted into his thoughts. Richard's sister was so frantic about her little brother's safety and whereabouts, that Tristan felt morally obliged to take a chance and approach. In such inclement weather he had good reason to seek refuge in the shadows of their overpass, and he made his way over.

"Hello there." A couple of heads turned. "Hello, do you mind if I huddle under your bridge for a while? I won't stay long." He had to shout to be heard above the din of the deluge that echoed off the concrete above and below. An old man smiled and waved him over.

"It's not *our* bridge," he shouted in kindly reply, "Come up by the fire and make yourself at home."

Tristan stepped onto the raised level and out of the rain.

"Welcome to our castle, young man."

Paper cups of tea were already being handed out, and Tristan accepted one gratefully, soon relishing the warmth on his cold hands. He'd been on the road a week now, and seen other homeless people. But these were the first he'd spoken to, and was surprised by how receptive they were, though he didn't really know why. He was drawn to the old fellow with the beard, who impressed him greatly, and from a handsome yet weathered face shone green eyes that sparkled. Two middle aged chaps sat close by, rugged men that looked as if they'd lived outside for decades, and just behind them sat a young woman of perhaps twenty. Beside her, Richard. No doubt about it. He looked tired and pale, and very thin, but otherwise he seemed to be holding up, and Tristan was inspired to see that such a young boy could make it so far alone and without being found.

Tristan desperately wanted to speak to Richard, especially after his promise to Anne-Marie, but he bided his time so as not to frighten him away. Besides, he could probably learn a lot from this kid, and moreover, though more in the realms of fantasy, they might even become friends.

To have found Richard there, of all places, under a drab

and dreary bridge on the fringes of a town that he had no plan to visit, was a huge coincidence. But he'd met Anne-Marie randomly too, and it was clear to Tristan that despite how vast he believed England to be, not to mention the world, the importance of luck and the unknown potential of fate would play a big part in him finding his own lost treasure.

*Chapter Thirty Nine*

Three days had slid by since Mark Trescothwick's visit to the cottage, and not a single drop of poison had passed Blyth's lips. With a mixture of shame and relief he'd watched on passively while Mark burned his shed to the ground, and the swirling inferno that had risen into the autumn blackness reeked from the fumes of his stockpiled alcohol. He told himself, had convinced himself, that it didn't matter that there wasn't any drink available; he wouldn't have touched it anyway. At least that's what he believed, and with no one else about to bear witness he was his own barometer of truth.

Those last days were spent in an almost meditative state, long hours sat contemplating life and how he'd ruined his own and the lives of his family. *How did it all become so bad? How have I become so vile?* He felt alone, desperately alone, but it was as it should be, the natural order of things after everything he'd done. Divine justice.

The beach as he walked felt softer beneath his feet than usual, as if trying to suck him down, drag him into its depths where he'd be lost and forgotten forever. But Blyth knew that those fates were coming to him soon anyway, were almost upon him, and he didn't need an early burial to be forsaken.

That reality, that his last years on Earth would be spent in pitiful isolation amid rasping loneliness, made him shiver more than the biting cold ever could. And shiver he did, as he imagined how intolerable life must have been for his wife and son under his absolute control. He had put them through hell on a daily basis for weeks and months and years, and it was time to face up to his heinous crimes and take responsibility for his hideous actions.

In his own mind Blyth had often blamed the circumstances of his life for his unjust behaviour, and he attributed his weakness for violence to the drinking issues which in turn were caused by the terrible bouts of bad luck he suffered. He'd always hidden behind those excuses, however valid he believed them to be, or at least he persuaded himself they were valid. But beneath it all he was not a good person. He knew he was weak and cowardly at best, and at worst a manipulative bully.

But that wasn't really the worst of it. Though he fought in vain to erase it from his mind, the memory of his daughter and what he'd done to her haunted him constantly. *How could I have hurt her like that, a tiny innocent child?* Blyth knew they were right to take the baby from him, but he also knew they'd made a mistake by not reporting him to the authorities. If they had, he believed, then his family's years of constant suffering probably would've been avoided.

And what of Ailla now? He wanted desperately to know where and how she was, and if she suffered any long term issues because of his abuse. But Blyth had long ago forfeited any rights to fatherhood. His immorality had bred so much pain into the lives of so many people; his beautiful wife Kerra. His daughter Ailla and son Tristan. His poor sister Bella, and her stricken husband Will. So much torment, so much pain. And he himself, he wasn't happy, and hadn't been so in almost two decades. And it was his fault. His own misery, and the misery he wrought over his entire family, was all down to him.

It was way too little and way too late, but after years of ignorant and drunken denial Blyth would finally accept what he'd done during his unholy life. The question now, was, would he ever be able to make it up to them all? But even as the question formed, a cold reality struck him; he didn't know where a single member of his family was, not one, and the realisation wounded him deeply. They had all left him, and with good reason. The isolation he created for Kerra and the boy, he understood that now. Was it a coincidence Kerra named their daughter Ailla, the Celtic word for *isolated*. Perhaps she knew what was to happen, the name symbolic. He didn't know, and in that instant Blyth truly felt that he no longer knew anything.

His constant truculence and the living conditions he'd contrived for his wife and son haunted his every step, but unlike the living ghosts of Kerra and Tristan, those ghostly echoes would never leave. But humbled as he now was, Blyth took a measure of comfort in embracing his comeuppance, and that manifested loneliness he faced would be a worthy penance.

*Chapter Forty*

Wind and rain lashed all around, but the bridge gave good protection from a storm devoted to misery. Tristan huddled close to the fire, and the chat among the group was pleasant. When he was asked about the whys and wherefores as to how he found himself on the streets, he politely denied them the details, and in turn they didn't push him into answers, for which he was grateful. Tristan sensed a healthy amount of quiet respect among that small contingent of unfortunates, with compassion and empathy the currency of the homeless.

Though he didn't give away much about himself, Tristan did learn about the others. The sad young woman had recently fled her vicious boyfriend. She arrived only yesterday and rarely spoke, only enough to say that she felt safer among those strangers than she had in years and was thankful for their acceptance. The two middle aged men were long term street dwellers who had each battled issues with various vices but were thriving among the non-judgmental people of the streets. They were comfortable on the road, and had been happy there at the bridge for several weeks.

And there was the old fellow with the beard. The others referred to him as 'Tramp,' and despite its negative connotations, he didn't seem to mind at all. Tristan couldn't help himself.

"May I ask, why do they call you Tramp?"

The man needed little persuasion to launch an eloquent rhetoric.

"My friends," he began, and his voice was strong. "Society labeled me a tramp, and the authorities confirmed it. They judged me, and presumed to know me, yet knew nothing of my past. Their ignorance as to the reasons why myself and many of my fellows here are homeless is shameful, and rather than support us, they discriminate against us. Rather than feed and shelter us, they declare us problematic. In their wisdom they labeled us freeloaders, when many of us have never asked for anything. So, my dear boy, this country of ours believes me a tramp, so that is what I am. I am 'Tramp,' and it's my pleasure to make your acquaintance."

Tristan was intrigued. At first glance Tramp looked well over sixty, and behind that scruffy beard was a handsome face from which green eyes shone like lustrous beacons and sparkled with an intensity both alluring and magical. He seemed to be the unofficial leader of that band of vagabonds, but when he spoke it was always in the calm and approachable tone of a wise patriarch. And his words carried weight. Tristan liked him immediately.

Slowly warming up due to the radiating fire and a donated blanket, Tristan listened intently as Tramp's poetic voice told romantic stories of life on the streets and of long ago lived adventures. And not once did he speak negatively about his predicament. They all clearly respected the man, and he understood why, for he too was in awe of the erudite, warm and father like figure before him.

But mostly Tristan wanted to speak to the shy young kid in the red jacket. He'd uttered barely a word in hours, and when he did it was in a painfully timid manner. But Tristan sensed an astute individual beneath the shy and cautious exterior, and believed him to be a tough, determined boy...tougher than he considered himself, anyway.

One or two of the bridge dwellers stood up to prepare more tea, and seeing his chance Tristan took a seat next to Richard. The younger boy mumbled a softly spoken greeting, and Tristan held out his hand, which Richard took reluctantly, as if it might be a snake. But when Tristan proffered a smile, he smiled back. Tristan began with casual small talk, asking subtle and covert questions though he believed he already knew the answers. He first had to earn the boy's trust before he could tell him about meeting his sister Anne-Marie, due to a very real concern that he might take off. But once he had sensed Richard relax a little, he decided to reveal his secret.

"Richard, I've something to tell you, but please, hear me out, okay?"

A momentary look of concern flashed in his eyes, but slowly he nodded.

"I met your sister, Anne-Marie. She goes out in her car everyday to look for you, and gave me a ride after mistaking me for you."

Richard looked back in disbelief, and for a moment, Tristan expected him to run. Swiftly he raised his hand to his chest in an, '*it's okay, you can trust me*' gesture, and Richard settled. A few seconds passed, but finally, and with teardrops forming, he spoke in a cracking voice.

"How is she? Does she hate me because I left her alone? Is she worried about me?"

"Believe me, she doesn't hate you. Anne-Marie loves you, and is terribly worried. Every day since you disappeared she's been driving around the south looking for you, because she never believed what the police said, that you drowned in the storm. She just misses you, Richard."

Once the tears started they wouldn't stop. First of all, he was overjoyed his sister didn't hate him for leaving, and that she hadn't believed the police and knew he was alive gave him immense relief. But there was also a deep sadness. What Tristan had told him proved his parents had given him up for dead. He hated his father, and didn't care about what he thought, but he was devastated about his mother. *Really? She believes I'm dead?* The boy was clearly distraught, and now Tristan questioned his wisdom of telling him.

Tramp was sitting quietly, observing the two youngsters in conversation. He saw that Richard was upset, but once the weeping had subsided he took over a cup of tea. The man exuded a constitutional calmness, and within a minute Richard smiled his gratitude. Tramp hadn't uttered a single word.

Tristan took the opportunity to mention his vow to Anne-Marie.

"When me and your sister parted ways I made her a promise. She was so worried about you, and so sad, and I just wanted to encourage her and give her some hope, even though I didn't really believe I'd ever see you, so I told her that if I ever came across you I'd try and persuade you to contact her, and that if you wouldn't, then I would."

There was real sincerity in both Tristan's face and voice, and Richard knew he had only good intentions.

"But I really think you should contact her yourself," he continued, "it would mean so much for her to hear your voice, even if it's just to tell her you're okay." Tristan placed his hand on Richard's arm, and the two of them knew that each could be trusted. "Will you do it?"

A pensive quality pinched Richard's features as he considered his difficult options, and clearly he was torn. But the boy loved his sister more than anything, and was guilt ridden to have caused her so much worry. Ultimately that swayed his decision, and he and Tristan made a plan. Tristan would call Richard's home first, and if Anne-Marie answered then Richard would speak to her. He didn't want to call himself, just in case one of his parents answered. He never wanted to speak to them again. Also, he would insist Anne-Marie make a promise to keep their contact secret. She had to.

Tomorrow. Being a Monday, his father would be at work. They would call then.

With the welcome and surprising news that his sister

believed he was alive and was actively looking for him, Richard at last cast aside some of his defenses. A lot of the reason he was so subdued was the guilt he felt over leaving her alone, but now Tristan had come along and told him about her searches and how she believed he was okay, the world was suddenly a much brighter place. And not just for Richard. The two boys chatted on, and they soon realized their lives ran along many parallels; abusive fathers, no friends, dark and dingy futures. They didn't know it yet but the signs were definitely there; destiny had brought them together and, aside from Anne-Marie, soon they would be each other's first and only friend.

Against all the odds the atmosphere under the bridge felt like a party, and the centre-piece of the festivities was the old oil drum. Like some fiery elixir, the blaze that roared constantly radiated heat and energy into the group, and as stories were told and songs were sung as if beside a friendly campfire, Tristan felt strangely at home. There would always be hunger living on the streets, and it would obviously get colder during the night, but he wanted to spend more time in their company, and was keen to get to know Richard better.

They were a group of virtual strangers, but he had never felt safer and more welcome anywhere in his life. *I guess that's why Tramp called it 'the castle,'* he mused with an inward smile. He would remain vigilant...the incident at the hotel taught him that. But the smile on his face was wide and, he hoped, he'd made his first real friend.

Hours had passed, and without Tristan realising it night had fallen beyond the castle walls. The perpetual rain had caused the near side of the road to flood, effectively trapping him under the concrete shelter, unless he wanted to wade knee deep into the darkness. And he was delighted…a real life castle with a working moat. Tramp and the other two men were getting steadily drunk on bottles of cheap red wine, and Tristan soon learned that when they did have a little money, they would rather spend it on alcohol than food.

"It helps warm our cockles," they chuckled, "and makes us forget about our miserable, hopeless plight." They jested with tongue in cheek, but for the two middle aged men it was probably true.

"Well, if you lot are miserable," said Tristan, "then I'd better stay too, because I've never had so much fun." And that was also true.

As they listened to Tramp's tales, while ably aided and abetted by his two thirsty cohorts, Tristan and Richard were in fits of giggles, and only Winston had ever made him laugh as much as he was then. He truly was enjoying himself, and he was smiling, not the weak smile of someone who wasn't really listening, nor was it the fake smile of someone expected to do so. No, it was the smile of a young man who for the very first time in his life was understanding freedom.

He recalled standing in the cottage's garden, watching the gulls soar effortlessly above, and envying them their freedom. And now, there he was, free from the lonely and restrictive…destructive…life he'd known just weeks before, and at last aware what it meant to be free. He didn't have to stay there at the castle. If he chose to, he could simply stand up and walk away and nobody would try to stop him. He'd have to negotiate the moat of course. But if he wanted to jump on a train to London, or Glasgow...anywhere, well, he could. In theory he could do anything and everything he wanted to do, and for a boy so long imprisoned in a cycle of violence and darkness, it was a wildly enlightening notion.

Tristan did have obligations now, though they were self imposed. He had to find his mother. He missed her terribly, and he owed it to both her and himself to try his utmost with his search. And after that, his second mission; track down his sister. He was still coming to terms with the fact that she even existed, a sister kept secret from him for sixteen years.

But he was starting to realise that life was full of strange events and coincidences, and actually finding his sister would be like a kind of miracle. Long ago he had stopped believing in magic and religious myths, his belief being beaten from him and his mother by the loose fists of a drunken father. But he couldn't deny that to actually meet his sister would certainly seem like a miracle.

Spirits were high in the castle as Tramp took centre stage behind the drum, the fire's glow adding to his already lambent persona.

"What do you boys think I used to do, you know, before I chose to become a tramp?"

"Pardon?" Tristan was incredulous. "You mean you chose to become a tramp?"

"Of course I did, and why not? Very sagacious of me, and I don't mind saying so."

The boys didn't understand such a big word, but it sounded good, and they believed him regardless.

"It's a great lifestyle. I come and go, whenever and wherever I please. I travel all over the place, and I get to meet interesting people...like you. Like all of you." Tramp looked around, and addressed each one of them individually. He spoke with passion and from the heart, and with such earnestness that his truth held power.

"Look here, lads. Peter, a hero among men. Pete was a firefighter in London, but society and the government let him down, and he was forced to fend for himself. He saved the lives of many men, women and children over a long career, but sadly suffered a bad leg injury on the job and had to retire early. Do you think the authorities under the tory government help people like Peter? No! The government constantly turn their back on real men and women, the ones who risk their own lives on a daily basis to save those of strangers they've never met." Tramp waved his arm respectfully in Peter's direction, and raised his paper cup of wine in a toast. "True heroes."

The small group clapped and whistled their approval, and Peter tipped his hat in bashful recognition. Tramp had them rapt.

"Next we have Old John here. Johnny fought in World War Two, and is a decorated soldier. He retired from active service but, unqualified beyond his army training, Johnny couldn't find a job. With no support from the government, another of our heroes wandered down the wrong dismal path to drinking in order to fend off his depression…a more powerful adversary than the Jerries, right Johnny?"

"That's right, Tramp," replied the war vet, and raised his cup with a wink. Tramp continued.

"We all know it's wrong, turning to the bottle, but it's an easy and all too common choice. Society labeled him a lazy drunk, but it was that same society that created his problems in the first place. Where were they when he needed their help? Nowhere, hiding behind their bureaucratic desks and broad sheet newspapers, while the rest of the country struggled on. Well Johnny old friend, we're all here for you now."

Johnny smiled his wide, gappy smile, and took another swig from his cup. Again the band of strays applauded, and all eyes were on Tramp as he pushed on.

All eyes, that is, except Tristan's, who now sat lost in

thought. At the mention of alcohol related problems, his mind turned to his father who for so long was a slave to the whisky. All his family's problems had stemmed from that, and Tristan wondered if he should have more empathy with his father's issues. *Perhaps it wasn't all his fault?* Tramp said Johnny drank to escape depression, and Tristan felt sure his dad did the same. But had Johnny continuously beaten up his family? Beat a scared and defenseless wife and kids? He would never ask, but somehow he doubted it.

"Tristan…Hey, son? Are you with us?" Tramp's serene voice drew him from his melancholy, and he looked up at the old man.

"I'm sorry, I was just thinking about someone."

"Are you okay lad?" The friendly old timer oozed tranquility, and Tristan's smile returned.

"Yes, I'm fine thanks."

"So Tramp, how about you? What's your story?" It was Peter that probed, though he knew the story well and asked only for the benefit of the boys. Tramp's eyes sparkled like emeralds in the firelight, and he bellowed a laugh that was loud and strong.

"Well my friends, I thought you'd never ask. I was deposited into this world, feet first and screaming like the proverbial devil, in Wheatley, a small village in Oxfordshire, the first and only child of a ridiculous Reverend and his puerile wife, in the monumental year of nineteen hundred and one, monumental because Queen Victoria died, and well, because I was born. I've given away my age, I realise, but remember, age is just a number, never a curse, and I feel as young as I did as a child and my heart beats just as strongly…stronger, in fact!" Tramp beat his chest like King Kong, which raised a chuckle in the group.

"Anyway, where was I? Oh yes, Oxford! So I was a prodigious young boy and a gifted student, so of course my parents had high hopes for me, with father fully expecting me to follow in his holier than thou footsteps to the clergy and to God. I had other ideas however, and spent all my free time reading the brilliance of Darwin and Spencer. I knew very young that I wanted to be a science or philosophy teacher, and as you might imagine, that was much to the chagrin of my father's peace of mind." The words streamed from Tramp as if he'd told his story a thousand times. Tristan thought he probably had. Peter and Johnny knew it, though they never tired of the telling.

"I eventually graduated from Oxford with a Master's Degree in Scientific Theory, but by that time my father had practically disowned me. So very Christian of him, wouldn't you agree?"

A ripple of laughter echoed beneath the bridge, and Tramp's wide eyes seemed to illuminate the very air around him. The man was in his element.

"Aged twenty five I became the youngest ever Professor at Oxford, and probably the most handsome too," he added with a wink, "and was all set for an inglorious career, quashing the imagined words of God and the fairytales of our saviour, Mr. Jesus Christ. Eventually though, the good fellows at Oxford felt I became too partisan, and asked me to tone down my rhetoric, at least in my lectures, but I would never dilute my beliefs and kowtow to high paying parents or archaic lords. So I quit!"

Again, whoops of appreciation filled the air. Tramp surged on.

"But I loved to teach, and felt sure I would find another university to lecture at and, quite frankly, life at Oxford was stale. I was thirty years old and needed a new challenge, so I took a year's sabbatical, and like some wealthy hippy I travelled the world. I leaned so much and met so many inspiring people, and I knew I would never be the same again. Despite my own humanist beliefs, religion and its art fascinated me, and on my travels, I did all sorts. I knelt with the monks in Burma and painted rocks with the Australian aborigines. I bathed with saddhus in Varanasi, and hiked to Machu Picchu in The Andes. I was becoming enlightened to the mysterious ways of the world and wanted so much to share it all with my students. But when I returned I was in for a shock. My wise and blessed father was disgusted by who I'd become, and sent letters to all the major universities in England. He told them I was a blaspheming homosexual, hell-bent on corrupting their precious students. Well, my brethren and sistren, nineteen thirties England was ultra conservative, and so my career as a passionate and dedicated lecturer was over. What my father told them was an outright lie, but that's irrelevant…gay or straight, man or woman, white or black; I was a damn good professor that no one would employ. Oh, have no doubt, my father sinned, and may he forever burn in infernal damnation." A wide and mischievous grin spread across his glowing face, his eyes ablaze as they reflected both the fire's glow and radiated his own fire that burned within.

"But if you think that setback prevented me from sharing my knowledge with others, then think again. I've been teaching cultural philosophy ever since." Tramp spread out his arms before him to illustrate the point. "And you, my friends, are my newest students."

The group erupted in raucous applause that echoed back at them from the castle walls. And Tramp milked it. It mattered little that one or more of his audience remained quietly skeptical about the authenticity of his story, because all bar none were enthralled, and the two young boys had hung on every single word.

Tristan believed everything he'd heard, but even if he didn't, Tramp had still demonstrated that there was another world out there, a world beyond the expectations of others, beyond the confinement of family and tradition, a world in which you sought rather than await your destiny, and where everyone's destiny was unique only to them.

"You know, when I was young I had such high and lofty ambitions, things I wanted to achieve, places I wanted to go, things I wanted to say. But to tell you the truth, I was so determined to rush headlong into the future that I missed out for so long on the precious privilege of living in the moment. Way too long. So believe me when I say that life starts today, boys, and then tomorrow it starts again. Live everyday as if it's your last, and then, one day in the distant future when you look back, you'll have lived ten thousand lifetimes."

A philosophical hush descended as the avid listeners absorbed what the apparent sage had said.

"But to finish today's class, my friends, I want to share with you my favourite poem. It was written over two thousand years ago, and is so powerful and important that the whole world should know it. When I first read it I was enthralled, and quite honestly it changed my life forever. It was written in antiquity by a Roman philosopher poet who went by the name of Horace, and it became my mantra. To this day it remains my motivation. Here goes;

*'Happy the man, and happy he alone,*
*He who can call today his own,*
*He who, secure within, can say,*

*Tomorrow do thy worst, for I have lived today.*
*Be fair or foul, or rain or shine,*
*The joys I have possessed, in spite of fate, are mine,*
*Not heaven itself upon the past has power,*
*But what has been, has been, and I have had my hour.'"*

Tristan and Richard were as spellbound by the words as if Horace himself had spoken them. For Tristan it was like a bombshell. Life was for living, pure and simple, and should be lived, regardless of the consequences. The poem suggested that as long as you did all you could to live a good, meaningful life, one day at a time, then nothing anyone did could ever take that away from you. The simple yet revelatory words showed him with clarity that his life truly was his own.

And it was true. Ever since his mother had left, only he had power over his actions. Only he had decided what to do. Only he had confronted his father.

Tristan was now the true master of his destiny.

Though the fire burned close by, the two boys huddled together for warmth. Tristan's eyelids pressed heavy, and sleep came easily, comfortable in the knowledge that he was safe, and he slept throughout the night until the early commuter traffic roared above and roused him from sleep. The other members of the castle community were still buried beneath their tatty blankets, and sometime during the night they'd been joined by a couple more drifters. To Tristan's surprise, the fire still burned.

His last act before sleep was to ask Richard if he would travel with him to London. He wasn't sure what response to expect, because he knew his new friend didn't want to be found. But he was delighted with the speed and certainty of Richard's simple answer; *Yes please.*

Once the others were roused, they all enjoyed a simple

breakfast of tea and flame toasted stale bread.

"The breakfast of Kings and fit for a castle," declared Johnny as he handed it over. After, the boys thanked Tramp and the others for sharing their shelter as well as their stories, fare-thee-wells were said, and as the boys stepped out into a bright new day, the rain gone and not a moat in sight, Tristan couldn't shake the strange feeling that his and Tramp's paths would one day cross again. He knew, somehow, that there was more to the enigmatic old man than met the eye.

They climbed the bridge's steep embankment to the highway above, and Tristan held out their new sign.

It was plain and simple: 'LONDON.'

*Chapter Forty One*

Quite simply, Ailla was overwhelmed. The very first exhibition of her own work had been an unprecedented success, and visitors to the gallery had purchased almost every painting on display. She herself had little interest in actually making money from her own art, preferring to help other young artists further their careers. Thus, she'd labeled each piece with an extravagant price, certain she wouldn't sell anything. So surprised was she by her success, that when the last guest left the gallery and she and Jack were alone, she jumped around giggling with joy. Jack though wasn't at all surprised.

"I knew it would go this well, I just knew it," he told her as she danced around him, spilling wine as she went.

"I just can't believe it...it's...well, it's amazing." Worn out, she slumped once more in the same spot as the previous night while Jack refilled their glasses. Looking down at her from the facing wall was the same boy, his joyless expression the antithesis of the evening's celebratory atmosphere, and despite plenty of keen customers it was the one painting Ailla chose not to sell. For a while the two of them sat in quietude, Jack waiting patiently for her to enlighten him about the boy. He was sure she knew who it was. Finally, Ailla broke the silence.

"I'm so sorry for last night," she said, "but it was a very emotional moment for me. Life has changed so much since I was a kid, and you asking me to marry you, well, it's almost like the last piece of the jigsaw." A doleful vision of melancholy spread over Ailla's face. "I've been meaning to tell you about that boy up there." She pointed to the child opposite, and as she did a solo tear slipped over her cheek.

"I've kept a few secrets from you, but please believe me that it's not because of you, the sweetest most kind person I know. And they're not even really secrets…it's just…well…it was always too painful to talk about until now."

Jack edged closer to his love, and squeezed her hand gently within his.

"You needn't explain anything to me, it's okay," he responded, and his voice was soft and sincere. But Ailla was ready; it was time to unload her burden.

"Thanks, but it's okay…I'm okay. That boy…he's my brother."

Jack turned to her, expecting more tears, though the couple that did fall were caught by a smile.

"You have a brother? That's great Ailla, and he looks just like you."

"Yes, he does, but that's the weird thing…I've never even seen him." The smile faded a little, but her resolve held, and over the next hour Ailla explained to Jack all the missing details from her past; about her parents, and the abuse; about her aunt Bella, and her subsequent guardians; about New York, and why she returned to England; and lastly, about her brother, and the guilt she always carried internally regarding her good fortune and his almost certain lack of it.

Jack was amazed by a story that was such an undulating passage of ups and downs leading all the way to Brighton. She went on.

"It seems so long ago now, but I remember it like it was yesterday. It was my sixteenth birthday and I was feeling especially sad about the brother I'd been denied, and was so worried about what he might be going through. I was in New York then, and, far removed from all that torment, I just had to do something, so I wrote a letter. I just tried to explain that whatever it was he was going through, there was someone in the world who was thinking about him. With no address other than my wonderful aunt Bella's, that's where I sent it, hopeful that somehow she could forward it on." Her eyes closed as if in deep sorrow. "But I don't know if he ever got that letter, or if it even arrived? I don't even know if..."

She broke off, and her breaths came in short, panting gasps. It took her a few moments to calm down, and when she looked up at Jack he saw only pain and anxiety in her wide and heartbroken eyes. "Oh Jack...I don't even know if he's alive."

Jack wrapped Ailla up in his arms and comforted her the best he could, trying to share and thus ease her pain. Their conversation continued late into the night, as questions were asked and answered, and occasional teardrops wiped away. Ultimately, and with Jack's heartfelt support, Ailla's deep store of guilt, though not entirely lifted, was considerably lighter. Most importantly, they resolved to try and make contact with the boy, and though he probably had no idea she existed, they would try.

Ailla was genuinely moved by Jack's obvious love and compassion, and it only confirmed to her what she'd always known about him. She stood and grabbed him by the hand.

"Jack, now you know everything there is to know about me. I'm sorry I kept those things from you, but I know you understand why I did. Do you still love me?"

"I've always loved you, and now that I know your story, I love you even more. You are truly amazing Ailla, and I'm a very lucky man."

"Well in that case, Lucky Jack, isn't there something you wanted to ask me?"

*Chapter Forty Two*

Mollie was missing. Four days she'd been gone, and Kerra was frantic, especially after the nightmare she'd had about her friend's dead body. No one had seen or heard from her, and in her heart she knew something terrible had happened. She even went down to the factory to ask Billy Boy if he knew anything. He said he hadn't, but she noticed a dark look pass across his narrow, scheming eyes, and she wanted to push him further. But that snake of a man was nasty and unpredictable, and she was afraid of him and his equally shifty sidekicks, so although she felt sure he was hiding something she had little choice but to let it go. Kerra had learned that the police in the area could be just as shady and corrupt as any East End gang, but if Mollie hadn't shown up by the following evening she would report her friend as missing.

It was barely mid-afternoon, but despite the hour Kerra

was tucked in bed, the only place she could stay warm. She was broke, and there'd been no heating for a week... so cold inside she could even see her own breath. The factories weren't hiring and the pantry was devoid of food...things were getting desperate.

Worse still, at least to her ears, were the street rumors, as caliginous as the East End streets themselves; that more and more girls had turned to prostitution. But Kerra couldn't believe Mollie would do that, not with her sharp wit and brains, and so much else in her favor. Then again, her friend as good as intimated that if it really came to it, she might, and thoughts of her stripped and bloodied body replayed in her mind like some macabre horror movie.

Kerra dozed fitfully for the rest of the day, but at five o'clock she awoke to the sound of the flat door squeaking open. Standing there, in all her fiery glory, was Mollie, and she was grinning from ear to ear.

"My god, you're back. I'm so relieved. I thought you... you know, you'd done something stupid."

"Maybe I did," came the sharp reply, and with a wicked smirk, Mollie emptied her bag onto the bed. Kerra's breath caught in her throat as she stared at the piles of cash in front of her.

"It's a monkey, before you ask, five hundred of your finest English pounds."

"But where did you get so much money? How did you...you didn't! Did you?"

"Listen love, times are hard, especially round 'ere. Needs must, my girl, needs must! We need food, and we must eat. We need heat before we freeze in this ice box of a flat, and the factories are all laying off. We need to survive, and you need to be ready for when your boy arrives. I won't steal, and I'll never beg! However, I do have some tools that can still perform a decent job, and believe me, there are plenty of willing customers out there who'll pay handsomely for the services I can provide." Mollie cast her eyes over Kerra's body, though it was buried in the sheets. "And if I might say, sweetie, looks like you're packing a fairly complete set of wasted tools under that shabby old blanket of yours."

"But…I can't believe it…I thought…I was worried about you."

Mollie saw that Kerra was struggling, and tried a less humorous approach.

"Listen love, sometimes a girl's got to do what a girl's got to do, and anyway, it's hardly the first time. It's not a regular thing, mind you, and only ever as a last resort. And let's be honest, we really needed some money, right?" Mollie grabbed another bag from the floor, and took a seat on the bed. With raised eyebrows and a devious smile that dared Kerra to turn her down, she asked, "Hungry?"

"What? Sorry, yes. Yes, I'm hungry."

"Of course you are love…me too." Mollie laid out several boxes from the bag; chicken balti; lamb korma; a giant container of saffron rice; freshly cooked naan breads; two bottles of thunderbird, a cheap wine as fiery as Mollie herself. It was a feast, and as Kerra's belly growled it all smelled like manna from food heaven.

She looked on, amazed, but it was against her morals to accept food bought from the spoils of prostitution, and she considered a long moment. Yet hunger is a powerful and provocative force, and her hollow stomach soon got the better of her fading morals, and as they feasted, morally flawed Mollie filled her in on the details.

*Chapter Forty Three*

As the undulating grassy downs of Sussex flashed by unnoticed, the two new friends chatted unhindered as they rode east in the back of a farmer's pick-up truck. A mutual trust had soon formed between them, a connection based upon understanding and shared childhood miseries. Their conversation though reflected the polarities of their otherwise similar experiences, with one boy longing to have attended school, and the other saying he had hated every moment of his. They laughed at the contradictions, each sympathetic to the other's reality. Yet neither boy had ever felt more positive about the future than they did then, both exulted that for now, at least, they were headed into it together.

A little after noon, and they had thanked their overall clad chauffeur and were striding the last two miles into Brighton on foot, when Richard soon spotted the ubiquitous red of a public phone box. He shot Tristan a glance, but his new friend's smile and nod confirmed that he'd seen it too. Lunchtime. It was a good time to call Richard's house. His father should be out at work, and his mother wouldn't become suspicious if a random boy called asking for Anne-Marie. They leaned on the red but rusting phone box, and Tristan appraised his slightly younger friend, who seemed unsure, perhaps unwilling to make the call. Tristan tried to encourage him.

"You really do look like her, you know, except she's far prettier...and I've seen more muscle in a sparrow's leg than you've got."

They both grinned, and Tristan rested a reassuring hand on Richard's shoulder.

"Look, she really loves you, Richie, and she looked so

sad and worried when I saw her. As long as she believes you're alive, she'll search for you, and until she finds you, all you're doing is breaking her heart. I think you owe her this. Let's call her, hey, and tell her you're okay."

"I know it, I know you're right…it's just, well I can't go back there, I won't."

"And you won't have to, at least until you're ready. We took control of our situations the moment we walked away. We are in charge now, always remember that."

Tristan's face wore a compassionate yet sincere look, and it was all the encouragement Richard needed.

"Okay…make the call. And Tristan…" Richard took Tristan's hand and shook it firmly and with equal sincerity. "Thanks a lot."

Tristan dialed as Richard dictated the numbers from memory. The phone rang its muted ring.

Two hundred and fifty miles away in Penzance, a girl rolled over in her bed, confused by the muffled ringing from downstairs. Fully thirty seconds passed before Anne-Marie recognised the harsh bell of the phone, and she immediately jumped up and flew down the stairs, almost stumbling as her heart pounded in her chest.

It was weeks since anyone had called the house, and the police had long turned their attentions elsewhere. Even the sympathetic calls of friends had stopped. She snatched the phone from its hook.

"Hello...hello?" She was too late, and in tearful despair shoved the receiver back on its perch.

"No answer. Sorry," Tristan said as he hung up.

"Try again, please," Richard replied, "maybe she was asleep?"

So Tristan did.

Anne-Marie was slumped on the stairs, grabbing a coat from the bannister to beat the chill. *What if it was him and I was too slow and stupid to answer? He may never ring again.* She wept, gripping her head in her hands and shaking with sadness and frustration. When the phone shocked her again a minute later, she snatched it up before the second ring.

"Hello? Richard?"

"Hello. Is that you, Anne-Marie? It's Tristan. Do you remember me?"

Her heart sank. She'd hoped beyond hope that it was her brother, but it just was the boy she'd met while out searching a couple of days ago. Though Anne-Marie was momentarily confused. *Didn't he say he'd call if he ever saw Richard? Yes...that's what he promised.* Her stomach was assaulted by a thousand butterflies.

"Hello Tristan. Yes...yes it's me. But why are you calling?"

"Hi. Are you home alone? Can you talk to me?"

"Er...yes, there's no one else here. Mum and dad are at work. Why, Tristan, what is this?"

There was a moment's silence, followed by an indistinct shuffling noise down the line. Long seconds passed, but then she heard a voice that sent the goose bumps crawling.

"Anne-Marie, it's me! It's Richie!"

She almost passed out with happiness, dizzy with emotion. Her bottom quickly found the stairs.

"Is it really you? Richie? I knew you were okay, and I never believed the police. Are you alright? Where are you? Are you coming home?"

"Slow down Annie, slow down. I'm fine, really, I'm

doing fine, but I'm so sorry I left without warning, and I'm sorry to have worried you so much."

"I'm just relieved you're okay, that's all that matters. Oh Richie, I missed you so much and I never gave up. Are you really okay?"

"I'm really okay, Annie. But no! I'm not coming home. I won't come back there."

His voice was different, stronger somehow, and he spoke with a conviction she didn't recognise.

"Where are you now? Can I come and see you?"

Tristan stepped away from the phone box and sat on a nearby bench. He felt happy to have helped them, and was glad he'd kept his promise. But he was sad, too. If Richard now decided to go home, he may lose the only friend he'd ever had. Alone in the world once more.

Ten minutes later, Richard came and sat beside him, and he looked so happy right there and then that Tristan felt a little jealous. But it was a good natured envy and he couldn't have been happier for his friend, though he expected the worst. What Richard said next took him by surprise and bought a tear to his eye.

"I'm not going back, Tristan, not ever, and if it's okay with you I still want to come to London and help you with your search."

Tristan was elated. "Of course it's okay, but are you sure? You're sure you don't want to go home?"

"I've never been more sure of anything! And I really want to help. I'm so grateful to you, because if you hadn't cared and kept your promise to Annie, we may never have spoken again." There was genuine feeling in his voice, and the two friends embraced like brothers.

Several days of wintry gloom were finally being usurped by the sun making a rare but welcome appearance. It was still cold…in their own ways, both lads had felt cold their entire lives…but as they headed into town they sensed a great energy about the place, a warm and alluring magnetism difficult to fathom.

Tristan knew he was naïve, no more so than in the culture of the young; how they dressed, their language, their mannerisms. But even with his candid ignorance, Tristan thought that the youngsters around Brighton looked strange. Young men with wild hair wore tough looking leather jackets and shiny boots, and alongside them their girls also sported leather, and inconceivably despite the chill, miniskirts. Other youths wore long coats, their hair slicked down with what appeared to be cooking lard, while their girls wore flowery scarves and what looked like dead animals draped about their shoulders. To Tristan, he might as well have been on the moon with how conspicuous he felt. And on every street, motorbikes and scooters whizzed by, all bar none of their riders decked out in one of the two distinct styles; mods and rockers, or so he learned.

The friends wandered on. They passed book shops and art galleries that oozed vibrant colour from their windows, as cafés spewed the rich aroma of fresh coffee while bakeries sent mouth watering smells wafting out onto a high street literally swarming with people. Tramp's tales of travel came to them as they nodded in greeting to people of myriad ethnicities, and from where they couldn't guess; India? Turkey? Kenya? Brazil? They had no idea, but just seeing and hearing those people transcended the boys far away from England's cold November, and they reveled in it.

They finally came to a stop outside another bustling yet down to earth café, and as their noses were assaulted by the tantalizing smell of frying sausages and bacon, a forgotten hunger jabbed them in their empty stomachs. In the eventful day they'd had other things on their minds, but now they needed food. Neither made a move to step inside, though, and after an uncomfortable moment Richard turned to his friend.

"Tristan, I've been scavenging up until now and I don't have any money." He smiled, and a surprising flash of mischief shone in his eye. "No money, but I do have an idea."

"I'm almost out too," Tristan replied, and with a hint of trepidation, he asked, "what do you have in mind?"

Richard beckoned him to follow, and to say Tristan was surprised about what happened next is an understatement of the greatest order, because never had a transformation been so complete. Richard crossed the busy street and stood outside a small but industrious post office, the customers striving to get their Christmas cards off early this year. Ignoring the cold, he then laid his jacket on the floor, which drew more than a few curious looks from the endless stream of passers-by.

Then, and with a quick glance at Tristan and a deep breath, he launched into this:

*"Oh yeah I, tell you something, I hope you understand,*
*Oh yeah I, tell you something, I wanna hold your hand,*
*I wanna hold your ha-ea-ea-and,*
*I wanna hold your haaand."*

Tristan stood slack jawed, his mouth a perfect oval. There stood his new friend, who until yesterday, so far as he knew, was a painfully shy and timid kid, singing his heart out in public. Unbelievable! Not only that, but Tristan recognized the song as the one that so enthralled him at the book store in Penzance. The Beatles.

And the surprises continued, as one by one the people on the street gathered around and tossed coins onto Richard's jacket. Half a dozen songs later, and a fair pile of silver coins shone bright in the afternoon sun. And what that shine meant to the boys was a late lunch with all the trimmings. Finally, and with a sheepish grin, Richard bowed to the applause of his small but appreciative audience, and Tristan raced over and grabbed his friend by the shoulders.

"Where did that come from, eh? You were brilliant, and all these people loved it. I'd no idea."

"To be honest, me too. I sometimes sing at home, but only when everyone is out. But today feels like…well it feels like a new start, and nobody here knows me except you, so I gave it a try." He gazed down at the lake of shiny coins on his jacket. "I guess it went pretty well." Richard bowed briefly again, and then looked seriously at his friend. It was short lived.

"My Lord Tristan...may I buy you breakfast?"

They cracked into fits of laughter.

Full up on greasy sustenance and at least three warming mugs of tea each, the boys went over to look at the sea, and on seeing the magnificent pier that stretched far out across the dark water, they simply had to investigate. Tristan had never seen anything like it before, and his excitement was enough to overcome the icy wind as they made it all the way to the end.

"What do you think is out there, Richie? I mean, out beyond the horizon."

The low sun was sinking toward that imperceptibly curving barrier, that to Tristan marked the edge of the world.

"Well, France is straight ahead, then Spain, and after

that, Africa. What do you mean? Countries?"

"Yes, countries, but more than just names. I mean, do you think there's a life for us other than that which we've known. Seems like we've had similar lives so far, and we've both managed to escape it somehow. Can it get even better for us? Not just out there across the sea. Anywhere. Here, even?"

"I don't know. All I do know, is that right now I'm having the best time of my life, so as long as that continues, then it's better than before. Right?"

"Right. I understand that, and I agree...but what if I don't find my mum? I can't even imagine my life without her, and I've only ever though of her absence as temporary. And then, what if I can't find my sister either. I'll never go back to St. Mary's, and you're my only friend in the world. What will I do?"

Tristan was suddenly swamped by a tide of sadness, as the very real possibility that he wouldn't find his mother hit home for the first time. Richard put a comforting arm around his friend's shoulder.

"Look, we will find her, I'm sure of it. I don't believe in much. Not God, not fate...not anything, really. But I believe in this, I believe in us, and I believe in you. You deserve to find her, after everything you've been through, so just give it time, and you'll see. You've come so far, and now it's just the next challenge in a life of challenges, and so what if it's the most difficult yet, like finding a human needle in the giant haystack of London. But you can do it. You *will* do it!"

Richard's enthusiasm worked, extracting a smile from the forlorn face. Tristan stood, retrieving his long legs from where they hung ten meters above the English Channel, and breathed deeply of the crisp ocean air. His eyes were clear and bright.

"You're right, we will find them, and it starts today. Remember Horace? *'He who can call today his own?'* Well, today is ours, and tomorrow do thy worst!"

"That's the spirit. *'Tomorrow, do thy worst, for I have lived today.'*"

The two boys set off down the pier at a sprint, whooping and shouting as if in some kind of tribal war dance. Anywhere else in England at that time, they might have got some mystified looks. Not in Brighton.

They arrived back in town just as the last rays of the winter sun glistened on a street hewn with cobbles, and as they strode with purpose toward the highway, both were intent on making it to London that very evening. But without warning, Richard halted outside a large illuminated window belonging to one of the myriad galleries. He stared for a few seconds before Tristan even realized he'd stopped. Bemused, he casually walked back to his friend, and what he saw caused the breath to stick in his throat. There before him, hung on the opposite wall and clearly in pride of place, was a large painting of himself.

In the hours and days since Mollie's shocking revelation, Kerra couldn't stop thinking about it, and those thoughts were abhorrent. Sleeping around with random men was bad enough, but selling her body to the sleazy kind that needed to pay just wasn't right, even in their dire predicament. And not only that…the weight of long kept secrets was crushing Kerra's soul. Her innate goodness seeped from her pores like ancient water seeping from a rock, and when she cried it evaporated from her tears. She knew she was good…was born good, at least, yet that goodness was souring, curdling like forgotten milk as she considered Mollie's idea.

Kerra knew that the strain of one more salacious secret would one day become too much to bear, and eventually, after grinding its keeper down, a secret would be shared, killing its power, emancipating her. But she could not and would not ever share this secret, not ever, and if she did what she was considering doing it wouldn't even matter anymore because her slaughtering shame would bury her soul in the greedy dust of ruin.

*But I'm so cold always, and my God I'm hungry.* Her mind repeated it over and over, and it was true because she was cold and hungry. But! *I'm an honorable woman,* she'd declare silently in an effort at stoicism, though immediately her sub conscience would retort, *really, Kerra? Are you sure?* And Mollie had made it all seem so easy...five hundred pound in a matter of days was incredible. It was a horrible conundrum, because above all else, Kerra was desperate. Her son would be there soon, and she had to provide for him, and not under any circumstances would she let Tristan share that damp and miserable space with herself and Mollie.

Riddled in the midst of a oneway whirlpool, her plight ate away at her principles, feasting like starved rats at a fresh corpse. She'd finally escaped her tyrannical, abusive husband, only to find herself destitute and demoralized in stinking London, broke, frantic and all out of options. With what felt like an icy fist clutching at her chest, she contemplated her choices. And it came down to only two; either do it or not, and both left her damned. It was a good job she no longer believed in hell. A good job. She wept with shame as she gave serious thought to following Mollie and becoming a whore.

By the next morning a painful decision had been made. It was Tuesday. If by Friday night Tristan hadn't arrived, she would ignore her shriveling moral code and speak to

Mollie. Mortified about the looming prospect, she screwed her tortured eyes up tight and hid herself from judgement beneath the blankets. Kerra hadn't prayed for a long time, her belief in the existence of any God beaten out of her by the fists of a cruel drunk. But in the rattling darkness of her tiny flat, she whispered a few prayer-like words that Tristan would arrive soon. Time was running out, and Kerra Annis knew what she had to do; she would turn her life around, or she would die trying.

Disbelief. That's the only way to describe the looks on both boy's faces as they gawped through the window at the painting. They simply could not believe it. Of course they knew it wasn't really Tristan…that was impossible. But the resemblance was uncanny, there was no denying it. Tristan was transfixed. The boy seemed so lost and forlorn, and stared back at him with a sadness and vulnerability that stabbed his own heart with an icy blade. The boy's face carried the same shadow of sadness he conceived in his own reflection, the same silent cry that no one heard, and he couldn't take his eyes away. Finally Richard broke the spell.

"You okay?"

Tristan blinked, and with effort dragged his gaze from the boy to face his friend. With a knowing shrug, as if to say *why not?* they stepped inside the gallery. It was empty. After a cursory look around it seemed as if the place was closing down, and in fact only a few paintings remained on display. Just as they were about to leave, the gallery door slowly opened behind them, and the oldest lady the boys had ever seen hobbled in, stooped over an equally old walking stick.

"Good afternoon," she said in a warbled, cosy voice. "How may I help you?"

They were unnerved. The old woman looked beyond them as she spoke, and her thick glasses resembled a pair of jam jars attached to her face.

"Hello miss, are you the owner? I want to ask about that painting over there." He pointed towards his lookalike, but she didn't follow his hand.

"I think she's almost blind," whispered Richard, and the two of them stifled a giggle.

"I might be blind, but I'm certainly not deaf!" Her reply was terse, but the boys also sensed an underlying trace of humour. "Which painting do you mean?"

"There's a young boy with reddish blonde hair. He looks very sad. Who is he?"

"Well, young man, I've no idea which painting you refer to, and I certainly don't know about any boy, so you'd need to speak to the boss about that, but she's not here at the moment. After the success of the exhibition yesterday, she and her boyfriend…fiancé…have gone away for a few days." At the word fiancé she cracked a wide smile. "I'm just guarding the gallery while she's gone. She'll be back after the weekend."

More than a little disappointed, the two boys thanked the woman and left the gallery.

"I doubt that poor old lady could guard anything," Richard said with a grin, "not that there was much to guard."

They chuckled, and their thoughts soon returned to more pressing issues. London was beckoning, and without another moment's pause, the boys made haste to the highway.

Back in the gallery, Vera Wright sipped a cup of tea as she listened to The Archers on the radio. Otherwise, all was quiet, and except the curious young boys there were no further visitors. Vera was virtually blind, but if she wasn't, she'd have noticed an unerring familiarity between the boy in the store and the boy on the wall. And not only that. Her boss, the pretty and talented Ailla Annis, could so easily have been their sister.

## Chapter Forty Four

They were in luck, as after just five minutes, a rusty heap of a car pulled over, and the crazy looking guy inside shouted out to them; "Alright lads, getting in? Ain't got all day!"

The friends exchanged a bemused glance and jumped in, unsure of the car's ability to travel ten miles, let alone all the way to London. But to their great surprise the car accelerated away smoothly and was soon speeding north. *This is it*, thought Tristan. *After all the miles and the disappointments, I'll soon be in London*. The notion both thrilled and terrified him. He was desperate to find his mother, and excited about going to the 'Big Smoke,' as Ernie had put it. But it was the biggest city in the world, and he was daunted. *How will I find her? Is it even possible?*

"How's it going, fellas? The name's David, but friends call me Butch. A pleasure." Butch held out one hand while steering with the other, and the boys took it in turns to shake it.

*Who was this man?* He was early twenties, and had his spiky hair dyed a shocking combination of red, white and blue. Tristan thought he looked like something from a circus side show, but he was friendly, and exuded total confidence. They liked him instantly, and also admired his unique appearance.

"This must be what 'cool,' looks like," Richard

mumbled to Tristan, who nodded with a mix of baffled yet willing agreement. As the ramshackle Ford Anglia sped north, Butch had to shout over the engine's roar.

"I could see it in your eyes…you thought she was a heap of junk, didn't you."

Both Tristan and Richard blushed, ashamed at their transparency.

"And you're right, she is a heap. But I don't like to spend money on her appearance, not when I can spend it on my own, 'cos appearance is everything, isn't it?" Butch laughed out loud, then added with a disconcerting two handed sweep over his chest, "I mean, just take a look… what girl could ever turn me down, looking like this. Eh?"

Despite his laughter the boys believed he was serious, so they kept their real opinions to themselves. In reality, Richard thought he'd have more luck attracting a parrot than a girl, and Tristan though the name Butch was a cruel joke. However, they liked him a lot, and listened intently as he continued their education.

"Lads, Brighton's the place to see and be seen, these days, so many cool kids, and the drinking, and all the concerts. And the girls, man! So many girls! If you promise to look me up while you're in London, I'll take you down to London-by-the-sea for a party. You'll be amazed."

Their imaginations ran wild; first ever party; the music; and the girls, though the latter filled them both with dread. And the drinking. But Tristan remembered his personal pledge to never to drink alcohol, and instead focused on music and the girls.

An hour outside Brighton and the countryside melted away, soon morphing into the sprawling red-brick and concrete suburbs of outer London. A little further north, the day's last light was lingering on, and for now Tristan's anxiety was dominated by his barely contained excitement. Out to the west they saw aeroplane after giant aeroplane criss cross the ever darkening sky, their lights evoking imagined U.F.O.s as Butch spewed out more commentary.

"Those are flying to and from Heathrow, the world's biggest airport." Then he pointed out the front left window. "And over there, the magnificent twin towers of Wembley Stadium, the home of football, and lads, mark my words…that's where Ramsey's boys will win the world cup for England in a couple of years." Suddenly, he wound down his window and, raising his arm to the sky, chanted at the top of his considerable voice, "Come on England! Come on England!"

Tristan and Richard loved Butch's crazy personality, and it was so infectious that they joined in the chant, though they didn't really understand what it meant. *This is life*, Tristan thought…*real life. This is a real man, and we're approaching a real city, where millions of real people live real lives. And one of them is my mum!* He couldn't suppress the giant grin that spread across his face.

Butch dropped them on the banks of the Thames, flowing west on a rising tide like torrents of spilled ink. He had an appointment soon and didn't have the time to take them any further, but told them of a tourist information desk he knew of in Piccadilly Circus station. He wished them well, and they bade their grateful farewells. Free and unbridled, they took their first tentative steps in London.

The sheer size of the city was mind blowing to kids that hailed from sleepy coastal areas. Tristan, who just a week ago had been awed by modest Penzance, felt tiny and insignificant, and it wasn't only the obvious magnitude of the city but the scale of things. Buildings scraped the sky, their summits only known by aircraft warning lights. Its people swarmed everywhere, like so many ants on a concrete anthill, each busier than the next and all in a mad rush to somewhere. And the noise, too. People had to shout over the throb of the raging traffic, and sirens rang out everywhere like the mating calls of some prehistoric beasts. It was wild and it was wonderful, and the boys thrived amid the chaos.

They jostled their way into a nearby subway station and imagined they were on some grand adventure, which in reality, they were, and their feet barley touched the ground as they rode deep into the depths of some Jules Verne underground kingdom on a writhing mass of humanity. It seemed as if a different breed of people dwelled down there, and as Tristan looked about he knew he wasn't far from the truth. Languages were spoken he didn't understand, and people of every colour, age, shape and size shared one common emotion; anger. If you inadvertently bumped someone, they glared as if you'd stolen their arm. If a seat became free, what followed was like a mad scramble for the Crown Jewels after the queen had declared, 'Come and get them.' Preachers, beggars and buskers vied for a yard of space, and babies screamed in the pandemonium. It felt like organized anarchy.

By the time they emerged from the bowels of London it was almost six o'clock, and after the snug glow of the underground the temperature seemed to have plummeted, and the reality of their situation dawned as darkness lay heavily across the city. They had only two possible contacts; Butch and Winston. Butch was probably drunk already, and Winston could be anywhere along the south coast, but they were rightly nervous about spending their first night in London on the streets, and hunted down a phone box. With luck Winston might just be able to help. Tristan dialed his friend's number, and immediately a woman's voice shouted down the line.

"Hello. Who that be calling 'ere at this time o'night?" It was five in the afternoon.

"Hello Miss, my name's Tristan. Could I speak to Winston please."

"Why you wanna speak to that no good lazy boy for?"

"We're friends. Is he home?"

"Y e a h ,   h e ' s   ' e r e .   J u s t   a   m o m e n t . WWIIIIIINSSTAAANN!!!"

The receiver fairly shook in Tristan's hand. Thirty seconds later a familiar voice came on the line.

"Tristan? Is that you kid? No way, man. I guess you made it, eh? How goes it, brother?"

Tristan was relieved his friend was home, and so happy to speak to him again.

"Hi Winston. Yeah, I made it."

They chatted and chuckled for a few minutes, and before Tristan could even ask, Winston had offered the boys a bed for the night with directions south of the river to Brixton where he'd meet them outside the underground station in an hour. But before he hung up he offered a caution.

"Tristan, listen brother, don't be too early, and if you are early stay inside the station. There are certain elements of society out here that, shall we say, aren't too keen on white fellas like you hanging about. But don't worry, old' Winnie 'ere will take care of ya, just like I promised. Don't be late, pal. Oh yeah…don't be early, neither."

The boys once more ventured into the subterranean world of Verne, and like two sardines in an undersized tin they crossed London in the unimaginable bedlam of rush hour, and were finally ejected onto the platform at

Brixton…twenty minutes early.

With Winnie's words fresh in his mind, Tristan was a little nervous as they climbed several crowded staircases up to ground level, and they soon understood what he meant; they were two of only a handful of white faces in the heaving station concourse, and being so young and so obviously outsiders, they might as well have been Winnie's cricket loving aliens.

Winston was the only black person Tristan had ever known, and he was so nice that he wondered what all the fuss was about. But he trusted Winnie and would be careful. They made their way over to the entrance to wait, where pretty soon a group of black teenagers sidled up, though they didn't speak, and simply looked at them. A couple of minutes passed. Finally the tallest of them stepped forward.

"What you doing 'ere, milky."

Some of his group laughed. Others scowled. Tristan didn't realise the boy was speaking to him and so didn't reply.

"Hey boy, don't ignore me!" This time, the mean looking lad's tone was aggressive. When Tristan again didn't answer, he moved so close that Tristan had to look up to see his face. "Boy, I said what you doing 'ere? You deaf, or just dumb?"

"Are you speaking to me? Sorry, I didn't realise. I'm just waiting for my friend, Winston, do you know him?"

With that, all the young black kids cracked up laughing.

"That's funny, man! Reeeaaal funny…everyone 'n his brother's called Winston in these parts."

The laughing continued, and Tristan and Richard joined in, but the leader's eyes suddenly narrowed and his face turned serious. As he leaned in close he slipped a hand into the pocket of his jeans.

"Fun time is over, milky, gimme ya money."

From his pocket he slid a short, shiny knife that glinted orange beneath the street lamp above. With his eyes wide in horror Tristan backed away, but the gang circled in. There was nowhere to go.

"I…I haven't got any money. It was stolen already." That was the truth.

"Hear that, boys, the white kid ain't got no money. Well, why don't I use this knife, and check beneath your skin."

The knife edged closer to Tristan's stomach, but just then two hands grabbed the other boy's shoulders and yanked him away.

"Hey, what the…"

"Kid, you better get outta 'ere right now before I kick your ass again. You get me?"

In a flash the gang were gone, and the boys had never been happier to see anybody in their entire lives. Winston's beaming smile leaned in between them.

"Didn't I tell you kids not to get here early?" He winked as he threw an arm round their shoulders.

"Boys," he said, "welcome to Brixton."

*Chapter Forty Five*

Just a short walk down a few back streets from the station led them to Winston's family home. He'd promised them a good feed when they arrived, and even before they did the boys smelled delicious food wafting across the entire neighborhood. The streets were well lit, but still Tristan sensed a mean element in the atmosphere, and felt his instincts sharpen, his senses on full alert. He was glad Winston was there with them, as beneath street lamps on every corner stood gangs of youths and young men that glared at the unlikely trio as they walked by.

"You don't need to worry about those kids, boys. Most folks round 'ere are sweet and won't pay you no never mind, though some of the youngsters are caught up in some gang shit, and it makes me sad, but it's often white against black, or West Indians against Indian. But relax, 'cos you're with me, and I'm the unofficial King of Little Kingston."

Tristan had missed Winston's friendly nature since they'd parted ways in Brighton, and was relieved his friend wasn't out on the road. Climbing the three wide steps up to the town house, they entered into a world full of voices and laughing, and were engulfed by tantalizing aromas and a unique kind of music that vibrated throughout the entire house. They could tell immediately that it was a happy home full of laughter and love, and the boys secretly envied Winston and his family.

Within five minutes they'd been introduced to what felt like two dozen children and adults, and after an endless round of handshakes and a few tight squeezes by some rather rotund and colorfully adorned sisters and aunts, it seemed as if at least four generations of Winnie's family lived under that one roof.

And then they heard it.

From somewhere towards the back of the house came the loudest most clamorous laugh the boys had ever heard, and it continued on like some burgeoning rumble of thunder, so loud in fact that they assumed it must have emanated from the lungs of a giant man, and it grew louder still as it approached, and when a short but lumpy woman wiggled into the room, neither could believe that such an impressive noise could come forth from such a small woman. Winston shook his head in mock annoyance, then held out his arms and bowed slightly.

"Tristan, Richard...meet my mother."

"Boys, I reckon a stray dog would turn its nose up at them skinny bones of yours, so sit down 'ere, kids, and let me put some meat on ya flanks."

When Pearl Brown spoke, people listened. At least twenty people, with an age range of between one and one hundred, crowded around the dining table, and dish after spectacular dish of West Indian food was placed before them. The hospitality shown was incredible, and as the hungry boys gorged on the magnificent feast, neither had ever felt more welcomed.

Dinner in the Brown household was a boisterous affair, and it seemed like there was a never ending supply of food. But some two hours later, and most of the group had disseminated around the large house, leaving only the two boys, Winston and his mother Pearl at the table. Winnie was on grand form.

"You should've seen the look on that innocent white face, ma, classic! It was like he'd climbed in the van with a dinosaur driving. Oh, and Stonehenge...you would have thought he'd spotted a million quid in the grass, the way he sprinted over there. Go on, Jesse," he shouted, "our very own Jesse Owens."

The laughter was loud and hearty, and the boys were having a great time. But the conversation ultimately turned to the reason why Tristan was really in London, and the Brown family, who in Pearl had a wise and strong matriarch, wanted to help. Pearl was a small lady, but she possessed that rare gift of being larger than life. In that household, she commanded respect.

"Firstly, you boys are welcome to stay 'ere as long as you need. I only ask that ya pitch in with a little washin' up and baby sittin'. Secondly, we'll make some enquiries around the hood, see if anyone's heard anything of your mother's name. But I warn you, it's very unlikely in this area, because unless you didn't notice, this 'ere is a black neighborhood. Still, we'll spread the word."

"Thanks so much, Mrs. Brown, I really appreciate it."

"Please boys, the name's Pearl, and d'ya know why folks call me Pearl? Obvious, innit? Round n' shiny, just like a pearl."

There was laughter all round, none louder than Pearl herself. The small group chatted and giggled late into the night.

Winston didn't usually work at the weekends, so the next morning he was free and happy to drive the boys around in search of clues, at the same time promising to show off the city's highlights. And probably its lowlights, he guessed, though he kept that dismal thought to himself. Winston was pessimistic about Tristan's chances of finding his mother...London was a city of five million people, after all. But he hid his negativity beneath a positive attitude.

Winston edged his white van through south London' stop start traffic, and although the mood inside was good, a very solemn sense of duty and importance wasn't lost among them. Tristan kept his eyes wide, and scanned every road and path and doorway they passed. In the first hour he spotted his mother a hundred times, but, he soon realized, sad eyes were seeing only what they longed to see. Via the Chelsea Bridge they crossed The Thames, now swirling its way back east, and Battersea Park was an oasis of green to the left. But the streets were jaded, and it looked and felt a little sketchy in that area, the big ugly power station dominating the bleached grey skyline and trash blowing in the polluted breeze. As they crept north in ever arresting traffic, the streets slowly became tidier, the houses subtly more grand.

Richard and Winston were still vigilant in their searching, but London's grayness was taking its melancholic toll on Tristan, and his positivity wore off as time slipped by. He stared out blankly into the drabness, buildings passing unseen as he became lost in thought about his mother. *She must feel scared and alone in this huge scary city. Does she have any friends? Where is she?* That was the biggest question, of course; where was she?

Slowly they passed along Buckingham Palace Road, the Queen's massive house materializing out of the gloom, and Winston sensed Tristan's demeanor matched the equally murky skies. In an effort to lighten the mood and raise a smile, Winnie spoke, and his voice was pinched and nasally.

"Ladies and gentlemen, if you look out on your right hand side, there you'll see the Queen's palace, the house of Buckingham. Look carefully if you will at the far, top right window, and you'll see our gracious queen sitting on her royal throne...depositing last night's vindaloo." In his most clipped accent, difficult with a heavy Caribbean twang, he continued. "Oh, come now Philip, hurry here with that loo paper. I don't have all day...I have taxes to collect, what, what."

They laughed so hard, including Winston, that the van swerved dangerously across The Mall and narrowly missed a group of real tourists. But it worked, and Tristan snapped out of his doleful musing.

They surged through the vast white edifice ofAdmiralty Arch and came onto a riot of colour in bustling Trafalgar Square. Winston pulled over to the kerb. Upon seeing the masses, hundreds, maybe thousands of people all clustered together in organic hoards, Tristan was once more disheartened. Like one giant flock, people were literally shoulder to shoulder as far as he could see, and he knew in his heart that the mission was futile. To look for his mum this way, he knew, he'd need more than just a major slice of luck. Winston placed a hand on Tristan's shoulder, and pointed out the towering structure of Nelson's Column.

"D'ya know who that is, kid?" He didn't. "That's Lord Nelson, mighty victor over the French at the Battle of Trafalgar, and a national hero. He had only one eye, one arm and one leg, or so legend has it, yet he still won his fight. D'ya see what I'm saying kid? Anything is possible."

Once more Winston had done the trick, and Tristan couldn't fail to smile, even to the point of adding a little banter of his own. He looked up again at the statue far above, and then back at Winston, before saying, "I bet old Nelson up there is still better than you at cricket, no matter how many arms and legs he's got."

"That's more like it, kid. No matter what happens here in the city, Tristan, you can never give up. And you deserve some luck…perhaps you'll get it sooner than you think."

All three of them hoped that was true.

Back in the van they drove east along Victoria Embankment, and Richard commented on how dirty the river looked. Though he hadn't seen it before, he imagined some glorious stretch of shimmering water, stippled by the luxurious yachts of London's rich and famous.

"Yeah, well London ain't what it used to be, Richie. There are rich folk of course, like actors and musicians… politicians, mostly. But now there are too many unsavory types, and gangsters largely control the streets these days, 'specially out east and west where organized crime is almost an epidemic. You ever heard this name before? Kray?"

Both boys shook their heads.

"Reggie and Ronnie Kray…The Krays, as most people know 'em as. Shit, the very name is enough to scare most people in this city. They own night clubs in the West End, and hardly any crime takes place in London without their knowledge. Nasty pieces of work, those fellas are, though some say they're good for the city, you know, controlling the criminal aspect and saving the coppers a lot of time and bother. Well I don't know about all that, but either way, I hope I never piss 'em off."

Now they were entering the run down area of east London, and though he didn't say it, Winston guessed that if Tristan's mother was even in London at all, because there were no guarantees, it was likely she would've ended up there. A lot of illegal factories employed newcomers to the city, and natives and immigrants alike descended there for work like ants on an ice cream.

No doubt about it, there was definitely a seedy element about the East End. Gangs dealt drugs, and though he didn't want to think about it, prostitution was a common way to make ends meet. But communities were tight down there among those grimy, crooked streets and back alleys, and family meant everything. Winston hoped for the best, but despite his best wishes, he couldn't help but fear the worst. They stopped to eat.

"It's going to be difficult to find her, but you've got to stay positive," he told his friend, "because it's a huge city and we've no clues. This area draws in loads of the new people that come to London looking for work or a new life or even to escape something, so it's as good a place as any to start making enquiries. Besides, it's the cheapest place to eat in all of east London."

"And the best," came a hearty riposte from the waitress who had a body some might call cuddly. Richard guessed she ate there everyday herself. "Allo, Winnie, nice to see ya, love"

"Hello Marnie. Nice to see you too. These boys are my friends, and I'm helping them look for someone. Thought we'd come here and refuel before we set out on foot."

"Oh yeah? Who ya looking for, boys? I was hoping it might be me." Marnie planted her considerable bum on Richard's knee, who squirmed instantly and felt sure his chair would collapse under the strain. She was a big and buxom girl who wore enough make up for five women, and the amount of noxious perfume she wore stung his eyes and caused a bout of sneezing. Still, he'd never been that close to a girl before, and couldn't suppress his enamored smile.

"Be careful, Richie, that one'll make mincemeat out of ya. Ain't that right, Marnie?"

"That's right, love. If he were just a couple of years older, sweetheart, I'd eat him for my second breakfast… better than these 'ere eggs n' bacon, anyhow." She turned and whispered in Richie's ear, but when Marnie whispered, anyone within twenty yards could hear it. "But you'll make some girl a lovely breakfast one of these days, know what I mean?" Her laugh was loud, and had the rat-a-tat-tat of a machine gun, and the mortified kid's cheeks blazed the colour of ketchup. Winston linked arms with his friend, and led her smiling from the table before the boy could die of embarrassment. They chatted in hushed tones.

"Look Marnie, Tristan believes his mother is somewhere in London, and he's desperate to find her. The kid and his mother have had such a tough ride, and the poor buggers really need a break."

He summarized Tristan's unlikely story, and described Kerra as Tristan had described her to him. Marnie promised to keep an eye out and speak to her friends.

"A lot of women come in here," she said, "to eat cheaply and escape the cold and, if I'm honest, it's as much to do with being around other equally worn down and lonely souls as they themselves are."

Her heart went out to the kid as it went out to the women she saw through those doors on a daily basis, and she would do what she could. She wished the boys well as they headed out into a now bitter east London afternoon, but not before giving Richie an almighty slap on his skinny behind.

*Chapter Forty Six*

Kerra's sleepless night of waking nightmares ended in tears at dawn. Throughout the small hours, while the sky was black and the stars passed slowly across the void, she lived through visions of masked men and rapes and violence, and of Tristan standing helpless and alone in the storm, and of Mollie and black eyes and blood. Lots of blood, and it was her own.

Friday had passed, and the worst case scenario was now upon her. Saturday had arrived; Tristan had not.

Kerra was crushed. She was disgusted with herself just for considering prostitution, and had never felt so low, but as the hours of that now fateful day evaporated into the past, Mollie was there encouraging her about the task at hand. Finally, and in mortal conflict with her now flimsy moral conscience, Kerra accepted that she was emotionally and physically strong enough to get through it. Besides, it would just be a couple of times, maybe a few days. She knew that. And when Tristan arrived, they would start to rebuild their new lives, free from tyranny and abuse, together.

Mollie dragged Kerra from the bed and, handing her a dress, watched as she tried it on. She appraised herself coyly in the mirror, and stared for a long moment, twisting left and then right, and then, with her back to the mirror, looked over her shoulder at the woman looking back. Her thinning coppery hair lacked life these days, hanging limp and loose as if just another burden she couldn't bear. But she couldn't stifle the grin that appeared. It was a smile tempered with shame, and it was soon gone. But Kerra still looked good. For as long as she remembered she hadn't worn nice clothes, certainly not a pretty frock like the one she wore now. She simply hadn't been allowed. If she did wear a dress, Blyth would call her names, accusing her of tarting herself up like a whore. Though it was ridiculous, because the dresses were nothing more than loose and flowery, perfect for the long hot summers on St. Mary's.

But paranoia and jealousy controlled the man, and his threats of violence were never idle. Kerra shook her head at the unmissable irony, and it seemed Blyth's words were prophetic after all. There she was now, dressing to impress. *How had it come to this?* she thought, and a flush of anger rose at what her husband had caused her to do. But *she* controlled her destiny now, and would do what needed to be done. Options ceased to exist, and the most difficult decision she'd ever had to make had finally been made. And she wept, inconsolable, because today was the day that Kerra would take to the streets.

*Chapter Forty Seven*

Sunday, and the search in London was into its second day, but as yet there'd been no breakthrough. Nothing! Tristan tried not to despair, but it was proving tough, and in such a vast city with six million people, the chance of success seemed just that; six million to one. But he vowed to continue. *What else can I do*? he thought.

Winston reluctantly returned to work on the Monday morning, and Richard also had to leave. Anne-Marie was driving into London later that day, and they'd arranged to meet at a friend of a friend's house in Camden. He was obviously excited to see his sister, but was sad to leave his new friend alone on his search.

"I'm really sorry for leaving you now, but it's just for a few days. We haven't known each other long," he said, "but it feels like we've been friends forever, and I know we will be. I truly hope you find your mother, and I'm sure you will any day, but if not I'll be back by your side before you know it. Just stay positive, and Tristan… thanks for helping me contact my sister…it means everything. Good luck."

They embraced like brothers, and Tristan of course understood that Richie had to see his sister. He himself would do anything to see his mother again, and was happy for his friend. With their own important missions ahead, they said their farewells, both boys fighting vainly to suppress a tear or two. One way or another, however, both knew they would see each other again soon, and with good news to share.

Tristan spent that night back at the Brown's house in Brixton. Tomorrow he would continue on foot, making door to door enquiries at shops and cafés in the East End while showing his mum's picture around. The photo was a little creased and faded now, and with a hint of a smile that he thought his mum would appreciate, he guessed she was a little creased and faded too. But she didn't look all that different now from the photo, and he hoped it might lead to a shred of information, some trace of hope he could cling to as he searched.

They sat once more around Pearl's table, and Tristan listened intrigued as she shared stories of life in Jamaica under a hot sun and swaying palm trees.

"You should see the golden sand, miles and miles of it," she said, "and fish so fresh it wriggles on yer plate while yer eating."

He could barely imagine such an exotic place existed, and asked Winnie to take him someday. Most of the lively household had turned in for the night, and it was quiet throughout, an unusual occurrence in the Brown house. Suddenly the phone rang, and judging by the surprise on Winston's face, it was equally unusual. He grabbed the receiver up before it woke the kids, and spoke in a hushed voice. Moments later he hung up, and motioned for Tristan to follow him with a very serious look on his face. That too was unusual, and Tristan's pulse quickened.

"What is it Winnie? Who was that?" He hoped it was about his mum.

"Don't get too carried away, kid, it could be nothing."

Tristan nodded.

"So that was Marnie, you know, from the café. She said she'd had a call from a friend in the East End, and she warned that it may be nothing, but the friend someone matching the description of your mother was seen, and that's all she told me, except to say that the person didn't know her, and that she was probably new to the area. Like I said, it may be a false alarm."

Butterflies flocked in Tristan's guts. He knew he shouldn't get carried away, but at least it was a potential lead. He could barely suppress his excitement.

"Maybe it's her, Winnie, it's possible, isn't it?"

"Yeah kid, it's possible. But, maybe…"

"I know, I know, don't get carried away."

They shared a smile.

"Thanks Winnie, and thanks for everything you and your family have done. How can I ever repay you?"

"Kid, just being our friend is enough. You know brother, us West Indians are getting a real bad rap around here these days, so for a young lad like you to come here without judging us…well, it means a lot, and we could equally thank you just the same."

Days started early in the Brown residence, and even before seven o'clock reggae music drifted throughout the old house, and the now familiar smells of West Indian cooking permeated the air of every room. Kids scampered about getting ready for school, and as he made his way downstairs the older family members greeted him warmly and with respect. Tristan again compared that atmosphere to the home life he'd known, and the bitterness he felt toward his father was still ripe. He admired the Browns, and loved how open and honest they were, both to each other and to him, a young and seriously naïve white kid from what felt like another world.

While more or less force feeding him a spectacular breakfast, Pearl made him promise something.

"Listen kid, whatever the outcome of the next few days, you must come and see us again before leaving this filthy city."

Tristan dutifully…happily, promised to do so. Pearl then burdened him with a giant package of more food, which he accepted as he told them how grateful his mother would be, adding that he was sure she'd get to meet them all soon to thank them in person.

Pearl threw her short, meaty arms around Tristan, practically squeezing the breakfast out of him and, waved off by what seemed like a full classroom of children, he climbed into Winston's van, and was gone. At Brixton station, Winston looked squarely at his friend.

"Good luck, kid, but I think today's gonna be a good day for you, I can feel it in the air. You've come a long way, and destiny is waiting." Winston grabbed him in a tight hug. "Don't forget about us, you hear me, and you'll always be welcome at our place…your mum, too!!"

It meant the world to Tristan to know that he had friends like the Browns. Just a week or two ago he didn't think it was possible, but now he could count on friends like Mark and Bobby, Winston, Pearl and the others, and of course Richard. Maybe even Anne-Marie. With an untapped ocean of love swishing around in his under used heart, Tristan hoped they could count on him, too.

But in reality he was alone again. With a deep intake of the raw November air, Tristan plunged once more into the Vernian world on what he hoped with all his heart was as Winston had just said; his day of destiny. Tristan missed his mother so much, and the sixteen-year-old boy didn't think it was too much to ask of the world for a little slice of luck.

## Chapter Forty Eight

Night had almost fallen across the city, and though barely four o'clock it was the charcoal coloured afternoon of a winter now arrived. With no gloves and only cheap shoes, Tristan's fingers and toes were frozen, and his back ached from constant tensing against the intense chill. His father's indifference to his welfare had provided him with a spartan array of clothes, and he had on every item he owned. It wasn't enough. Shivering as he walked, he recalled reading in his mother's encyclopedia about the Spartans of Greek history, that fearless breed of tough warrior men and women who fell so bravely at Thermopylae, and he wished he was more like them. They wouldn't complain about the cold, he knew that, though in fairness he probably wouldn't be hacked to bits on the battlefield by a sword.

He didn't know whether to laugh or cry at the irony as he sought sanctuary in the bustling warmth of a fish and chip shop. Inside he enquired about his mother, and when the boss learned of his plight he took pity on Tristan. But when he showed the man his picture, his eyes widened in instant recognition.

"No doubt about it son, no doubt, it's definitely her. She's been in here a few times, lovely lady and really polite."

"Really?! In here? When was the last time?"

"Oh, maybe three or four days ago. Comes in with that friend of hers…what's her name? Hmm…nah, it's gone. They only bought chips, mind you, said they didn't have much money, so I piled 'em high. Nice girls, they are, and the one you say is your mother, a real pretty gal, for sure, but kinda sad. That's how I'd describe her, anyhow, really sad."

Tristan was consumed with emotion after that first positive sighting, and to learn that she had a friend comforted him no end. At least she wasn't alone. But the man had stressed how sad his mother looked, and his own distress was clear.

"Take a seat, son, and I'll shout you some grub. On the house. Go on lad, grab a seat."

Tristan took a seat in the small dining area, grateful for yet another show of kindness. But the upbeat smile from the morning had slipped from his face, and the freezing weather had worn him down. *She must be worried about me, and is sad because I haven't found her yet, or worse, she thinks I'm not coming. I have to find her soon. I must.*

"There you go, son, get stuck into that lot, the finest fish n' chips in London, I don't mind tellin' ya!"

"Thanks, it looks great."

"Listen son, I wish I'd more information for ya, and I'm sorry I don't, but I reckon your best bet is to try in a few of the pubs in the area, get amongst the locals. Someone is bound to know something, and they love a bit of gossip round 'ere. And take this." The man handed Tristan some money and a big old fisherman's jumper. "It's just a few quid and an old rag...way too cold out there for that flimsy jacket of yours. Buy yourself a beer or two...how old are you? Sixteen? Plenty old enough in these parts. Good luck, lad."

With that he ducked back behind the counter and through a door, deliberately denying Tristan a chance to decline. He was truly grateful and awed by yet more gracious charity. But there'd be no beer for him.

With a full stomach nestled snugly beneath his new jumper that was nothing like an old rag, Tristan made for the nearest pub. It was clear that times were hard in most of London, but he soon realized that when the chips were down the East Enders looked out for one other, and folks could always find a few spare coins for their beer. With renewed hope he slipped through the doors of the first pub, The Blind Beggar, and though it was still early, a few customers chatted idly at the bar. Two young men in sharp suits…mean looking men that might have been brothers… merely stared at him as if to say, *you shouldn't be in here, son*. He showed them his picture anyway. No luck, but the older looking man handed him a one pound note and told him to scarper. Tristan pressed on, unaware that he'd just met the Krays, London's most notorious criminals.

Pub after dingy pub he went, but with no further success, and by ten o'clock he was crestfallen. After talking to the man in the chippy, he felt sure he'd get the breakthrough he so desired, but at least a hundred locals had seen his picture, and not a glimmer of recognition. Exhaustion sagged his shoulders as he traipsed back to the cheap hotel he checked into earlier. Pearl Brown insisted he borrow a little money for lodging, which he'd accepted reluctantly but was glad of now. It would've been treacherous to sleep outside that night. Winter was upon the city, and had seeped into his heart.

He trudged through the lobby of the grimy hotel, but somehow made a wrong turn and found himself in the dingy and desolate bar area. The young barman was barely awake as he idly washed a few glasses. But he soon spotted the forlorn look on Tristan's face as he caught sight of his reflection in a glass cabinet.

"Evening mate…blimey, what's wrong with you? I've never seen such a miserable face."

"Hello. I'm okay, thanks. Just made a wrong turn, that's all. Goodnight."

"Then let's drink a toast to our mistakes, you for choosing the wrong door and me for choosing the wrong job."

Tristan ignored him and turned to leave.

"Hold on mate, why don't you sit down for a minute and tell me all about it? Besides, I'm bored out of me mind here, can't ya tell? Come on, kid, humour me."

Too tired to protest, Tristan sighed and took a seat at the bar, his head resting wearily in his hands.

"You look like you could use a drink. You're eighteen, right?" He winked. "Course you are. What'll it be?"

"I don't drink."

The barman laughed a little, genuinely surprised. "Pull the other one, son, everybody drinks, and people who say they don't drink usually drink like fish. Let me guess... you're a whisky man, am I right?"

Tristan's throat went dry and a knot formed in his guts. He valiantly held his tongue, reckless after all the disappointments. Jim winked again.

"I knew it...one whisky, coming right up."

Tristan wanted to say no, was desperate to decline. He'd vowed long ago never to touch alcohol, knowing first hand the damage it caused.

But...

He was so depressed and tired of feeling that way, and his mood rendered him dilatory. He waited. Jim placed a small glass on the counter. Whisky over ice. Tristan's stomach flipped, and his father's wild face filled his eyes. Adrenalin surged. He stared at the glass as if it contained poison. In a way, it did. His hand shook.

"What you waiting for, kid? Looks to me like you *really* need that drink."

Tristan raised his hand, unsteady, daring himself to reach for the glass, daring himself not to. *I'll just try it, see what it's like. I know I'll hate it, so it'll be just once.* In his mind's eye he saw his father smiling, taunting. *Do it, son,* he whispered...*drink it!* He grabbed the glass. Eyes closed tight, denying his father. The glass at his lips. He paused a moment. A battle of wills.

And then he drank, small quick gulps...one more, and

it was done.

Tristan stared blindly at the rows of bottles behind the bar. He balled his hands into tight fists, the blood draining as his jaw clenched shut. *Another drink?* but the now trembling boy didn't hear, Jim's voice an irrelevant hum. He'd broken his oldest and most sacred promise to himself, and a horrifying realisation hit him like thunder as his worst fears came crashing down.

*I am weak, just like my father.*

A dormant expression settled on his face, hands now gripping the bar to keep himself from falling.

"His blood is in me…his poison is in me," he whispered, barely audible. "We *are* the same. I *am* my father's son."

Jim tried to speak to Tristan, whose rigid frame now leant precariously on the bar. But the boy just didn't hear him, as if he was lost in a trance. Somewhat unnerved, he spoke louder, and this time, as if awaking from some kind of dream, Tristan's eyes came into focus. Slowly, his frail and taut body relaxed, and his shoulders slumped as if the weight of the world was suddenly upon them.

And then the teardrops came. In torrents. He fled from the bar, fled from dangerous territory, and bounded up the dark stairs to his room, devastated, leaving behind a concerned and bewildered barman. For the first time in many months, Tristan cried himself to sleep.

A couple of hours later, just before that traumatic and eventful day ticked around the clock into tomorrow, Tristan awoke, and an acute shame of what he'd done filled the room, suffocating him with guilt. It was his first ever drink, and he felt sick with a regret that dug deep into his soul.

"Why? Why did I do it?" he whispered to himself. The blackened room was tiny, but the void around him suddenly felt endless, as if the very walls were backing away from his sinful aura. He'd never felt so alone.

Midnight came and went, but Tristan knew the memory of that evening would never leave him as he stood shivering at the window. A harsh wind rattled the glass, a pathetic barrier that did little to keep out the winter, and his thoughts turned to Tramp and the others. He imagined them huddled together at the castle, gathered around the fire in the old drum, and sadness fell upon him like an icy shroud, knowing full well how cold they would be despite it…how dangerously cold.

Through his clouded thoughts he recalled something one of them had said; *It helps keep us warm*, they'd said, *and helps us forget about our miserable, hopeless plight.* There were smiles as they'd said it, and at that moment an imperceptible grin spread over his own dispirited face.

Then he spotted the mini-bar.


*Chapter Forty Nine*

Tristan woke very late after dreams of his father and violence and…and drinking? With difficulty he opened his eyes, but immediately screwed them shut because the dim light that filtered through the shabby curtains blinded him. And his head ached. And then he remembered.

Slowly he leaned up on his elbows and glanced around a room now bathed in the dullish light of late morning in winter. He was horrified. Scattered all about were small, discarded miniatures, vodka, gin…whisky, shining glass carcasses of the monsters of his youth. He'd emptied the entire mini bar…eight bottles in total. A lot for anyone. But he was just sixteen years old.

Tristan was mortified. But something else was obvious.

His head throbbed, but not badly. He felt okay. Tristan wasn't hung over.

Each day that passed broke Tristan's dwindling spirit a little more. He slept poorly, and exhaustion clouded his mind and judgement. There hadn't been a single further breakthrough in his search since the man at the chip shop, and he'd knocked on a thousand doors and shown his picture in every shop and pub and hotel. Tristan was utterly demoralized, and without realising it he had turned smoothly to alcohol in order to smother his anguish. Initially he laughed it off. *Just for warmth*, he told himself. But when the laughing stopped, the drinking didn't.

With a shrinking appetite now quenched by whisky, Tristan had more or less stopped eating, and he spent as many days hidden behind the mouldy curtains of his seedy hotel room as he did out looking for his mother. He had known misery before, had lived among it his whole life, but the overwhelming emotion he'd now adopted was, quite simply, abject wretchedness. He would never find her, he knew that without any doubt, and slumped into the dirty and unmade bed, whisky in hand and not a trace of hope in sight.

Later that day though, Tristan did venture out. He convinced himself it was for some fresh air, to try and shake himself out of the slump, but he knew the truth; he needed more whisky, because right then the future beckoned with as much warmth as Death's extended finger. On he lumbered through a darkening day with nothing but fading hope and a shadow lengthening under the early winter sun, and as the light diminished, so did his hope, while a howling wind stung his face as he skulked wearily through the cloying East End, sucking him deep into its shadows, and he felt a true denizen of the narrow alleys and gutters clogged with shit and filth and broken dreams.

And then, out of nowhere, he veered onto Tower Bridge, the Thames dark and intimidating far below. He found himself in the middle of the ancient crossing's wide expanse, after what must have been several hours of aimless and unconscious wandering. His chest ached, and inside that chest his heart was broken. His body was cold and malnourished, and though he didn't feel it, Tristan was numb all over.

He'd tried so desperately hard to find his mother, yet it had proved futile. London was just too vast. There were simply too many people. He thought when he left St. Mary's that the hardest part was over, and he'd soon find his mother.

That is what he believed. But he was very, very wrong. Tristan had failed.

And guilt seeped up all around him like a choking and sinister mist from the unforgiving dirty river below. He had let himself down. His aunt Bella too. But mostly he had let his mother down, and knew he could have tried harder, arrived in London quicker, knocked on more doors. *Did I spend too long at the castle with Tramp? Too much fun with Richard? The whisky!*

*She thinks I deserted her, and she's right!*

Tristan leaned over the railings and stared into the mysterious swirling grayness beneath the bridge. How far was it down to the filthy river below? Ten meters? Twenty? At least that. It was raining now, the dreadful wintry drizzle that lasted weeks, yet Tristan didn't even notice. He stepped away from the ice cold rails and reached into his pocket. When he looked at the picture of his mother, the one thing that had kept him from a total breakdown, his face contorted into a grimace of sheer pain, and anguish etched into every cell of his being.

And then the unthinkable happened; Tristan dropped the picture. An extra powerful gust of wind snatched away the final link to his mother, but when he reached out in desperation to grab it he was too slow. The photograph slipped agonizingly between rail and concrete, and came to rest on a steel girder several feet below. Tantalizingly out of reach.

Another gust and, as if in slow motion, his mother's smiling face receded into the mist. Gone.

Tristan was sixteen years old, his entire life visible in bloodshot blue eyes that had seen nothing yet felt everything. Now, that childhood world was lost to the winter wind as the faded photo of his mother fluttered slowly into the icy, treacherous filth of the Thames. In that moment he felt like an actor, flitting among the scenes in a pageant of death and misery, and he screamed in frustration, his voice along with the photo carried off into forever.

With ice in his heart he stepped back from the rails, pausing a few seconds by the roadside. His mother was lost to the city. His sister, maybe the other side of the world. A father that would beat him if he ever returned to St. Mary's. He couldn't even trust himself now he'd started to drink. All his dreams had shattered in the last few weeks.

He noticed for the first time the rain and the forming puddles, and in them he saw his own death smiling at him, beckoning him down. Really, what was there to live for? Nothing! Nothing at all!

Twenty meters? Probable death, combined with the frigid water. His pain and suffering would be over at last. He breathed deeply, and the world around him slowed. He heard nothing, but saw with crystal clarity.

This was his destiny. He contemplated dying and fancied it, and blinked twice and decided to.

Tristan ran at the rails.

Winston was getting anxious. He'd neither seen nor heard from Tristan in many days, and on a hunch went out in the van to look for his friend. The city's traffic was thick in rush hour, especially with the dismal sleet that now fell. His route from Brixton took him north, and Winnie was happy to be on the relatively free flowing north bound side of Tower Bridge.

He ignored it at first, the vague notion that he'd just seen Tristan. *I must be tired*, he muttered, blinking it away. But the thought could not be shaken, so he looked again, and there he was, no doubt about it, standing on the side of the road across the bridge, looking lost and confused.

"No," he said, but in his heart there was no mistaking the unfolding scenario as an ominous look crept onto his friend's face. Then Tristan faced the railings. Winston slammed on the brakes and his van skidded to a halt, he abandoning it in an instant and launched into a desperate sprint across the busy road.

Then Tristan's feet left the ground.

"NNNOOOOO," Winnie screamed, though he knew it was too late.

A millisecond of subconscious recognition of the voice as he jumped…it was the first sound he'd registered in many minutes…and two feet of icy air now separated his feet from the concrete, his left hand planted firmly on the ice cold steel rail. Wind rushed past his ears from the void beyond the rails.

And then it was over. Only blackness and silence. He was gone.

Winston's every sinew strained to breaking point as he flung himself through the air at the boy. And in a moment that he would never forget in all his long years, he slammed into his friend's body, smashing them both into the railings in a tangled heap of arms and legs.

*Chapter Fifty*

After the incident at Tower Bridge Winston insisted that the broken hearted boy stay with his family for a while, and he wouldn't take no for an answer. Physically he was okay, but Tristan was a mental wreck. Knocked out cold in the collision with the rails, what he though was his welcome death was nothing more than temporary unconsciousness and a heavy concussion. He had slept poorly ever since, the long nights filled with haunting visions and fractured images of his mother, and his unhealthy few days of whisky fueled lethargy had left him weak and more morose than ever. He barely spoke to anyone, both out of shame and the realisation that he was lucky to be alive.

And he *was* lucky. Tristan didn't want much from life, only a little luck that had as yet eluded him, evidently until now. But it wasn't the kind of luck he wanted. He wanted to find his mum, and if he'd used up his only luck so he himself had survived, then…well, he'd rather be dead.

Eventually though, exhaustion got the better of him, and by the fourth night he sunk into deep sleep, slowly and thickly at first, like mercury creeping uphill, but when it came, it came with finality to render him lifeless as the darkness swallowed him, and denied the whisky his body had come to rely on, it spat him out in disdainful chewed up clumps and kept him there until the morning light at last prized him free, and delivered him from the night and its torturous nightmares of abuse and violence and destruction.

When he finally roused, Winston informed him he'd slept for nineteen hours straight. Rested and somewhat cleansed, and with the Brown's good hearty food forced upon him, Tristan rallied. Pearl Brown had plenty of wise words.

"Depression is a powerful emotion for anyone, young or old, and believe me when I tell ya, that channeled well, it can be a potent ally, a driving force, but adopt it badly and it'll suck the life from ya bones and leave you in ruin. You're not the first child to find themselves adrift out in the great big scary world, but I believe in you, kid, and I warn you with ya best interests at heart…don't let this drain the spirit from your good and decent soul."

Tristan took great encouragement from the kindness and support he got from the Browns, and felt ready and secure within to resume his search. They gave him some more money for food and hotels, and he swore never to touch alcohol again, with Winston and Pearl to bear witness. He would not let them down, and they could see it in his eyes.

"But most importantly," Pearl told him, "if ya grab the bottle again you'll be betraying both your mother and yourself. Just stay off the whisky, kid, and stay positive, and all of this will work itself out, I promise."

His smile was genuine, but deep down Tristan could not shake off the doubt that had crept into his mind. He had no idea how anything would turn out, or if he'd ever see his mother again.

Two days later he received a surprise call at the hotel. He left within two minutes.

The same sleet that he was oblivious to on Tower Bridge still lashed down, and London buckled under the weight of heavy skies as Tristan hurried into the sanctuary of the nearby café. It was crowded, with every table chock full of working men guzzling tea and devouring bacon sandwiches, but he caught Marnie's eye as she took orders, and snagged the last remaining seat. A moment later she waddled over, trailing spilled tea as she came.

"Hello love, how ya doing? Enjoying the weather?" She smiled at her own joke, but her look soon turned solemn. "To be honest love, I don't have much to tell you, and it could be nothing, okay. I'm sorry I can't be more positive."

He nodded at the cuddly waitress, and smiled back as he remembered Richard squirming under her hefty bulk.

"I understand, so please just tell me what you've heard."

"Okay kid. Look, one of my friends, a driver just like Winnie, said he'd seen a woman that looked like your mother. She was attractive, he said, in her late thirties, maybe forty, he couldn't be sure. Long, wavy hair, too...not ginger...how'd he say it? Darker than ginger, but less than red. That's it, that's how he described her."

Tristan straightened and his pulse raced. It sounded like his mother...*and the hair...it had to be her*.

"Please go on Marnie, tell me everything."

"Well, he said he'd seen her a couple of times out walking the streets. He didn't recognise her, he said, which surprised him, cos he thought he knew everyone in the East End, and both times he saw her he had to look

269

twice…said he couldn't believe how few clothes she had on…not slutty, like, just that she looked cold and poor. And one more thing."

Tristan stared off into some unknown place, lost in thought and his emotions shredded. It had to be his mother, but if it was then she was having a really tough time.

"Tristan?" He gazed blankly through the downpour. "Tristan? You okay love?"

"What? I'm sorry. That last thing, what was it?"

"My friend, he said…well, he said that he'd never seen a more forlorn looking person in all his days, and let me tell ya kid, from someone raised in the miserable East End, that's an ever so bold statement."

Across the hard grey edge of London, and deep in the narrow grimy alleys of the East End, Kerra was scared. The moment she dreaded had arrived, and she was soon to meet her first client as a prostitute. She knew nothing of who the man was, only that he was wealthy, was from out of town, and he regularly came to the city on business.

"And to spend blissful time away from his wife, I expect," Mollie had chuckled as she explained. "He's known to stay with the same woman for days at a time, and by all accounts, according to a couple of my 'associates,' is a charming and well paying bloke."

Kerra believed her friend, but it didn't ease her nerves and her stomach flipped in somersaults.

She waited at the pre-arranged location, and went through a whole spectrum of emotions as she counted down minutes that felt like hours. A deep shame unlike any she'd ever known clung at her chest for what she had committed to do, and the guilt she felt lodged like a pound of lard in her guts. *What if Tristan ever finds out? How could I ever look him in the eye again?* But if she was to pull through such a desperate time, there really was little choice but to go ahead with the plan, though the internal struggle was intense as the pending reality approached.

Kerra had heard about women far better off than she who'd chosen prostitution as a positive and financially rewarding career. They hobnobbed with London's high society, she'd heard, and dressed in designer clothes and fancy high-end jewelry. But there was little comfort in that for a woman who just wanted to make ends meet and provide for her son.

And she was afraid, too, and not just for her safety. Mollie had convinced her that she was still attractive, though it was years since she'd felt pretty around Blyth, and the cold fact was that she hadn't had sex in more than a decade. *What if the man doesn't even like me? What if he thinks I'm not attractive enough?* They were reasonable enough questions, she told herself. *Would he pay me? Dismiss me like an old toy?* That would be the ultimate humiliation. But then she scolded herself for her selfishness. *I'm a whore*, she thought barbarously, *why should I expect to be treated nicely?* Kerra was in turmoil with her own thoughts.

But she also recalled her years of heinous suffering at the hands of her husband. She'd been beaten by Blyth so many times that physical abuse didn't scare her, and worse, she'd endured mental punishment for a decade and a half. *What's the worst that* can *happen?* she thought. No, she was tough. She could do it.

Still Kerra waited. She felt dolorous, but forced herself to focus on the task ahead. Beneath a thick fur coat, Mollie's loaned dress clung tight, and she barely felt the bitter air that besieged her exposed skin. Fixing her eyes only on the road from where the stranger's car would soon emerge, she fought in vain to stay calm as she thought about the plan. They were to go for a drink. Then they'd spend the afternoon at a hotel. The rest she could only guess at. Hot blood pounded in her numbed temples.

Twelve o'clock came and went, the time replaced by pressing uncertainty. *It isn't too late,* she thought. *I could be away from here in seconds. It's only money.* The internal dialogue almost activated a defence mechanism that would have seen her flee in an instant. But Tristan's serene and innocent face flashed in her eyes, his eyes seeming to give her a reassuring look, and she calmed herself by breathing deeply of the Siberian like air. *It's not about money,* she told herself. *I'm doing it for our future, our survival.* She only had to wait a moment longer.

Seven minutes after midday, and glowing through the drizzle shone the strong beam of a Jaguar's headlights. The large silver car cruised up, and Kerra's heart rate accelerated from double to triple. As the magnificent machine slowed to a stop, the tinted window descended, and the little breath she could muster caught in her throat. An extremely handsome and well dressed man spoke in a voice as sleek as his car.

"I'm sorry I'm a little late. Kerra?"

Struck dumb like a robot, she only nodded.

"Well hello, Kerra. My name's Max…please, climb in."

With an unconscious glance around, Kerra managed to suck in a deep breath as she closed her eyes in shame. *I'm sorry son*, she whispered into the wintry mists, because now there was no turning back. Now she was committed.

Kerra climbed into the car, and as she did so, all the virtues that she'd ever considered sacred were left ingloriously behind.

Tristan marched out of Marnie's café, energized and

refocused on what he now considered his duty. Before he was searching for his mum because he missed her and because he needed her. But now he realized that she probably needed him as much, if not more, than he needed her, and the shame he felt at succumbing to the whisky so easily in a show of weakness clearly inherited from his father had really heightened his sense of responsibility to a mother who had sacrificed so much for him for nothing in return. Besides, it was the first genuinely positive clue about her whereabouts, and he didn't intend to waste a moment.

With a rigid wind at his back Tristan headed directly to the area of The Blind Beggar pub, where Marnie's friend claimed to have seen his mother. He knew he'd been in there before, but with no joy, and he hoped for more luck second time around. As the houses got smaller and the streets narrower, he was getting close. Everything…the buildings, the cars…even the people…seemed more run down…dilapidated, as if the daily grind of the East End was getting the better of them. Tristan was torn. He wanted nothing more than to find his mother. But it was a tough area…dangerous, even, and his apprehension rose as an icy rain fell to accompany the now shrieking wind.

He hustled on through the greyness, shoulders hunched against the ferocious elements, warnings resonating in his mind while below his feet, deepening puddles shone with misery. *Be careful Tristan*, Bobby had said, *there're some bad people out there*, and just an hour before Marnie insisted that her news *might lead to nothing*.

Yet he remained upbeat and confident about the prospects of finding his mother, and in the growing gloom, Tristan didn't even notice as a large silver Jaguar materialized out of the mist and cruised slowly past.

Max looked at her. But it wasn't the sleazy look she might have expected.

"The word is that you're a newcomer to the East End and, shall we say, to this profession." He smiled, and it was disarming.

"Yes sir. I mean, yes to both." Her voice barely rose above a nervy whisper.

"Well, Kerra…may I call you Kerra?"

She nodded again, this time less robotic.

"Please, try and relax. I'm not going to hurt you, and honestly, I just want to have a fun and relaxed afternoon. Can you relax for me?"

She nodded once more, and now a half smile formed on her rouged lips.

"That's good. So what do you like to drink? Wine? Cocktails? The choice is yours. We'll grab a couple of bevies, and then go for an early dinner. How does that sound?"

Since Blyth's own drinking had ruined her life, Kerra no longer drank, and she had definitely never tried a cocktail before, and couldn't name one if she tried. Even the thought of it seemed comical, exotic even, in an ironic kind of way. But why not, why let the past dictate her future? This strange man was probably going to pay her for sex, and yet before that, she might just have the time of her life.

"Cocktails," she said.

Max really was charming. Over the next couple of hours they enjoyed a pleasant afternoon chatting over a couple of drinks, and Kerra was soon relaxed, so much so that she'd almost forgotten why she was there. It was many years since she'd even spoken with another man, and the fact that Max seemed genuinely interested in her was almost overwhelming.

Nestled in the corner of a quiet bar, he listened intently as she told him a little about herself...where she was from, her love of art...but she kept most of the darker details to herself, as she didn't want to mention her torrid past or the terrible plight of her children. And Max didn't push her to say more than she wanted.

Kerra couldn't deny it; she was having fun. In fact she couldn't remember the last time, if ever, she'd had such a lovely afternoon, and it was a surprise to her when Max announced it was already five o'clock and probably time for dinner. He then drove them to a tiny restaurant, and the impeccable host greeted him personally.

"Mr. Bartholomew, so nice to see you again. How's business, sir?"

Pleasantries were exchanged, and the host was equally polite to Kerra. The restaurant was beautiful, clearly expensive, and it was the finest meal she'd ever eaten. But when it was time to leave, reality settled back upon her as the bewitching effects of the cocktails quickly wore off, and she could no longer ignore what was obviously expected of her. Kerra tried to hide her nerves, but Max sensed her apprehension. Calmly, he eased her fears.

"Listen, Kerra, I can see you're apprehensive, and I understand, I really do, but it's not too late to change your mind if you need to. It's not only intimacy that I wanted, though I do find you very attractive. If it was, I wouldn't have bothered with all the fancy drinks and dinner. I simply wanted a good time, and in that regard, well I've certainly had it. You are beautiful, it's true, but more importantly you're excellent company. You know, things aren't going so well for me at home...haven't been for many, many years..." A momentary look of sadness flitted onto Max's clean cut face, but was soon blinked away. "Honestly, if you'd like me to take you home, just say the word and I will, no questions asked. And of course I'll still pay you handsomely for your time thus far."

Kerra was confused. It wasn't supposed to be like that, all manners and charm and generosity. She'd always assumed that men who paid for sex were dirty, horrible people who treated women badly and expected them to give them what they wanted. But Max could not have been more different. Part of her wanted to take his money and run, get out of there while she could and forget about the whole thing. She trusted him at his word to pay her for the afternoon, and her dignity would still be more or less intact, whatever was left of it. And besides, she'd had a nice time. *I could think of it as a date*, she mused, in a derisory effort to console herself.

But she liked Max. He'd been so nice to her, and she had thoroughly enjoyed her afternoon with him. Her own husband Blyth hadn't been nice to her in fifteen years, yet this stranger had treated her like royalty. She hesitated, just long enough for Max to put a gentle and considerate arm on her shoulder.

"Relax my dear, I'll take you home. It's fine, and I won't take it too personally, honest." His good natured wink was genuine.

Kerra looked into his eyes. And she trusted him.

"I'll go with you, Max." She smiled inadvertently as he held out her coat. This guy Max, whoever he was, was the finest gentleman she'd ever met.

By nine o'clock the next morning, Kerra was safely tucked up in her own bed, smiling and giggly from the champagne she now shared with Mollie, as she told her friend all about her first job as a prostitute.

In her purse was one hundred and fifty pounds. It was a lot of cash, and it was easy money. The worrying thing about it, though Kerra was too relieved to notice it yet, was that it hadn't felt like work at all.

## Chapter Fifty One

For the first time in months, probably even years, Kerra slept soundly. The late night with Max followed by early champagne with Mollie had left her exhausted, but when she awoke in the wintry darkness of late afternoon, she felt rejuvenated. Mollie was out, now, so both the flat and the neighborhood were quiet, and as she brewed a mug of tea she struggled to keep the smile from her face.

Kerra pondered what she'd done. It had gone so well, and after her initial fears she had enjoyed a wonderful afternoon...and night too, she thought with a slightly embarrassed chuckle. But perhaps it had gone too well? She had to remind herself that not all clients could be...wouldn't be...as nice as Max. *Don't get carried away*, she thought. No doubt about it, though, Max was lovely. He had told her later in the evening that he and his wife were having some difficulties, and that he was so lonely, and they'd even arranged to meet again when he was next in town...for a date, no money involved.

And why shouldn't she have some fun, fun she'd been denied for so long. She deserved it, and she couldn't wait to see him again. But that was two weeks away, and meanwhile she intended to keep her next appointment with another man tomorrow night. Kerra had to make more money before Tristan arrived, that was the reality, and why she'd even contemplated doing it in the first place.

She skipped dinner and went to bed early, mind drifting

uncomfortably between thoughts of Max and of Tristan, of shame and of excitement. Tristan weighed heavy on her mind, and she felt disgusted with herself for having fun with Max while he was out there somewhere, alone on the streets, probably hungry, and certainly cold, and that giddy sense of childish happiness she'd basked in for a few hours now drained away into the night as she wondered if they would ever be reunited.

Tristan had no plan other than to start at the pub, and if that didn't help, then to walk the streets and search, asking in newsagents and cafés, and describing his mother to as many people as possible. Since he had lost his one and only photograph, it was all he could do, and with luck it wasn't only Marnie's friend that had seen her. Sadly, the folks in The Blind Beggar were of no real help, though one greasy middle-aged man smirked, saying in a gruff voice, *she sounds familiar*. The slimy innuendo was missed by the naive Tristan.

A couple of hours on and a lot of sullied ground was covered. The streets were grimy and tough, but the East End natives were a friendly breed, and most wished him well. But his mood worsened with each disappointment, and his delicate spirits dropped like a big stone in a small pond and as he sank his hopes sank with him. Even the sky looked troubled, as if nervous or angry and might collapse at any moment, but it didn't and he continued on beneath it looking troubled too, almost as if by bearing such a weighty burden, he too might collapse.

But at last Tristan found someone whose one good eye sparkled in instant recognition. Wilfred was an aged, worn-out fellow that owned a corner shop he'd rebuilt from the rubble of the Blitz. He recognised Kerra's description immediately.

"Why yes, young fellow, I reckon I've seen that pretty woman before. In here only yesterday she was, buying tea bags...or was it the day before, or coffee? You know, son, the old memory ain't what it used to be. I put it down to the bombings, and all that racket during the war. But I ain't crazy, I've definitely seen her, from the way you described her, and besides, I'd never forget a beautiful young woman like that. Few and far between they are, especially round 'ere...and I don't need two eyes to tell you that."

With two more positive sightings that afternoon, Tristan felt a tempered surge of confidence. He was definitely getting close, but he still had no address, and as yet nobody could confirm his mother's name. Strangely though, the closer he felt he was getting the lonelier he became, and that loneliness accompanied him on his walk in the form of stalking shadows and imagined whispers, taunting and teasing him as lonely footfalls echoed on lonelier streets. *Just have to keep going*, he sighed, and shrugged off the melancholy beneath a sky that was now clamping the city in its grip of blackness.

Things began well. Kerra's new client was equally as dapper as Max, and apparently as wealthy. Though short and stocky, his hard features were handsome and rugged, the look completed by a couple of significant scars, one above his right eye, and another that cut a cleft in his squared chin. His eye scar, she noticed, almost matched her own, a sickly and untimely reminder of her husband's brutality. She hoped this wasn't evidence of a similarly violent man, and the thought caused an involuntary shudder she hoped he didn't notice.

Michael was a softly spoken man, and though a little aloof he seemed nice enough. But after an hour in his company Kerra's thoughts turned to Max. It was crazy, she knew, and she felt deeply ashamed at her feelings for a man who had, one way or another, paid her for sex. But she couldn't help it, and almost laughed aloud at the ridiculous situation she found herself in. *What kind of woman,* she thought, *falls in love with a customer of whores?*

But it wasn't long before Michael realized Kerra didn't want to be there, and he didn't like it one bit.

"Are you going to talk to me, or shall I talk to myself?"

"Pardon me? Oh, I'm sorry."

He proffered a weak smile, but she could see he wasn't impressed and quickly forced the image of Max from her mind. After that moment Michael's affable manner changed, the previously gentle tone of his voice replaced with a flinty edge.

"Let's go to the hotel. I'm tired of this useless conversation." The look in his eye made her nervous, and she tried to stall.

"Couldn't we stay for a while longer, just a couple more drinks?" Kerra didn't want to upset the man, but if she had to satisfy him physically, she would need to drink a lot more. Michael laughed at her as if she were nothing. Then his eyes narrowed.

"You think this is some kind of charity? I'm paying you for a good time, and it's not working, so let's cut the bullshit and get to the real business."

She thought of protesting, but he was right; she was his whore. Kerra bit her lip and walked quietly, almost obediently, out to his car.

They drove away from the bar in a welcome silence, but Michael's demeanor had changed so dramatically that Kerra was now seriously on edge. She hadn't really noticed before, but Michael was a mean looking man, and clearly very strong. It wasn't a fear of being beaten up that worried her, as she was more than used to that. There was just something about him and the situation in general that was causing her to panic. Perhaps it was simply that she was alone with a tough looking stranger, she didn't know where she was going, and the only person in the world that would know if she went missing happened to be a newly acquired friend, herself with a morally suspect set of principles.

Suddenly the idea seemed a totally different prospect, and Kerra resolved not to offend the man any further. She had a job to do, and a duty to her son. She would not mess it up.

They arrived at the backstreet hotel and, like the one with Max, it was small and discreet. Michael hurried her up to the room, and glared at her from the doorway.

"I'll be back later. If you want to get paid, don't go anywhere." And then he was gone. Kerra wasn't expecting that.

She relaxed a little and sat on the bed, thinking she was just being paranoid. Looking around she knew that it wasn't a cheap hotel, so Michael clearly had money. *It's just business*, she thought, and reminded herself that it was only temporary, a part-time job, and while degrading and against any principles she'd once had, it was necessary and well paid.

*For Tristan*, she assured herself, *for my son.*

It was Mollie who'd recommended Max. She'd heard about him from some of the other girls, and they told her they trusted him completely, that he was a safe bet. But Michael had been set up through a friend of a friend, and Mollie had gone only on a word of mouth recommendation. Kerra knew absolutely nothing about him, and she knew she was being reckless. But she recalled one of Mollie's well worn phrases, and she had to smile at the truth of it. *Needs must,* said her friend, *needs must.* And Kerra really needed the money.

Significantly calmed, she felt secure enough to take a bath, and ran a steaming jet of water into the lavish tub. It was many years since she'd had that rare opportunity, and Kerra lay back blissfully as the water rose over her naked and, for the first time in far too long, her bruise free body.

Amidst the lulling combination of steamy water and fragrant bubbles, Kerra soon drifted off into a peaceful sleep. But when she awoke two hours later the water was cold. Momentarily confused, she remembered where she was, and now alarmed she stepped out and quickly wrapped herself in a towel. She listened at the door for a sign that Michael was back, and hearing nothing walked through into the bedroom...just as he staggered into the room.

"Oh, hello. I hope you don't mind, I just…"

"In bed! Now!"

In a split second Kerra's heart pounded and her stomach knotted in the grip of fear. She immediately recoiled from the foul stench of whisky breath from three yards away, and in his cold, malevolent glare she saw her husband looking back.

"What're you waiting for, bitch?" he said leering. "Do as I say!"

The fact that he didn't shout was even more frightening, and his tone was void of emotion.

She was frantic and wanted only to run, but his massive body blocked the only exit, and the danger of her situation exploded into her mind with diamond clarity; alone; back street hotel; a very drunk, very powerful man. *I'm so stupid...so, so stupid!* Thinking quickly...almost naked... if I dress now he'll get angry...he'll know I'm afraid...he won't let me leave…I have to submit…it's the best chance…my only chance.

Michael glared passively from across the room, and his cold yet amused expression taunted her, dared her to run. He could see she was scared, could sense her fear, and he smiled a warped and crooked smile that betrayed his handsome face. Michael was having fun.

Kerra's adrenalin surged, and she tasted the all too familiar metallic taste she associated with her past and with violence. With fear. Desperate, there was only one option left to her.

"I just wanted to freshen up for you, be a good clean girl." She let the towel slide seductively to the floor, then walked to the bed and slipped under the covers. "Are you going to join me?"

Genuinely amused, Michael laughed a callous, indifferent laugh, and then he glared a little longer, as if he'd known all along how things were going to play out. But what he did next stopped Kerra's heart. Without taking his penetrating black eyes from hers, he edged backwards, and with a wicked smile that froze the blood in her veins, Michael bolted the door.

Slowly he approached the bed, like a tiger sizing up its helpless prey. His eyes bore deep into Kerra's with an intensity that made even Blyth look meek. And then he spoke, and his voice was pure ice.

"I fucking hate hookers."

*Chapter Fifty Two*

Yesterday, the owner of a café who empathized with Tristan's plight promised him a free breakfast if he returned, and when he was warmly greeted as he entered the Woodbine Café at just after nine in the morning, he was again awed by the kindness of strangers. The owner was a real East Ender, loud and gritty and with a wicked sense of humour, and Tristan could hardly understand him when he spoke. In fact, Arthur didn't really speak at all, rather, every time he opened his mouth, a torrent of foul mouthed shouting poured out, much to the delight of his equally rowdy customers.

Middle-aged, bald and with a massive belly bulging out of his grease stained t-shirt, he was clearly a very popular man in the area, and greeted all his punters with an '*allo mate*' or a '*mornin' love,*' when they flowed in from the rain. Arthur was a natural storyteller, and addressed anyone who'd listen.

"Ya see, that's the trouble with them cheeky arsed kids, ain't it."

"What's that?" replied an equally well fed patron.

"Nowadays, they all want sumthin' for nuthin'." He glanced over at Tristan, and included him with a conspiratorial wink. The rant continued.

"Remember that gobby kid, Harry wotsisname, Frankie's boy, always coming round 'ere and asking for a free fry up. Well, I gave him his fry up. Then I charged him double, and sent him off sharpish with a clip round his wing-nut ear. Kid scarpered quicker than you can say Flash 'Arry."

The Woodbine's regulars laughed in unison, and their host and entertainer gave respectful bows all round.

Later, after the morning rush had subsided, Arthur joined Tristan at his table laden with two mugs of tea.

"So, sonny boy, I may've heard sumthin' about ya mum…well not about her, but maybe another woman who might just be her friend. An old pal o' mine came in and mentioned a girl named Mollie, right firecracker she is.

The two of them have been seen together more than once."

Tristan's eyes lit up. "Really? Where? Do you have an address?"

"Actually, as it 'appens I do." Arthur told Tristan what he'd heard, but like Marnie, he too warned him about setting his hopes too high.

"You see, sonny, this Mollie gal has a bit of an unsavory reputation in these parts...hangs out in, shall we say, less than charming company. And there's sumthin' about these streets...people tend to, well, they change people, and not always for the best, know what I mean?"

Though he didn't really understand what Arthur meant, Tristan was sure this was the final clue he needed to find his mother. And despite the warnings, he couldn't help but get carried away. After all these weeks, and all the hundreds of miles, the robbery, the sleeping outside, the hitchhiking, the misery...Tower Bridge...finally, he had something solid to go on. Tristan had an address.

He thanked Arthur, and literally ran into the mean streets of London's East End on a wave of delirium and adrenalin that protected him from the cold and surged him onward. And though he'd developed as an individual since the escape from St. Mary's, beneath it all he was still the naive Tristan from the island who knew nothing of the world, rendering him oblivious as to just how mean life on the East End streets could really be.

Kerra was stricken with terror. Michael had no real reason to lock the door. If she wanted money, which was the only reason she was there, obviously she'd stay. Yet lock it he did. More ominous than that though was what he'd said; *I fucking hate hookers*! And it was with those words, and the flat and heartless finality with which he'd said them, that she knew she was in serious trouble.

Michael made a quick lunge forward, just one short step, and Kerra stifled a scream. He was toying with her, relishing her fear.

"There are no other guests here," he said, "Just you and I. And the manager is...well, he knows how I like to play."

In other words, screaming was futile. Kerra's mind worked frantically for a way out of the escalating nightmare. The manager was in on it. No other guests. No way out of the room. She waited, stalling for time. Waiting for what she didn't know, but now she feared the worst.

Kerra studied his face. Was it mere anger she saw, or genuine hatred? She would settle for a little anger. He stumbled forward as he kicked off his shoes, shoulder muscles rippling as he unbuttoned his shirt. Kerra gasped in horror. Across his now exposed chest was a gruesome scar, at least eighteen inches long and, though she couldn't believe it, so long it might even have been caused by a sword. It seemed that he was lucky to be alive. Michael looked at her. And smiled.

"What, you never seen a scar before? Don't worry, his was worse, had himself a little accident with a meat cleaver. I expect you want to scream, just like he wanted to." He laughed, and the sinister sound sent her skin crawling. "Difficult to scream, though, with his tongue lying in the dust. Fucker got what he deserved...just like you're going to."

Kerra now knew, without any doubt at all, that she was at the mercy of a psycho. Her mind raced. She was a hooker now...weren't they supposed to be tough, feisty? And she thought of Mollie. What would Mollie do? The answer to that question was easy; fight. Mollie would fight to the death.

She launched herself from the bed, and flew at Michael with all the rage she could muster. But she'd lost so much weight recently, both from stress and malnutrition, that her barely eight stone frame was smothered in an instant, and easily pinned to the bed by a man twice her size.

Kerra was literally helpless. He was just so strong that she couldn't move an inch, and as one hand clutched at her throat, the other slowly balled into a fist like a wrecking ball. Though her once pretty eyes were wide with terror, Kerra didn't see the devastating knock-out punch coming her way.

Blindfolded and paralyzed, Kerra came to in a world of hurt, with the familiar smell of her own blood filling the air. She tried to call out, but pain screamed from broken ribs. She fought for air through a swollen windpipe. She couldn't see Michael, but knew he was close, his stale whisky stench filling her broken nose. In a struggle to calm her terror, she ignored his heavy breathing just inches away. *Is he asleep?* But escape appeared futile, with both her hands and feet tightly bound, the circulation all but cut off.

Kerra stared into the muffled darkness of the blindfold, as all her dreams of a better future unraveled right there in that hotel room. The horrific irony wasn't lost on her either, despite her delirious state, that she had finally escaped the tyranny of one psychotic man, only to end up the victim of another. In all her years of unmitigated suffering, Kerra had never once felt pity for herself. Somehow, for reasons known only to her, she deserved Blyth's punishments and had accepted them for the sake of her son.

But Kerra Annis knew one more thing; she did not deserve this indignity. Not here, not now, and not from this man. She might die tonight in a hotel room, and nobody would know. Never again see her children. Never get the chance to atone for her mistakes.

For the first time in her forty years, Kerra wept from pure, unadulterated self pity.

Tristan hurried along dreary, almost funereal roads towards where he hoped to at last find his mother, but if he wanted to take any optimism about her situation from the area as he passed through it, he found none on such empty and desolate streets. The address he had was in a rundown area of town known to house most of London's immigrants and emigrants, and as a magnet for the poor and disenfranchised, it was cheap and it was nasty, and rife with crime of every sort.

None of this mattered though, and Tristan thought only of hugging his mother soon. He could barely contain his emotions as he pressed on, the rain unnoticed as the sunless sky above denied him even a shadow for company. Corner after sketchy corner he turned, next crossing a rusted railway bridge overgrown with vines and nettles and covered in obscene and poorly spelled graffiti. Skinny stray dogs yapped at his heels as he rushed by, and he had to dodge reams of garbage that drifted past on a stiffening wind. And the few people he did see offered nothing but a scowl.

But Tristan ignored it all as he followed the directions fanatically, his focus narrowed, and oblivious to the thundering deluge and the lightning that illuminated the sky every few seconds. Finally, and after an hour of almost trance-like dedication to the task, he found what he was looking for.

Tristan's heart sank. The three story concrete block looked as if it hadn't been maintained in twenty years, since the Blitz had decimated most of the city. Every second window was boarded up, and one in three doors was only half repaired. Graffiti stained every available wall space, and the weed strangled courtyard between the road and the stairwell was strewn with trash and bottles and the shit of a thousand stray dogs. It seemed simply unfit for human habitation.

He rechecked the address to be sure, but knew it was right. This was it. This was where his mother lived.

Three at a time he took stairs laced with smashed glass and that stank of fetid piss, and he almost dashed past the correct door in his haste through the squalor. But there it was; number 15. Tristan shivered with nervous emotion, and with another look around him at the atrocious bombed out look of his mother's new home, part of him wished that she had moved on. But only part of him. The selfish part of his still childlike mind was desperate for his mum to throw open the patched up door, and then throw her loving and relieved arms around him and to never again let him go.

*Finally, I'm here,* he whispered, and watched as his fogged breath dispersed onto the moldy ceiling of the doorway. Tristan stepped forward and knocked on the door.

By rubbing her battered face against the pillow, Kerra managed to slip free of the blindfold. She blinked beneath bright lights, and surveyed the scene through swollen eyes. Michael was passed out. Try as she might, she couldn't stand up, and desperation dulled her intense agony. Blood had spilled from too many different places, including her most private areas, and she was weak and on the verge of throwing up. Kerra didn't know how many times he'd raped her, twice, maybe three times? *How do some men become so evil?* She had always thought her husband was the epitome of immorality. He beat her with untamed violence, and had tortured her mentality for close to twenty years, and though Blyth's abuse was never sexual, she didn't believe it could get much worse.

How wrong she was! Michael was an animal. His indifference to her fear was obvious, and he'd taunted her before the attack. *How many other women has he beaten and raped?* She felt sure she wasn't the first. *And what happens now? He can't just let me walk out of here. Of course, he won't.*

Panic shook her to the core, and in the warm room a cold sweat trickled down her bruised back. Kerra legitimately feared for her life, and sensing that Michael was beginning to stir, she struggled wildly, thrashing against her bonds, despite the likelihood of it waking him up completely. After fifteen seconds of constant writhing about, one leg somehow broke free of the gaffer tape that clinically held her hostage. If she could just get a hand loose…

But it was futile; she simply couldn't release her hands from the inflexible ties on her wrists. Exhaustion rendered her useless, and when the last ounce of will and fight and desperate courage had slipped away, the magnitude of her all encompassing pain consumed her.

Unconscious, Kerra was once more at the mercy of the beast.

No answer, and the only sound came from rattling wind and hail that clanged on a nearby tin roof.

*Asleep? Not home?* He knocked again, a sustained and heavy knock. Some slow shuffling inside, like someone roused unwillingly from bed. No lights came on. His heart pounded. The flickering glow of a nearby street light only added to his tension, and when a scrawny black cat suddenly screeched angrily at him from the top of the stairs, as if in warning to the dumb fucking kid to stay away, Tristan almost jumped out of his skin.

But overriding it all was a desperation to see his mother, and he forced himself to calm down. He'd come too far to lose it now. She had to be in there.

"Mum, is that you?" he called, "It's me, Tristan." Emotion laced his cracking voice, and he wondered why she didn't rush to him. He studied the door, willing it open, and noticed its fading, blistered green paint that barely clung to the wood and the mould that crept across it like a cancer. It didn't bode well. If it was possible, his pulse rate notched up a level as at last he heard a key turn inside. Just another second. Tristan felt his legs weaken in anticipation, as the door slowly opened.

It wasn't her.

Michael awoke slowly from his slumber, and eyed Kerra with amusement, the way a cat toys with a tiny mouse...just before the kill. He jabbed a strong finger at her, but she didn't register. Again he prodded, harder this time, and this time she grunted, delirious from pain and physically ruined. Very slowly, Kerra's puffy eyes peeled open, cracking the dried blood and causing an agonized wince. She almost vomited from pain. And then she remembered, as her wildly dilated pupils struggled to take in the demonic look that told her everything; she was about to die.

With nothing more in her hellish life to lose, Kerra screamed.

Quick as a flash he was upon her, his speed and ferocity horrific as the heinous coward battered Kerra to within an inch of her life. And then he battered her some more.

Unconscious again, the lifeless form slumped back onto the bed, and just a mile away, at the very moment tears of disappointment flowed from her son's eyes, the blood of life flowed from her crippled and corrupted body.

Mollie's bleached hair was wild and her makeup garish and smeared, while her clothes looked as if they'd been slept in for two days. But upon seeing the tall young lad standing at her door, whose face looked so much like her friend's, her own face lit up like a beacon and she threw her arms around his neck in a powerful, emotional hug. Stood before her was Tristan Nancarrow.

Tristan could barely breathe, his stoicism on the verge of collapse.

"Tristan," she said, "thank God you're here."

Upon hearing his name, he wrestled the tiny woman's arms from his neck and took a step back, his disappointment soon displaced by concern. This woman clearly knew him, but who was she, and where was his mother?

"Where's my mum?" His mature voice belied his adolescent features, and his eyes shone with emotion.

"Oh kid, I'm so glad you've made it. Your mum's been beside herself waiting for you, but she's gonna be so happy. Just wait 'til she sees you."

"She's not here?" he asked, quickly followed up by a more urgent, "so where is she?"

"No kid, she ain't here, but don't worry cos' she'll be back soon. Ya mum's been…well…she's out…working a night shift. Why don't you come in out of that miserable weather."

Tristan had become more sensitive to people's attitudes and dispositions these last difficult few weeks, and could sense she was clearly hiding something. And he certainly didn't miss the shadow that crept guiltily across her face.

But he only really cared about one thing. He had found his mum. He was at the right place. And that small yet effervescent woman who called herself Mollie had just said she'd be back soon. He would see her at last, and as the realisation hit him that, after everything he'd been through, and all the trials and tribulations had almost reached their conclusion, his shoulders shook with unbridled emotion.

Mollie sensed his emotional overload, and prayed he hadn't noticed her own discomfort. But try as she might, she couldn't prevent her own tears from falling, though for an entirely different reason. She was sick with worry about Kerra, who hadn't shown up home from last night's job, and only earlier that day she'd heard rumors on the East End grapevine that some lunatic had murdered a prostitute somewhere out west. In an effort to conceal her fears, she dragged Tristan into the flat and shut the door on the world outside.

Mollie had at last managed to get the gas reconnected in the tiny flat, and gently positioned Tristan in front of the fire that offered just enough heat to take the chill from the room. But as she looked at the boy, despite the welcome heat she felt a very real shiver creep up her spine. What on earth could she say to him?

"You know, she said you was a good looking boy, and she was right. You really look like her. Beautiful, your mum is, a real stunner, and a proper good friend to me. Let me get you a cuppa, kid, you look freezing."

Swamped with relief yet tainted by an uneasy sense of disquietude, Tristan sat by the fire and glanced around at the humble flat. It was shabby and sparse and, shared with Mollie, it was tiny. But it was at least warm…at least she wasn't on the streets. It was a home. He leaned back on the threadbare couch and relaxed, if only just a little.

Mollie took her time making the tea, stalling before facing the poor boy in the lounge and now realising the significance of Kerra's possible disappearance. She hadn't given it all that much thought before, as girls often stayed overnight with the client, even two nights, if the money was right. But Kerra would've told her somehow, got her some kind of message, if that's what she'd done. Yet she'd heard nothing. And just that afternoon she'd heard about the poor girl out west.

Now Tristan was finally there, and the situation was serious. Mollie was at her wit's end. But not being able to wait any longer, she sat with Tristan as they drank tea and he told her of his adventures since escaping St. Mary's Island.

It had been only a few weeks, but it seemed to Tristan like a transitory lifetime. He was the same boy, but changed, somehow. He felt different, grown up, stronger maybe, though he wasn't sure. The weeks since he'd left behind his father and the island had taught him much, illustrating so clearly how isolated from reality he really was. Now he'd found his mother, he imagined a continued time of evolution and discovery, and despite the apparently constant storm that had followed him east from his dark and traumatic past, the future looked altogether brighter.

*But where was she?*

Alone, brutalized and dying, Kerra's sad and slanted life passed before her swiftly fading eyes.

She heard laughter and saw sunshine as a handsome young man took her hand. Blyth! The beach and the blue skies and sea. Home. Her hand holding a delicately poised brush as she contemplated her next painting. Passion. Friends, her family, and the innocence and ecstasy of youth. Happiness.

Then…

Kaleidoscopic images of babies glowed…a boy, a girl, but never together. The boy she knew and the girl she lost, her son with a clear face, her daughter's face, elusive. Tristan and Ailla. She hadn't set eyes upon Ailla since she was a baby. She'd never known her face. Had never known her daughter. Regret.

Sorrow and regret.

Images came and went, grainy, unclear. A slow, single tear slid from a swollen, bloodshot eye.

A child's laugh punctuated the sounds of violence that echoed in her soul as they'd echoed throughout her life. Punches and screams, glass smashing, things breaking… things were always breaking. Those nightmare sounds formed the wretched soundtrack of Kerra's wretched life. The child's laugh again, a laugh always…always… followed by crying. And she saw no more smiles in her mind, her mind being the only place she remembers ever seeing them.

The final image she saw was the mortified face of her son. Her Tristan.

His hand reached for hers now, he now a young man, just like he had as a child, only now she couldn't reach back to him. Yet in vain she tried with her one loose arm…limp, broken and free of its socket.

She had failed him. In life, she knew she had failed him. Her daughter, too. She'd failed them all. Even Blyth.

As the concluding beats of her life ebbed and waned, that haunting image of Tristan evaporated, and a last tear nestled on her smashed cheek.

In death, as the grave beckoned, like in life, as she

fought it off, Kerra knew she'd failed.
And then she was gone.
Tragic and alone.
Kerra was dead.

# Part III

# The Unforgiven

*Chapter Fifty Three*

Blyth Nancarrow was a changed man, and both he and the cottage were unrecognizable from just a few weeks before. He hadn't touched alcohol in a month, hadn't even craved it, and now he devoted his time to doing repairs and restoring his home to its former civilized and pleasant state. Whisky had for too long rendered him useless and ignorant of the once attractive cottage, and its broken down state of disrepair, he realized with numbing shame, matched that of his failed relationships with his wife and son. So much needed repairing in Blyth's life, including his relationship with God. For years he had felt the forsaken one, but now, he knew, it was he who had done the forsaking.

Over the course of several days and weeks, and once he'd regained both his physical and mental strength after the close call with an inglorious and lonely death, Blyth got to work. He shored up stone walls and tidied ramshackle and weed choked rockeries. He built a new shed, this one containing only tools and not the poisons of his past. Tristan's beloved plants had slowly recovered, because, rather than destroy them as before, Blyth spent long hours caring for them. Even the old truck had been cleared of the inch thick mud, and stood shiny and gleaming on a freshly raked driveway.

The incessant stormy weather had hampered his progress, but the exterior of the property was vastly improved. Inside too, things were rehabilitated. Walls had been repainted and broken floor boards replaced. There was no cracked glass to be seen, and furniture stood straight and repaired. Beside the hearth in the kitchen, a space that had seen far too much suffering, was a constant pile of recently chopped wood, and never was there anything less than a perfectly blazing fire to keep the cottage warm. Yes it was cold, but Blyth knew the real reason that the fire had to burn.

But his proudest achievement so far was the artist studio he'd created for his wife. For so long he'd denied Kerra the opportunity to paint, and had long ago killed her passion for art. The shame of that cruel suppression burned him deeply, and in repatriating the mouldy, stale and never used junk room into a lovely, light work space for her, it did more than anything to keep his sliver like hope of redemption alive. That, and of course his prayers.

Deep down though, and in the depths of his deflated heart, he knew Kerra would never come back to him, and she would never lay her eyes upon what he had done. But whenever he opened the once neglected door to that beautiful and ambient room, his restored pride solidified just a little more, and his wish for total rehabilitation became just a little bit more real.

Kerra had loved him once, a long time ago, and the memory of her smile kept him focused on his recovery. Blyth often took to his knees, too, and prayed to a long forgotten God to once again cast some light in his direction, and banish the shameful and sinister shadows from the cottage. But as he looked about his property, finally looking as it should after too many years of selfish neglect, Blyth's one great fear remained; his family's home would never again be home to his family.

But he kept the fire burning anyway. If he was to be forgiven, by either Tristan or Kerra or Ailla, and one day, one or more of them walked back through his door, there would be a beautiful home warmed by that fire, and a reincarnated father or husband to greet them. That fire, that blaze that he so vigilantly kept alight, became his main symbol of progress and rehabilitation, and the moment the flames died, he knew, would be the moment that all hope was lost and he'd once and for all been cast adrift by God and by the world.

In her panic about what to say to Tristan, Mollie had blurted out something about Kerra working a night shift, which, in an incongruous kind of way, she was. It was totally misleading the kid, of course, but at least it had bought both her and Kerra some time. With sleep elusive, she tossed back and forth in her bed into the early hours, terribly concerned about her friend. Kerra should definitely have been home some time that day, and it was so out of character for her not to have made contact. Mollie was beside herself with worry.

Meanwhile, despite the uncomfortable and bony couch, Tristan did manage sleep, and it was deep and welcome. He drifted off knowing that he was in his mother's home, and that in the morning he would greet her at the door when she got in from her job and hug her until his arms dropped off. He wanted so badly to see her again, and they had so much to talk about and catch up on that his mind was whirring with anticipation. But soon sleep engulfed him, and he was lost to the night.

Morning came and went. Tristan had awoken at dawn and sat waiting on the couch, but as the stormy night gave way to a wet and silvery winter morning, his mother had not returned. By mid-morning he was pacing about the flat in a state of serious agitation, and last evening's dull anxiety about her whereabouts was now droning like an air raid siren in the Blitz.

Mollie, weary from barely two hours sleep, was now fearful for her friend's safety, but she was just as nervous about how to approach the subject with her son, who stalked about the lounge with a look of steel in his eyes. She tried to hide her anxiety from Tristan, but it was in vain. The boy was perceptive, and he knew something was being kept from him.

"So where does my mother work? Is that really why she's still out? Tell me the truth."

"Listen kid, I'll be honest. I did expect her home by now, but…well, perhaps she got kept back late at the factory." It was a weak lie, and Tristan knew it. "Probably just doing overtime, as God knows we could do with the extra money."

Tristan was sure there was more that Mollie wouldn't say, but decided to let it go for now. However, if his mum didn't show up in the next hour, he would demand answers from her so-called friend. *She's my mother…I deserve to know the truth.*

The minute hand crawled up the clock in an agonizingly slow death march to midday, both of them watching it as if, at midday, the very world might end.

18446744073709551615

Mollie was frantic. Kerra should be home by now…
yesterday, in fact. Sometimes clients kept a girl for a
second night, but it was unusual. Kerra wouldn't even
agree to that, not when Tristan could have arrived any day.
Deep in her simmering guts, Mollie knew something had
gone horribly wrong.

When the clock finally struck twelve, Tristan fixed
Mollie with an unwavering glare. He'd waited long
enough.

"Where is she? The truth, Mollie!"

She sighed, both from the strain and from resignation.
The boy was right. She owed him some honesty.

"Listen, Tristan, when I met Kerra she was lost and
lonely, and I saw it clearly, for I knew that look well and I
wore it myself." Mollie gulped, her throat dry and
constricted. But she had to tell him. "She's been out with
a man. She went two afternoons ago, and she said she'd
be back yesterday. I'm not sure where she went, and
honestly, I don't know where she is. I'm so sorry." She
held back the exact nature of Kerra's association with the
man, at least for now, and in a last desperate attempt to
allay his fears, added, "But I reckon she's just fine, love,
and she'll be back in no time." She hoped that her voice
didn't betray her lies, but knew instantly she'd failed. Her
hands shook and her brow creased in distress.

Tristan suddenly felt weak, and had to sit on the sofa
before he fell. Unravelling. Could his world be
unravelling again? Here in this shit hole flat in the asshole
end of this shit bound neighborhood? His head dropped
into his hands as he fought to maintain his waning
composure, and his breathing came in short sharp
discharges. After a while images of the people in his life
flitted about his mind. He saw his father, who looked at
him with an expression of sorrow. Bella, her face sick yet

proud. Ailla, pretty but unknown, and yet somehow known. Richard and Winston, Bobby, Mark and Marnie, all with smiles of encouragement. And then his mother. Lost and alone, just as Mollie said. Forsaken.

And himself, weak and afraid and ready to quit. Broken.

A failure.

But then he was surprised to see the image of Tramp. He hardly knew the man, yet there he was in his time of need, right in the forefront of his mind. Why Tramp? But he knew. It was the words he'd heard the mysterious old man say. That poem he'd delivered. Horace. The final words, something like this; *'what will be will be, and I have had my hour.'*

Those words, combined with seeing himself looking so defeated, snapped him from his slump, and he stood with purpose from the couch. This was it. This would be his hour. And it started now.

"I'm going to look for my mum. Right now! With or without you. You know the area, Mollie, so where might she be? Give me options!"

Tristan hustled into his shoes and coat, and hurried out into the harsh afternoon. Mollie was seconds behind him. It was bitterly cold, so they rushed at speed between all the pubs and cafés within walking distance of the flat, even the old factory where they'd worked. No sign. Mollie secretly thought that by now there were two options; either Kerra was still in a hotel somewhere, though that was unlikely after so long, or she'd actually left the area with a client, but that was even less likely with her son imminent.

There was one other possible scenario, and it filled Mollie with horror; something vile had happened to her friend. It wasn't unknown in these parts, and of course there was always some risk. But nothing serious had ever happened to her, and other than the one prostitute apparently murdered last week, most working girls considered it safe enough to continue making a living on the streets. Besides, that one incident was as yet unconfirmed, and was way out west, anyway.

Still, Mollie couldn't shake the notion that something sinister had happened. And if it had, she was to blame. *Poor Kerra,* she thought, *she was against the idea from the start. But I encouraged her. It'll be all my fault if any harm has come to her*. She shuddered at the possibility.

Their trawling of the cafés and pubs had yielded nothing, so the best option was to check out the hotels. But that would need some explaining to the young kid, and she just couldn't face that at all. It took some pleading to persuade him, but frozen and, with a promise to try again when the pubs would be busier later, they headed back to the comfort of the flat.

Mollie had no idea what to do. Call the police? That would alert Tristan to her fears of some catastrophe, and she just couldn't do it to the he poor kid. *After all he's been through so far, and then his mother goes missing again.* Her heart wept for those two desperate souls, who'd been through so much together, and now faced life alone. Mollie knew only this; she would pray for Kerra's safe return.

"Hello. Hello, it's the cleaner." The stooped old woman knocked as loud as her frail arthritic knuckles could manage, but after several unsuccessful attempts at rousing the occupants, she concluded they were out.

"Good," she muttered in a wispy voice, adding, with a bucketful of sarcasm, "one doesn't like to trouble the lovely guests."

The veteran maid fumbled with her skeleton key and unlocked the hotel door. In the darkness she found the room's light switch by touch and, letting her cataract diminished eyes adjust to the glaring brilliance, waited a moment by the door. When at last her vision melted into focus, what she saw caused the tiny old woman to emit a warbled scream that filled the room with the sound of horror.

Like a flashback to the war, there before her and sprawled in unnatural contortions on the bed, was the naked and destroyed body of Kerra Nancarrow. Unrecognizable as the sad but attractive young woman she'd seen arrive a day or two ago, she knew beyond doubt that the girl was dead. No person could survive those injuries.

Her face was a purplish mass of angry cuts and grazes, and blackened crusts of blood hid most of her once pretty features. Rampant bruises screamed agony around her neck, and one arm hung from the bed in a crazed and twisted mess. Strangely, her clothes were folded neatly on a chair. But the blood stained sheets were grisly evidence to an obvious crime.

The old maid picked up a clean sheet from the pile she'd dropped on the floor, and cautiously approached the bed. Georgina Joyce Proudfoot had seen some terrible things in her seventy some years living in the East End. Just a kid when Jack the Ripper was terrorizing her neighborhood, she'd lived through two world wars, losing a husband in the first and two sons in the second, and witnessed from far too close the horror of the German blitz. She'd suffered perpetual flooding and fought off one disease after another, and hadn't even known the luxury of simply being poor; in her lifetime, Georgina had known only extreme poverty. But never before had she been as shocked and devastated as she was right there in that depressing and hellish hotel room. With a glance skywards, she started to make the sign of the cross over her chest, but didn't complete the motion.

"Oh, what's the damn point," she murmured. "If there was a God, he's clearly forsaken this poor woman." Bitter and angry, she respectfully covered Kerra's annihilated body. Dignity was all she could hope for now.

Mollie insisted he rest, maybe even take a nap…at least that way he couldn't ask more difficult questions. *That's right, Mollie,* she mocked herself, *fucking selfish to the last.* The tension was unbearable, and she wasn't dealing with it at all. But Tristan did as she suggested and curled his long legs up onto the couch.

He dreamt of his mother, and the dreams were horrible. Reds and blacks and blues morphed into a maelstrom of feral, grisly forms, unknowable though familiar and with the shadowy figure of his father always nearby. Blyth moved closer, and terrified, she opened her mouth to scream…just as the piercing screams of police sirens reverberated up the black and icy streets. His eyes shot open. *I'm awake?*

And instinctively he knew; the sirens were for his mum.

Mollie heard them too, and her blood ran cold. Despite the tough nature of the East End streets the police were rarely called, the natives largely preferring to deal out justice themselves, hence the Kray brothers being far more popular than they should in a world where they'd risen above the law.

She saw the colour drain from the boy's face, but before she could react Tristan was in his shoes and bursting through the flat door.

"Wait…where you going?"

But he was gone. Mollie grabbed her coat and took the stairs as fast as her little legs would take her and hoping that, wherever those sirens were headed, it didn't involve her friend.

Tristan sped after the bawling drone of the police sirens, and soon caught his first frightening glimpse of the flashing red and blue, the spinning lights echoing the swirling chaotic thoughts in his mind. He turned into a street at just the same time as an ambulance slowly pulled up beside a panda car, an ambulance that didn't seem to be in any hurry. He sprinted over and pushed through the gathering crowd.

Mollie panted hard as she rounded the corner, but when she realized where she was she let out an audible gasp; The Albion. That old hotel was really only frequented by working girls and their clients, and she herself had used it just last week. Her eyes closed, and without knowing it she tilted her head to the sky as if hoping for some holy intervention. Exoneration? But she knew it was a waste of time, and with her stomach in knots and a deep sense of foreboding that pulled them tight, Mollie crossed over into the fray.

Several policemen stood around the entrance to the hotel, with one officer positioned at the grand looking front doors. Tristan approached the nearest uniformed man.

"What's going…"

"Stand back, kid. There's nothing here for you today."

"What's happened? Why are you here?" His voice ached with desperation, but even as the words came out in rapid, foggy breaths, he knew. In his wildly beating heart, he hoped he was wrong.

"Listen son, judging by your accent, you ain't from around here, so I suggest you back off and let the boys do their work." The officer huffed, his warm breath evaporating in the frigid air. "Hookers," he said, with obvious disdain, "she's just another hooker, anyway."

Tristan possessed only a fleeting notion of the word *hooker*, but when the officer said '*she*,' his guts twisted in vicious knots.

*No...please, no...*

Beneath a sky that offered only more misery and amid a growing mob that couldn't give a shit about him, Tristan felt the world start to shift, as if the first rumblings of an earthquake were shaking his very soul. But he had to get inside those doors. Pretending indifference, he waited for the callous officer to walk away and, when the man guarding the door momentarily moved to the side to relight his cigarette, Tristan darted through the loose cordon and slipped unnoticed into the hotel.

From the midst of a morbidly fascinated crowd that now swelled like a cancer, Mollie saw him disappear into the hotel. Too late she burst through to the front of that swarming melee...too late!

No one was in the lobby, so Tristan quietly scaled the stairs to the next floor, where he saw several uniformed men standing close together in quiet but animated discussion. They hadn't seen him, so he ducked into a doorway and listened, fear spreading from the hollow pit of his stomach.

"Look fellas, I know she's probably a whore, but come on...no one deserves that. To do that to a person? Fucking animals, that's all I can say."

"We don't yet know that she was a hooker," said another man, perhaps older. "And I certainly don't recognise her. Maybe new in town?"

"No one *could* recognise her now," came a third voice in an almost apathetic chuckle. "But whoever she is I reckon she deserved it, cos' whores always get what they deserve, selling their bodies for drugs or booze. Dirty disgusting bitches should just get real jobs."

*Maybe new in town* suggested confirmation of his darkest fears. *Selling their bodies* suggested prostitution, and *was a hooker* morbidly suggested past tense. At those grisly words, whatever shred of stoicism Tristan clung to failed, and his heart threatened to smash clean through his chest. He just could not bear it any longer.

A careful look down the corridor beyond the three policemen revealed a door that had across it the ubiquitous yellow tape of a crime scene. Tristan bolted.

He was past the first officers before they had time to react, though they soon shouted after him, but he ignored their shouts and seconds later stood breathing hard outside the room. Time seemed to stand still, and all noise became white, the officers' thundering footsteps fading out to nothing. He paused, hand on the cool steel handle. Immense flashes of red and black and blue pulsed before his eyes, as if he could see right through the door to witness the reality of his recent dream; Tristan knew all too well the colour of blood and bruises. Visions swirled internally, and the powerful beam of an unnoticed Jaguar blinded him from within, then was gone, and somewhere nearby, a baby cried, maybe in his mind, as bile rose in his throat and the metallic taste of blood made him gag. He sensed more than saw or heard that the police offices were getting close.

Tristan knew with nefarious clarity that his mother was inside that room. He knew that he was too late. He just knew it...his mother was...

An officer skidded and reached for his arm, but missed, also too late.

Tristan had stepped into hell.

He locked the door and didn't hear the pounding of fists from beyond as silence roared all around him, and on weak legs he staggered two steps toward the bed, where a sheet clearly concealed a corpse. Reams of blood had suffused into the fabric, near black against the stark white cover, and there was no telling who or what lay dead beneath it.

But Tristan knew.

And there, protruding from beneath the sheet at the top end of the bed, a few wavy locks of coppery orange hair crushed a young boy's soul.

Tristan had found his mother. And she was dead.

The walls rushed at him in an eddying kaleidoscope of whites and grays, and as the door came crashing in under the blows of a policeman's battering ram, a sixteen year old boy whose world had stopped spinning crumpled ashen and unconscious to the floor.

No matter how she pushed and complained, Mollie couldn't penetrate the now solid police cordon as she saw two paramedics rush inside. Impatient, she shuffled to keep warm and felt sick from anxiety. She was also getting annoyed by some of the rowdy locals nearby.

"Probably a drugs bust," suggested one young woman.

"Nah, I bet it's some underworld gang shit," replied her boyfriend. "You know, them Kray twins teaching some dumb competitor a lesson." His eyes were wide with mock fear, but she wasn't finished speculating

"Did you hear about that girl that got murdered up in the West End? It was on the radio earlier, and the chap said she was a prostitute and had been raped and sliced up really bad. Probably the same man doing it to another cheap whore." On hearing that last comment, Mollie puked on the floor.

Fifteen minutes later the two paramedics emerged from the hotel carrying a stretcher transporting a partially covered body. The dense crowd gasped. Mollie squeezed forward, desperate not to know whoever was being carried. But she soon did, and to her horror it was Tristan, whose face was ghastly white, and if she hadn't witnessed the rise and fall of his chest to signify breathing, she would have believed him to be dead.

He was alive, but seeing him that way meant that she knew something beyond terrible had happened to Kerra. Mollie's own heart constricted, and as her legs buckled, only the crush of the morbid crowd held her up.

Moments later a senior officer called for quiet before he addressed the hushed crowd and the gathering press.

"Good evening. I'm Chief Inspector Woods of The Metropolitan Police Force. It's with great regret that I must inform you of the discovery of a body inside the Albion Hotel. Time of death is not yet known, but cause of the woman's death is almost certainly murder, and caused by trauma wounds to the head, multiple stab injuries and strangulation by one or more perpetrators. There's also evidence of multiple rapes. We'll be working closely with the local community and police in order to catch whoever committed this heinous crime, and rest assured, we at the MET won't stop until we do. Thank you. There'll be no further comment at this time."

As the crowd erupted in a cacophony of noise and swayed in a frenzy of excitement, Mollie sank to her knees and, turning her face to the dark and indifferent London night, she wept.

They hadn't said the victim's name, but she knew. It was her friend. It was Tristan's mother, and though she herself didn't kill Kerra, there was no doubt she'd played a big part in her murder. In that moment she did indeed feel as if she'd killed Kerra herself.

Some of the East End locals knew of Mollie and, helping her to her feet, walked her on unstable legs to a nearby bench. With the usually effervescent woman now apparently mute, they thought better of the bench and escorted her to the nearest pub, quickly forcing a couple of stiff drinks down her throat. At last she spoke, but it was the incoherent ramblings of a madwoman, something along the lines of her being a killer, and to the folks that partially knew her she seemed on the edge of some kind of breakdown.

They shared confused and concerned looks with each other, and for a few minutes were at a loss about what to do. Eventually though, and after the third shot of gin, Mollie's eyes fell into focus and she uttered her first intelligible words since they'd picked her up from the floor.

"The hospital...take me to the hospital."

Ten minutes later they were at nearby St. Bart's, and by then she'd recovered her senses and rushed into reception and asked for Tristan. Next she dashed up stairs and through starkly lit corridors as the sick and the dying blurred the edges of her vision, and she panted hard as she entered the ward.

And then she saw him.

Tristan looked so vulnerable then, lying in bed with tubes strapped to his skinny arms, the ominous red wires in stark contrast to his pale, milky skin. Mollie approached and remained silent, gazing at his innocent face and noticing how much younger he looked than when she first saw him. So recently, and yet a lifetime ago.

Her heart broke at the accursed kid's misfortune. How can one person have witnessed so much adversity in such a short life? All those beatings, and now this. And poor,

poor Kerra. Had any person ever suffered as much as her? Mollie shuddered, fully aware of the part she'd played in her misfortune.

*If I'd only respected her wishes more, listened to her fears, she'd be alive now, not on the way to some cold slab in some lonely morgue. Why was I so insistent?* She knew Kerra would be with her son at last, a boy who now lay unconscious in a hospital bed, maybe from shock, but probably from a broken heart! Mollie Noble had never felt so ashamed, and never had a name felt so inappropriate.

Later on and after a series of tests, a doctor reassured her that at least physically the boy would be fine. Mentally though he'd suffered a terrible shock, and would need a support network to remain close by. Wiping away teardrops from eyes now awash with smeared make up, Mollie leaned a little closer to Tristan, and casting a furtive glance about the ward, she saw that nobody was listening. She whispered anyway.

"Tristan, please believe me...I'm so..." Breathless snivels caused her to stop and her throat was desert dry. A deep, gasping breath, and she continued. "I'm very, very sorry about everything, about this whole mess, and it's all my fault. I'm to blame, just me, stupid fucking Mollie un-Noble. It should've been me, love, not your mother...it should've been me."

Her shoulders shook from pure sorrow, and she sobbed, though whether from relief that Tristan would be okay or devastation that his mother was not, she didn't know, and really, it mattered little. She had helped to ruin not just one life, that of her friend Kerra, but two, the life of Kerra's beloved son Tristan. She would never forgive herself.

One of those tears dropped onto Tristan's hand, which she gently raised and rested against her cheek.

She kept her vigil with him the entire night.

## Chapter Fifty Four

Tristan surfaced slowly from the depths of a heavily sedated sleep. He'd slept for almost two days, and had tossed and turned continuously, often calling out for his mother and startling Mollie in the darkness. She had barely left his side throughout that time, and was on hand with whispered words of comfort as he suffered through obvious nightmares.

Confusion lined his gaunt face as he blinked under the glare of the hospital's industrially bright lights. But like a leaking tap, the world slowly trickled into focus, and anxiety followed, as for a moment Tristan had no idea where he was. But over the course of a few minutes, he was thrust back into his living hell, the unimaginable scene he'd witnessed seeping agonizingly back into his conscience.

His mother was dead. As the stark realism gained clarity, a young boy's world that had always been laden with misery now filled to the brim with pain. Tristan was numb. He didn't know the details of her death, but had seen with his own eyes the abhorrent evidence that no child should ever see.

His mother was dead. Yet Tristan couldn't cry. As heartbroken and ashamed as he was, he could not cry. He had suffered; Alcoholic father. Years of abuse. Abandoned by his mother. His own flirt with suicide. Now she'd been murdered. Yes, he had suffered, and Tristan couldn't take it any longer.

His mother was dead. And finally, his young and fragile

mind shut down to despair and he wanted nothing more than to fall asleep and never wake up. Broken down and mentally beaten, a young man closed his eyes to the world and waited for its darkness to swallow him forever.

Maybe he would wake up again? He no longer cared.

Tristan slept for a further twelve hours, and when he finally woke on a morning illuminated by beautiful clear skies, he found himself alone on the ward, and other than an empty stomach that grumbled in protest, he felt fine.

As he laid there looking out at the blue sky, a colour that as he travelled east on his journey, he felt he might never see again, Tristan remembered not caring if he woke up or not. At the time he meant it. But now he had questions. And he wanted answers.

Mollie dashed over when she saw him sitting up in the bed. "Oh Tristan, I'm sorry, I only left for an hour, but I've been here since..."

"I know, Mollie, the doctor told me. I appreciate you staying with me."

She was visibly relieved, and he knew it. But he wanted answers, and for half an hour he spoke candidly with her about her relationship with his mother, and she explained how their friendship was borne from respective adversity. She told him about the factory, and sharing the flat, and the cold and the hardships they'd faced together, and through it all Tristan began to understand what his mother was doing to earn money. Although it shredded his heart to think about it, he had to know for sure. So he asked his final question to Mollie.

"Was she a prostitute?"

She blanched, not expecting that question so directly. But she knew it would come, and she wouldn't lie to the kid again. As gently as she could, Mollie explained how

Kerra had taken only two clients, and only after a long and tormented battle with her conscience. Mollie also admitted her role in it all, saying how she had urged Kerra into believing that 'desperate times needed desperate measures.'

"And they were desperate times, love. We simply had no money, and were so cold and hungry in that miserable flat. What your mum did she did only out of her unstinting love for you. She left you alone back there on that island with only one goal in mind, and that was to make your life better. She had to make some money so as she could support you when you arrived in London, and there just weren't any jobs. It was a desperate last resort that made her do it. But I...if I hadn't of pushed her..."

Mollie broke down in an unmitigated outpouring of anguish and guilt, her exhausted eyes bloodshot. Tristan looked on, but he said nothing. He was distraught, and clearly Mollie was distraught too.

His feelings about the woman before him were confused and off balance, and he'd need time to reconcile himself to a person that had contributed in some way to his mother's death. But he admired her honesty, and was grateful she'd stuck by him in the hospital. There could be no one else, he thought with a cold heart.

Ultimately though, he knew it was his mother's choice, and believed with all his heart that she only did what she believed she had to do. By placing his hand over Mollie's as she wept, he internally absolved her of any blame.

Tristan was discharged from the hospital the following day, and agreed to Mollie's offer of staying at the flat for a few days. His mood was melancholic, and it was strange to be in a place that resonated with his mother's absence. But he needed to be there, and spent several days resting while huddled in his mother's blanket. Somehow, and though he didn't believe in spirits, he knew that she was there with him.

Over several conversations, Mollie spoke a lot about his mother and the love she had for her son. He glowed with pride.

"Your mother worshipped you, you know that, don't ya? Everything she did was for you...everything. She didn't leave your father for her own benefit, though goodness knows she should've. It probably doesn't look that way right now, but believe me, if there was any other way, she would've chosen it."

Mollie was sincere, and Tristan was glad to have his selfish wishes confirmed: s*he did it for me...it was all for me.* He only wished he could have heard it from his mother herself.

Mollie continued. "I have to tell you, Tristan, your mum told me all about you, and she wasn't wrong when she said you were a smart and handsome young fella."

He was glad. He didn't care about being handsome, but to be called a smart young fella meant he'd started to grow up, and he knew he needed to. But in his heart he was still his mother's little boy, and that would never change. But she was dead...how could it ever change now?

That thought really crushed him, and over the course of the next few days Tristan slumped. The immediate shock of his mother's murder had softened, but what followed was a period of deep grief and depression. He barely ate and rarely spoke, and then only reluctantly. And he felt so alone, despite Mollie's constant presence and genuine kindness.

Tristan missed Richard, and he longed to hear Winston's voice. Just to see Tramp's kindly face would be enough, but to hear Pearl Brown's riotous laugh would be music to his ears. He was yet to shed a single tear about the tragedy that had happened, and his shame about that only heightened his misery.

And worst of all…he needed a drink.

Mollie had gone to bed early, worn out from her nursing vigil and confident that the kid would be okay. In the other bedroom, Tristan sat in his mother's bed, back against the wall and severely agitated, and for hours he fought the growing temptation to hunt down some alcohol. He was ashamed to even have those thoughts, knowing it was a terrible, even fatalistic idea, but this time, some small part of him felt justified. He was probably still in shock. Something unimaginable and devastating had just happened. He was grieving. He would never get over it. And crucially, he knew, his father's poisoned blood polluted his veins.

Emotions raged, first one way and then another, and he swayed between them all; weakness and strength, shame and indignation, sorrow and indifference, turmoil and peace. Tristan was overwhelmed by his sadness about not crying, until suddenly, and after days of bottling it up, his grief arrived in floods, and didn't stop throughout the small lonely hours of the night until at last the dawn approached, and his heavy eyelids clamped shut and he was drowned in an ocean of shame and loss and loneliness.

When he awoke, the world outside his small and crooked window was buried beneath a blanket of white. In a flurry of colour he saw kids on sleds, others throwing snowballs and making rotund snowmen complete with faces, hats and scarves. Everyone was having fun, including the adults that watched on. Tristan was mesmerized, watching the action as if in a daze.

And then the sorrow hit.

All his life he'd been denied the simple pleasures of childhood by his father; the friendship, the playmates... the normality. But his sadness was quickly replaced by a rage that set his heart racing and ground his teeth together in frustration. He paced the small room, his father's face a flashing, taunting image before his eyes, and in that moment he wanted to smash that smirking face with the very fists that had previously failed to protect him.

He stalked into the tiny living room. Mollie was out. Into the kitchen, and he quickly found what he was looking for. Tristan Nancarrow was an angry young man. He would have that drink.

Twenty minutes later, and two thirds down a bottle of cheap scotch, he fumbled on his shoes and staggered down to the street, ignoring the hissing black cat as he wobbled past. It wasn't yet ten o'clock in the morning, and he made quite a scene as he swayed about drunk and looking for an outlet to vent his rage. Hot, confused teardrops slid over reddened cheeks, and the icy air turned his breath to steam. He looked into the sky, where white emptiness shrouded a long forgotten sun.

Then something caught his eye. One of the snowman the kids had built stood out from the others, its red scarf identical to one his father sometimes wore. Tristan had found his target. He stepped toward it, bent on violence, the scarf's red matching the red mist that descended upon him. He stared at the inanimate yet smirking creation before him, yet it was his father he saw, and he wobbled as he raised the bottle to his lips. Empty. He cursed, and tossed it away so it smashed on the ice yet he heard nothing above the thunderous rush of blood pounding in his temples as he blinked away stinging tears of misplaced vengeance.

On the brink, Tristan took a step toward the icy, almost life-size manifestation of his father. He looked again into the nothingness above with what might have been a desperate plea for help, before settling his steely gaze on the nemesis before him. His Scotch blurred vision cleared, and his muscles tensed. His mouth was clamped shut, as his breath came in snorts like an agitated bull ready to charge.

And then, after a full minute of bristling, seething rage had passed without action, Tristan let out an animalistic roar from deep within his tortured soul that signified a wild outpouring of years of stored up pain and waste and sorrow and anger that spilled forth from the area of his mind reserved only for darkness, where memories were often put, but never…never…taken. Until now.

Raw pain. That's how the bewildered onlookers felt about that frightful sound that echoed off the dilapidated houses as they whispered and pulled their children in close. But abruptly it stopped, and Tristan dropped to his knees as a lifetime of anger and frustration and sadness and shame spilled to the ground in torrents. Yesterday he thought he was in control. Now he knew he wasn't. And he was scared.

Mollie emerged from around the corner, just in time to see the last moments of Tristan's near breakdown. She rushed over, and with a few encouraging words led him back to the relative warmth of the flat, once again appreciating just how tragic his young life really was. And for the part she had played, her own guilt resurfaced.

Mollie was from the old school, and felt Tristan's cold induced shivering and emotionally induced agitation would be calmed by a shot or two of warm liquor. She was aware to some degree of his father's history of drinking, but didn't know of Tristan's own brush with it and thought that just once would be okay. She offered the boy the glass. Tristan wavered. He stared not at Mollie but at the glass itself, transfixed on the brown swirling poison inside.

"Take it," she said, "it'll do you good."

Still he stared, his fists clenched together as if in secret battle with unseen demons. After what to Mollie seemed an eternity, Tristan closed his eyes and leaned back on the bed. Finally, he spoke, and his voice was clear.

"No, Mollie. Drinking's for the weak."

## Chapter Fifty Five

Later that day, Mollie told Tristan how she wanted to help him in the coming weeks, and handed him an envelope. Inside was almost two hundred pounds. He looked at her blankly. She smiled. It wasn't returned.

"It's the least I can do. Besides, it's not just my money, but…well, some of it was Kerra's."

"I don't want your money. Or hers. I know how you got it, and I know how my mum got it. I won't accept it, and I don't need it." His voice was harsh, yet beneath the firm tone she sensed bitter sadness.

"Listen kid, I know how ya feel, and it's admirable to think the way ya do. But you've a sister to find now, and no matter how your poor mother got the money, she got it for you. So it's yours, and you should take it to help find Ailla."

"No!"

"Okay. I'll try another way, and forgive my tone, but it's the truth." Her voice hardened. "You owe it to ya mum to make the most of this opportunity. You may not like it, but she died doing something for you. I know it's difficult to understand, but you *have* to take the money and find ya sister, if not for you, then for your poor mother."

He shook his head adamantly.

*This young kid's got more morals than his father ever had*, she thought, and admired him all the more. But she pressed on, and her voice grew passionate.

"Your mother was forced to give up her baby, something I can't even imagine, and has never seen her since. That girl deserves to learn the same things you've recently learned, and that responsibility now falls to you. The world, or at least your sister, needs to know what a good woman Kerra really was. The toughest life imaginable, she had, and despite it all she managed to raise a wonderful kid like you. Please, Tristan, it's not a lot of money, but you've got to take it, firstly for your own sake, and if not for you, take it for your sister. Go and find her, kid. Take the money, and go and find Ailla."

That impassioned plea hit home. Tristan didn't speak, but he didn't need to. His subtle nod gave her the answer.

On an unusually clear morning, with the snow now gone and even a little sunshine to warm the air, Richard and Anne-Marie arrived at the flat to pick up Tristan, and Richard's grin was so wide that Tristan smiled himself for the first time in weeks. Anne-Marie smiled too, but hidden beneath the smiles they shared his terrible pain.

Days before, during a tearful phone call Tristan told them about everything that had happened, and they were devastated. Richard had wanted to come sooner, but Tristan convinced him he was okay and to come along in a couple more days. It was an emotional reunion with his friends, and he was humbled by their compassion.

Tristan had helped make their reunion happen, and he was so happy to see them together. Not only that, but it empowered him with great hope of finding his own sister Ailla, especially as they had both committed to help him with the search. The days ahead were looking brighter.

With his few possessions stuffed into his bag, Tristan waved goodbye to Mollie. She was crying, and Tristan knew they were worthy tears of shame. Deep down, he believed she was a good person with a good heart, and if nothing else, she had been a friend to his mother in London, despite her obvious mistakes.

They parted on good terms, but he knew that Mollie would carry that heavy penance of her guilt around her neck forever, and nothing he could say would change that. But if it helped keep her on the straight and narrow, and make her never again risk her life as a prostitute, then maybe it was good thing, and maybe some semblance of good could emerge from the tragedy. And as tempting as it was, Tristan would not allow himself to wish it was his mother instead of Mollie that waved at him through the window.

As Anne-Marie's familiar car pulled away, Tristan didn't look back, anxious to put the painful memories of the cursed East End behind him.

And so the three of them set out on a new quest to locate Tristan's long lost sister. It was still a little surreal to him, the fact that he even had a sibling, but in the light of his undulating and troubled life, he guessed that he probably shouldn't be surprised.

In terms of where to begin, the only thread they had to work with was slim. Tristan knew that at one time Ailla stayed in an orphanage on the south coast. It was even possible that she now lived on the other side of the world in New York. Like his brave and tragic aunt Bella had told him, it was as if Ailla had disappeared completely.

Over mugs of tea at Marnie's café, they made a plan to visit all the orphanages along the south coast, either until they ran out of money, or they discovered some solid information. They might even get lucky, and actually find her. But that kind of good fortune didn't exist in the world of Tristan Nancarrow, and it was the one thing he knew for sure. Their plan wasn't the greatest of ideas, but it was all they had.

Kerra's murder was headline news, so of course Marnie had heard of the tragedy, and rather than risk upsetting Tristan by mentioning it, instead she did her best to lift his spirits. And what better way to do that by embarrassing his friend again by depositing her hefty bulk once more in his lap. The result was immediate, and to see Richie squirm under the combined weights of Marnie and embarrassment caused smiles all round.

The pain of the last few weeks would never leave Tristan. And yet, in the company of trusted friends he began to believe that he was going to be okay. He'd come through his ordeal, the toughest of his already tough life, and despite his obvious heartbreak, he felt good. And Mollie was right, he did owe it to his mum and Bella to find his sister, even if it was to bear the tragic news of both of their deaths.

But there was another reason, and this Tristan knew was justifiably selfish. He just desperately wanted to feel and experience that same sibling love that Richard and Anne-Marie so obviously shared, and as he knew that another painful chapter of his young but harrowing life story was coming to an end, yet again the emotive words of Horace, resounding loudly in Tramp's unmistakable and powerful voice, echoed through his mind;

Tomorrow do thy worst, for I have lived today.

'I have lived today,' he whispered to himself, then

thinking, *I will do everything in my power to find her. Everything! And every day I live, I live for this cause.* He meant every word.

With steel in his heart and conviction in his eyes, and his own pure blood pumping through his veins, Tristan stepped out of the long, dark and dying memories of his youth, and entered into a future, where every day the sun would rise so high and so bright that he would never again live in the shadows of the past.

*Chapter Fifty Six*

By the third day, and after checking out more than a dozen orphanages, Tristan was beginning to feel a little disheartened. But when they arrived at a children's home in Southampton, things took a positive turn. They were greeted warmly by an affable and breezy old woman who, as strange as it seemed at that moment, didn't appear at all surprised to see them. Slightly bemused, Tristan made his enquiry.

"Oh yes, I remember Ailla," she warbled, and Tristan's eyes widened with hope. "She stayed here with us for just a few months. Such a pretty and friendly young girl, and she was one of the lucky ones, too, being fostered by a really pleasant and loving family that lived, I believe, somewhere just outside of town, if my dwindling brain can remember correctly? She still came back in and played with the other kids sometimes after she left. Ah, such a sweet child, and I'll never forget the donations that her foster family made, either. So generous! Then one day she came in to say her goodbyes because the family was moving abroad. The other children here were so sad, as were all the staff, but we were also very excited to hear that one of our own was off on an exciting trip."

"Where did she go? Do you remember where she went to?"

"Why of course, young man, and how could I forget? And I don't mind telling you," she said with a smile, "some of us were more than a little jealous." The old lady had an airy, whimsical look in her pale green eyes. But Tristan couldn't wait.

"Where did she go?"

"Oh yes…that lucky young girl went all the way to New York City."

Finally, the solid clue Tristan so desperately wanted, and the three friends were momentarily delirious. But just as quickly as his hope soared, his heart sank. The money Mollie had given him was almost out, and a crushing reality became clear. How could he possibly go to America? He couldn't. It wasn't possible. The mood plummeted, and it seemed Tristan was destined for more misery.

The old woman gave him a moment. And then she surprised them all. Taking something from a drawer, Mary Miller rose from behind her desk and stood in front of Tristan. She could scarcely conceal the mischievous glint of joy in her eyes.

"I almost forgot. This envelope arrived for you a day or two ago. Anonymously."

Bewildered looks spread among the friends, and Tristan's amazement and apprehension was evident to them all.

"Who could have sent me a letter? And here? How could they know?"

Tristan took the envelope. On the front, and written in a flamboyant, cursive script, was a single word:

*Tristan.*

"Go ahead, love, open it," Mary urged him, as if she already knew what it contained. Tristan looked at his friends. Their raised eyebrows mirrored his own, and with a shrug he opened the letter.

"I...I don't believe it." His mouth gaped in genuine surprise.

"What...what is it? asked Richard.

"It's...it's money. A lot of money. Maybe five hundred pounds!" His tone was incredulous.

"But who's it from? Who knows we're here?" Yet even as Richard asked himself the question, a light bulb flickered in his mind, and then he knew. Both he and Tristan thought there was more to that old guy with the beard at 'The Castle' than he'd let on, and it made sense... a professor, world traveler, philosopher, rich parents. It was obvious now...Tramp himself was secretly rich.

Tristan turned to ask Mary. But she was gone.

A few days later, and Tristan was all set for his flight to New York. The decision to go was an easy one. Just a month before he'd never once set foot anywhere beyond St. Mary's, but his life had changed so much and in such a short space of time that now it didn't even seem that strange.

What did he have left to stay for, anyway? His mother was dead, as was his kind aunt Bella. His father had forsaken him, and the thought of ever returning to St. Mary's was...well, quite simply, he wouldn't. He would miss his new friends, no doubt about that, but he would keep them in his heart and knew they'd do the same with him. If and when he returned, they would be the first to know. Tristan was going on an adventure, and though the final destination may never reveal itself to him, he would search and search and search until he found it.

For too long he'd known nothing of life and the potential for happiness, and in recent weeks he'd known only misery and death. It was time to start over. The first step to emancipation had been taken when he left both that desolate island and his father behind. Now he would be leaving behind not only acute sadness and painful memories, but the country that had created them. He was turning his back on England, and as he did so, he wondered if it was for the first and last time.

Of course, there were no guarantees he would ever find his sister, or indeed, if she even wanted to be found. But getting that envelope stuffed with cash, the latest in a long list of shocking and strange events, had at least provided him with an opportunity to find out. And he was going to take it.

Inexplicably, some mystery benefactor had deposited five hundred pounds into his hand, and just when he needed it most. Tristan had no desire for money of his own, but he understood what a golden opportunity he'd been presented. Yet he simply did not know who the cash was from. He didn't even know that many people, and those he did he'd only known for a few weeks. In the last days, only Richard and Anne-Marie knew where he had been, and anyone else he cared for were either dead or oblivious. It was a total mystery.

Though it wasn't a mystery to Richard. Back in Southampton, the day before they'd picked up Ailla's trail at the orphanage, the three of them had gone to pay Tramp a visit at the Castle. Tristan had explained the horrific events of the last weeks to him, and he'd been genuinely distraught at the poor kid's plight. It was actually Tramp who'd pointed them in the direction of that specific orphanage, and he must have taken the money down there before they arrived. The world really is full of amazing people, thought Richard, and he smiled at his secret.

Overwhelmed. That's how Tristan felt as he stood in the departure lounge of the world's largest airport, being waved off by the most unlikely assortment of friends. Little more than a month ago, Tristan was all alone in the world, his only company a weak imagination and a loving but aloof mother. He blinked back a teardrop as he scanned the group.

Winston and Pearl, their smiles wide and proud, waved fondly and with passion, as if Tristan were a lifelong friend.

Mollie, too. As he knew his mother would have wanted, Tristan had made his own peace with the devastated woman, and she smiled as she waved, the relief in her eyes evident.

Anne-Marie, whose eyes were misted with sadness. They'd developed a closeness in recent days that stemmed from a common understanding of loss. She'd lost a brother, and he a sister, and though under very disparate circumstances the absence had consumed them both. Despite the relative age difference, a silent affection had evolved between them which they scarcely understood. Words were neither said nor necessary as she stepped forward and kissed him tenderly on the forehead. Tristan had brought her brother back to her, and for that she would be forever grateful. Her heart ached for what that brave kid had been through, and she stifled a sob as she edged back to the group, hopeful that someday they would meet again. It was a notion they unknowingly shared.

Even Mark and Bobby had made the long drive over from Penzance. Tristan had telephoned to explain what had happened, and Mark was obviously distraught at the death of one of his oldest friends. The fact that Mark had loved Kerra once wasn't an issue for Bobby, and she shared both his and Tristan's sadness.

They were good people, all of them, and Tristan would miss them dearly.

Richard was the last one to say his farewells. He and Tristan had become loyal and trusted friends, and an unspoken bond had formed that sprung from their similarly awful experiences of childhood; a father's abuse, a lack of friends, and a lifetime of loneliness with no sense of place in the world. The two of them shared a brother's love that would last a lifetime. It was Richard who at last broke the long embrace.

"Thanks for being my friend."

"It's me that should thank you, Richie. You were a friend to me when I needed it, and the fun we had helped banish the dark shadow that trailed me after I left my aunt Bella's house. I'll miss you."

"I'll miss you too. Be safe in New York."

They hugged again.

Tristan felt that he at last had some true friends, and that knowledge not only helped wash away the lingering shadow of sadness from his face, but helped restore some sense of stoicism that had been lost after his mother's death. He was ready for the next chapter of life.

Tristan turned to leave, went just a few steps, and then stopped. He looked steadily at Richard.

"You know where that money came from, don't you?"

Richard returned the gaze, eyes ablaze with the guilty twinkle of a happy betrayal.

"Maybe I'll tell you when you get back."

Tristan nodded. With a final wave goodbye to his friends, he was gone.

As he passed through the doors to the boarding gate he didn't look back, and for the first time in his short life he was truly ready to face the world alone. Everyone he'd met since he left that incarcerating and inhibiting island, people both with benevolent and malign persuasions, had taught him invaluable life lessons, and he was unrecognizable from the meek and contrived son of his father. There would be further disappointments, and that things would not always run smoothly was guaranteed.

And as for the unexpected? Well, that was to be expected.

With head held high and shoulders broad and straight, he walked between writhing queues of bustling people, dodging mums that barked at children and dads who wrestled with baggage, and as he negotiated the anarchic bedlam, a wide and unfiltered smile spread across his face.

And in that moment, that wonderfully free moment, where his will was his own and the monkey of burden was off his back, he was certain that for the first time in many months, perhaps for the first time ever, the whole world his for the taking.

Because he was Tristan Nancarrow, and at long, long last, he was the sole master of his destiny.

*Chapter Fifty Seven*

Tristan's muscles tensed as the giant plane roared to life. He was terrified, and looked around with nervy apprehension. To his left sat a middle aged man, flashy suit and barely visible beneath a wide newspaper. Businessman, he thought, and admired the man's calm composure. Behind him, a giggling young couple. Honeymoon, he guessed. Everywhere else, people read or chatted, and some were already asleep. *Am I the only one who's nervous?* It seemed like it.

Tristan speculated that about three hundred people were on board, and it was beyond his comprehension that the huge plane, with so many people and so much luggage, could even move along the runway, let alone fly all the way across a vast ocean to America.

Tristan gripped tight as the gigantic plane trundled down the apparently never ending runway. As it gradually accelerated his knuckles blanched under the strain, until with a deafening roar the behemoth lifted smoothly off the ground. His dry throat gulped even drier air, and he realized he hadn't breathed for about two minutes, but when he finally sucked in some air and recovered a little, he strained to see out of a nearby window.

"I'm flying...I'm really flying," he muttered in amazement.

"Well observed, kid, great powers of observation." It was a tubby man next to him that had spoken. "Bet you got an IQ above fifty, don't ya?" The man laughed loudly, and yanked his dark sunglasses from his eyes.

*Does he realise it's daylight?*

Suddenly the roar from the engines died, and as his stomach seemingly vacated his body, Tristan felt sure he was about to die too. But in seconds, the giant engines once more kicked in, and lurched the plane on toward New York City.

The initial shock and wonder of flying had passed, and Tristan relaxed. He'd been in the air about thirty minutes, and imagined St. Mary's Island wasn't too far below. From his seat in the aisle he had no way to see, but in his mind's eye he saw through dark clouds to a green dot in an expanse of grey blue sea, the rundown cottage and its small, unkempt garden, and his beloved asters, destroyed. The thought of his precious flowers being left to die caused a lump in his throat which wouldn't leave, but when he envisaged his father sat at the kitchen table, lonely, depressed and forgotten, Tristan felt nothing beyond complete and utter indifference.

Several hours later, Tristan woke with a start as the huge jumbo banked sharply to the left...too sharply, he was sure, and he clung to the seat arms as if his life depended on it.

"Relax, kid, just a little turbulence," said the fat man with a sarcastic wink. "Just dropping through the clouds. We'll land in ten minutes."

Tristan tried and failed to disguise his embarrassment with a smile. If the big man noticed, he didn't let on.

"Ever been to New York? Been my home almost fifty years. Shoot, I practically run this city, and not a lot goes down in the Big Apple without me knowing about it. The name's Hank...Hank Burroughs, but you can call me Mr. Burroughs." He chuckled at his own joke as he tipped his baseball cap, blue, with an intertwined N and Y on the front.

"You got a name, kid?" He's friendly enough, Tristan thought, *but does he ever stop talking?*

"My name's Tristan, Mr. Burroughs. It's my first time in New York. Actually, it's my first time anywhere, except London. I'm looking for someone."

"Oh yeah? Course you are. Everybody's looking for someone. Who you looking for, kid?"

"My sister. I think she lives in New York. She's twenty."

Hank Burroughs was big and loud, but he seemed sincere and friendly, and when he said he might be able to help, Tristan was all ears.

"Listen, son, I know a lotta people in New York, and frankly speaking, finding people is my specialty."

Tristan was unsure what he meant, but his curiosity

grew.

"So what's your job, sir?"

The big man once again removed his sunglasses, and winked a sly, conspiratorial wink. He leaned in a little closer.

"My job? Kid, you're talking to the finest P.I. in all of New York City."

Tristan replied, "P.I? What is that?" eliciting a patient chuckle from Hank.

"Son, a P.I. is a private investigator. My job is to find people. And I'm the best in the business." From his pocket, Hank slipped a business card that showed his name, and also had directions to his Manhattan office. "Why don't you swing by the ranch in a couple days?"

"Thanks. I will, I'll come and see you at the...the ranch?"

"Office, kid, it just means office."

"Ah. Okay then, the office." Tristan paused, his eyebrows raised in a hopeful arc. "Do you really think you can find her? My sister? She's all I have left in the world."

"Kid, if she's in New York, I'll find her. If she's left the city, we might still find her. Come see me in a couple of days, and we'll see what we can do for ya."

Hank had an oversized personality that more than matched his considerable frame, and he seemed like an honest and approachable man. Tristan already liked him.

The monster plane touched down in New York with a bone jarring bump, the brakes screaming for mercy as the pilot slowed it to a crawl. Hank bellowed with laughter at Tristan's palpable relief. It took nearly half an hour, but after making it through immigration Tristan met up with Hank in the main entrance.

"You need a ride into the city, kid?"

Tristan thought for a moment before replying.

"Thanks, but I want to make my own way from here. It's an adventure, after all."

"Are you sure? I mean, it's no problem for me, drop you at a hotel, wherever you want? No problem at all."

Tristan thought Hank looked a little concerned that he was going on his own, almost desperate to help him. But he wanted it to be that way, almost needed it, as if he still had a lot to prove to himself. He politely declined.

"Well, alright then, if you're sure?"

"I'm sure Hank." *Why is he so worried?*

"That's the spirit, kid. Well, I'll be seeing you in a day or two then, right?"

"I'll be there, Hank, and thanks a lot. I really appreciate it."

"Don't mention it kid, and kid...take care out there, okay. I mean it." And then Hank, with a forced smile and an automatic flick of the sunglasses, waddled off through the exit.

Tristan waited a minute, and then followed, out into a bright, chilly day. He sucked in great gulps of the crisp air, way colder air than in England, he noticed, and felt as alive as he had ever known.

"I'm in New York," he said quietly to himself, "are you here as well, sister?"


*Chapter Fifty Eight*

Tristan climbed into a taxi and had barely closed the door before it was flying out of the airport toward downtown, and weaving in and out of traffic that seemed almost entirely made up of the ubiquitous yellow cabs of that city. Even when the driver spoke, his words spewed out at a velocity that more than matched the speed of his driving, and Tristan couldn't understand a single word of it.

He looked out the window, and marveled at the size of some of the cars flashing by, huge roaring machines with bonnets that stretched out yards from their giant windscreens. The driver must have noticed his amazement, and reeled off names as the cab edged beyond them...*Mustang...Chevy...Cadillac...*while adding an impressed whistle that shrilled of longing as he ogled them in his rearview mirror.

Tristan stepped with relief from the taxi in lower Manhattan, and hurried to the relative safety of the sidewalk. With a swift glance up and down the street, he soon realized he was in a land of giants, because as far as his awed eyes could see, one impressive building after another scraped the sky, each taller than the last, and craning his neck toward their summits left him dizzied by their mesmerizing heights.

Tristan really wanted to see a sunset from the top of one of those skyscrapers, having spent his entire life on a small, flat island, so with just a few hours before dark, he checked into his hotel and rushed back out onto the chaotic and crowded sidewalks. Once in the hazy past his mother told him of a famous old building in New York, so famous that it had even been in movies, something about a giant gorilla. He approached an elderly couple walking by.

"Why, young fella, you must mean King Kong," said the lady, smiling beneath a velvet cap.

"Is that the building's name?" asked Tristan honestly.

After a pleasant chuckle that was in no way mocking, the old man replied. "You're not from around here, are you sonny. King Kong is the gorilla. The tower your mom told you about is The Empire State building." He took Tristan's arm, and gently spun him around ninety degrees.

"Spectacular, isn't she?"

Tristan couldn't hide his delight. It was truly magnificent.

"Wow. It must be…it must be a mile to the top."

The old couple grinned. "A mere four hundred and forty three meters, actually, but it seems like a mile when you're up there."

Thirty minutes, and one hundred and two floors later, Tristan stood gazing out over Manhattan. He'd thought London was big, but with his bird's eye view of New York it seemed like half the world was spread out before him, and he'd never imagined anything so beautiful.

The sky was starting to darken, and the crisp cerulean blue of the wintry day was replaced by thick purple clouds that scudded above his head, almost close enough to touch. Those racing, trail blazing clouds cast organic, effervescent shadows all about the open air observation deck, and whereas a bruised and purpling sky above England implied only a brooding, tempestuous night, there in that moment in New York City it was magical.

For just a few minutes, a troubled young boy from a small and tormented island was on top of and at peace with a world that, until now, had promised nothing and given him even less.

Early the next morning, Tristan headed out into a city bathed in golden red skies, and though the temperature was barely above freezing he was anxious to get out and explore. Manhattan in rush hour is not for the faint hearted, and twice in the first ten minutes he got whistled at by policemen for stepping onto the road where cars whizzed by in black and yellow blurs. During his time in London, he'd believed that nowhere could the streets and paths be as busy and hectic as that frantic city, yet it had nothing on downtown Manhattan.

The vibrancy of everything enthralled him as he wandered along wide and tree lined avenues and between buildings so tall they seemed to sway with the wind. A slowly rising sun spilled rays of mystical light through the dying autumn canopy above, and made the pavement seem to swarm as if alive, while autumn's fallen leaves swirled playfully at his feet. And on the breeze, the myriad smells of New York's ubiquitous street breakfast tantalized; coffee with bagels.

Mid-afternoon on his second day in New York, and Tristan headed to the offices of Hank Burroughs. The building was no Empire State, but was still impressive, and as he rode the elevator a modest fifteen floors and stepped out to face an impressive set of ornate glass double doors, Tristan was relieved to see a sign that read; 'Hank Burroughs Esq., Private Eye.'

*At least he's genuine*, he thought, and entered into an arena of frantic activity. An attractive young lady soon approached.

"Good afternoon. Mr. Nancarrow, isn't it? Mr. Burroughs has been expecting you."

"Thanks. My name's Tristan."

"It's a pleasure to meet you, Tristan. Go on through to his office and take a seat. He'll be right there."

He followed the secretary's directions through a hive of desks abuzz with two dozen or more men and women, almost all of whom were making animated and important sounding phone calls. The noise level was incredible. *How can they even hear each other?* he thought.

Reaching Hank's office he saw the door already open, and stepping inside the large room he found an oasis of calm. He looked about. Behind a huge shiny desk was an equally huge and well worn leather chair. On one wall a wide window afforded a view of the hustle and bustle of the street below, and on the window sill Tristan was surprised to see a pair of binoculars. *I wonder what Hank looks for?*

Framed photographs of the man himself and his young family dotted the walls and desk, and one grand and formal looking certificate after another occupied an entire wall. If there was any lingering doubt that this man was successful, it was quickly dismissed.

"Ah, the kid has made it. It's good to see ya, son. How you finding our fair city?" Hank seemed to fill the entire room with his personality, and his booming voice echoed off the walls.

"Hello, Mr. Burroughs. New York is amazing, sir, and it's good to see you too."

"Yes sirree, it sure is a fine city we live in. The Big Apple has its moments, but hell, what doesn't? Take a seat, kid."

They chatted for a while about his first days in the city, and Tristan was buoyed by the big man's even bigger personality. But he had a question for Hank and was keen to learn the answer.

"Mr. Burroughs...Hank. On the plane you told me you're in the business of finding people, but why are you so keen to help me, a random young boy from England?"

Hank's smile remained, but suddenly his eyes seemed lost to a distant and painful memory. For a few moments Tristan looked on as Hank stared out into some far off place, and witnessed the sparkle slip from the man's eye in a solitary silver tear. He waited.

But just a moment later, Hank sighed, his massive shoulders rising and falling like a vast tide of sorrow. And then he told his story.

"I'll tell you why I want to help you, kid, and though it's a story of sadness and regret, it's one I don't mind sharing."

Hank took up a photo from the desk and, pausing for a quick look himself, handed it across to Tristan. He looked at it for a moment, then glanced back at Hank, who seemed to read his thoughts as he smiled and patted his significant belly.

"That was ten years ago, before you ask, and the Mrs ain't shy when dishing up dinner. Besides, us Americans do love to eat." Hank winked, and both chuckled at a statement made obvious judging by his bulging shirt.

"That picture you have was taken in 1953, the year my son went missing. You see him there, on my left? Handsome ain't he. That's my eldest kid, Jesse, named after Jesse Owens."

At the mention of that name Tristan's eyes shot wide.

"Who is Jesse Owens, Hank?"

"You kidding me? Jesse Owens is one of my heroes. Why d'ya ask?"

"A friend once called me that, but I had no idea who or what he was talking about. He shouted it out as he saw me running somewhere."

At that Hank burst out laughing, but when sufficiently recovered, he explained.

"Oh kid, that's great. Well, you must be a pretty swift runner, because Jesse was the man who won four gold medals for the U.S. of A at the Olympics in thirty-six, right under Hitler's nose in Berlin. The man's a legend."

Tristan finally got the joke, and was proud to be called Jesse Owens by Winnie, despite not being swift at all.

"Sorry Hank, I didn't mean to interrupt."

"It's all good, kid, it's all good. So, mine and Jesse's father son relationship was, well, it was a little rocky to say the least. We were both strong, opinionated guys, and we clashed about most everything. He was a good kid, but at that time he hung out with what I thought were a bad bunch, a bad influence on him as he grew up. His mother said I was too harsh on him, that I should let him grow and learn by any mistakes he made. But I was over-protective, I see that now, and she was right and I was definitely wrong." The big man's eyes closed tight for a few seconds before he continued. "One day we had an especially heated argument, and as usual it was about Jesse's friends, though I thought nothing of it at the time. He barely spoke at dinner, which wasn't unusual, and afterwards he left the house, as he often did. That was just over ten years ago. We haven't seen him since."

Hank's anguish was clear, and Tristan could tell he was still distraught about what had happened. He took a sip of water, and then another. Tristan sensed the despair that resonated in his long sigh.

"I'm sorry, kid. Just a silly old man, I guess."

"It's okay, Hank."

"There's not a day goes by that we don't think of our son, and we continue to hope that one day he'll walk right back through our door. And you know, it's all my fault. I would never hit any of my kids, never, but on that day I did raise my hand to him. It was just a threat, and I would never have done it, but I've regretted that one, stupid and thoughtless action every minute since."

Hank's pain was evident in the puffy eyes and quivering lip, and Tristan wanted to offer some comforting support. He didn't have the words.

"The usual missing person reports failed to bring a single sighting of Jesse, and after a few months the authorities told us we were on our own. So I've spent years searching for him myself, using every spare minute by going from street to street, from door to door. But New York City is vast. Many times I thought we were close, you know, a sighting or two, whispers in the neighbourhood, but they all came to nothing. Ten years on, and I've failed to find him. I've failed my son."

Hank's despair filled the room, and Tristan read only pure sadness on the lines of his face. But after a moment, his eyes revealed their familiar glint and the long suffering man stood and came around the giant desk. To Tristan, the big man appeared bigger than ever.

"But, kid, lemme tell ya something. I will never give up, never, because Hank Burroughs never quits! And you know, son, there are a ton of happy families out there, reunited thanks to the stoic work that my great team does here. And we will always do it."

Tristan was so glad to see the big man smile again, rightly proud of his company's successes despite his own traumatic loss.

"You see, kid? Didn't I tell ya? Everyone is looking for someone…including me."

As they laughed together, Tristan felt sure that if anyone could help him in his own search, Hank Burroughs was the right man.

"Listen son, this will all take some time to set up," said Hank, "so rather than wait around like a spare part, you should go out and explore the city some more." His insistence, though, came with a warning. "Some shady characters out in Harlem and the Bronx, kid, and you gotta watch ya back. Most people are decent, but when the gangs get territorial you don't wanna be in the way. Lot of murders out in the 'hoods, too."

The dazed look momentarily returned, and Tristan could guess why; it was more than possible his son Jesse was dead. But Hank blinked away the dark thoughts, and was soon smiling again.

"Kid, you've got a lotta guts to show such spirit after everything you've endured. My heart goes out to you, and you should be mighty proud of yourself." There was real sincerity in Hank's tone, and Tristan was moved. "But we're all human. You try showing me a man who hasn't made mistakes. Lord knows I've made plenty…costly ones, at that, so I was thinking'…I dunno…maybe you should go visit your father when you get back across the pond, because he might just be worried about his son. Everyone deserves a second chance, right? Promise me you'll at least think about it?"

Tristan was doubtful. He'd seen what his father was capable of, and struggled to believe that such a complete turn around was possible. But having heard about Hank's own pain at losing a son, albeit in vastly differing circumstances, it did make him question the depths of his father's love. Hank was so sincere in his plea, that he was compelled to nod his acquiescence.

Before Tristan left, he had another question. "What do you look for with those binoculars, Hank?"

"Why d'ya think my office has such a big window, kid? My son. I look for son Jesse. You never know, right?"

And it was true. You never did.

While Tristan headed out to get lost downtown, Hank's team had to admit that they'd very little to go on; a first name, nationality, and the year she arrived in America; Ailla, English, and nineteen-fifty-six. A couple of potential surnames, too, in Nancarrow and Annis. Nancarrow was her biological father's name, but Tristan was sure she wouldn't be using that after all this time. And Annis, her mother's maiden name, was also a long shot. She was probably using her foster family's name, and of course they had no idea what that was. Hank knew his team had their work cut out, but immediately assigned a few of his staff onto the challenge ahead.

Tristan was still awed by the majesty of the towering buildings all around him, and felt the measure of his insignificance as he wandered in their shadows. After a few hours of walking on well known touristy trails, he found himself strolling over the golden carpets of Central Park, the autumn leaves blanketing the ground beneath. Many dramatic and weather stained statues dotted the park, some depicting soldiers, others the stony forms of characters from fairy tales. But Tristan was especially taken by one particular sculpture, that of a sad old man, apparently reading to a duck. Its carved caption was barely visible under golden leaves, but kicking them away, he read, 'Hans Christian Andersen.'

"Do you know why Hans looks so sad?"

Tristan turned in surprise to see a smiling yet disheveled young man, whose cheeks were thin and whose smile betrayed a cold and hungry desperation.

"No sir, I don't."

"Ah, a young English gentleman. Well, I'm no Shakespeare, but I'll tell you anyway. Hans here is a master storyteller, but the problem is no one ever listens to his stories...only that single, solitary and loyal duck that stands there and listens in all weathers. In the two years that I've lived here, that duck has never left his side."

"You live in the park, sir?"

"There are a lot of homeless in New York, my friend, many of us here in Central Park."

Tristan thought of Tramp, and once more felt a strong affinity to the unfortunate people that lived on the streets. He knew from listening to that wise old chap that they were often harshly treated by society, pre-judged and labeled 'undesirables,' and Tristan pitied them. Though he'd scarcely experienced the hardships of street life himself, he somehow felt a kindred spirit with them and their plights.

"And that's why Mr. Andersen looks so sad, and it would make me sad, too." The young man smiled again, and began to walk off.

At that moment Tristan got a delicious waft of something cooking nearby, and spotted a man selling hot dogs from a cart. He ran over, quickly bought five of them, and soon caught up with the park's resident historian.

"Thanks for the story, sir. Please take these...for you and your friends." He handed the hot dogs to the shocked young man, and before he had a chance to offer his thanks, Tristan was gone.

Later, he took a ferry to Liberty Island, a short trip that brought back mixed memories of his first ever boat ride; the escape from St. Mary's. As the boat rose and fell on the choppy harbour waves, he witnessed up close the majestic statue that shared its name with the island. The towering Statue of Liberty. As a cold wind howled and whistled about the exposed promontory, Tristan read the inscriptions dotted around, inspired by the visions of the founding fathers, names he'd heard of, such as Lincoln and Washington.

But reading them forced him to consider his own liberty. Did he finally have it, after the oppressive forces of his childhood? He certainly had a freedom he'd never before imagined, but how long could that last? And what did the future hold? And were all men really created equal, as it said on one of the plaques? It certainly didn't seem that way, when he considered his father compared to the likes of Mark, Winston and Tramp among others. And, of course, most recently Hank. Tristan had never been to school, and for every time his mother had told him he was smart and bright, his father had truculently called him stupid. That, and his father's other abuses, would undermine his confidence forever.

But now wasn't the time dwell on blackened memories of the past or worry about the brighter but unknown future. He had a sister to find.

At the office, two days had passed without any developments. Tristan tried to remain positive, and Hank's optimism was contagious as they met for lunch on the third day, at a small diner just on the fringes of Central Park. But Hank could tell Tristan was disappointed.

"You gotta stay positive, kid, you hear me, because optimism is the birth rite of the young, though it seems to me that you're missing a big slice of the positivity pie. Now, for many folks of my significant years, middle age is the catalyst of paranoia, as reality dents the faith we have or have had in ourselves and in our fellow men. But not me, oh no. Despite everything I've seen and learned, both by my own mistakes and the awful mistakes of others, I remain positive and hopeful, for without hope, what do we have? And while we're on the subject of age, let me tell you what I think. Desperate beliefs are reactionary to old age, usually a belief in God, for when even hope is lost, most people need someone or something to cling to. Look, son, I've spent close to ten years searching for my boy, and do you think I'll ever give up? Because if we give up on the things we care about in life, then life itself isn't worth anything, don't you see? I'll never quit looking for my boy, which is why I'll never get old, and as long as you're here, trying to find your sister, I'll never quit on you. And if you need something to cling to, well you can cling to the fact that

Hank Burroughs and his amazing staff are doing everything in their power to find what you're looking for."

Hank's patriarchal tone wasn't necessary for Tristan...he knew the man would never give up. But he appreciated Hank's genuine concern, and loved him for it. Also, he knew that in some way Hank had taken him on in a subtle, surrogate fatherly kind of way, and so the mission had become uniquely personal to him. He'd lost his own son, and had so far failed to find him. Uniting Tristan with his sister, Tristan himself sensed, would in some way ease the big man's obvious pain.

Whatever happened, Tristan would never forget Hank Burroughs.

*Chapter Fifty Nine*

During the night Tristan had a bad dream, more of an abstract flash back, really, in which he found his mother's brutalized body, but rather than on a hotel bed she was laid out on a slab at a beachside mortuary, even though she was still alive. She called out to him, and he tried desperately to reach her, his heavy feet trudging through wet and cruel sand, the waves washing up to his knees on the beach at St. Mary's, and in his nightmare, as in reality, he couldn't get to her in time and she died in front of him on the cold and lonely concrete. Tristan knew it was his fault.

Waking slowly he felt exhausted after a fitful sleep, and opened the window for some air, sucking in the cold breath as it wheezed through the narrow crack between door and frame. Hope, as it so often had as he searched for his mother, was diminishing.

He left the hotel in a daze, and above him, large icy

clouds threatened snow, and swirled organically, like gigantic marble slabs. Tristan recalled his awful dream, and couldn't shake off macabre thoughts of death and corpses. He glanced about, and found himself in a foreboding, ominous world whose buildings and people seemed distant, callous and cruel, and subconsciously he edged into the unwelcoming shadows of a gnarled tree, suddenly feeling the threat of impending doom.

*I'm just tired*, he thought, shaking his head to clear the exhaustion, but it didn't work, and the specter of death hovered over his conscious thoughts like an all consuming veil, shielding the lighted path ahead, and grounding him where he stood. A ferocious wind began to blow, rushing by him like a harbinger of sorrow as he slumped down against the tree that leaned at him with its branches menacing, his pulse racing, and he tried to control breaths that came in a staccato of ragged and discrepant bursts.

Tristan remained cowered beneath that tree for long moments, waiting for what he realized must be some kind of a panic attack to pass. His breathing eventually returned to normal, and the sense of fear and claustrophobia that so quickly overwhelmed him was gone.

And yet the feeling that all was not well wouldn't leave him. Picking himself up from the floor, he carried on his way to the office on legs that seemed forged from lead, the spring in his step with which he'd arrived in New York gone, and, exiting the elevator on the fifteenth floor, he trudged through the doors of Hank's offices, agitated and with a heavy heart.

Tristan was a familiar and welcome visitor by now, and he knew the faces that hovered over desks and spoke loud and fast into telephones. But he sensed something different. *What was it?* He looked about. The same people. Same frantic activity. But then it hit him. Everyone seemed happy. They were lovely people, but often appeared stressed, too busy sometimes even to smile. Not today. The atmosphere was lighter, and his heart galloped as he strode towards Hank's main office.

"Kid, come in and sit down."

He led Tristan to the couch, where he sat down weakly, like a child waiting for a scolding. Hank was business as usual, and Tristan was confused. The team was definitely acting different, exuding positive energy, yet here was the boss, business like and not a smile in sight. His throat dried as Hank stared at him with the guilty intensity of a broken promise. Then the bombshell.

"Kid, I've got some bad news!"

Tristan blinked and swallowed hard, his fists clenching shut in anticipation of the devastation to come.

"After an exhaustive search throughout this vast city, I can say with a fair amount of certainty that your sister is not in New York."

In that moment, all hope of finding Ailla was lost.

"I'm sorry to tell you that, kid. I know I promised I'd find her."

With his head bowed, Tristan fought back a surge of emotion.

"I...I know you tried."

"That's right, kid, we tried. We tried real hard. And you know what? Good old Hank never breaks his promises."

Tristan's head rocked up.

"Pardon? I thought...I thought you said you didn't find her?" He looked at Hank, and saw a giant smile spread over the face of his friend.

"You're right. I told you she wasn't in New York. I didn't say I didn't find her. Kid, we have found her. We know where she lives."

"Really? You've really found her? Where, Hank? Where is she?"

Hank couldn't contain his delight. He was so happy for the kid, and answered with a smile as wide as the Atlantic.

"Brighton, England! You know it?"

Tristan was delirious. After so much disappointment, at last some good news. Rushing round the desk, he grabbed Hank in a bear hug, though his arms hardly reached around the corpulent mass.

"Whoa there, kid, save that affection for the ladies...I'll need some air in my lungs."

He took a step back, and looked in awe at the big man.

"I don't know what to say, Hank, except thanks. I knew you'd do it, I just knew it."

Hank demanded they went out to lunch to celebrate at a pizzeria near Central Park, where he explained how he and his team had managed to track down Tristan's long lost sister.

"With such sparse information it was painstaking work," he said, "but the team jumped to it, one group making a list of New York orphanages while a second team contacted all the city's adoption and foster agencies. The list of families that now lived in New York but had at one time lived abroad was long, but when narrowed to families that had lived in England, it left us only a dozen names. Then it was just a case of contacting each of them and asking about Ailla."

It wasn't actually said in the offices, not even in private, but no one really expected a happy outcome. Yet they worked feverishly and with total diligence. The staff all believed in Hank and his work, and thrived off his undoubted passion and unstinting optimism; each and every one of them would have hated to let him down.

"My team are a hard working and caring bunch, and

besides, they've all grown fond of the shy, polite kid with the cute accent."

Tristan blushed just a tiny bit, but at the same time rolled his eyes in mock annoyance, because after hearing it several times on his forays around the city, he wondered why his English accent warranted such fuss.

"It took many days, and many hundreds of phone calls and false leads, but young Jo-Anne Barber finally got a breakthrough. After contact with one particular adoption centre, a series of calls led her to the CEO of an international investment company. Bingo! She'd located the foster parents of one Ailla Annis. She'd found your sister."

Hank couldn't miss the heartfelt and genuine gratefulness etched on Tristan's face, and seeing that the boy was more or less speechless, that was all the thanks he'd ever need.

"I know you're grateful kid, and you're very welcome. And ya know what, it's given me renewed confidence that I'll find my own boy Jesse sometime. Just gotta keep believing, right?"

"Right. I think you'll see him again soon, Hank, I can feel it."

Wide smiles followed, and there was genuine affection between the two unlikely friends.

Tristan couldn't finish his giant pizza, and perhaps more surprisingly, neither could Hank, but Tristan knew where he'd find some grateful recipients to help them out. He hugged Hank tight, arranged to see him later, and walked with that old spring back in his step across the street into Central Park to trade a pizza for a story or two, and feeling as happy as he had ever been.

*Chapter Sixty*

Mr. George Robins couldn't have been happier to meet Tristan. He'd always known Ailla had a brother, but it made her so sad to speak about him that they rarely did. George and his wife Sue loved Ailla as if she were their own daughter, and had always considered her that way, so they were terribly sad when she decided to return to her native England. But they completely understood her desire and need to return, and helped and supported her as much as they could. They were still in regular contact.

The Robins' took Tristan to dinner at a quaint place downtown, a restaurant that served English roast style dinners, sure that the boy was missing comfortable English food, but not totally surprised when he ordered a hamburger instead. Tristan liked them immediately, and despite their obvious wealth he sensed they were a loving and down to earth family. During the meal he hoped to learn everything he could about his sister, and Mr. and Mrs. Robins didn't let him down.

"Well Tristan, she was…she is…such a kind and gentle girl," said Sue, clearly proud of her foster daughter. "When we first met Ailla she was just eleven years old, and we instantly fell in love with her. She was beautiful, and a natural beauty, just like her mother, at least that's what we were told. But it was her sincere honesty and personality that melted our hearts, and one smile made even the grumpiest mood disappear while her bright eyes could light up any room."

Tristan listened with growing pride as George took over the tributes.

"And she was such a precocious young girl, and so talented. Some of her paintings were stunning, especially for one so young, and she still has great talent. In fact, she owns a gallery in England now."

A glow of comprehension began to form in Tristan's mind; *Brighton...gallery...it has to be...I was already there!* He bit his lip and waited for some confirmation.

"Which reminds me," George continued, "when Sue and I first saw you we knew instantly you were Ailla's brother, not any doubt about it, because the two of you look so alike."

Sue reached into her bag and pulled out an old sketch book, flipped through until she found the page she was looking for, and passed the book across the table with a wide and expectant smile.

When Tristan looked down at the page, he saw his own face looking back at him, an incredible likeness of himself as a younger boy. But more than that; it was undoubtedly drawn by the same hand as the painting he'd seen with Richard in Brighton. No question about it now, Tristan had already seen, and by some amazing quirk of fate, been, in his sister's gallery before.

Tristan was enchanted by stories of his sister, but was more sad than ever that he couldn't have shared his childhood with her. However, over the course of the meal he shared tales of his adventures that had led him all the way to New York. The Robins' were understandably horrified by his tormented childhood. They had very few details of Ailla's family, only fragments they'd garnered from Ailla herself, but the shocking reality was far worse than they could imagine, and they suddenly appreciated why Ailla was so troubled by her memories and her guilt.

"Ailla will be beside herself with happiness to meet you," said George. "All her life she's lived under a veil of guilt...guilty that you were left behind with that terrible...with your father. She knew she was the lucky one, first to be raised by her kind old aunt Bella, and next coming to live with us. But she's always felt bad about it too."

"But we're the lucky ones," Sue continued, "because Ailla has made us all so proud and happy, a real credit to our family and a pleasure to be a part of her life, if only for a few years. She was always so independent, and we knew that one day she'd leave to pursue her artistic dreams. But we're so excited to hear about her successes, and she truly is an amazing young woman."

Tristan decided to fly back to England as soon as possible. He needed to meet his sister and tell her not to feel guilty any longer. The Robins' generously offered to buy his ticket, but when Tristan politely refused, they simply smiled and thought, *just like your sister*. "Then if you won't accept the gift for yourself, just consider it a present for Ailla. Could you do that?"

"Yes, I can do that. Mr. and Mrs. Robins, thank you so much, I really appreciate it, and I appreciate how you took care of Ailla when she was younger. I know our mother would be grateful too."

Tristan's flight wasn't for two days, so he paid a final visit to his favourite place in the city; Central Park. It was a cold, biting winter's day, but there were plenty of people in the park, exercising and walking dogs as kids played and scampered about in the fallen leaves. They looked happy, and Tristan thought that for the first time, he was genuinely happy too.

His mind still reeled at the fact he he'd already been inside Ailla's gallery in Brighton, and he smiled to himself as he imagined what might happen the next time he'd step through that door. His life had new purpose now that he had a sister, and in spite of the recent traumas he'd endured and the devastation of losing his mother, hope remained of a better future.

He also for the first time had some good friends who'd be excited to see him, and that was another thing he never thought he'd say. The world was full of good people, he knew that now, and even as the icy air chilled him to the bone, he began to envisage a life in which he might never be cold and alone again.

The Robins' wanted to throw a party to celebrate the soon to happen reunion of the lost siblings, but Tristan declined, saying it wasn't right for them to celebrate without Ailla there, and they all agreed, admiring his sensibility. Instead, they went out for a farewell dinner, together with Hank and his family, and it was a lovely evening. Tristan thanked them all individually for everything they'd done for him and for his sister, and assured them that his mother Kerra, wherever she now rested, would be eternally grateful.

Through Hank, Tristan thanked the hard working team of Hank Burroughs Esquire, saying he would never forget their efforts.

And lastly, Tristan thanked Hank. Few words were necessary though, and anyone who saw their hug knew a deep and requited bond and respect had formed between them. It was a touching moment, and one they'd each hold dear forever.

Like a father and son.

*Chapter Sixty One*

Tristan's flight bumped down on time into London's Heathrow Airport, and this time it wasn't fear that jolted him, but a heightened sense of anticipation. Only two weeks had passed since he'd left, but both he and the world in which he lived were changed. He was no longer the frail, timid kid from the Scilly Isles, and the sky was no longer a perpetual and miserable grey. Instead, he strode out of the terminal with his shoulders squared and his head held high into a world of infinite white.

Heavy snow continued to fall, yet nothing could dampen his spirits as he rushed to the airport's bus station. Despite the weather, he was relieved to read a sign that said *All Services South Operating On A Normal Schedule*.

He boarded the bus to Brighton and soon relaxed into the two hour drive to the coast. His sense of excitement was palpable, but the journey south was slow and, though the roads were surprisingly clear, a strong wind whipped flurries of snow at the windscreen, making it virtually impossible for the driver to see more than a few yards. He would have to be patient.

Some three and a half achingly slow hours later, his bus rolled safely into the small station in Brighton, and just twenty minutes after that, Tristan was climbing the stairs of a hotel, echoing stairs that brought back memories of the robbery. But he smiled. He'd come a long way since then. In minutes he was passed out in his room, exhausted from the flight and eager to get the night over with. *Tomorrow,* he thought, *tomorrow's the day I will meet my sister.*

A chilly draft crept over Tristan's exposed flesh and woke him with a shiver. The room was cold, so he jumped out of the bed, jumped around a little more to get his blood flowing, and quickly threw on his clothes. Sliding open the flimsy curtains, he wasn't surprised to see only the rough outlines of cars and trees, their bulks completely covered in a foot thick quilting of snow. It had been a long dark autumn since he left St. Mary's. But that time was over.

Gulping down the lousy complimentary breakfast, then washing that down with equally lousy tea, Tristan didn't care. Nothing was going to spoil the day he now realised he'd longed for all his life, and a child-like excitement he'd never known as a boy surged him into town on a wave of adrenalin, and as fast as the treacherous, skiddy pavements would allow.

Tristan found the narrow, colorful street that Ailla's gallery was situated on from memory, and hoped that this time there wasn't only the blind and hunched old lady to greet him. His heart pounded, but this time it felt different. In the past when his heart pounded it was usually out of fear or expectation that things were about to go bad, but now, as it beat with fervor in his chest, it was the beating of a drummer leading men to victory, the anticipation of a great and imminent success.

He paused at the corner of the street and breathed in deep, oblivious to the cold and aware only of his intensified sense of purpose. The world around him slowed down, and he walked on, not hearing the crunch of snow beneath his feet. Gulls stopped cawing, all except one, squawking a familiar call that to a boy's ears had once sounded like *destiny*. Traffic noise had ceased on the narrow cobbled lane, and he glided along, his stomach turning somersaults.

And then the familiar bright red paint of that old wooden door came into view. He was so close. A string of delicate Christmas lights framed it prettily amid the white, and he paused again, trying to slow his racing breaths. The door's small glass squares were steamed up on the inside, blurring the muted colors and shapes beyond. Tristan reached out his hand, and with a final, gasping breath, as if about to step into a whole new world, he went inside.

The gallery was once again deserted, and Tristan's heart momentarily stopped beating, as if the lead drummer had been shot. But he soon glanced about and was relieved to see the walls covered in paintings...*Ailla's paintings*. The drummer revived, he then spotted a door behind the counter, slightly ajar, and he listened. Someone was moving about inside. *My sister.*

He called out gently. "Hello? Is anybody there?"

"Hi there. Yes, I'm here...I'll be out in just a moment. Please, take a look around." It was a clear and confident voice that replied, and though unsure how he knew, he knew it with certainty; it was his sister's voice.

Just how he'd imagined, kind and sincere, and Tristan was bursting with desire to call out and tell her everything. *Just another minute*, he told himself, and forced his way over to the familiar painting on the wall. *It's definitely me.* Wide blue eyes looked down at him. *What do they see?* he thought. *How does he feel?* There was no doubting the sadness in those eyes, and that's how he knew it had always been him; that sadness had been his own. Now, two silent tears fell. He couldn't prevent them, and didn't want to. And he smiled, because he knew what each tear represented. One fell for a sad, painful past...a tear of sorrow. And the other...it was a tear of pure joy.

Footsteps clicked on the wooden floors behind him. He turned, slowly, the drummer in his heart pounding with renewed energy. She was at the counter, head down, and still couldn't see him. But he saw her. His heart melted. It was Ailla.

"Good morning, sir. Awful weather isn't it." Her head still down, busy with some papers on the counter.

"Yes...yes, it's terrible." Tristan approached, and carefully removed something from his backpack. "I wonder, miss, could you please sign this for me?"

Finally, Ailla looked up, and her eyes shot wide open as if they were looking at a ghost. In a way, they were. The colour drained from her rosy cheeks, and she stared in utter disbelief. Tristan thought she might faint, as her body swayed a little and she staggered forward, clutching the counter for support. But those eyes never left his. Slowly, she took a small step forward. And then another.

Ailla opened and closed those big blue eyes a couple of times, as if to blink away the dream, but the dream remained before her until she had to accept it as reality.

And then by force of will, she spoke. "Tristan? Is it really you?"

Tristan's own breath caught in his throat. He was rooted to the spot. No words came forth, and all he could do was smile and cry at the same time. He reached out his hand, and passed her the picture she'd once painted of him, so many years before. She took it, and looked between it and the boy in front of her. Then she glanced at the painting on the wall, and though her eyes closed, it didn't prevent her from spilling teardrops onto the painting.

After a long, long moment, as if taking the time to piece all of the fragments of her distorted life and mixing them together to create this new reality, her eyes opened again, and after one more glance at the painting on the wall, she settled her eyes on Tristan's. They looked at each other in wonderment.

"My brother," she muttered, "My baby brother."

Now, they both stepped forward and, embracing for the very first time, Tristan spoke the magic words he never thought he'd say.

"Hello, sister."

Epilogue

**The Forgiven**

An inauspicious sky swirled grey and black, and snow seemed imminent. Few people braved the streets that afternoon, most likely in the pub drowning away the misery of London's winter, and in front of the hotel, an eerie silence hung over the solemn group as the dreary, crumbled façade merged with the sky.

The Albion hotel had been closed since Kerra's murder, and was no longer a crime scene. Its owner was charged with concealing evidence, and currently feared for his life in Brixton's notorious prison. The killer, Michael Monroe, was never caught by the police but was found dead and half buried in the mud on the banks of the Thames. Rumors in the East End said he'd fallen foul of the Kray brothers, who suspected him of the murders of at least three prostitutes, but Tristan took no satisfaction from the news given to him by Chief Inspector Woods, who stood with them on an icy day in late December.

They'd gone to The Albion to pay their last respects to Kerra. While Tristan was in New York, a cremation had taken place weeks before at nearby Plaistow Crematorium, and in the absence of any family, it was a small service attended by one person; Mollie.

But with Tristan now were Ailla and her fiancé Jack, Winston and Pearl, Mark and Bobby Trescothwick, Richard and Anne-Marie White and of course, Mollie Noble. Inspector Woods was there to say a few words on behalf of the Metropolitan Police. Nobody asked where Blyth was.

Leaning against the hotel wall, a single bouquet lent the only color to a dismal scene. Ailla read aloud its faded note. The message was simple:

*A beautiful young woman, taken too soon.*
*May she rest in peace.*
*G.J. Proudfoot.*

*Georgina Joyce Proudfoot,* Inspector Woods told them, was the poor old housekeeper that found their mother's body.

*Too soon,* Tristan thought. *Beautiful.* He realized then how deeply he missed his mother. In the first weeks after her death he was lost and in shock, and focused only on finding Ailla. Now he'd found his long-lost sister, he'd spent the next few weeks getting to know her and hadn't had time to grieve properly.

But as he stood side by side with Ailla now, near to where their mother was so brutally murdered, he believed...he hoped...that he could at last begin to accept all that had happened to him, accept that his mother was gone, accept that he wasn't to blame for her death, and begin to move forward with his own life.

Today was the first step.

He had thought of her as pretty, but Tristan had never

really understood that his mother was beautiful. But as he gazed at Ailla then, he not only saw his sister before him, but he saw his mother too. Ailla's pretty face was the mirror image of their mother's before life had stolen the glint from her eye. The high smooth cheek bones. Huge, azure eyes. Soft, unblemished skin that glowed, even in the dim light. Thick, wavy hair the color of a cornfield under a fiery sunset.

And that sparkle. So long lost from his mother's eyes, snuffed out by a vicious father and tyrannical husband, that sparkle he saw shining bright in his sister's eyes would be the light to dominate any future darkness and keep the memory of his mother alive forever.

The journey from London to Penzance was slow. Tristan fought hard to suppress a shadow of anxiety that journeyed west alongside him. He was nearing St. Mary's, the place where he'd witnessed and endured so much suffering, and who knew what lie in wait for him there? A snarling, vengeful beast, or a harmless, broken man?

Tristan spent long hours on that trip thinking about how he felt towards his father. Hank Burroughs had persuaded him to visit Blyth, offer him a chance of redemption, and though at first he was more than reluctant, he agreed. He'd grown up a lot, thanks both to his own experiences, and to the words of several people for whom he had the greatest of respects, not least Hank, Tramp and his aunt Bella. Tristan knew that his father's blood ran in his veins. But he also knew that everybody made mistakes, and not all was what it appeared to be with the world.

Most of all, though, it was his sister who'd led him to the decision to go through with the visit. With her gracious heart, and her limitless compassion and dignity, Ailla told him that she'd long since forgiven the immoral imperfections of her father. And, if she could find it in her heart to forgive the man that had caused so many people so much pain and sorrow, then he too could rise up and do the same.

Lunch time, December twenty third, and no sooner had Tristan stepped into the gloomy yet busy pub, Bobby bounded over and almost crushed the air out of him with an affectionate hug.

"Merry Christmas, Tristan...well, it will be in a couple of days."

"Same to you, Bobby. It's good to see you."

Over her shoulder he saw Mark coming to greet him, and the gentle giant shook his hand and led him to a seat in the corner. His friendly face soon took on a more serious expression.

"Are you sure you're ready for tomorrow? We can wait until after Christmas if you'd like?"

"I'm ready Mark. I'm a little nervous, but I have to go. I know you and my father have had your differences in the past, and I appreciate your concern, but I want to give him a chance to make it up to me and Ailla. We're both ready, and besides, I think it's what mum would want. We can go alone, if you would rather..."

The hint of a shadow passed over Mark's face, as if a cruel memory had suddenly come to him. Quickly, perhaps too quickly, he replied, and his voice was harsh.

"No! I'm coming with you! Definitely." But then his face softened, as if the memory was gone, or at least shut away somewhere. "I don't think you'll have any trouble over there, I really don't, but I want to come, with you just to be on the safe side."

Mark's apparent hostility towards his father did little to ease Tristan's own concerns, but he was glad that he'd be alongside him when he finally returned to the prison of St. Mary's Island.

A creeping, icy mist shrouded Mark's van as they made their way slowly into Penzance ferry port, and then up onto the same boat that had emancipated Tristan from the island what felt to him like a lifetime ago. While Mark went off to buy hot drinks for them all, Tristan, Ailla and Jack sat huddled against the chill. As the ferry rocked on a winter swell, there was little conversation, each of them in quiet contemplation of the hours or days ahead. There was no real danger of violence, they believed, but emotionally, the strain was starting to show.

Several hours later Mark's truck lurched down the well worn ramp from boat to dock, and as their lurching stomachs settled, the silence inside the cab was conspicuous as the two siblings each came to terms with facing up to their childhood demons. Tristan cast his eyes out the window. *It looks the same,* he thought, *grey, miserable...sinister.*

Trundling along country lanes, the old truck skidded where snow had melted into slush, and progress was slow. Tristan's warm breath swirled playfully into the cab's icy air, like smoke from a chimney, and as the miles to the cottage gradually lessened, it brought back painful memories of the day his mother went missing. Except that day, no smoke puffed from the cottage's chimney.

Tristan felt his hand squeezed. It was Ailla. Comfort in numbers.

Sometime later, whether five or fifty minutes Tristan didn't know, Mark's deep voice told them they were close. Tristan knew those roads, and in a few moments knew they'd crest a small hill, and the cottage, scene of so much cruelty and loneliness, would emerge from within the gloom.

And there it was, stood alone in the mist, like a haunted theatre of anguish whose show had no witness. Ailla let out an involuntary gasp, and squeezed her brother's hand tighter as, in the coming dark, the muted angles of the cottage cast a ghastly silhouette against the smooth ocean beyond. Low and mostly hidden, the setting sun's ethereal light penetrated the mist like daggers, and though the high cloud was thick and black, the waxing moon threw an unearthly glow across the entire vista, where the surreal mix of light shone out forever across the vastness of the horizon. Whether the scene was baleful or beautiful, Ailla couldn't know.

Just like he'd been once before, Tristan was surprised by the absence of smoke curling from the chimney, but even stranger was the lack of light from inside the old stone walls. It was barely three o'clock, but winter always brought an early dusk to the island. Lights should be on. Mark too noticed the anomalies, and he and Tristan shared a curious glance. The tension rose.

The cottage stored only lonely, unhappy memories for Tristan, and under the heavy, malevolent twilight his thoughts turned as dark as the sky. *He knows we're coming...he's waiting for us.* A shiver crept up his spine, but he tried hard to suppress his vivid imagination. Rolling to a stop, in the isolated area the gravel crunched loud beneath the truck's wheels.

Mark turned to face the others. "I'm sure everything's going to be fine. But your father's an unpredictable man...just wait here while I check it out."

The three passengers silently nodded their ascent as the reality of the situation loomed over them. Things had suddenly become real. Grabbing a torch from below his seat, Mark stepped from the truck and disappeared toward the cottage. In the murkiness, only the jerking beam of torchlight betrayed his position.

Mark Trescothwick was a brave but cautious fellow. Blyth was older, a weaker man than he, but Mark had witnessed in his eyes a genuine, unhinged rage, some inner demon on the verge of escape. Anything was possible.

Back in the truck they spoke in hushed tones. "What happens if he's not here?" Ailla whispered, "What will we do?"

"I'm sure he's here, though something feels different," replied Tristan. "I can't explain it, but he's definitely here, I feel it."

Ailla was more than anxious. "What do you mean? Like he's here, but it isn't good?"

"I don't know. But I sense something, some change in the atmosphere…something strange."

After treading carefully through the darkness, Mark had reached the cottage. Allowing his eyes to adjust to the less than half-light, he then peered through a couple of windows, confirming that there were no lights on inside. Despite himself, the big man was on edge. Something was amiss here. *Shit,* he thought, *something had always been amiss here,* but it wasn't a thought that gave any comfort. With a giant fist, and much in the same way as he had when he visited Blyth a month ago, he banged twice on the heavy wooden door and stepped away. Mark waited, his pulse throbbing in his neck. Nothing. His jaw clenched tight, rippling his jowls, and his eyes narrowed. Just in case.

The weak sun finally dipped over the western horizon, and total blackness descended. It seemed darker than he remembered, more sinister. He knocked again, this time a sustained and heavy banging. Ten seconds. No response, so he walked around the side of the small house, and saw Blyth's truck parked up in it's usual spot. *Very strange*. He continued round the back, pausing to shine his light in the few windows with open curtains.

Mark had been gone less than five minutes before nervous tension got the better of them. They could no longer see the beam of his torch, and with the sun now departed they found themselves in complete and utter blackness. Stepping from the truck and careful not to slam the doors, the three edged their way towards the cottage.

Mark completed a full circuit of the house. No lights and no fire in the hearth. The truck's engine was cold, and there was nowhere to walk at this late winter hour, which suggested Blyth was home. Back now at the front door Mark looked around for clues, and found some partially snow covered old work boots that hadn't been worn for many days. But there was no sign of life. Deserted. It didn't add up.

He was reluctant to break down the door, considering whose house this was, because he might just get himself shot. Just then Tristan emerged from the shadows. "The door is never locked." His voice was calm.

It was a surreal moment. For so many years that door had held him captive. It was just a door. But as a kid it had seemed so much more. Impenetrable. Permanent. The difference between freedom and captivity. For the first time in two months and without another word, Tristan turned the handle and stepped inside his former prison.

It was just as cold inside as it was outside, colder even, because no fire had warmed that hearth for days. He turned on the light, and two things immediately caught his eye; it was impeccably tidy, and a crucifix hung above the mantelpiece. Tristan was shocked. His father never cleaned. And he'd renounced God in a distant and faded past.

The others followed him into the kitchen, and Jack closed the door on the winter. Despite the tidiness a thin layer of dust coated everything, and a stack of firewood stood by the cold fireplace. That there'd been little activity in several days was obvious. *And no lights?* But with the truck outside, and his father's boots in their usual spot by the door, Tristan was mystified.

Mark too was perturbed, and in his guts something felt very wrong about the house. "I'm going to take a look around. Why don't you start a fire, Jack, get some life in this old place?"

Jack nodded as Mark walked slowly from the kitchen, and Tristan made to follow, but Ailla urged him to wait with her at the table, she too feeling uneasy. They all did. But nobody understood why.

Tristan had a dire feeling, and couldn't shake the notion that something was terribly awry. He'd returned to the scene of all his childhood nightmares, and now cast his mind back to one of the last times he was in that room. His father beat him savagely, and just as he closed his eyes then, he closed them now. Despite the heat from Jack's now blazing fire, a powerful chill crept up his spine as his father still haunted his mind. And they all felt it, Tristan and Ailla, Jack, and Mark too, something in the atmosphere, an innate, vestigial cold presence as mental as it was physical.

Nobody was prepared to say it. But the cottage felt haunted.

Slow steps took Mark down the corridor, ears and eyes strained and alert for any notion of life. All was still. He knocked on the first door and got the expected silence. With a shove he opened it and stepped inside what was the modest master bedroom, where he was surprised by the smell of fresh paint. A framed picture of Blyth and Kerra sat on a side table. It was a nice picture, and for Blyth, the antithesis of sensitivity, it seemed so out of place. A small crucifix hung from a wall lamp, matching the one he'd seen in the kitchen. He shook his head, baffled.

Next along was the bathroom. The same knock, the same silence. The same surprise at the apparently new decor. Photos. Blyth, younger, and cradling a baby girl. Ailla? Another cross.

Jack's heart pounded as he sat by the fire, trying to imagine how Tristan and Ailla felt. He'd never experienced anything like the trauma these two had been through, and shuddered at the thought, only now realising just how brave they really were. He edged himself closer to the now roaring flames, vainly hoping they'd vitiate the goosebumps that rose all across his body. They didn't, and if anything he was getting colder. *What's going on here?* he thought, dread growing by the minute.

Two more doors to try. At the end of the corridor, Mark entered what was obviously Tristan's room. It seemed like a wonderful space for a young kid; maps adorned the walls, beautifully crafted model airplanes hung in mock battle, a football sat in the corner, though sadly un-kicked. More photos. Tristan with his dad, enlarged images of Kerra...all smiles. It should have been a great place for a kid. Mark knew it wasn't. On a wall, the ubiquitous cross.

A macabre thought crossed Mark's mind as an inevitable scenario formed. Blyth's only transport was outside. His only boots, Tristan confirmed, were present. The neglected hearth. A newly decorated house. Family photos everywhere. The crucifixes. He reached for the cross, and held it loosely in his fingers. *Blyth must have known his family would never return,* he thought, *so many ominous signs.*

Back in the hall Mark faced the final unopened door, almost certain of what he would find beyond it.

At the kitchen table the three of them sat in a silence broken only by the crackle of the fire. Shadows danced, taunting them from the walls. Jack looked at his fiancé with an even measure of admiration and concern, but with a subtle smile she assured him she was fine. They both looked at Tristan who sat opposite them, and whose eyes remained closed as if straining to hear what the others couldn't. After a moment they opened, and he stood up with a surprisingly tranquil expression on his face.

"He's here," he said softly but with absolute certainty, "our father is here." Tristan turned towards the corridor.

Mark jumped a little as his torch faded and then died, and he smiled wryly in the now dim light, shamed his imagination had gotten the better of him. *I'll look inside...just to be sure.* He checked nobody was coming down the hall, and with an unconscious glance up to a god he'd never believed in, Mark opened the door. Just to be sure.

The stench hit him first. He'd never seen a dead body before, but he knew that smell. He fumbled for a light switch, and what he saw when the room lit up dropped the big man to his knees. On instinct he shut the door, unable to remove his eyes from the scene before him.

He'd imagined Blyth's body, dead but untarnished.

That's what he imagined.

That is not what he found.

Tristan walked the hall slowly, conscious, yet somehow outside of himself, like a spectator at a show, involved, yet out of reach. His mind, free of emotion. Calmness he'd never before known.

No rush. He knew what he'd find.

At the door, now. Clarity of motion, every atom of his being in tune with his shallow, rhythmic breaths.

Déjà vu. Tristan opened the door. Destiny.

"NO!" Mark shouted, but it was too late. Tristan had seen.

"It's okay." Tristan's voice was definitive. He placed a gentle hand on Mark's shoulder. "Just give me a minute, please."

"Should I tell your sister?"

Tristan nodded, and calmly closed the door behind Mark as he left the room.

Tristan looked down at his father's dead body. He wasn't shocked and felt little emotion. He stepped closer. The air was filled with the potent scent of gunpowder and misery. And to Tristan, the now familiar scent of death.

From the front Blyth appeared unscathed. Eyes open, he looked straight ahead, and Tristan followed his gaze to the facing wall, where a large crucifix hung ironically from it's own nail. But where the back of Blyth's head should be remained only a pulpy mass of dry black blood and obliterated skull. The pale wall beyond wore an intricate web of sprayed blood and fragments of brain.

Yet Tristan didn't flinch.

The fallen man before him had caused years of untold suffering to all those he loved and who had once loved him, and while rage and paranoia had controlled Blyth's household, it had broken all of their spirits as well as his own. His son knew he was a troubled and tortured man who had lost control of everything, and looking now at the destroyed body, Tristan understood what he was seeing; peace. At last. And the peace was not his alone. It was his mother's. It was Ailla's, too. And now, finally, it was his father's.

That tormented family, that went by the unusual name of Nancarrow, was finally at peace.

In ancient Cornish the name Nancarrow meant 'valley of the deer,' and perhaps, Tristan thought, the deer might finally return now that the dangerous humans were silent?

He removed the old shotgun from the couch and sat down beside his father, the dark irony causing a bitter smile; not in a decade had he been afforded that privilege. Then he spotted something in his father's clenched fist. An envelope wrapped around a crucifix. He took only the envelope.

Long ago Kerra had encouraged Tristan to stop wasting his time on God, and recent events had only served to vindicate her stance. If God was supposed to be sympathetic, Tristan thought, then why had he forsaken so many; his mum, his sister, Bella, and for too long, himself? And now, of course, his father.

What he had felt in his heart all those years ago was right; a father should love his son. A father should love his daughter, and a husband should love his wife. That was how it should've been. Tristan had no doubt his father loved his family, but by some unseen power that controlled his emotional behaviour, Blyth had lost the ability to show it. In some ways, that helped. Looking back now, being irrelevant was preferable to being relevant yet unwanted, oblivious then to the love he wasn't shown. Depression and alcohol had cruelly beaten his father, and he in turn had cruelly beaten his family.

They were all victims. He could see that now.

Tristan had a vague memory of something Gandhi had once said, along the lines of, *the weak can't forgive, only the strong*. Something like that. Hank had said something similar. He, Tristan, would be strong, and stood and faced his father for the final time.

Clutching the envelope to his chest, he spoke the three words that would set them all free.

"We forgive you."

Tristan returned to the kitchen, finally warm from the blaze, as if at last the malevolent chill had been driven from the cottage. All eyes were on his. He caught his sister's gaze, and saw only love. His smile reassured her, reassured them all. He addressed the vestiges of his family.

"Everything's going to be okay."

He took a seat at the table. It was the position his father occupied when king and master. It was a poignant decision, understood only by himself. There would be no more masters in that house.

"I found this envelope."

"Should Jack and I leave you two alone," Mark asked, "give you some time?"

"No Mark, stay."

Tristan read the letter for all in the room to hear.

*07:30a.m*
*Tuesday, 24th December, 1963*

*My dearest Tristan,*

*By the grace of God you've returned home to where you belong. I know this is true because you have found this letter, my penultimate act on God's earth. That also means you have found my body. My final act. I'm so sorry that you had to find me this way. But in all life, where there is effect, there was always a cause. Remember that, Tristan.*

*It's the best lesson I've ever taught you.*

*It's been two months since you left me here, and rightly so. You have forsaken me as I had forsaken all whom I've loved. But I prayed you'd come back, that you'd all come back. Did you notice the house? Beautiful, isn't it, just how it used to be and just how your mother always wanted it to be. I ruined all her dreams, I know that now.*

*Mere words cannot accurately express what I need to say...as you know, I was never much for words, and they in death, much like my actions in life, do not begin to tell my story.*

*So I will be as forthright as possible.*

*Tristan, I truly loved your mother, my beautiful wife. We were married only a year when she became pregnant with Ailla, our first baby. Kerra was so happy. We had some issues, as all families do. I'm sure by now you've learned all about that. And then you came along, and that happiness briefly returned. But for what I am about to tell you, you must decide yourself whether or not to forgive your mother. You are a brave and pure soul, Tristan, and I love you with all my heart. I know you will do the right thing. Can you forgive your mother her sins?*

*There was one thing I never told her, and it's a secret I've always kept. That is, until now.*

*I'm incapable of having children. It was a childhood accident, and the doctors told me at a young age I would never be a father. I always longed for children, and was devastated, so when Kerra got pregnant, I kept my silence. She had her reasons, I'm sure, but the reality is that your mother sinned against me. Twice.*

**I am not Ailla's father. I am not your father.**

*Kerra always loved Mark, even back in school, I knew*

*that, yet she married me. But I know it was him she ran to when things were sour between us. I tried my hardest to make it work, I really did. But in the end, the reality of raising another man's children became too much. I got so depressed, and when the whisky took hold of me, it never let me go. Kerra was unaware that I knew about her and Mark. But I did know, and the torment of it created the depression that hurt my family and created the monster I became.*

*So son, if you didn't know already, Mark Trescothwick is your real father. When you see him, take a look at his eyes. They're blue. Like yours. Like Ailla's. It's so obvious when you know, isn't it? Mark's a good man, an honorable man who was seduced by Kerra, but he deserves your love. Again, whether or not she gets that love is up to you.*

*I'm eternally sorry for everything that you've suffered at my hands. I have asked God for forgiveness. At the time of writing this letter, I'm still awaiting His answer.*

*And so I turn to you, Tristan, my son. Can you forgive me? I believe you can. And I remind you again, where there is effect, there was always a cause.*

*And to the rest of my family, I beg your salvation-*

*Bella, darling sister. Your heart of gold deserved a better brother.*

*To Mark, a better man than me. You deserved the truth about your children sooner.*

*To beautiful Ailla, for a chance to turn back the hands of time, I'd sell my soul. You were always loved.*

*To Tristan. I hope and pray that today you become the man I could never be. I trust you to put right all of your parent's wrongs, and then forgive me. Forgive us both. I beg you.*

*Goodbye,*

*Love your loving father,*

*Blyth.*

**The End**

And finally…

I'd like to take this opportunity to thank you, first for downloading this eBook, and secondly for reading it to the end. I sincerely hope you enjoyed reading it as much as I did writing it.

If you did enjoy it, then I have a small favor to ask. Would you be kind and courteous enough to leave a good review on Amazon?

For a debut novelist good reviews are even more valuable than the small but welcome monetary rewards from sales, and I would truly appreciate you taking the time to write a review for this book.

I'd like as many like minded people as possible to read my novel, and more reviews will help me accomplish that.

**THANK YOU**

*Steven*

Made in the USA
Charleston, SC
25 October 2014